TOUCHLINE SAMURAI

TOUCHLINE SAMURAI

Guy Stanley

Book Guild Publishing
Sussex, England

First published in Great Britain in 2007 by
The Book Guild Ltd
Pavilion View
19 New Road
Brighton, BN1 1UF

Copyright © Guy Stanley 2007

The right of Guy Stanley to be identified as the author of this work has been asserted by him in accordance with the Copyright, Designs and Patents Act 1988.

All rights reserved. No part of this publication may be reproduced, transmitted, or stored in a retrieval system, in any form, or by any means, without permission in writing from the publishers, nor be otherwise circulated in any form of binding or cover other than that in which it is published and without a similar condition being imposed on the subsequent purchaser.

All characters in this publication are fictitious and any resemblance to real people, alive or dead, is purely coincidental.

Typesetting in Baskerville by
SetSystems Ltd, Saffron Walden, Essex

Printed in Great Britain by
CPI Antony Rowe

A catalogue record for this book is
available from the British Library

ISBN 978 1 84624 159 8

For Fred Varcoe

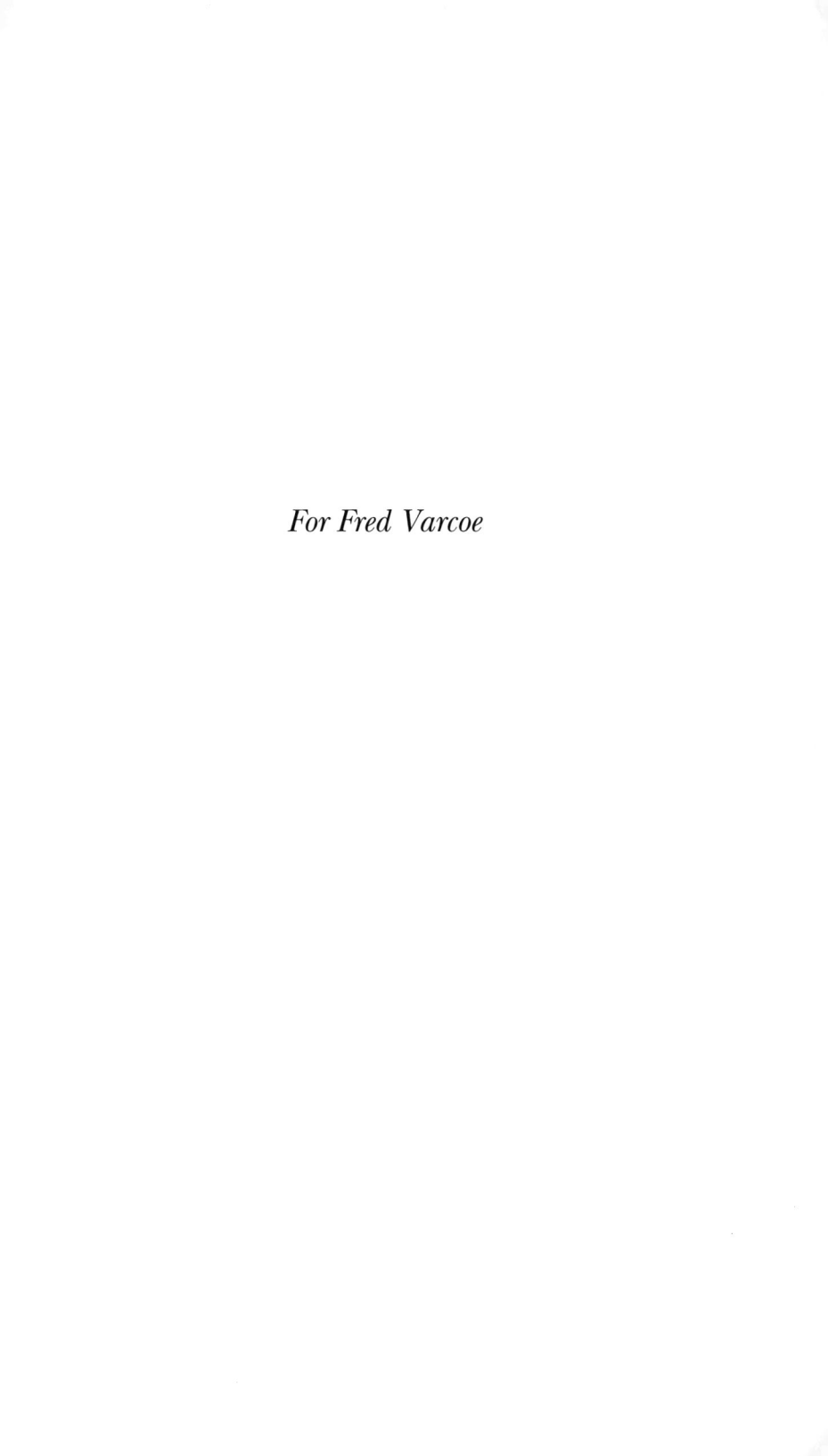

Prologue

Balls are not cheap, and when Moby McNally peered down into the darkness and saw the checkered sphere in the greasy, filthy water between the lock gates he hissed a triumphant: 'Yes'. Billy Pickwich had hoofed the football petulantly over the canal-end wall and refused to retrieve it, so coach McNally, seizing a corner flag, made his way through the rear turnstile to the slippery towpath of the Grand Siddley Canal. He trod gingerly, helped meagrely by the pewtery half-light from the bruised three-quarter moon. Seeing the ball among the debris in the lock, and smelling the foetid dankness, his feeling of elation quickly dissolved. He had dragged balls out of the canal water before but never from the forbidding confines of the stinking lock pool, with its flotsam, rotting food, supermarket trolleys and the odd dead rat. And certainly not at night. He shivered, the chilly air fuelling his anxiety, and zipped his tracksuit top. The fragile steps of a ladder, as ancient as the waterway itself, clung to the algae painted walls and disappeared into the watery blackness. Floating between a polystyrene fish and chip tray and a half-submerged gin bottle, the ball would be just about within reach of his corner flag pole if he stretched from the last rung. But the ladder ran down from the opposite side of the lock and he'd have to cross the canal by way of the leaking gate, with only a rusted, low rail for support and protection.

He'd come this far, he reasoned, and the ball was only five weeks old. Come tomorrow afternoon, it'd be gone, sellable booty for a fisherman or one of them youths that race up and down the towpath on stolen mountain bikes. Taking a very deep breath McNally hauled himself onto the narrow crossbridge and fixed his eyes on the old mill wall ahead, desperate to avoid the seductive lure of the coal black water below. The only sound came from the water seething and hissing between the warped gates and splashing 20 feet into the pit of the dock. Both hands on the rail, he inched across the gate. When a dog's muffled howl startled him he stopped to clutch his racing heart, and it was then, as he measured up the potential horrors of an uncontrolled descent into the stinking water of the lock, that he failed to hear the swish of the undergrowth or perceive the movement of a figure rising behind him. He'd never know it was a numbing blow to his skull from a baseball bat that impelled him into the lock, where he drowned quite quickly and painlessly.

1

Monique knocked lightly and opened the door just enough to introduce the upturn of her delicately powdered nose and a profile of rich, tousled blonde hair. 'Are you expecting a Chinese, Mr Hardcastle?'

The chairman of Siddley United Football Club, the 'Pitties', jolted upright in his deep leather chair, his chalky face quivering, his slumbering reverie ruined. His daydream, suffused with latent, sexual tension, betrayed the fear and anxiety of his profession. Where others scored the winning goal at Wembley, Walter Hardcastle dreamt a plague had laid waste to the population of Siddley and he was the last person alive. The city's most prestigious funeral director was walking naked through the body-strewn streets of the city, a young man's fresh corpse draped over his shoulder, desperately searching for his hearse.

Monique rolled her eyeballs and clucked. 'I said, are you expecting a Chinese?'

'No love,' the chairman said, regaining his composure and shifting a folder on his spacious desk. 'I've just had a sandwich.'

'No, Mr Hardcastle. Not a take-away. It's a man.' Suddenly, Monique's face froze in the doorway. 'Then it's him,' she uttered at length, her voice a bemused whisper.

'It's who?' Hardcastle said irritably.

'The Pitties' new manager.' Remembering the envelope

in her hand, she said: 'He's brought this letter with him.' Monique's petite, hourglass body bobbed across the room in a swish of Calentissimo fragrance, her subtly patterned tartan mini-skirt high on her thighs, her stiletto heels clicking on the aged floorboards. She stood where she could read the letter, a full breast resting on the chairman's shoulder. He slid open the thin envelope and perched his half glasses on the hump of a bulbous, pitted nose, a corner of an eye on the mound of ecstasy under the white, lacy transparent blouse, not a coffin handle's length away. If only she were dead, he thought wistfully.

Usually calm and composed in his dark suit and ever-ready black tie, Walter Hardcastle exuded the practised compassion of his calling, but as he read the letter from the visitor his rotund frame seemed to swell and his rheumy, oyster eyes bulged fit to burst, like the time he won the Royal Infirmary's unclaimed body disposal contract. But that had been a time of joy. The deltas of purple, broken veins that were his nostrils flared and an aspirant rumble, like the last breaths of a consumptive geriatric, erupted from deep in his chest. 'Does David know about this?' he said, assuming correctly Monique was reading it over his shoulder.

'I don't know, Mr Hardcastle,' Monique said, admiring her own ghostly reflection in the window glass. Outside, on Siddley United's scarred football pitch, in the fading light of a late September afternoon, a dozen figures in tracksuit tops and shorts kicked balls around lethargically, waiting for their coach with the cigarette and the deep cough to call it time. 'He's around somewhere. Should I get him?'

'Please, love,' the club chairman said, with a heavy tone of desperation. 'We'll soon sort this out. Where is this ... this oriental bloke now?'

'I put him in the visitors' changing room,' Monique replied, shifting snappily. 'It's cleaner than ours.'

The day before a Saturday match, the football club's board of local worthies gathered at the Pitt Lane ground for a little morale boosting session with the coaches, the part-time staff and whichever players felt like staying behind after training. They met in the hospitality lounge, where they drank and, in the continuing absence of a full-time manager, wrangled and argued over team selection with the interim coach, Terry Dribble. The chairman was still in the club office finishing off a bit of paperwork. He rolled on the balls of his feet by the window, hands thrust into the pockets of his funereal trousers. On the touchline below, Terry Dribble balanced unsteadily on his walking stick. Around the walls, from more than 30 picture frames, a century of firm-jawed Siddlean heroes, arms folded manfully, filled the boardroom with the timeless echoes of their exploits. Chairman Hardcastle felt the pride welling in his chest. 'What's up, Walter?' he heard, turning to face the tall, square-jawed man with the slick, badger-streak hair and wearing a grey double breasted checkered suit. The ice in David Broody's crystal tumbler clinked as he crossed the room.

'Sit down, David,' Hardcastle commanded gravely, returning to the desk. Siddley United's chief executive threw a glance at the shimmering, retreating figure of Monique Wainwright and drew a chair up to the chairman's desk. 'Listen to this.' The chairman read the letter from the English Football Association with the same voice he used to tell the bereaved that the elm-veneered coffin they ordered for their dear deceased was unfortunately not available due to a deadly outbreak of meningitis in the West Midlands and he hoped the oakwood alternative was acceptable, regrettably at a slight premium. ' "Dear Mr Hardcastle," ' Hardcastle intoned. ' "This is to introduce Mr Ken-ichi Ohara. As you have agreed, he will join Siddley United Football Club as player-manager on a one year contract. Mr

Ohara's papers have been received from the national football association of blah, blah, blah . . ."' He looked up, his face a slurry of confusion. 'Did I know about this, David?'

Chief executive by self-interest, property developer by self-description, avid speculator in practice, David Broody examined his manicured fingernails. 'You most certainly did, Walter. We spoke on your mobile on Monday, and I told you the papers were on your desk at the club. You were a bit busy this week so you had Monique call me to say you'd read the proposal and fully approved.'

The chairman's plump, livid fat lower lip quivered. Busy wasn't the word for it, what with the multiple pile-up on the ring-road and the tragic conflagration at St Werburgh's Rest Home, both providing welcome injections of income at a statistically low point in the annual human expiry profile, and a couple of promotional dinners for local hospice managers. He did remember flicking through some papers at Pitt Lane but nothing remained in his head except a name. Wasn't it O'Hare or O'Halloran? He tugged the drawers in his desk, pulling out and fiddling with folders and envelopes. 'Here it is.' He scanned a paper. 'But we're expecting a bloody Irishman. Kenneth O'Hara.'

Broody steepled his fingers. 'Not exactly, Walter. There is a Kenneth O'Hara. He was a candidate for the job but I believe he is talking to Rangers. I don't think Siddley's high on his calls pending list at this moment in time. Besides, we've got ourselves a real bargain with this chap. He's Japanese, by the way.'

'He's what?' Hardcastle's voice broke into a disbelieving, manic cackle. He snatched off his glasses and brought the letter to his nose.

'He's Japanese,' Broody said casually. 'Very famous over there, I hear. And besides, the Japanese Football Association's paying Ken Ohara's wages and all his accommodation. They want him to get experience in top flight English football.'

'Top flight, eh?' Hardcastle muttered pensively. 'People with perspicacity and foresight, these Japanese.' Then his face collapsed. 'But O'Hara's a bloody Irish name.'

'Japanese as well, it seems. Means "little field" or something. The pronunciation is, as near as damn it, identical.'

'This has got cock-up written all over, David. Can't we get rid of him?'

Broody sniffed. Your cock-up, casket man, he thought, laughing inwardly behind a stern exterior. You should have taken your mind off the obituaries for a minute and read the papers I gave you. 'We'll look like right bloody fools if we try. Besides, at least twenty-six Japanese journalists have requested press facilities at tomorrow's game and there's more on the way.'

'What?' Hardcastle's face turned purple, consuming the scabby liver spots. 'Then there'll be more of them than spectators.' He pretended to read from a stapled batch of papers. What had Broody said to him on the mobile last Monday when he reached him at the funeral home? The usually sombre premises of Hardcastle and Sons, Funeral Directors, had been humming with noise and people. Phones were ringing, grieving, impatient relatives cluttered the reception desk seeking burials, cremations and sympathy; the Royal Infirmary had just delivered a vacuum-sealed bag of human hard and soft core from the bypass accident for funerary reconstruction; and there were coffins and caskets to order and hearses to position. As he struggled selflessly to dignify the aftermath of the weekend carnage, the managerial vacancy at Siddley United FC had stayed firmly on the back burner. All he remembered of the untimely phone call was Broody saying something like: 'We've got O'Hara,' and he himself saying something like:

'That's perfect'. Now, confronted with the consequences of his lapse of attention, he tried to pedal furiously backwards, 'I've had so much to take on board this week,' he said, his eyes scrolling a page. 'Solid background, I see. Managed the ... the ... Kinki Princes.' For an instant, his finger froze over the paper. When he spoke, his voice was an octave higher. 'The Kinki what?'

'A big team in the J-League,' Broody explained. 'That's the Japanese professional system. 'Unfortunate name, though. Apparently, it's a place name. Like Siddley.'

Sounds like a troupe of male strippers, Hardcastle thought, gathering the papers. He cast a rueful glance at the portrait of Len Grate, who, with a broken big toe, once scored three goals, and had one disallowed, in the first round of the Paggett Aggregates Trophy. With the Pitties facing a big cup game in four weeks he felt humiliated, if not completely deflated. We are the Pitties of Pitt Lane, he reminded himself, and no sodding foreigner is going to destroy the heart of English football. 'We'd better go and meet him, but I've got a horrible feeling we're going to be the laughing stock of the RoustaRodent Solutions League by tomorrow night.'

A few steps behind the mumbling, retreating figure of the chairman, David Broody turned from the door and drew Monique to him with a finger hooked under a button of her blouse. 'I'll thank you properly tonight, my love,' he whispered. 'The Duck and Prime Minister at seven?' It was Monique who, at her generous lover's insistence, had deep-filed the papers on Ken-ichi Ohara and made sure that when the harassed chairman dashed in and out during Wednesday's training session the envelope on his desk contained the papers on the Irish managerial candidate. 'Then a spot of dinner before we have a look at the new dipper lights in my penthouse.'

Monique closed the door on the two men, turned towards

the window and threw her arms into the air, fists clenched. 'Yessssssssss!' she screamed. 'The messiah has come to Siddley. The Pitties are saved.'

A light, beige raincoat drawn around him, Ken-ichi Ohara sat on a bench clutching a sports bag in his lap, his knees between two mismatched suitcases. Topped with neat, off-centre parted hair, his taut angular face was a picture of confusion. Squabbling voices invaded his agile mind, the strongest urging him to leave the cold room, with its cracked paint and the odorous reminder of unwashed men, infused disinfectant and lavatories. Go back to Japan, unwind the journey that began in Yokohama and ended in Siddley, a town somewhere in central England. Surely the damp, chilly air and the rusty, corrugated metal sheets surrounding the Pitt Lane ground did not constitute the end of a road that had brought him from the Kinki Princes Wakayama Stadium, with its retractable roof, thermal bath and 30,000 squealing, shrieking supporters who smashed their clackers in unison, waved cerise and white banners as one and gathered up their litter as they celebrated a victory or cried over a defeat?

The host nation's heroics in the 2002 World Cup apart, when they reached the quarter-finals, it was 1998 in France, for which Japan had to qualify through skill and samurai determination on the pitch, that constituted the greatest achievement in the brief history of Japanese professional soccer. Glorious defeat after three bravely contested games electrified scores of millions of people watching them. Ken-ichi Ohara, a veteran at 25, was a right-sided wing back on that national team and he provided the pinpoint cross that was converted into Japan's only goal of the tournament. He became a national hero in a country desperate for sporting heroes, but elimination after the first round made it all a bitter-sweet experience for the proud country: in the true spirit of Japan somebody had to take responsibility for the failure to progress and the coach was handed the metaphorical sword and sportingly fell on it. His resignation left a big hole, and the Japanese soccer association agonized, seeing how poor in depth was the national team, how short of experience were the players and coaches. In the short term they took the unpalatable step of hiring foreigners, a Frenchman, then a Brazilian, as the national coaches while they set about seeking a local remedy for the longer term. Ken-ichi Ohara had played for the south Japan team, the Kinki Princes, and when a knee injury two years after the 1998 World Cup made regular 90 minute games impossible to bear he became their player-manager, guiding them to their first league championship and adding the Nabisco Cup in his first full season. It was then, when consensus had been reached in the Japan Football Association that managerial experience could only be obtained abroad, someone discovered Ken Ohara spoke English. It was a sign from the *shinto* gods: Ohara would carry the dreams and ambitions of Japan on his shoulders and he would be sent to England, the cradle of soccer, so that he might learn. Inviting a top English team to meet Racing Rio Juniors, or some other greedy South American show-offs, in a Euro-American super champions showdown in Japan provided enough of a bribe for the English football association to offer to find a club where the young Japanese could hone his skills.

'Why Siddley?' Ohara was wondering when a ruddy faced, *dango* pudding of a man in a three piece black suit bobbed in, his hand outstretched.

'Mr Ohara,' Walter Hardcastle beamed, professionally estimating the slender oriental at five feet eight, slight of shoulder, the perfect complement to the new line of Eternal Promise walnut veneered caskets. 'Welcome to Pitt Lane.

May I call you Ken?' He gripped Ohara's hand. 'I'm Walter Hardcastle, chairman of this great football club.'

'I am very happy to be a Pittie,' the Japanese replied. He'd practised his opening line on the plane. 'Please call me Ohara.'

'Wonderful, wonderful, Ken. Meet our chief executive, the power house and inspiration for our club.'

'Dave Broody,' Broody said, showing his perfectly capped teeth. 'Anything you need whilst you're with Siddley United, you come to me. Understand, Ken? Can't help you if you want to eat the black pudding raw, though.'

The two Englishmen chuckled mysteriously. Ohara smiled his incomprehension and followed them up a narrow stairway to a long room panelled in knotted wood and decorated with photographs and paintings with a football theme. Young men in tracksuits clustered around a corner bar, some of them smoking. They nudged each other and turned when the exotic newcomer and the club's senior officials entered. 'The Pitt Lane hospitality suite,' the chairman explained to Ohara, nodding authoritatively at the drinkers. 'The lads are just finishing their last training session before the big match tomorrow.'

'They are players?' Ken Ohara's eyes fell on the tall glasses and the golden liquid inside and the smouldering ashtrays. His façade was crumbling. 'They play game tomorrow?'

'They do, Ken, they do,' the chairman said grandly, mistaking Ohara's bewilderment for admiration. 'A big one. Cogworth. The lads are really up for it.'

David Broody released a cautionary cough. 'Not the lads round the bar, Walter. They're recovering from minor injuries.'

'Oh, right.' Hardcastle placed a hand possessively across Ohara's shoulders. 'Come and meet the other directors. We always meet up at Pitt Lane before a match. Pep up the players, like. Show them we care.'

At the end of the room, under the frowning portrait of a Victorian gentleman carrying a be-ribboned scroll, three men watched the new manager approach. 'He doesn't look Irish,' the slim, effete man in the blazer and club badge said. Ronald Townrow, slender, elegant city councillor and prominent solicitor with a suite of offices in Iron Gate. He held ten per cent of the shares in the football club. 'Nearer to your part of the world, Harry.'

'I'm African, Ronnie, a refugee from Uganda,' Harry Patel, the king of Siddley and district discount sports equipment, declared for the hundredth time. 'I've never been to India.' His smooth, pale brown skin stretched as he smiled. Harry also had a ten percent stake in the Pitties. It was not a marketable investment in reality, more of an intangible gesture of goodwill, good for his image as a sports promoter, entrepreneur and philanthropist.

'It was Walter's call,' the third man said, surveying a piece of twisted lemon in his otherwise empty tumbler. 'We agreed to leave it to him and his contacts in the FA.' He was Geoffrey Osborne, a hunchbacked, arthritic meat merchant and possessor of another ten per cent shareholding and a man who claimed he saw the epic 5-4 win over Cogworth in 1938. The others muttered and nodded. 'Walter's decision. Yes, of course. Fine choice. Yes. Very nice to meet you, lad,' he said when moments later he was presented to Ohara, enunciating in loud syllables, as if speaking to a deaf Martian.

No one at this point considered it worth mentioning that the club's honorary president, a baronet called Sir Reginald Pitt, did not bother with team affairs, even the appointment and presentation of a new manager. He rarely attended the club's board meetings and had no interest at all in football and was rarely seen in the hospitality lounge, never in the stands. The Pitt family had owned all of the shares in Siddley United until the 1970s when the current baronet's father began selling down his interest until just 20 per cent remained in the founding family, although tradition still required that a Pitt fill the honorary club president's chair.

Someone thrust a glass of whiskey into Ohara's hand and the chairman made a toast to the future success of the Pitties with much bravura. 'Let me show you the ground while it's still fairly light,' Hardcastle said to the Japanese when the smattering of applause had faded. Leading a short procession, he described the function of each room along the hollow, cold passages. 'You'll have seen the changing rooms,' he reminded his new manager as they descended a set of steep, concrete steps. 'And this is the manager's office,' he declared portentously, opening the door to a cubicle between the home and visitors' changing rooms. 'It's all yours.'

Ohara ran his eyes over the bare metal schoolroom desk, the battered filing cabinet, the wall calendar with the Siddley United team on it, stuck at July, and the single bulb hanging from the ceiling. He managed a smile of gratitude.

They climbed a short flight of steps and emerged onto the pitch through a tunnel. The figures running patterns or practising shooting stopped when they noticed the directors of the club on the touchline with an odd-looking stranger. Ohara took in his new workplace. The old-fashioned floodlights hung over the corners of the ground like preying aliens and the wooden stand behind them boasted lime green plastic seats, except for those in the directors' enclosure which were padded. The words Pitt Stand were just legible in faded white paint across the sloping corrugated roof. Ohara peered at the other stand, a ramshackle shelter at one end of the ground, backing, he was told, onto the Grand Siddley Canal, and then the steep concrete terracing opposite. It was studded with handrail posts of the like he'd only seen in soccer history books. The other end of the ground was a gentle stepped slope, apparently abandoned to nature. It must have been a big, popular club once, Ohara thought, as he took in the flat and broadly proportioned pitch. Looking harder, in the thin light, he saw that the grass was thin and patchy, and badly scuffed after only a month and a half into the season. It told him the Pitties trained and played on the same turf, or invested little or nothing in its maintenance and drainage.

'I can see you're overwhelmed,' Hardcastle beamed. 'We are rightly proud of Pitt Lane.'

'Forty two thousand here when we beat Cogworth in 1938,' Geoffrey Osborne commented. 'And I was one of them.' He didn't hear the others groan.

'How many come tomorrow?' Ohara wondered, an image of teeming stands and terraces coming alive in his mind.

'Yes. Tell us, David,' Harry Patel said, a mischievous smirk on his light brown face as he turned to the chief executive. 'Has the ticket hotline been overwhelmed?'

David Broody smiled thinly. A few weeks from now, certainly by Christmas at the latest, when Siddley United FC contemplate another empty season and the last bloody football fan has squeezed his pie-and-ale bloated gut through the rusty, temperamental turnstile, it will already be over. Pitt Lane will be a heap of rubble. The syndicate was ready with the money, the contracts were drafted. Only one small, technical issue remained to be resolved, all that stood between him and the greatest property deal in Siddley's history. 'Cogworth will bring a good contingent, of course,' Broody told the confused Japanese. 'They're only six miles away. I foresee a good five hundred bums on the seats.'

Had Ohara heard right? Five hundred? A whistle shrilled across the cavernous enclosure and as the thin autumn light gave way to darkness behind the main stand roof, the players drifted towards the tunnel.

A thin, balding man in shorts, his left leg swathed in bandage, hobbled up first, supported on a walking stick. He flicked a cigarette butt onto the pitch. 'Terry Dribble,' the chairman announced. 'Terry. Meet Ken Ohara, our new team coach.' To Ohara, he said: 'Terry's been interim coach since Moby McNally's untimely death. I gave him a lovely send off. Solid oak, with a satin polish finish, if I remember correctly. Anyway, Terry's soldiered on for us, in spite of the accident with the roller.'

David Broody leaned over the newcomer. 'We've not been very lucky with managers at Siddley lately,' he breathed, as if to suggest bad karma went with the job.

'Terry will pick tomorrow's team,' Harry Patel announced. 'While you get your feet under the table, assess the players' skills, soak up the atmosphere.'

'And we'll present you to the fans before kick-off,' the chairman declared. He turned to the crippled coach and asked him to introduce the players, who had formed a sullen, ragged semi-circle. 'Then bring him upstairs. See you shortly,' he said, patting the Japanese protectively before leading his fellow directors into the tunnel.

Another blur of names and faces: Billy, Les, Lucas, Kevin, Gary, Omar, Dean, Darren, Scott and something Pitt. Pitt? The name was everywhere, Ohara thought, as he fell in line with Terry Dribble's painful shuffle.

In the club bar, Walter Hardcastle was standing expansively before a glass-fronted cabinet. At the return of the new manager he drew an open palm across his body, luring Ohara's eyes, like a bullfighter would a bull. 'Your job, Ken, is to fill this trophy cabinet.' It looked empty, but as the club chairman stepped aside to complete his sweeping gesture he revealed a small wooden shield in the centre.

'The 1982 Siddley and District Senior Indoor Five-a-Side Trophy,' Councillor Townrow said grandly. Ohara stooped appreciatively to read the inscription.

'Let's drink to the future again,' Chairman Hardcastle erupted, his face inflamed with passion. 'To a trophy cabinet full of silver.'

'Hear, hear,' Geoffrey Osborne blurted, followed a beat behind by Patel and Townrow, all suddenly aware of the enormity of the challenge posed by the chairman.

Only David Broody stood back, barely separating the glass from his lips as he mouthed his empty agreement with the sentiment. What a useless bloody football club, he was thinking, just like an old, worn out brassiere: no cups and no support. Nobody'll miss it for more than a day.

2

'Welcome to Pitt Lane, home of the Pitties, for another ninety minutes of scintillating ballet-on-grass from Siddley's gladiators in the famous lime and tangerine strip. This is Saturday football on Radio Siddley with Nigel Wensleydale, brought to you today by Uncle Dunny's Incredible Edibles, purveyors of Siddley's finest meat and vegetable pies. And what a Saturday it's going to be! The rumours are true, and you heard it first on Radio Siddley. The Pitties have a new manager. He's continental, but from which continent?'

Ken Ohara sat in his musty office, like a monk in his cell, a folder of papers open on the desk. He rubbed jet-lagged red-rimmed eyes. The room, with its battered steel cabinet and two old office chairs, was even smaller than his temporary lodgings at the Five Winds Motel just off the motorway spur. He hadn't slept well. The noise from the traffic was nothing to the unease in his mind, and he'd woken early, leaving the motel in his suit as milky sunshine washed the stark barrack-like building. He walked towards the town, aiming at an imposing church tower, a Kinki Princes scarf wrapped high up his chin. Last night, in a gesture of welcome, the directors of Siddley United had taken him to Nicola's Trattoria for dinner, and the spicy chicken calabriana, with a heap of fried potatoes, had not lain well with the gaseous wine Geoffrey Osborne insisted was Tuscany's finest. While Walter Hardcastle was describing how his technicians had sewn back the severed head of the most distressed of the bypass accident victims, Ken Ohara's thoughts were on Siddley United and the circumstances that had seen him parachuted into it. He had to know how, and more than how, he had to know why it had to be Siddley?

When the Japan Football Association urged him to help Japanese soccer at its most critical moment he'd searched the internet for Siddley, scrolling through the mass of leagues and divisions and imagining himself bawling instructions from the touchline of a tradition-soaked club. Realistically he knew he would have to start the learning process by coaching in the lower levels but hadn't realized how much lower. Below the Premiership and the three senior divisions of the Football League was the Conference, a league of semi-professional teams with big squads and bigger dreams. Below them lay the matrix of feeder leagues from all over England, with hundreds of town and country teams, and it was there, near the bottom of the premier division of the RoustaRodent Solutions League he found Siddley United. The league table after the season's first five games credited the Pitties with four defeats and a draw, level bottom on points with three other teams. The league's sponsors, he went on to discover, provided a range of household cleansing and pest control services, the name, once Ohara had found someone to decipher it, betraying its original speciality. In another internet link, leading to Siddley's daily evening newspaper, the *Sentinel*, he read about the tragically bizarre accident that had robbed Siddley United of its ambitious manager, Moby McNally. From where, Ohara wondered as the stalks of the floodlights appeared like ghostly predators above the rooftops, was he going to find the inspiration to meet the chairman's great expectations for a trophy?

A cold mist hung in the air as Ohara approached the

weathered old stadium along empty streets of brick terraced houses, almost all of them in darkness, their windows boarded. In the window of one of the houses still occupied a handwritten sign pleaded: 'Save Our Homes'. Pitt Lane, the home of the Pitties, he soon realised, was in the dilapidated heart of the old industrial city, with the cathedral and its cobbled close a short walk away. Six hours still to kick off against Cogworth and the football ground was deserted. Had he half expected a grand reception, a crush of fans desperate to be the first to greet their team's exotic saviour? Or the team and staff, anxious to impress the new manager? He sighed, raised his jacket collar against the chill and walked around the old corrugated fencing until he reached a rusted gate in a high brick wall. Alone and with time he eased the gate open, finding himself on a set of worn stone steps leading to a towpath and a brackish, long-redundant canal. He stood between the water and the chipped sooty brick wall of Pitt Lane's Canal Stand and had to back against it to pass an old man in a flat cloth cap who, fishing rod between his legs, sat in a low folding chair, dribbling cigarette smoke as he stared transfixed at the whorls on his float. Stirred by the movement behind him, the huddled figure half-turned his head and mumbled a greeting at what he assumed was another fisherman. But unclouded by age his senses engaged and logged onto the young, smartly dressed oriental male with the briefcase.

'You the new foreign manager?' he said hoarsely. ''im they talked about on Radio Siddley this morning? You that Chinese Irish bloke?'

Confused, it must be the dialect, Ohara's head dropped respectfully in a brisk bow.

'How do you do? I am Ken-ichi Ohara. And I'm Japanese Japanese.'

The old man nodded sympathetically, showing a row of

brown, uneven teeth. The cigarette had burned out in his mouth and the remains were stuck in a crevice. 'Alfred Widdison's the name. Japanese, eh? Name sounds Irish. It don't matter. The Pitties need more than them *geisha* girls to perk up their game.'

Ohara smiled his incomprehension.

'You a *sam you ray*, then?'

Ohara backed against the wall, shivering as a drip of icy water breached his jacket collar. 'I'm sorry? I . . .'

The fisherman trapped his rod with his knees and made a two-handed slashing motion over the water. 'I've seen 'em with them swords on the telly.'

'What am I doing here?' Ohara moaned in Japanese. 'You mean, *samurai*? They were swordsmen many years ago. No more in Japan.'

'Pity. The Pitties could do with some sharp steel up their backsides.'

'Are you coming to the game today, sir?'

The old man chuckled. 'Not bloody likely. There's more chance of me catchin' the Loch Ness monster in this 'ere canal before I see the Pitties win.' He reeled in the hook with a skewered maggot dangling from it. 'Good luck to you anyway,' he told Ohara, who was setting off again. 'Enjoy it while you've still got the ground to play on.'

Ohara tugged a heel from a deep crack in the path and turned. What had the old man said? 'I'm sorry. What's the matter with the ground?'

The reel spun and line swished across the canal. 'No more than rumours.'

'What rumours, may I ask?'

Alf Widdison's face twisted into a bitter snarl. 'They want to pull the stands down, sell off the old ground and put up fancy flats and offices and all that. It'll mean the end of the club. And sooner rather than later.'

'That's very strange.' Ohara was thinking about his one-year contract and the challenge of the chairman to bring a trophy to Pitt Lane.

'Haven't you seen the houses round here? Most of 'em empty, boarded up. They're all comin' down. Not mine, though. I'm going to fight the wreckers. They'll have to take me out in a coffin.'

'Is that your house, with the sign?' Ohara wondered. 'Save our homes.'

'In Church Street. Yes, it is. Only three of us left.'

'Is the stadium going to be broken?' He was struggling for the right words.

Alf pointed a finger menacingly. 'You ask that club bloody chief executive chap of yours. What's his name? Brady.'

'Mr Broody?'

'Right. David Broody. He's got his fingers in every crooked piece of property business in Siddley. He'd know what's goin' on with my house and the football ground.'

Crooked? Ken Ohara was muddled to distraction. 'Have you always lived here, Mr Widdison? Close to the Pitt Lane ground.'

'I'm Alf,' Alf said stiffly. 'I've been here for ever, man and boy, same street, same house. Seventy five years. My dad, Endymion Widdison, played for the Pitties when he was a lad, on this very ground. More than ninety years ago. Would've played more were it not for the war. Not the one against your lot, mind you. That were me. The others, your German mates, the first time round. When dad came back from France he was too old to play any more. And, course, he only had his right leg left.' He shook his head sadly. 'Siddley's a true football town and this is the Pitties' centenary season. Now they're goin' to chuck it all away, take the heart out of the city. We haven't got much of a team and soon we won't have the grand old ground either. Me old dad's turnin' in his grave.'

A splash, a sudden flash of translucent turquoise, jerked the two men's eyes to the water. Alf's line flew out of the reel. A fin split the surface, carving a vee of ripples that raced towards the canal banks as the shimmering creature headed towards the bridge over Talbot Street. 'I've got it,' he hollered, on his feet, his rod bowed. 'I've caught Nessie.'

A wiry, 60-something man called Charlie Wharton, with deep set eyes and pale skin on an oddly youthful face, finally responded to Ohara's knocks and calls and let him into the ground. Charlie cleaned Siddley's public toilets for a regular living and undertook manual operations at Pitt Lane for pleasure and pocket money: pitch care, boiler maintenance and turnstile oiling.

On his way down the chilly passages to the manager's spartan office Ohara took in the home team's changing room. Unironed match shirts waited on locker handles for the players; boots, left where they fell and stuffed with shinpads, still bore the mud and grime from yesterday's training; a lager can used as an ashtray had fallen over and bits of tobacco lay shredded in a patch of dried beer. In the joining room, a broad, deep, tiled bath reminded him of home, and the steaming, clear waters of a Japanese *ofuro* tub, at least until he saw the scum around the rim and the muddy stains on the sides and floor, conveyed from pitch straight to pool.

A list of tasks, not all about football, formed in his mind as he walked through the tunnel and out onto the pitch. It was windless, the misty rain had lifted, giving way to thin sunless light. He sniffed the air appreciatively. A perfect day for football. He only had to think about playing to feel a surge of excitement, to hear the rising roar of the crowd as two lines of men spilled from the tunnel and fanned across the pitch. And then, as always, came the pain, imagined or real. That needle prick twinge nesting deep in his right knee to remind him of the old injury that had ended his playing career and tell him to keep his tracksuit on for ever. Even as he saw the deep rich turf of Kinki Prince stadium the morning light was revealing the wasteland that was the Siddley United playing surface, now without the deceptively flattering radiant glow from the floodlights. Scuffed, thin turf formed an oval over most of the central playing surface, reaching the two goalmouths. The grass was thicker along the wings and in the corners but it was slashed and torn, the divots and tufts unattended. Another sigh, more like an audible groan. The season was barely six weeks old. In the Kinki Prince stadium you didn't train on the pitch you played matches on and when you gouged out a divot in a game you apologised later to the groundsman. He noticed a fork left propped against a dugout and, removing his coat, seized the tool and zigzagged around the pitch, pressing back the divots with a heel and forking the patchy turf busily. Working his way around the ground, and with a sheen of sweat on his pale olive face, he noticed several figures in the main stand, watching him.

In the manager's room, with the door opened, occasional echoes of footsteps on bare concrete or an outburst of laughter told him that Pitt Lane was coming to life. On the scratched metal desk club and players' files had been readied for the new manager in coloured folders that suggested freshness and hope, shortlived emotions soon dashed by their desperate contents. Siddley United FC had a shallow pool of 18 regular players, most with full or part-time jobs, a few with higher league experience. Two were over 30, the senior goalkeeper, Kevin Stopham, a plumber, and the left back, William 'Billy' Pickwich, a taxi driver. The team captain was currently Simon Pitt, a common English name, Ohara guessed naively, having seen it on doors, walls and stands. Lucas Mandrake, a left sided wing back, had even signed youth papers with Newcastle from the top professional rank but when he was told he might have to play on Sundays he retired at 16 to train as a teacher and pursue his religious destiny. A piece of paper clipped to the file of a player called Clint Hopp simply read, 'parole expected in November'. Parole?

Ohara had reached the last file when Terry Dribble hobbled into the manager's office with his final team selection, grateful to slump in the spare chair. He ran through the names, which Ohara was beginning to recognize. 'We usually play four-five-one.'

'Shouldn't we be more aggressive at home?' Ohara wondered.

'We've lost three away and lost one and drawn one at home. I'm trying to plug the holes before we get too far into the season.'

Ohara studied the teamsheet. 'So that's Breakin, Pickwich, Diamond and Fisher at the back.'

'Right. With Drummond, Grant, Omerod, Pitt and Mandrake across the middle. Mandrake's a good attacking option, if we need it.'

'Just Dean Slutz up front.'

'Pitt can play just behind him if he has to,' Dribble said pessimistically, his voice dribbling to nothing.

Ohara's arms were folding over the desk. 'Is he a good captain? A good leader of his players?'

Dribble scratched an imaginary itch on his ear. 'He's got a degree, and he's an estate agent by profession.'

'Like selling houses, property?'

'Yeah, that's it. I suppose you call it real-estate, like the Yanks.'

Ohara remembered what the old fisherman had said about the sale of the football ground and the houses around it. Was Simon Pitt the broker in Broody's plan, he wondered? 'Is he connected to the Pitt family of the club?' he asked.

'Simo? Course he is. His dad's the club president. Simo's

the great grandson of Sir Abraham Jerusalem Pitt. That's him in the picture in the hospitality suite. He made his fortune in the textile mills. Put Siddley on the map did Sir Abby. He built all the houses around here and donated the football ground to the people of Siddley. Course, he stipulated it had to be used for football and his descendants, the males of course, always got a place on the team.'

'Is it true the stadium's going to be destroyed and the land sold?' Ohara asked timidly.

Dribble scoffed. 'Just silly rumours.'

'I heard Mr Broody is in real estate business so perhaps he sees big opportunity here.'

Dribble dismissed the idea with a sardonic scowl. 'They can sell the old terraced houses around the ground, what they call the old Pitt Estate, but not the football club land and what's now the car park. They're held in trust on behalf of the town. For ever, I understand.'

Ohara pondered the point, not really understanding.

'So what does the chief executive do?'

'Runs the place like it were his business. Looks after all the legal things, the players' interests, the money side. We're a small club so we all have to do whatever's needed.'

'So he is the chief executive, secretary, treasurer?'

Dribble nodded. 'Monique Wainwright runs the administration day to day, she's the only full-time employee, apart from you now that is, but David's got overall responsibility. Of course, he's not a director, and he doesn't have any shares in the club.'

The phone rang, summoning Ken Ohara to the hospitality room. 'I will leave the game completely to you today, Mr Dribble,' the Japanese said. 'And wish you luck. By the way,' he said, patiently matching the injured man's laboured movement up the stairs. 'How did my predecessor die?'

'Moby McNally? Tragic it was. It were at night near the end of training. He went down to the canal to get the ball

Billy Pickwich kicked over the stand roof. He must've slipped and fell in. They didn't find the body till morning. In a horrible state it was, but the chairman did him a lovely funeral. And we got the ball back.'

'What about you? The leg.'

Dribble chuckled. 'Daft really. I were leading the lads in some press-ups when the mechanical roller ran over me. Charlie Wharton said it started up on its own, apparently. I've only been off crutches for a couple of weeks.'

'Did it happen at night as well?' Ohara wondered, swamped by a miasma of cigarette smoke when he opened the door to the lounge for the injured coach.

'Night? Yeah. Well, it were dark. We train late and don't always turn all the floods on.'

'Two coaches have accidents,' Ohara murmured in Japanese. 'Strange. I must be careful.'

Heads turned as Ken Ohara entered the crowded long room, and Walter Hardcastle led a prolonged round of applause. The mood was cheerful, full of optimism. A table under the portrait of Sir Abraham Pitt was laid for the directors' pre-match luncheon. Ohara sat next to Walter Hardcastle and noticed the place on Geoffrey Osborne's left was set for lunch but the chair was empty. 'That's for Sir Reginald Pitt, Sir Abraham's grandson,' the chairman explained. 'He's with us in spirit. As the saying goes, while there's a Pitt in the boardroom the Pitties are indestructible.'

Florie, who had fed three generations of Pittean dignitaries, fussed over the new manager, serving him a heap of fried potatoes, boiled vegetables and a pie. With its hard, ribbed crust and dark brown, gelatinous mucus oozing from a fissure in its swollen belly, it looked to Ohara's untravelled palate like a dying, punctured prehistoric reptile. 'Do the players eat this before a game?' he asked Harry Patel on his right.

'It's also part of the tradition. The lads eat Florie's famous

Pittie pie with chips before every home game.' He saw Ohara's eyes fall on the potatoes, peas and carrots on his plate. 'Not me, though. I'm strictly vegetarian.'

Winnie, Florie's twin in height, advanced age and black and white lace apron, brought another tray of beer and Ohara's lemonade. Through a gap Ohara saw three young men at the bar. The same three injured players he'd met yesterday. They were all laughing, flushed with drink, and two were smoking. 'Excuse me,' he told the table and sidled his way across the room.

'Hello, Boss,' the three men chorused.

'Or should we say, Hitachi afternoon? Or is it Kawasaki, Mitsubishi?' Lenny Hampton guffawed, his voice cracked by a deep cough. He was a tall, lithe man, his head shaved, like most of the team. The other two were Mike Groot and Alan Blink.

'Shouldn't you be with coach Dribble, preparing for the game?' Ohara said.

'With Tel?' Hampton shrugged. 'Nah, Boss. We're injured. Blinko's got a bit of a groin strain, Mickey's carrying a knock on his knee and I've got a virus on me chest.' He stubbed out his cigarette. 'It's keepin' me off work as well.'

'Why do you not stay in bed?'

'He came in to support the lads,' Blink said. 'Like me. Big needle match today. Cogworth.'

Ohara drew himself up. His bean-size nose was level with Lenny Hampton's scrubby chin. 'Virus is very serious. Only by resting will you recover. What did the doctor say?'

'Same as you,' Hampton confessed, unable to stifle a smirk.

'We are short of players and the team needs you to be fit very soon. Please go home now and rest.' The barmaid froze, a cloth stuck in the belly of the dimpled beer mug she was wiping. Drinkers, club members and their guests, who had followed the new manager from the corners of their eyes, prodded their companions.

'We'll walk you home, Lenny,' Mike Groot smirked. 'Tuck you in, we will.'

Ohara put a hand on the injured midfielder's bare forearm. 'He doesn't need help. But do you want to support the team, in spite of your knee injury?'

'Of course I do but—'

'Thank you. Please find a suitable implement and clean all the boots in the changing room. They are very dirty from yesterday's training. You can sit on the bench and rest your knee while you work.'

Groot's mouth fell open, but his new manager had turned to the third player, Alan Blink. A semi-circle of space had opened around them and the entire room was suddenly stilled. Ohara's rather high, irritated voice easily reached the board luncheon table. 'Please find the tool by the coaches' dugout and fork wet places on the pitch. I pressed the divots myself this morning but I notice some remain on the long terrace side. But please take care not to strain your groin again.' Blink could only nod, his chin limp. 'Oh, another thing.' Ohara was looking at the pretty young woman with large brown eyes behind the bar, but his words were directed at everyone. 'Players must not drink alcohol or smoke here on game days.'

'The lads usually let their hair down a bit in here after a match,' pleaded a fit-looking man of about 50 called Matt Dennis, but he didn't press the point. He was the physio, trainer, scout, kitman and general dogsbody in a club short of resources.

'We have meeting instead after matches, including today,' Ohara said emphatically. 'We must remember our mistakes before we forget them, even if we win.'

Blink looked round, mouth agape, but the room was still, the pride of sporting Siddley frozen as they stood. Slowly,

Tina the barmaid's hand began to revolve again inside the glass and then, as if snapped from a hypnotic state, she reached out and snatched the brimming ashtray and dropped the contents in a bin liner.

Terry Dribble eased himself between the Japanese and the three scolded players, weight dripping from his shoulders, his leg suddenly feeling better. 'You heard the gaffer,' he said imperiously. 'Get off home, Lenny, and you lads to your jobs.'

'This is what we need in this club,' Councillor Townrow opined loudly at the directors' table, as the gathering picked up again. 'Oriental philosophy and discipline.'

'It's called zen,' Geoffrey Osborne informed his fellow directors. 'He'll have them sitting naked under the Siddleworth weir in January for some spiritual purification.'

'It'll take more than cold water to purify Legs Diamond or Gary Omerod,' Harry Patel chuckled.

'Be serious, gentlemen,' the chairman commanded with a self-satisfied smirk. 'We have unearthed a jewel in Mr Ohara. A *samurai* who will grace the lime green and tangerine of Siddley United.' He had found the papers on the new coach. 'Ken played for Japan in the last but one World Cup, you know, and he was a star player coach with the, er . . .'

'The Kinki Princes,' David Broody said flatly. The others grinned.

Hardcastle coughed. 'Yes, of course. With the Kinki Princes.' He brightened. 'He's a legend in his own life-time in Japan and of all the teams in all the football universe he chose to bring his skills and fame to Siddley. And he won't only manage and coach, he'll be on the pitch once graced by the likes of Len Grate, inspiring by example to make our centenary year the one the citizens of Siddley will forever remember. The Pitties will be the team to beat in the RoustaRodent Solutions League.'

'Bravo,' Harry Patel cheered.

'I'll drink to that,' the butcher Osborne offered, clinking his glass of port against Councillor Townrow's.

'Hear, hear,' Broody uttered lamely from the other end of the table. What the fool Hardcastle hadn't seen was Ohara's medical report, conveniently retained by Broody, along with the trifling detail passed on to him by his contact in the English Football Association that Ohara's knee injury limited his appearances to dire emergencies, and even then he couldn't play for more than 15 minutes before the pain flared and crippled him. No, gentlemen of the board, hiring a fit player manager wasn't in his plans at all when he set out to replace the unfortunate Moby McNally.

Ohara excused himself, and when he'd gone, Chairman Hardcastle led the board's loyal toast to their benefactor, Sir Abraham Jerusalem Pitt, and in the vainglorious portrait thought he saw, in the euphoria of the moment, the old philanthropist wink.

In the home team changing room Ohara wished Terry Dribble the best of luck on his last day in charge and addressed each player personally. The mood was strangely subdued, uncomprehending. Word of the new coach's first managerial commandments in the hospitality suite had sped to the dressing room, and they were all wondering what kind of persuasive power the Japanese possessed to cause Grooty to come down and scrape and rub their shoes in silence and place them tidily under the bench.

On her petite but voluptuous frame, and over leggings of loyal tangerine, Monique Wainright wore an outsize lime-green replica shirt. She was in a flustered state when she found Ken Ohara leaving the boisterous visitors' changing room, where he had greeted the manager of Cogworth Town. 'Help, Mr Ohara, please. There's lots and lots of reporters from your country outside. They don't speak any English. Can you come, please? Quickly.'

They'd come in cars and a hired bus, journalists and cameramen with huge lenses and tripods from the three big Japanese national dailies, from the sex and sport tabloids and the mass circulation weekly magazines. They milled outside, in front of the single ticket window and the hut selling Pitties key rings, lime green scarves and lapel badges, watched by sniggering youths drinking beer outside the Pitt Lane Arms and rumpled old men gathered around the hamburger and pie stall. The Japanese could have come from Mars. Reporters from the *Siddley Evening Sentinel* took pictures of them and interviewed fans and the curious; a jeep bearing a small antenna on top and sporting the logo of Radio Siddley spilled journalists who made straight for the oriental visitors.

On the word from Monique, David Broody was there, speaking loudly and slowly to the uncomprehending Japanese and the locals, promising them the appearance of Japan's first overseas football team manager. He herded the Japanese into the ground and onto the pitch where they waited on the touchline, weighing up the drab stadium, and the scattering of spectators, until Monique arrived with Ken Ohara. The directors and their guests watched the unique event from the verandah at the top of the Pitt Stand.

Nerves on edge, Ohara read a short statement in English and a much longer one in Japanese. 'It is an honour to be at Siddley United,' he told a battery of microphones and mini-recorders in Japanese.

A reporter from the *Hochi Sports*, who three days earlier had watched a Japanese player play for Juventus, asked: 'How do you find the fans' support in this club?'

Kick-off was 30 minutes away. Cogworth supporters were dribbling into the Canal Stand, enough so far to occupy about two buses. The central part of the main stand was dotted with spectators, many more than usual, but the wings were empty. A few dozen people leaned on the barriers on the long terrace and a smattering of Japanese flags on the end terrace suggested the Japanese effect had been triggered. A couple of old men took their seats in the empty rows behind the makeshift press conference. Perhaps it was still early, Ohara hoped. 'I hear the people of Siddley are passionate about their soccer. I want them to come and show that passion here at Pitt Lane.'

'Did you pick the team today?' the *Shukan Sports* reporter asked.

'No. Our first team coach, Mr Dribble, is in charge today. I only arrived yesterday and must study the players and evaluate their skills.' A string of Japanese style questions about the new manager's emotions at leaving the homeland followed. Finally, a man bundled in a puffer jacket caught Ohara's attention, and he began with a statement.

'Siddley Town is not a full professional league team, as I think the Japanese people expected. Is this the best place for a future Japan national team manager to get experience?' It was Tanaka, from the *Kanto Daily Sports*, a racy tabloid with none of the constraints of the staid, national press. He'd also done his homework on the league structure, and where Siddley fitted into it.

The hairs on the back of Ohara's neck turned to ice. He knew Tanaka, and a good few others who understood football, had wondered publicly why the only offer to take on a Japanese coach had come from Siddley. Nobody in Japan had expected Real Madrid or Inter Milan, but a team of taxi drivers, painters and unemployed somewhere deep in England, nowhere near Manchester or Chelsea? They didn't know that the reception he received yesterday from the chairman, Walter Hardcastle, was strangely distant, uncomprehending, as if he'd been expecting somebody else. 'Siddley United is a very ambitious club in a big city, with some very talented players, and it is normal for them to be part-timers at this level until they reach the higher leagues.' And he had a positive scrap for them to feed on. 'Apart from challenging for promotion this season, I understand Siddley United have reached the semi-final of an important knockout competition and it is my dream to take them to the final.' Most of the Japanese journalists nodded and smiled as they held out their pocket recorders and microphones. Was it a shared feeling of compassion and understanding for a compatriot in professional peril overseas, or was it out of pity?

Tanaka was readying a second comment or question but Ohara was saved by an interruption from a thin woman with high, blushed cheekbones and square sunglasses. 'Yuki Enomoto from *Fashion Up Japan*,' she squeaked, poking the air with a rolled copy of the slimming and shopping magazine. Ohara was still something of a pin-up in a land short of heroes. 'When do you play against Beckham?' her readers would want to know.

Karen Saddleback imposed herself over the shorter foreigners. The last question had drawn a very brief answer. 'Do you have a word in English for the listeners to Radio Siddley, Mr Ohara?'

'It is an honour to serve Siddley United and the great fans from this great city,' he said carefully, just as he had rehearsed. 'I ask them to be patient. I will do my best.'

The Japanese journalists were taking photos when David Broody broke up the touchline press conference and directed the media to the main stand and Ohara to the directors' enclosure. Pathetic, he was thinking, scanning the thin spread of spectators.

It turned out to be Pitt Lane's biggest crowd for 7 years, topping 617, conspicuous among them the Japanese media in the Pitt Stand and employees from local Japanese companies, rooting for the Pitties from the town end terrace. David Broody was punching numbers into his mobile phone; Harry Patel was lighting Councillor Townrow's cigar; Terry

Dribble was trying to find a comfortable posture for his injured leg in the dugout; and Monique Wainwright was applying lipstick. They all missed the first goal of the afternoon.

'We'll be back with the deputy Prime Minister on Radio Siddley shortly,' Nigel Wensleydale breathed, his voice rising in an inevitable crescendo, 'but there's already been a goal in the match of the day. Let's go straight over to Karen Saddleback in the white heat of Pitt Lane. Karen.'

'And it's gone to the Pitties after only forty seconds. The ball came back to midfield magnet, Omar Grant, from the kick-off. He sprayed it to Gazza Omerod who'd gone wide on the left and he threaded it to Luke Mandrake who danced round two Cogworth defenders and hit it hard past the Cogworth goalie. Only the Pitties' third goal in five games. It may have taken a lucky bounce on the way but it's a goal that's going to set the RoustaRodent Solutions league alight. What a start for the Pitties in front of their new Japanese manager, Ken Ohara. Back to you, Nigel.'

The home team's lead lasted 13 minutes. Robby Breakin, caught for pace, clumsily brought down Cogworth's left winger in the penalty area and Kevin Stopham was left immobile by the bullet spot kick into the roof of the net to his left.

'The Pitties are going to have to score early in the second half if they're to stay in the game,' Karen Saddleback told the listeners of Radio Siddley as the team trooped off, 3-1 down at half time thanks to an own goal by Simon Pitt, who, to be fair, was not a natural defender, and slack marking by Billy Pickwich which allowed a shot that deflected in off Les Diamond. 'At least we're holding them to three,' Ohara heard Harry Patel tell a friend. 'And what about Lucas Mandrake's strike?' somebody enthused. 'Wasn't it a stunner?'

The Pitties failed to score early or at all in the second

half, while Cogworth were racking up another two. Ohara noted that both goals were scored on the break during sustained pressure by Siddley, and if the veteran goalkeeper, Stopham, had been a bit quicker on his feet he might have narrowed the angle more effectively. Good spirit, he wrote of his team, poor tactics, some useful individual skills, but watching a team of ball chasers, Ohara had been numbed by the energy they expended and wasted on fractious indiscipline, petty niggling, incomprehensible cursing and arm waving and useless, vein-bulging appeals. The captain, Simon Pitt, had tried to rally them but his voice was high and unimposing and after his own-goal he was too humiliated to cajole or enthuse the others. The Pitties played their football for the price of a meal and a few beers and it showed, and all this after a century of evolution at Pitt Lane. When the final whistle blew, Ohara stayed in his seat, filling in a notebook, trying to find a positive comment or two. He watched his players leave the pitch. Two were sharing a joke when they entered the tunnel but most had their heads down. Not Omar Grant: when the big, black centre back had shaken the hand of the referee and a few opponents he headed for the dressing room, slamming a fist into a palm, his face full of anger and defiance. Simon Pitt's empty smile towards Ohara said it all. The Japanese made a final note.

His head was filling with ideas and he stood with his chin in a hand for a moment as another intruded. A young Japanese woman with flowing, glossy hair and thin-rimmed glasses was caught in a bottleneck of people on the stairs, just outside the directors' box, a few rows below Ohara. She wasn't a journalist: she'd been sitting among the Pitties supporters and wore the club's lime-green scarf over her narrow shoulders. When she turned to file through the exit tunnel their eyes met and both raised a tentative hand of mutual understanding, like compatriots stranded abroad do. Ohara moved to the front of the directors' enclosure. 'Mr Dribble,' he called, seeing the temporary manager on his last day in charge come limping along the touchline, a man broken in body and spirit, his face ashen. 'Well done, today. Please tell the team I'll talk to them in the dressing room in five minutes.' To his surprise the Japanese woman had turned and was heading up the steps towards him.

'Ohara *san*?' she chirped when she reached the edge of the directors' box. Under a leather jacket, she wore a tight black jumper tucked into her jeans, with a little pouch attached to her belt. Her compatriot nodded the slightest of bows.

'Ken-ichiro Ohara. *Hajimemashite.*'

'Rika Yamaguchi. Nice to meet you too.'

'You're not a journalist,' he remarked as she fumbled in her belt bag. Glancing behind him, he saw the Japanese press contingent had dispersed with their pictures and stories and no doubt as bewildered as he was about life with Siddley United in the RoustaRodent Solutions League. She handed him a business card which told him she worked in the president's office of Uno Electronics Europe, a subsidiary of Uno Electronics, Japan.

'We make computer components on St Elphin's estate.'

'I don't have a card yet,' Ohara apologised.

'Don't worry,' she said pleasantly. 'We all know who you are.'

He gave her a thin smile. 'Are you a regular Pitties fan or were you drawn by the historic occasion?'

She tossed her head sideways, her smile as wide as Tokyo Bay. 'I live in a flat over there, overlooking the marina. An English boyfriend brought me to Pitt Lane first and I liked it. Now I just come to home games when I'm not working. I couldn't miss today, could I? Your appointment. The news has only just hit Siddley, but it's been all over the Japanese media.'

'Ken,' Harry Patel called from the doorway above. 'We're in the boardroom when you're ready.'

'I will join you later, Mr Patel. I'm meeting the team first.' To Rika Yamaguchi, he said, 'I'm sorry, I have to go. I have a few things to say to my players. Thank you for supporting me and my team.'

'It's my pleasure. I used to watch you when the Kinki Princes played my team in Osaka. Do you remember a player called Taro Suzuki?'

Ohara was about to turn away when a needle of pain speared his right knee. 'Taro Suzuki? The Pompanol Osaka striker?'

'Yes. When he retired he joined Uno and now he's a quality control manager here in Siddley. He's the star player in our company team. I'm sure he'd like to meet you again.'

Like hell he would, Ohara thought. He stroked the imagined tenderness in his knee. Suzuki's tackle in a cup game four years ago was so late it was in the wrong decade and it put an end to Ohara's regular playing days. The operation on his cruciate ligaments was only partially successful and when he returned to the field six months later, he found the pace that had made him Japan's sharpest right-sided wing back was still there but every game played needed three weeks for the pain and ache to subside. Suzuki was only 28 when he retired, the common rumour having it that he gave up the riches of the J-League as a gesture of remorse for the tackle. 'Perhaps he will support Siddley at my first game in charge next Saturday,' Ohara offered.

'Away to Molecroft, isn't it? We'll all try to be there, mister manager.'

The chairman's office extended into a long boardroom and here the directors mixed with shirt sponsors and chums from the chamber of commerce, all with a drink in their hands. David Broody slipped into Monique's empty office at the purring of his mobile phone. 'You took your bloody time getting back to me,' he hissed into a cupped hand. Leaning against a filing cabinet, he had his back to the door and failed to hear Monique Wainwight's quiet entry. 'We can't take any chances with this bloody Japanese ruining things. He's lecturing the team now, and he's banned 'em from boozing, for God's sake.' He nodded impatiently while the other party spoke.

Monique approached him stealthily, her arms spread, ready to embrace him from behind, perhaps to unbutton something. Then she froze.

'I know I got him appointed here, but only because it's easier to keep a foreigner with a fucked up knee under control. He won't know what we're going to do to this club.' Another pause, then a vigorous shake of the head and the same hushed conspiratorial voice. 'Now look here, Reggie. We need those old papers like yesterday. The consortium's got the money ready and the bulldozers are waiting to move in.'

Bulldozers? Where? Monique didn't like the sound of any of this. Reggie? The only Reggie she knew was ... Sir Reginald Pitt, honorary president of Siddley United Football Club.

Broody was too engrossed to hear the click of her heels as she tiptoed backwards. He said: 'The only thing that's keeping you from a lot of money is ... Okay, okay, let's talk this over tomorrow. Drinks at the Duck and Prime Minister before lunch?'

Surely not *that* Reggie, she thought, closing the door carefully behind her. 'And they're meeting in *our* pub.'

The last two players were leaving the bath, emerging through brown, frothy scum that clung in braids on their bodies. Matt Dennis was massaging Darren Drummond's lower back on the treatment table, the young centre-back wincing at each probe of the physio's fingers. Dean Slutz was pulling on his jeans. Seeing the Japanese coach watching him, he snubbed his cigarette under the bench, muttering: 'Sorry boss, the last one.'

Ohara raised his arm and called for attention, coughing until they were quiet. He spoke in nervous, slightly broken English for 22 minutes, first thanking Terry Dribble for filling the gap since Moby McNally's untimely death and talking of his respect for the British football tradition which had spread to every corner of the world. He begged for time to understand the situation in Siddley United, to get to know the players, their skills and potential as well as pinpoint the weaknesses he had seen in today's performance and work on strategies for improvement. He confessed he was used to a bigger playing squad but, on the other hand, he hadn't worked in such a ground as Pitt Lane, a unique monument to the home of football, pounded by studs and irrigated with the sweat of local heroes for almost a hundred years. Darren Drummond was falling asleep on Robby Breakin's shoulder. Working in such an environment, with its dedicated staff and players, was an irresistible challenge Ohara was saying, drawing breath deeply for his finale. 'I will meet with each of you in the next few days according to your busy working schedules and work out a training schedule to suit you individually and as a team.' When he finished he lowered his chin to his chest and held it there for a few seconds. Simon Pitt lifted an arm tentatively.

'I'd like to welcome you, Mr Ohara, on behalf of the players and myself, to Siddley United.' Omar Grant led the applause, but it was tepid and not universal. No one moved when Ohara turned and left.

'Where does he bloody think he is?' Alan Blink wanted to know through a scowl, as he and a bunch of the players enjoyed a post-match drink in the Pitt Lane Arms. 'Bloody *reel* Madrid.'

'Mine's a pint of *rarger*,' Gary Omerod bellowed, pulling his eyes until they narrowed to slits. Blink roared, slapping his thigh. '*Rarger, rarger brudy funny, Galy.*'

'Give over, lads,' Darren Drummond grumbled at the chortling and the bad mimicry. 'Let's give him a chance. It can't be worse than having a crippled trainer, dozy, ego-tripping directors and that mean-arsed Broody for a chief executive.'

'Yeah,' the substitute goalkeeper Tony McDonald agreed. 'He talks a lot of sense for a foreigner. Sounds like he knows his football as well.'

'Moby McNally knew all the fancy tactics and words an' all,' the overworked veteran goalkeeper, Kevin Stopham, sniffed, twisting a finger in his ear. 'And where did it get 'im?'

Lucas Mandrake clutched his Bible and refused a second glass of orange juice. 'Amongst other things, it got him killed.'

3

After three days in the Five Winds Motel, Ken Ohara and his cases were transported in Walter Hardcastle's reserve hearse to a detached Edwardian house in an avenue bordered with lime trees in a suburb separated from the weathered tower blocks of a council estate by Siddley's inner ring-road. The back door opened onto a patio of cracked paving stones and a garden of tired grass bordered by shrubs and wilting perennials. A pair of gnomes grinned from the foot of a potted laurel. With a photo of a smiling woman in a kimono, an incense dish and a prayer tablet, he set up a makeshift Buddhist altar honouring his late mother on a bookshelf in the living room. Three packing cases containing his clothes, tracksuits, football boots, coaching manuals, DVDs, sachets of green tea and miscellaneous foodstuffs arrived by airfreight to his new address and a low-mileage Honda Accord was placed at his disposal.

With the team and staff telephone numbers input into his new mobile phone and the players' routines and availability on file, he was ready to manage the Pitties of Siddley, from the foot of the RoustaRodent Solutions League. He had stayed at Pitt Lane after the Cogworth match, and when the directors and everybody else had left, he sat in his little office, the desk covered in folders and files. He read every piece of paper on every player, their histories, performance evaluations, disciplinary and injury records and their pay and bonus terms, thanks to the orderly and precise records left by the unfortunate manager, Moby McNally, and updated and maintained by permanent and dedicated employee, Monique Wainwright.

While his mind drifted more than once to the dark canal and his drowned predecessor, his job now was to get to know the players, make them fitter, and more disciplined, more tactically aware, but it was clear from the files that 18 players had 18 daily routines. A few players were officially unemployed but he found they had 'commitments' which were not clearly specified; others were self-employed with flexible working hours and those in full employment had fixed working hours or movable shifts. Apart from the estate agent, the taxi driver, the plumber and the teacher, the small playing fees and occasional bonuses from Siddley United constituted a welcome and in some cases needed contribution to the players' lives. By splitting the days into time modules he would offer the players the slots of their choice three times a week with a full or near full squad turnout expected at least twice a week.

The Ohara era started in earnest on Sunday, the day after the Cogworth loss, when the small squad, including the walking injured, gathered at Pitt Lane. Lucas Mandrake agreed to appear but for religious reasons would not participate on the pitch; Gary Omerod hurried over from the DIY superstore when his shelf-stacking shift finished at 2.30p.m. Ohara called the players in turn to his office while the others trained under Terry Dribble and Matt Dennis. He repeated to each of them the words he'd laid on the directors. 'I only know one way to work, whatever the task, and that is with all my heart. In case of this football club it means very hard training, much discipline on and off pitch and to play together as a team. If you do not have the time and the will to be a Siddley United player, please do not hesitate to leave the club now.'

Siddley's squad was small by any standards, even the RoustaRodent Solutions League, and the available players and substitutes on Saturday had used up all resources, except for the reserve goalkeeper. Ohara had brought his boots from Japan and he was still technically a player-manager and eligible to play. But just imagining a torrid break-out from defence, a thrusting forward run ending with a sudden, ligament-straining stop or a clever change of pace climaxed with a joint-twisting cross, and from behind or the side an unyielding centre back or careless forward hurtling at him with feet flying, was enough to send another surge of imagined pain from his thigh to his fragile knee. Out of courtesy he called in the scion of the Pitt family first, the issue of the captaincy to be addressed. As a senior partner of Reilly-Pitt Prestige Estates, the honourable Simon Pitt sold upmarket property in Siddley and turned out for the Pitties for fun. A team place and the captaincy were apparently bestowed on the current young male Pitt heir by some unwritten right. 'Now I understand,' Ohara had smiled when Pitt explained. The young businessman seemed quite relieved when Ohara politely suggested a change to tradition. Pitt was a striker, but hardly a leader, and they both knew it intuitively.

'Are you taking on a triple role?' Pitt wondered. 'Manager, coach and captain?'

Ohara forced a thin smile and shook his head. 'Tell me about the players, please. Your assessment of their skills.' Pitt drew his chair to the desk, Ohara scribbling in his notebook while he spoke. When Pitt had finished, Ohara looked at him with a frown. 'I cannot understand what the players are calling each other. Is it a code?'

Pitt flashed his intelligent eyes, pleased to help. 'I'm "Simo", Les Diamond is obviously "Legs" and Robby Breakin is "Robba".' It wasn't obvious at all to Ohara. 'Darren Drummorid is "Dazza", Dean Slutz is "Deano". And so on.'

'But why is the goalkeeper, Kevin Stopham, called something like, "*Noee*"?'

Simon chuckled. 'It's short for, "no he doesn't".'

Ohara closed his eyes and shook his head in desperation. 'He doesn't what?'

'He doesn't live up to his name. He doesn't stop 'em.' Simon enunciated, as if to an idiot. 'He lets goals in.'

Ohara smiled, still deep in darkness, and turned a mimeographed paper with the season's fixtures, the results so far helpfully added by Monique, towards Pitt. Between the five league losses and the draw Monique had proudly drawn his attention to the good news by underlining several scores in red ink. 'Miss Wainwright told me that the Pitties have reached the semi-final of a cup competition.'

'Amazing, isn't it?' Simon Pitt declared. 'The Golden Mousetrap Trophy. We had a lot of luck in the earlier rounds but I think it's about to run out. We're at home but we've drawn the semi-pros of Yattock. They're joint top of the Conference. It'll be like Real Madrid against the Fat Cow pub team, but we'll have fun, make a few quid for the club.'

Omar Grant's skin was already glistening from his short training session when he followed Simon Pitt into the manager's office. Ohara calculated he'd run at least 15 kilometres over the heavy Pitt Lane ground on Saturday, covering every patch, exhorting, cajoling, cursing, defending, attacking, overlapping, running off the ball, intimidating the opposition, and he was the only player who seemed to show a profound hatred of defeat in his face when he left the pitch. In Siddley United's five loss one draw league season, they had only managed five goals, two of them by Grant from midfield. Muscular, well-balanced, he was a Ramleigh's store security guard in daytime, a bouncer at the Taste of Heaven club in Cooper's Lane on Fridays and after games on Saturdays and a part-time student of accountancy. He'd once had a trial with the Conference team Kidderminster, and had played for Siddley United since he moved to the city five years ago. Ohara knew he was a driven man, hungry to win something, starting with a football game. He went straight in.

'Simon Pitt has resigned as captain. May I invite you to take the role?'

Omar shrugged, producing a huge, toothy smile. 'Great, boss. What can I say? I hope it goes down well with the lads.'

Speaking as coach to captain, Ohara explained the no-smoking and drinking rules and his wish for better food awareness. 'Okay, we're not Manchester United or Chelsea, but a few simple changes, requiring only self-discipline, will really show through on the pitch.' In a uniquely Japanese way, he requested Omar Grant's co-operation in establishing a consensus of opinion with the players and support staff in relation to health and discipline so that harmony, trust and mutual respect became synonymous with Siddley United. He showed Omar the piece of paper Monique Wainwright had kindly printed out before she hurried off in a swirl of black fabric and sunglasses for a Sunday lunchtime date. 'This is a schedule of training slots which I will ask each player to consider and choose. I am available for every session. We will train here at Pitt Lane until I can find another place.' Grant hummed his approval. 'By the way, where do you work out, Mr Grant?' The Kinki Princes had their own gym, sauna and rehabilitation unit in the stadium and use of a sponsor's indoor and outdoor pitches: all he'd seen at Pitt Lane was a single dumb-bell and a ragged skipping rope in the machinery room.

'The Old Silk Mill gym at Mackworth. I'm Omar, by the way.'

Ohara smiled. 'Okay, Omar. I suppose I'm "Keno". But I prefer Ken, or boss.'

'Ken Ohara.' Grant nodded thoughtfully. 'You played for Japan in the World Cup in France, right?'

'Thank you for knowing it.'

'Are you going to turn out for us? We're a bit short of pace down the right.'

'I hope I don't have to, but I'm worried about the small squad.'

'We were twenty-five or six when I joined the club. We even put out a reserve team. No problem.'

'Eighteen players not enough,' Ohara declared. 'And I must find another ground to train on. Pitt Lane is very badly damaged.'

'We used to rent a council pitch but gave it up last year. Broody said it cost too much.'

'The club has no money?' Ohara wondered.

Grant shrugged. 'The directors put as much as they could into it, especially Mr Hardcastle, the undertaker. And the Pitt family, of course. They gave the land to the club. When we were in the Conference we had gates of ten thousand regular like, the biggest in the league. Never won anything, but we had a bit of pride and a lot of passion, and the town joined in. Not like that now, though. Lucky if we get four hundred at Pitt Lane. And that's a lot for this league.'

'Who do I talk to about money?' he asked Grant.

Omar's face creased into a rueful smile, and a derisory scoff erupted from his chest. 'Only one man in it. David Broody. Nobody belches at Pitt Lane unless the chief executive agrees it.'

Long absorbed into sprawling metropolitan Siddley, the old brick Victorian workhouse was situated near the edge of the city, converted from a nursing home by David Broody's property development company into a hotel. Its restaurant offered classic chip and pie-based English heartland cuisine and was popular with travelling sales executives. Its in-house pub, the Duck and Prime Minister, with its themed traditionality, attracted the city's professional classes and adulterers. In her black, crinkled shell suit, Uma Thurman-in-*Pulp-Fiction* wig and octagonal, rimless sunglasses, Monique Wainwright sat behind the wheel of her red Ford Contacto, relieved not to find David Broody's BMW in the car park after her dash across town from Pitt Lane.

She'd been there in the pub with him on Friday, only two days ago, after the club directors had taken the new foreign bloke to dinner, David feigning illness before dessert and leaving. After the Hawaiian seafood platter with the lovely bottle of wine, it was over to David's penthouse flat in his Sunriser Heights development where he changed into his referee's strip and she into a Siddley United number six shirt and nothing else but a generous splash of Calentissimo. She'd prowled around the lounge growling, cursing his parentage, his private sexual behaviour and then begged him not to send her off for such foul and abusive language. She'd do anything to avoid a red card. It's not that she loved the man. David looked freakish, his face taut from cosmetic surgery and perma-scorched from tanning sessions using colouring lotion. He was as lecherous as he was loathsome, and she really only submitted to his fetishes because the relationship left her free to run Siddley United, her real love, on a daily basis, full-time. But what was going on with him? He'd been tense for weeks, the simmering volcano of passion of six months ago now definitely dormant; and it hadn't worked on Friday either. Sensing his anguish, she'd taken desperate measures, changing into an Arsenal kit she'd kept for emergencies and then circling him, her bare feet lashing out cynically from behind, jabbing at his ankles and knees, an elbow finding his chest, a fist threatening his crotch. Serious foul play, she'd breathed huskily. But no: she checked his shorts and knew it wasn't going to happen tonight. Should she try violent conduct and wrench his testicles? Wielding the punishment cards limply, he seemed beyond provocation, and when she held his clammy face in her lap afterwards, it was clear from his eyes that his mind was elsewhere. Had he found another dalliance, she wondered, or did the problem lie with the secret Sunday date he'd made with 'Reggie'? Reggie could only be Sir Reginald Pitt, grandson of Siddley United's great benefactor. What was he up to, Monique was still thinking, when she spotted a familiar car.

David Broody arrived first, in his black BMW, and within minutes a dark green Rover pulled into a space two cars from hers, driven by a man with a florid, bulldog face who tried and failed to button his blazer over his stomach as he straightened. 'So I was right,' Monique murmured.

'Reggie' was indeed Sir Reginald Wetheral Henry Pitt, squire of Pitt Manor and wayward, absentee president of Siddley United Football Club. Thanks to the generosity of Sir Abraham, the Pitt family was for ever tied to Siddley United and while some of the descendants, like great grandson Simon, contributed gladly on the pitch, grandson Reggie found his duties irksome and was rarely seen at the ground. The fortunes of the Pitt dynasty were at their lowest ever: the eighteenth century mansion, re-named Pitt Manor by Sir Abraham on acquisition, was in need of serious repairs. It had neither ghosts nor a decent garden centre to attract the urban masses, and money had been squandered by Sir Abbie's less driven descendants without meaningful economic response, the present family living on rents, fishing rights on the estate's stretch of the River Siddleworth and dwindling capital. The family still held a 20 per cent share in the football club but only the absence of a buyer prevented Sir Reginald from breaking with tradition and selling out. Monique was slowly realizing that Broody had never revealed his true feelings towards the football club. Even in his most defenceless moments of passion with her he had never talked of ambition or success on the field or shared her dream of promotion and trophies. After Monique, he was the person most involved with club management and day-to-day business but where Monique lodged her heart at Pitt Lane, she wasn't at all sure what inspired Broody. Lately, she'd seen him at the ground a lot more than usual. He'd looked distracted, opened drawers and rummaged, absorbed in something he wouldn't reveal and she'd seen him taking measurements when he thought he was alone. So was her under-performing lover plotting some mischief with Sir Reggie Pitt? Were they plotting to screw Siddley United?

Monique gave them a few minutes, time for her to ponder the state of the football club she loved more than sex. Missing the manly pleasures of a son, her father had taken her to Pitt Lane as a toddler, when the Pitties played in the Conference in front of 10,000 fans. At 16 she gave herself to the goalkeeper of the day after the Pitties beat Crabmorton 3-0 and avoided demotion to the then Everwarm Cavity Insulation League. She would wait at the players' entrance on match and practice days, greeting them and club officials by name, and travel to away games in the team bus as a kind of mascot. When the full-time post of executive assistant arose at Pitt Lane the name of Monique Wainwright was already familiar to all at the club, including David Broody, who interviewed her. With her love for and intimate knowledge of the club, promise in her eyes, and even more in the body-moulded sheath of a dress, she brushed the other candidates aside. With Broody busy with his property business, the chairman with his corpses and the other directors choosing to belong and be seen rather than participate and manage, much was left to her judgement and she was soon running the club administratively. For a modest salary, she ran the payroll, paid bills, organized match day help, hired the coach to away games and lied to Mrs Broody for her husband. It was paradise: no monetary value could be attached to the privilege of hanging up the famous lime green and tangerine kit on match days, starched and rampant, or to inhaling the intoxicating smell of spent testosterone in the sweat-soaked, grass-streaked mudded shorts and shirts after a knife-edge local derby. But eight years on, and two months into the Pitties' centenary season, foul rumours about its future enveloped and polluted the atmosphere, and her lover was suddenly having trouble getting it up.

Adjusting her sunglasses and wig and smoothing the line of her shell suit, Monique felt invisible as she followed her football club's honorary president and its chief executive into the Duck and Prime Minister. Spacious, with low ceilings and walls girded with flock wallpaper patterned in mauve, floral variations, the pub had been tastefully refurbished. Warming pans and brass horse trimmings decorated the walls and mock coal fires in each of the themed bars imbued it with the timeless, unsullied spirit of old England. Shimmering carefully between the murmuring groups of Sunday lunchtime drinkers, she saw a profile of David Broody's head in a corner booth on the quieter lower level. Smoke from a cigar curled over his gin and tonic. Across the table, Sir Reginald Pitt was insisting silently with a stabbing finger. She bought a large glass of Hungarian chardonnay and edged stealthily towards the empty booth behind David Broody's, her buttocks brushing tables and knees. But it wasn't empty: the high backboards that would hide her also concealed a young couple, who, entwined obliviously, did not hear Uma Thurman in black when she breathed: 'May I?' and sat down opposite them and clamped an ear immediately against the partition. Mouths joined, eyes closed, hands busy below the table, the lovers made no contribution to the low rumble of chatter and the outbursts of shared laughter in the pub, allowing the conspiratorial conversation between David Broody and Sir Reggie Pitt to filter audibly through the latticed panel.

'I haven't found anything in Pitt Lane.' The voice was David Broody's. He was speaking through clenched teeth, hissing with suppressed intensity. 'I've been in every corner, in every crevice, cupboard, locker and drawer, under every floorboard, sink and pipe. If the deeds to Pitt Lane are in the stadium we'd have to take the fucking place apart, brick by brick.'

Monique drew breath so sharply it almost stirred the engrossed couple, but each thought it was spontaneous eruption of pleasure by the other and simply took in air and proceeded. Monique suddenly understood why she'd seen David Broody so often in the last month, rummaging in the files, tapping the walls, asking for keys to long unopened cupboards, boxes and doors, out in the stands, hands on hips, surveying the seats and terraces. He was looking for something, and now Monique was almost certain it was the documents, believed by most to be mythical, that had bequeathed the Pitt Lane ground and the land used as a car park to the town for ever. Why on earth was he looking for them suddenly? Everyone believed the charitable bequest had been made by mouth and it had been honoured as a legally sound situation for a hundred years. Which was because, Monique suddenly realized, nobody had tried to challenge the validity of it. Until now. She felt heat rise to her face; beads of perspiration tipped the fringe of her wig. She took a long drag on the buttery chardonnay, a dribble escaping to her chin when she cocked her head against the slender backboard.

Sir Reggie coughed and when he spoke in that deep, theatrically forced posh voice it was easy for Monique to separate him from the earthy, flat vowels of her lover, even above the hum of the drinkers. 'So without the deeds or a legal affirmation of the old bugger's intentions the land can't be sold. But I desperately need that money, David. Unless I get a very prompt cash injection of several hundred thousand pounds from you or persuade another two hundred thousand irks in anoraks to spend a fiver each on my Pitt Manor mugs and own-brand organic heather honey from Nicaragua I'll have to sell up. At this moment in time, David, getting a bucket of milk from a bull seems a lot easier a prospect.'

Broody's shoulders shrugged. 'Your grandfather must have left a letter or something. You can't just give away a prime chunk of Siddley for ever without spelling it out for the next generation.'

Monique used a pause to lift her petite frame onto the seat, kneeling as she stretched her neck until her eyes reached the latticed panel that gave height to the partition and the booths their privacy. Lover boy Broody, whose wiry hair she could touch if the holes had been big enough, paused to take a drink and was off again. 'Because he didn't leave the ground and car park to the town forever, did he? He had a little prank up his sleeve. He left a time-bomb under Siddley United.' Monique's heart stopped.

'I'm still not convinced about that,' Pitt said.

'Well let me remind you,' Broody persisted. 'I was chatting to your dear departed father, Sir Lionel, at the Siddley Yeomanry reunion last December, only three weeks before he died. Well into the port and apropos of nothing at all, he told me that his father, Sir Abraham, your grandfather, actually put a proviso against his famous in perpetuity donation to the effect that the club and its land could actually be disposed of in certain circumstances.' Behind the screen, Monique sucked in air, her eyes popping. 'I'd had a few myself, Reggie old son, so I didn't think I'd heard him right, but Sir Lionel, bless him, confused as he was, said it again. Where's the proof? I pressed. I told him a wise old bird like Sir Abraham wouldn't leave anything so important to chance, but your father couldn't recall a written proviso or a covenant, nor even the deeds to Pitt Lane.' Broody drained his glass and looked ruefully at the leftover scraps of meltdown ice and lemon. And in a low conspiratorial voice which Monique had to strain to hear, he said: 'So when I heard all this I straight off thought of you, Reggie. Together, I fancied, we could pull off the biggest property deal in Siddley's history. No. In the county's history, if not the whole of bloody central England. But we have to have evidence on paper, proof that we can sell off Siddley bloody United before we can do the property deal to end all property deals. Unfortunately, your father had that accident with the Jack Russell terrier and the shooting stick at the county show before I could talk to him again and I can't find anything like a covenant at Pitt Lane.' His voice was barely more than a whisper. 'This is the bottom line, Reggie. I've got a syndicate ready to sign on the dotted line. They're reputable Russian businessmen looking to invest up to half a billion dollars into cast-iron British property, like modern Siddley. The money could be here at the press of a couple of computer keys and it's life or death for both of us, as you know, Reggie. The small fact is, like you, I'm well short of the readies. I've mortgaged and re-mortgaged everything I own in this county and I've pushed my credit facilities to the limit in order to borrow the funds to buy every sodding slum terrace and house within a five hundred yard radius of the Pitt Lane ground, right up to the cathedral, but there's no deal without Siddley United's land. It's the jewel in the crown, the *sine qua* bloody *non* of the whole deal, and I'm going to lose everything if I can't get my hands on it. All I have to do is prove it can be legally sold.'

'*Cinema* what?' Monique wondered, as the head of David Broody leaned forward to press a point.

'So you can see, Reggie, I need to have legally binding confirmation that your grandfather deliberately left a written proviso to his so-called donation. I have not found it at the ground and so the only other place it could be is Pitt Manor. Are you certain you've been over it thoroughly?'

Hot from burning ears, Monique's head was in danger of rising over the top of the partition. 'Please, please,' she breathed. 'Talk about the proviso. How can Pitt Lane be sold?'

Broody went for fresh drinks, giving Sir Reginald Pitt time to think and Monique a moment to stretch. A very large scotch against his cracked, purple lips, Pitt could only shrug. 'To be honest, I've been looking for something for years, old boy. There were all sorts of rumours in the family.' A rueful smile spread the deltas of broken veins on his cheeks. 'Do you know how big the manor is? It's got twelve bedrooms for a start.'

'Now go for the improbable. Check for secret passages, look in the coffins in the fucking mausoleum, in the stuffed animal heads, the armour. Shove a servant up the chimneys. It's got to be somewhere. I'll come over myself, with some of the lads, if you like.'

The baronet still wasn't convinced, or perhaps he'd heard Monique's breathless plea. 'Are you absolutely sure what my father said? He *was* the worse for drink, you said.'

Broody sniffed the air, causing Monique a spasm of panic. She had injudiciously applied his turn-on tonic, Calentissimo. Holding her breath, she waited for the familiar face to peek curiously into her booth. But he sniffed again, apparently clearing cigar smoke from his nostrils. 'We'd all had our share of the regimental claret, but Sir Lionel suddenly became perfectly lucid. I think we were talking about the club's impending relegation and lack of support.

"We can always sell the bloody place," he said. I was about to remind him that the ground was a gift for eternity to the town from his father when he cut me off. "Not necessarily for eternity," he said, pulling me by the lapel. "My father, Sir Abraham, once told me the football club was entirely at liberty to sell the ground if a hundred years passed without the Pitties winning a trophy. Like the league championship or a bit of cup silverware, that sort of thing." I could hardly believe what I'd heard, what with the regimental songs and the shouting, so I asked him to repeat it, and damn me if he didn't say the same thing again.' Broody wiggled his heavy glass and the ice clinked triumphantly in Reggie Pitt's face. 'We're celebrating the club's centenary this very season, aren't we Reggie? You reckon the superstars in lime green are going to break the habit of a century and win something? The hundred years is not actually up till next summer but as far as winning anything it looks like it's already all over for the Pitties.'

Sir Reggie Pitt's thick lips curled scornfully. 'Supposing this new Jap chap wins the league, or tin cup or glass bowl or whatever?'

'Win? You should watch them play sometime. We're second bottom after six games so you can forget the RoustaRodent Solutions League division championship.'

'But aren't the Pitties in the semi-final of some cup competition or other?'

'You mean the Golden Mousetrap Trophy? Yes, but we got there virtually by default. The other three teams left are all from the Conference and we've got Yattock, currently top of that league. They'll put us out without breaking sweat.'

Bastard. Full of venom, the word almost escaped Monique's peach pink glossed lips.

Sir Reginald Pitt leaned forward. 'Okay. Supposing the Pitties fail to win anything and we find the codicil that proves what old Abraham said, you're forgetting the little matter of my fellow directors. You'd have to buy them out before you could flog the place to the Ruskies and I somehow doubt old bodybags Hardcastle will agree to give up his shares, let alone councillor Townrow, Patel and Quasimodo Osborne.'

Broody released a knowing, sarcastic snort. 'Leave the board of directors to me, dear boy. They'll be begging to sell up when I've finished with them.'

Ohara flipped the lock on his big suitcase, even as his mind struggled with tortured hopelessness on a strategy plan for Siddley United. How easy it would be to pack up and sneak away in the night, back to the comforting motherland across the world and into the embrace of the harmonious Nipponese people who forgave their own against the treacherous foreigner, whatever the circumstances. A rueful smile creased his face. He knew in his heart all this harmony stuff and unconditional unity was all crap in modern Japan. The mobile phone was lord and scandal the religion. The weekly tabloids would tear him apart, question his manhood and his right to be Japanese: Tanaka, the *Kanto Daily Sports* journalist at the game yesterday, had already hinted at a cock-up at the pitch press conference. Television comedians would mock him, call him the loser, the man who surrendered Japan's honour. They wouldn't care if he'd been tricked into a job in a lost world, with a lost team, nor bother that he'd been cheated and humiliated by his own people and by foreigners. No, only revenge could purge him of the wrath of his people. Revenge, he snarled, slamming the case shut. No fucking *hara-kiri*, just white-hot revenge before he abandoned this soaking, foetid town and country for ever. And it started now.

*

Ohara issued his ultimatum to the players: put your heart into the Pitties or push off. They would train more often and longer and on a timetable made to suit those who worked and those who didn't. Players without declared employment and those not actively seeking it were asked to clean gear, tend the pitch, clean the stands and terraces and do other helpful tasks for pocket money. Matt Dennis, the physio, was instructed to monitor the players' health and physical development systematically under new diet and training routines. Florie was freed from pie and chip production by a shift of the food budget to the contracted delivery at Pitt Lane of trays of grilled fish and chicken, pots of lightly cooked vegetables and home-made sauces from PastaBasta, Siddley's leading Italian food purveyors. Florie's similarly liberated twin, Winnie, was delighted to be given responsibility for washing, ironing and laying out of team kit, a cosmetic touch aimed at giving the players pride in their appearance. Ken Ohara himself would take over most of the on-pitch training from Terry Dribble who, as his mobility returned, would assist and prepare intelligence on opponents. He made it clear to all the new rules on diet, drinking, smoking and match discipline were not negotiable. He was passing the changing room after Sunday's training session when the inevitable voices of dissent from inside halted him.

'I ain't stoppin' smokin' for no fucking Jap.'

Ohara thought it was Billy Pickwich, but most of the players sounded the same.

'And what about this bloody wop food he wants to shove down our throats?' someone bellowed, inviting agreement.

'Winnie thinks the pies are going vegetarian,' another said.

'Put that fag out,' Omar Grant's voiced boomed.

'Who says so?'

'I do. Your new captain.'

Ohara let a bitter sweet smile break across his face. He trod softly as he left the ground, tugging up the zip on his jacket against a chill breeze, and when he slid into the Honda he noticed his hand was shaking. Was it the cold air or the tension oozing from the feeling of isolation and loneliness he was trying to suppress? Japan was mostly about trees and mountains, about three quarters of the whole country was made uninhabitable by them, and now his homeland would be embraced by cool autumn weather that turned the maples in gardens and temples into spectacular flaming reds, the forests into golden, bronzed explosions. Siddley, with its trees already almost bare, was the Siberia of his expectations. From the recess under the dashboard he took a small, crumpled, silver grey packet and, as a ragged, bruised cloud drifted over Pitt Lane, he lit his last Seven Stars cigarette and sucked in deeply. The rush of nicotine sent a sensation of lust and triumph through his body. He smacked the steering wheel with the heel of a hand and wished he could summon up something of the disciplined samurai spirit, but his grandparents had been lowly Kansai rice growers. Deep down he knew it was his loathing of defeat, his fear of unbearable humiliation and the memory of his mother that kept him from driving straight to the nearest airport. No. Failure was not an option: Siddley United had no choice but to go forward and upwards. That would be his revenge.

On a mild Tuesday afternoon, eleven players responded to the coach's call, including all the back and central defenders whose play was to be the focus of the training. He wanted in particular to try out a sweeper system, not for deep strategic reasons but because all else seemed to have failed, and he'd penned in the student, Scott Fisher, who had impressed him against Cogworth, for the main role.

The system had been used often and successfully by the Kinki Princes in Wakayama. Without the height of men like Pickwich, Breakin or Grant to head away, balls tended to bounce capriciously over Japanese defenders, and a diligent, swift and well-drilled sweeper was an obvious strategy. Japanese players don't threaten in the air but in their favour they are lithe, fast, very fit and a low centre of gravity allows them to keep their feet when all around the big, imported foreigners are losing theirs. In his second year as the Princes' coach, he brought in an Italian with shot knees to teach the tactic of the sweep, and the Kinki's defence responded magnificently, winning the prized league championship in the same season. It was his ability to learn and adapt that marked Ohara as a future national coach. Siddley United's needs were just as urgent: they leaked goals. The strikers couldn't strike because they were too occupied defending.

Ohara marked out a short pitch with poles for goals, and split the eleven players into two teams, with himself making the sixth player on Dean Slutz's side. Fisher, his designated sweeper for the next game away to Molecroft, played behind Omar Grant and three of the Pitties' regular defenders. He put the young goalie, Tony McDonald, in Omar's goal, which made Kevin Stopham a little sulky. 'We play game now,' Ohara declared after a warm-up jog. 'The four front players on each team must mark one particular opponent and can only tackle him. If you tackle a different player it's a free kick to the other team. The free sweepers, Scotty and Les Diamond, cannot cross the halfway line but they can tackle any opponent who enters the defenders' half and breaks away from his marker. Right. Line up and pick your marker.'

Gary Omerod and a couple of others needed a re-run of

the rules but finally, with Terry Dribble marooned on the halfway line with a whistle and a limp, the game started, slowly at first then with pace. Ohara lined up with forwards Lucas Mandrake, Dean Slutz and Simon Pitt and as he wanted most of the play took place against the defensive players in Omar's half. It was Ohara's first serious on-pitch run for months, he had to show the way, and after half an hour the knee was holding. Billy Pickwich was his marker, but the veteran bought dummy after dummy and, happily, Scott Fisher was over to cover for him smartly, allowing Ohara only one decent shot on goal. Big Omar was marking Dean Slutz out of the game but Lucas Mandrake tormented Robby Breakin, keeping Scott busy on the left as well.

They played for an hour without a break, changing ends and interchanging players, except for the two sweepers. The tackles went in harder as the players tired, and when Ohara nutmegged Billy Pickwich once too often, the taxi driver put his foot in half a second too late, catching the Japanese on his unreliable right knee. The Japanese hobbled off the pitch, his next objective on his mind. Charlie Wharton had heated the huge deep bath until it drew steam into a thick, ghostly mist. Ohara showered, cleansing his body of every possible trace of sweat, grease and dirt, showered again and was about to enter the overflowing tub when his players arrived. They found Ohara naked but for a hand-towel draped over his head.

'Excuse me for bathing before you,' he told his audience, 'but I could not wait any longer to take a Japanese bath. I will try to understand your customs and eat your pies but I regret I cannot possibly sit in water where people have not washed before using it.' He stepped gingerly into the hot water, his skin colouring, and spread his arms, sinking, luxuriating, the towel slipping over his face. 'I will not take long, but you are welcome to join me if you wish.' Except for Billy Pickwich, they all did, after a long shower and scrub, of course.

During his first week at Pitt Lane, Ken Ohara spoke three times on Radio Siddley and gave a long interview to Paddy Brick of the *Siddley Evening Sentinel*. Praising the football culture of the town and the hundred year history of the club, he implored its people to support the Pitties, if not away to Molecroft on Saturday by all means at home to Grittley Mills the following week and then the incredible semi-final of the Golden Mousetrap Trophy against Yattock of the Conference. National dailies, alerted by the intense interest showed by the Japanese media, arrived in Siddley and the likes of the *Guardian*, the *Sun* and *The Times* profiled the first Japanese, and indeed the first person from the orient to manage a foreign soccer team. In between, Ohara took the Pitties towards his next goals, working on speed and cardio-vascular performance with short-burst sprints and slower, longer runs along the canal, greeting Alf Widdison who always seemed to be there with his rod. He wanted his team to run for 90 minutes on the pitch. Defensively, he was insisting on concentration, watching advancing strikers and springing the offside trap in a disciplined, tactical line, not as an afterthought. He had begged off another dinner invitation after the late Thursday training session and was watching a football video when Rika Yamaguchi called. Would Ken-ichi Ohara *san* be available for lunch with the president of Uno Electronics tomorrow?

The Uno complex, a long, broad flat-roofed assembly plant flanked by high security chip storage buildings, offices and staff recreation facilities occupied most of the St Elphin's industrial park and was separated from the municipal boundary of Siddley by a swath of woodland and an oxbow bend in the River Siddleworth. Pronounced properly, Uno would sound exactly like the Spanish for 'one' but the citizens of Siddley and district rendered it as '*you know*'. Ohara's car was admitted through electric gates onto a short curving drive. Beds of jaded geraniums, marigolds and begonias circled an ornate fountain in front of the tinted glass fronted office block. The Uno corporate flag flapped limply in an indecisive breeze against a sky of high, shredded clouds.

Wearing the company's loose, sky blue uniform jacket, Rika escorted her visitor with pride. Japanese technicians passed him with a '*gambatte, Ken san,*' and from the English it was 'good luck mate'. Leading him to the assembly building she described proudly the scale of the investment, employment figures, the output and export percentages and the sports and recreation facilities for the staff and their families.

'Is there a football pitch?' Ohara wondered, his interest suddenly perking.

Rika Yamaguchi beamed. 'We've got two floodlit outdoor pitches, grass for football and rugby and an artificial surface we can use for whatever. There's also a gym, two tennis courts and a small indoor swimming pool.' They had entered the long assembly building and climbed a short stairway to an observation platform fenced with glass.

Ohara hummed. 'A gym? Really?'

Below him, along rows of tables in the clinically ordered hanger-like hall, Uno staff in caps and surgical masks leaned over computer mother boards, little welder pens snapping and blinking in their hands. Rika's deep brown eyes scanned the figures and the faces. Finally, she tugged his sleeve and pointed to a group of people, all in light blue smocks and masks. 'Over there, Ohara *san*. By the ventilation shaft. The man with the clipboard, the second from the right.' Ohara was close to her shoulder following the line of her finger to a figure of his own height. The hair

was no longer spiked and streaked blond but in its natural black, trimmed smartly above the ears and parted at the side. 'That's him, Ta—'
'Taro Suzuki.' A psychosomatic twinge, a sharp deep ache, nudged its way into Ohara's knee.
'He plays football for the company team,' Rika commented.
'Oh really?'
The president of Uno Electronics Europe, Eisaku Ishida, was an amiable, round faced man with warm eyes and the easy smile of a successful manager. He wore the same sky blue work jacket as everyone else, and while Ohara waited at a table in the staff refectory, signing autographs and accepting the greetings of the Japanese and local staff, he stood in line with Rika and collected their lunch trays. 'On Fridays we have a special Japanese dish,' he beamed. 'And today it's *tendon*.'

What pleasure! Two large battered prawns and *tempura* mushrooms and onions, sauced with soya on a bed of boiled rice, in a lacquer box, accompanied by a saucer of bright pickles and a mug of bitter green tea. Ohara scooped and sucked while president Ishida recalled the World Cup tournaments in Japan, Korea, Germany and Ohara's heroics so long ago in France. He claimed to support Iwata Jubilo of the J-League but Ohara knew he was lying politely. Mr Ishida looked baseball and sumo, both run in the feudal, tyrannically paternalistic way of old Japan, while football in Japan meant youth: screaming girls with pompoms and plastic clackers, youths with drums and flags, a stadium of noise and colour, a celebration of the new spirit, players with dyed hair, strutting with arrogant confidence in imitation of the European and South American stars they worshipped. Over the kindly man's shoulder Ohara saw Taro

Suzuki at the food counter. The man whose tackle cut short his playing career had been looking towards him but quickly turned away. Suzuki hadn't played in the J-League for six years at least, Ohara guessed, but he still looked fit, his face still burnished from wind and sun. Was he still in self-imposed penance? Did he see Ohara as a ghost that had followed him from Japan to Siddley to haunt him? His eyes followed Suzuki to a table by the window, then out to the football pitch and tennis courts.

'Does Uno Electronics sponsor sport locally?' Ohara asked Ishida, when their tea cups were refilled.

Ishida thought he heard a plea tinged with desperation in the young Japanese's voice and turned to his personal assistant for the public relations angle.

'We're involved in many youth projects in many areas. Schools can use the hardcourt for soccer, hand and netball and the gym for basketball. We sponsor several trophies.'

'What I mean is, does your company provide direct financial, or similar support?' Ohara remembered seeing big English clubs with the names of Japanese firms on their shirts.

The president of Uno Electronics sucked in air noisily. Far from home, burdened by an expectant nation's hopes and dreams, the new manager of Siddley United was requesting his help in an absolutely responsible Japanese way, and it required a Japanese response. 'I must admit that when we established the production facility here three years ago we were approached by the chairman of your excellent team who wanted us to sponsor Siddley United in a positive manner. I can't remember his name, but he was very earnest, and generously offered to conduct any unforeseen company funeral requirements with a special discount. But . . .'

'But you were unable to find Siddley United in the sports

pages or on television,' Ken Ohara interrupted politely. 'I fully understand your situation.'

'I'm so glad,' Ishida replied sincerely, bringing his hands together. When news reached him through the Japanese media that a famous countryman was giving up the successful player-managership of the champion Kinki Princes to run an unknown, run down, unambitious minor league team of part-time has-beens, amateurs and unemployed loafers, the 32 Japanese staff at Uno Electronics were dumbfounded. 'But you are here in Siddley,' president Ishida was saying, 'and committed to make the soccer club a success just as we are committed to the success of the local economy. So we must help each other.'

Rika Yamaguchi glanced at her boss, then at Ohara. 'The Japanese media has already been on to us, asking what we're going to do for you.'

The Pitt Lane spectator capacity was 20,000, the biggest in the three divisions of the RoustaRodent Solutions League and, thanks to the vision of Sir Abraham Pitt a century ago, higher than most teams in the professional leagues above them. The vast confines now echoed with the screams of agony and ecstasy of its regular 420 paying fans.

Ohara's chin dropped to his chest in a crisp head bow of respect. 'Your co-operation and assistance would be of immeasurable benefit, and I think you can support me best by putting fans in the stands and on the terraces. What I remember most is the noise of the supporters when I played for the Kinki Princes. It drove us forward, and that's what we need at Pitt Lane.'

The president's arm spread expansively. 'Of course, of course. I will come myself to your big cup game. In about three weeks, isn't it?'

Eyes closed, Ken Ohara gathered his courage. He couldn't stop now, but he didn't want to cause embarrassment. A plural can only be expressed in Japanese from its context with other words, and so when Ohara respectfully said he had *onegai* it could have meant he had another request or several. In fact, he had three more. He gave two a good chance of success, the third zero. 'May my players have use of your gymnasium, please? At agreed times, of course.'

President Ishida's head jigged. 'Why not? It's hardly used during the day.'

'And your soccer field? The Pitt Lane turf is very damaged because it's used so much for practice.'

Ishida looked at his assistant. 'What do you think? Who's our team captain?'

'Mr Gavin Rowley,' Rika said.

'Would he mind, do you think?'

'Like the gym, *shacho*, the pitch is rarely used during the day. I think he'd be honoured if the Pitties trained on it.'

'Just one more thing, Ishida *san*.' Ohara placed his hands on the table and bowed his head low to the Uno Electronics boss. 'I want to ask Taro Suzuki to play for the Pitties.'

Monique Wainwright closed the last file from the last scratched and dented cabinet in the dusty storeroom and sighed. When David Broody came by he mistook her coolness for peevish annoyance at his sluggish game play performance last Friday and by way of apology said he'd bought a Burnley home shirt for her to wear, which should be enough to inflame the passions of anybody, even Walter Hardcastle's stiff clients. When she was alone she'd searched the Pitt Lane ground, knowing she was following in the club chief executive's predatory footsteps, looking for something, like him, but with violently opposing motives, searching for the document which, if it existed and the proviso exercised, could destroy her football club. Surely it couldn't be in the fabric of the structure because the terraces, stands and interior arrangement of rooms dated from the 1930s, long after Sir Abraham Pitt's death. She looked anyway, in crevices in the stanchions and supports where a pouch or a container could be concealed and in obscured spaces and gaps where a piece of paper may have been secreted. She had access to the great mahogany desk that had served every chairman for a hundred years, but sadly the deep drawers revealed nothing of interest, apart from a paperweight made from human bone. From the way Broody and Sir Reggie's conversation went in the pub on Sunday, it was unlikely anyone else knew about the destructive codicil which had ticked away menacingly across the decades, and with her search proving futile she almost reached the conclusion that if it had existed at all it would have faded beyond legibility or disintegrated after a hundred years in Pitt Lane.

On Friday, before the players, directors and staff arrived for the ritual end of week bonding and training session, she was sitting pensively in the chairman's leather chair, her delicate feet crossed on his desk, wondering what Broody had meant when he told Sir Reggie he could get the other directors to agree to sell their shares in the club to him, when her eyes drifted to the oldest of the elaborately framed photographs on the opposite wall. It was a blurred sepia image of three men with drooping moustaches on the pitch at Pitt Lane. One of them was surely old Sir Abraham himself. But she was staring at the thick frame. Very thick for a simple photo, she was thinking. Was it hollow, doubling as a box, a hiding place? Emitting a screech of delight, she looped her legs off the desk and tripped across the room in a swirl of hope. 'Clever bugger, old Sir Abby,' she said, aiming a finger at the three figures, not sure which one was the great man. The secret documents had been staring at every chairman for nearly a century. Easing the frame gently off its hook, she examined the back. A thin piece of stained cork covered it, held in place with bent, rusted pins, two of which had broken off at the head. It didn't look as if it had been tampered with recently. Using a steel letter opener, she prised the remaining pins until she could slide part of the board from the back of the frame. Heart racing, she slid a hand into the space, feeling the parched back of the old photo against her fingernails as she explored. Empty. Then, in an absurd piece of melodramatic timing that would haunt her nights, a voice behind her said:

'Magnifique Monique. What on earth are you up to?'

Clutching the dismembered photo frame, Monique turned slowly to face David Broody who stood in the doorway holding aloft in his fingertips a claret and blue shirt. Think fast, think hard, Monique. Fixing her eyes on the shirt she screamed, dropping the frame onto a foot. As she hoped, the glass didn't shatter, but the undipped back board fell out silently. 'Oh God,' she said, her voice a breathless whisper. 'That's the shirt! What position is it?'

'Number three,' Broody trumped. 'A bad, bad defender who's asking for trouble and needs serious discipline.'

Monique snapped a button on her silver satin blouse. 'I've gotta put it on. Now.'

Broody spun in the doorway, his passions under restraint. 'Save it for later,' he said quietly. 'I think I'll be all right tonight.'

'I can hardly bear it until then,' she breathed, looking down at the separated frame and backing. 'But I've broken the picture. I was only trying to straighten it. Mr Hardcastle's going to kill me.' Her tight apricot skirt rose up her thighs as she went onto a knee. She was wearing a black thong under her tights and made sure he noticed.

'No he won't,' Broody said caringly, kneeling beside her. 'Let me fix it for you.'

What can I do, Monique worried, chewing a knuckle while he squeezed the pins back over the frame cover? I need to talk to somebody, but who can I trust?

'It's all right, I can manage it,' said Monique.

'Okay, I'll see you in the Duck and PM at seven.' Broody turned from the door. 'I was there last Sunday, actually. Some weird woman looking like Uma Thurman knocked a lot of glasses over when she dashed out of the pub. About your height, she was. Reminded me of you.'

4

Ohara sat pensively with Terry Dribble in the back of the old, grinding bus, its seats and fittings infused with the aromas of cigarette, beer and fried food. The new no smoking, no drinking rule only seemed to bother Billy Pickwich, whose petty discontent was becoming more open, and he threw the manager an occasional sneer as they drove between lumpy, harvested fields on their way home to Siddley. Perhaps being substituted upset him. The others were quietly subdued, worn out after a week's unaccustomed vigorous, programmed training and a tough, physical match against Molecroft.

Ohara was quietly pleased with his managerial debut in charge of a team whose players' language he barely understood and whose results went unnoticed outside Siddley. Was he turning soft? Did he feel a touch of pride for this run down city team? Was a fear of failure greater than a thirst for revenge? Certainly playing at Molecroft had put things into perspective. Pitt Lane was a genuine football ground, with two stands, expansive terracing and an amazing tract of parking space in central Siddley, while Molecroft played on a bumpy park pitch with a bit of stepped concrete terracing along one side. The Molecroft manager personally thanked him for attracting 300 plus people to the game when his home average was 72. Among the dozens of Pittie supporters who had made the 20 mile journey, Ohara saw

Rika Yamaguchi with a group of Japanese, all wearing lime and tangerine scarves, the colours of a bad tropical cocktail, Ohara thought secretly. He also picked out a group of Japanese reporters, silently watching the spectacle that had brought them 7,000 miles to see, and they included Tanaka of the *Kanto Daily Sports*. Was Taro Suzuki watching, Ohara wondered when the Pitties' forwards fired their tenth blank, an effort by Simon Pitt that scraped the foot of the post as it bounced wide?

The sweeper system worked well in the first half, Scotty tidying up behind Breakin, Pickwich and Diamond like a demented vacuum cleaner. Calling for a flatter defence near the end of the first half, Ohara patrolled the touchline, arms waving his men forward when he wanted the offside trap sprung. The defenders were kept busy by Molecroft's aggressive bullying tactics, but Dean Slutz and Pitt the younger had themselves good chances from slick movements instigated by Omar Grant and Lucas Mandrake. Perhaps Mike Groot found boot duty too much like work and he declared himself fit on match day, and when Ohara brought him on for Billy Pickwich at left back, the Japanese was pleasantly surprised at the man's coolness under pressure and his low, flat clearances. The team in general were not as fit as Ohara wanted but they played with more sense, like men who knew they were being watched and analyzed. His sushi-making father would practise molding vinegared rice until his hands were bleached white and then serve only six customers on a slow night. But he never stopped learning, improving, and Ohara wanted this spirit from the Pitties. Pride, passion – and goals. He knew already he wouldn't get these from Dean Slutz in the next two league games, let alone in the semi-final of the Golden Mousetrap Trophy, if the papaya-sized swelling on his left ankle didn't respond to ice.

He'd have to remind the team about his uncompromising

position on pitch discipline, which they'd forgotten in the heat of battle. The wasteful verbal and physical violence, he'd told them, must be channelled into more purposeful and productive aggression. He showed Omar Grant his black list as soon as they got on the bus. The niggling back tackles, mindless energy-sapping screaming accompanied by snarling faces and insulting gestures. Les Diamond and Pickwich were the main culprits in the revenge attacks and Dean Drummond with the vile verbals. He smiled inwardly when he remembered how Japanese players imitated their western role models when the J-League started in 1993, dyeing their hair, harassing the poor, inexperienced referees with false claims, diving balletically and celebrating goals with flamboyant abandon. Sitting there on the bus, it occurred to him that the Pitties were also imitating, and their models were the swaggering millionaires from the professional squads way above the RoustaRodent Solutions League. With the Kinki Princes, he just about eliminated the useless intimidation of officials, punishable dissent and petty fouling, and the improvement in performance and work-rate was immediate. He wondered if his methods would work in the land of individualism. He stabbed his notepad defiantly. He had nothing to lose.

The bus driver turned up the volume on his radio, watching in the rear-view mirror as the players looked up. The voice of Radio Siddley's Nigel Wensleydale buzzed from the speaker. 'From Old Trafford, let's go straight over to Karen Saddleback in the radio car, returning from Molecroft after another pulsating performance by the gladiators in lime green and tangerine. Karen.'

'Yes. Thank you, Nigel. I'm just passing the old Cracko biscuit factory on Sackville Road, and I can see the majestic columns of the floodlights of Pitt Lane, standing like beacons of hope behind the cathedral in the misty dusk of a mid-October . . .'

'Another cliff hanging loss for the Pitties I hear, Karen,' the presenter broke in tenderly.

'Yes, but they deserved more. I have never seen such a display go unrewarded, and neither have hundreds of Pittie supporters who packed the ground. And so many of them Japanese. If I remember correctly, Nigel, only twenty-three of our fans made it to our last away game. The fans who made the journey today will one day tell their grandchildren they witnessed the managerial debut of their own son of the rising sun, Ken Ohara, and saw their majestic team come within five minutes of a famous draw or even a victory. It was all Moleys in the first half, but Siddley Town rallied in the second as Ken the samurai coach patrolled the touchline, scenting blood and his first points. Sadly, Kevin Stopham made the crucial slip in the eighty-fifth minute when he sliced a Scotty Fisher back pass into the path of Molecroft's poaching striker, Hooper, who punished the error with clinical precision. Until then, Omar Grant had commanded the midfield like Horatio at the bridge, under pressure all the time but managing to spray the ball to both wings where Lucas Mandrake in particular looked sharp. Simon Pitt went close for the Pitties on the hour and the old war-horse, Dean Slutz, was short of a yard of pace when he beat the off-side trap on eighty, the ball being smothered by the Moley goalie. Deano took a bad knock in the follow through. Still, the Pitties can be proud of their performance ahead of the big Golden Mousetrap semi-final at Pitt Lane in three weeks.'

'I don't remember a player called Horatio at Stamford Bridge,' Les Diamond told Mike Groot as the bus passed Siddley railway station. 'Lots of bloody foreigners with weird names but not Horatio.'

At daybreak on the day after the Pitties' loss to Molecroft, David Broody led ten loyal employees on a treasure hunt to Pitt Manor. In a systematic and minutely planned operation they split into teams to search for an unspecified family document of great historical value, described only as being in folded, rolled or flat form. Each hunter received £100 for the long day, with a promised bonus of £500 if the document was recovered. At the end of the day, the only treasure given up by Pitt Manor was a newspaper, the last edition before the general strike of 1926; a mummified mouse, circa 1950, behind a boiler; and a batch of recently published gay encounter magazines, under a mattress in a room Sir Reggie insisted was used only by guests. A few sheets of yellowed, dried-out paper from the bottom of long unused drawers lifted hopes but they were just that – old drawer liners.

Broody drove testily to his Alma Heights mock-tudor mansion, tapped in an entry code to his private quarters and secreted himself behind locked doors with the books, papers and models of his work in progress around him. A muffled scream startled him, until he remembered the first Sunday of the month was the day for Camilla's seance in the lounge, and the current Bishop of Siddley's wife, who attended in secret while her husband conducted evensong in the cathedral, usually managed to contact a relative while trying for Jesus, thus provoking an outburst. He fixed a vodka and tonic from the bar and contemplated the old plans and blueprints of the Pitt Lane football ground spread on his teak desk for the twentieth time, looking in the lines and angles for inspiration. 'Sir Abraham left something in there and I am going to find it.' Then his eyes rounded, as they often did, on the intricate, small-scale mock-up of the grand Pitt Lane project, on the twin towers that represented the chrome and glass edifice of the Siddley financial centre, currently the football club's car park; on the hotel and leisure complex to be built where the football field now lay, on the shopping mall that would rise from the rubble of the ancient, malodorous terraced houses; and the stepped, south-facing block of executive apartments overlooking the canal. It was all too much. Blood flooded his sensitive region and the image of Monique in a Lazio strip suddenly swamped him in a surge of unbearable pleasure.

Changed into a tracksuit bottom, he was stirring a second drink when an odd thought intruded, triggered by his fantasy. Why was the gorgeous Monique so edgy when she dropped that old photo? Why was she so nervous, all of a sudden? What had she seen – or found?

Training at Uno Electronics began in the gym during the day and drills to improve passing skills on the floodlit artificial surface at night. Driven by Matt Dennis, the club's battered minibus shuttled between the town and St Elphin's all day, picking up players and returning those who had to work. By the end of the session 15 players had participated in indoor weight and cardio-vascular exercises and in a range of drills outdoors from Ohara's coaching manual and some of his own invention. He bought the players spaghetti and beer at di Rapido's PastaBasta restaurant when they returned to the city centre, making a mental note to approach the club's board of directors for a serious injection of their cash. The following day it was back to Uno for a seven-a-side involving conditional passing skills, where players followed through with one-two return or hit passes of more than 15 metres. The Japanese *ofuro* bath became a popular feature at Pitt Lane, so much so that Charlie Wharton agreed to come in and heat it up for players who might otherwise have been at the pub. A more potent attraction was Clarissa, a qualified sports masseuse Ohara had met at the Uno gym and who administered *shiatsu* with the skill of an experienced Japanese, her slender body belying the strength in her fingers as she straddled the players and depressed the pressure points in the shoulders and along the spine.

Dusk left Pitt Lane bathed in pale moonlight, the still air tempered with autumnal crispness and suffused with the sniff of coke smoke from the chimneys of the few remaining inhabited houses in the terraced streets around the football ground. With Matt Dennis timing cross field sprints in one half of Pitt Lane and Terry Dribble orchestrating man-to-man marking drills in the other, Ken Ohara sat morosely in his office, checking again figures he'd prepared for his upcoming meeting with the club's directors and chief executive. The causes of his depression were a selection of Japanese and local newspapers on his desk. 'Sandlot Soccer for Japan Ace Manager's Debut,' was the kindest headline. It lay poignantly beside a photograph of Molecroft's muddy, lumpy pitch. 'An Insult to Japan,' screamed a right wing sports and sex tabloid. 'Japan Shamed on Coach Ohara's Debut,' wrote another. The *Mainichi*'s kinder story was backed by a photo of the flag-waving Japanese supporters. The *Yomiuri*, with the largest circulation of any newspaper in the world, said: 'We did not expect coach Ohara to gain the experience Japan needs at AC Milan or Manchester United but Siddley is not . . .' and then speculated that the Golden Mousetrap Trophy semi-final against Yattock might be televised live in Japan. Ohara's face collapsed when he read this and he called Rika Yamaguchi at Uno Electronics to see if she'd heard. The British press reaction was generally kinder, and they had also picked up the broadcast rumour. They were bemused and intrigued by the impossibly surreal image of an oriental calling the shots at a nondescript provincial football club in a game televized live to a country with a population of 125 million people. 'Hara-kiri for Siddley Samurai,' ran one caption, above a photo of a morose Ohara leaving the field at Molecroft. 'See Siddley and Die,' said another, the nuance of which eluded him. He tossed the last of the newspapers aside as Florie tapped and entered. 'The young lad who delivers the spaghetti stuff from PastaBasta wants a quick word, Mr Ken. Shall I send him down?'

'No, Florie *san*,' Ohara said, thankful for the interruption. 'I'll come up.' With the next game against Grittley Mills three days away, the blows to his pride were nothing compared to the health problems in his meagre squad. Dean Slutz was definitely out, the ankle was badly bruised; Lenny Hampton's viral complaint was clearing but he was still too weak to play; and Alan Blink's groin injury was not responding very well to treatment. Simon Pitt's bruised shin from the Molecroft game was still painful but he was optimistic about facing Grittley Mills. Gary Omerod's self-inflicted injury was more serious. A loose five kilo weight had slipped off the bar as he benched-pressed in the Uno Electronics gym and fallen on his left foot. The left-sided mid-fielder was resting, with a less than a fifty-fifty chance of fitness by Saturday. Right-sided Ohara saw himself in lime green and tangerine on Saturday but didn't know who to move over to the left. A real or imagined ache moved into his right knee; and he could hear it laughing. Where could he get players? Breaking Clint Hopp out of prison was beyond him and three days of silence had followed his request for his old national team mate, Taro Suzuki, to play for the Pitties. The club needs a quick injection of money, he thought, as he made the last notation for the board meeting.

Wearing a tight pectoral-enhancing black T-shirt, Marco di Rapido introduced himself. He was a slender, muscular young man with high cheekbones, heavy eyebrows over brooding eyes and thick, slicked-back hair raked with comb trails. Checking off his delivery of raw pasta, sauces, chicken cuts and vegetables in the kitchen, he told Ohara he was the son of the owner of the PastaBasta chain, with the two restaurants in Siddley, a catering business covering the town and the county and an import arm bringing in cheese and wine. 'What part of Italy do you come from?' Ohara asked casually, as Florie packed the fresh food into the refrigerator.

'Italy? Me? Only been there once, for me grandma's funeral. No, I'm from Siddley. Dad's from Calabria. He came here a long time ago and met me mam in the Locarno dance hall.'

Ohara smiled away the gaps in his comprehension and took from him a long, itemized piece of paper headed with the PastaBasta logo of entwined tagliatelli. 'Your invoice, Mr di Rapido. I'll see it's paid as soon as possible.'

'I didn't just come to give you that, Mr Ohara,' Marco said sheepishly. The athletic Anglo-Italian looked over at Florie and lowered his voice. 'Can I have a trial?'

'A trial?' Ohara searched his memory bank. Trial was *saiban*, a law court. *Wakaranai.* I can't understand him. 'What have you done?'

'Got four against Ampleton's Brewery at the weekend. I'm top striker in our Sunday league. I was awarded the Silver Shinpad twice in the Siddley schoolboy challenge competition but then I broke me leg and I missed out on all the trials with the big clubs. When me leg was completely better, I'd already joined dad's business and sort of lost out on a professional football career. But I still play a lot, and I want to play for the Pitties.'

Ohara shook his head and glanced at his watch. 'Excuse me. My English is not adequate yet. And I must attend a meeting.' Marco followed the Japanese into the empty lounge. 'It's very difficult for me at the moment, Mr Di Rapido.'

'It's Marco. I turned down Grittley Mills this year, and Penditch.'

'I don't have money for new players yet, Marco. I've only just arrived here. Perhaps—'

'I'll play for nothing.'

'Perhaps next week I will have time to—'

'That woman on Radio Siddley says that Deano Slutz is not fit for Saturday. Please give me a chance.'

'He's fifty-fifty as of this morning,' Ohara lied.

'I have a Japanese motorbike,' Marco pleaded.

'Thank you. But most motorcycles in the world are Japanese.'

'I saw your World Cup goal in France '98.'

'I didn't score.'

'It looked like you.' In desperation, Marco had inched forward, ready, Ohara thought, to touch or attack him.

'We all look the same, Marco. Please excuse me. I have emergency meeting with the club directors.' He swayed past, leaving Marco anchored to the floor with disappointment, the Golden Mousetrap semi-final on his troubled mind. He knew the reality of his situation in Siddley and he was hurting from the mockery and criticism reaching him from Japan. On television, in the dailies and tabloids and in the wickedly uncompromising weekly magazines. He called on all the hundreds of Shinto gods to confound the rumours about the game being televized live there. Head pounding, he threw a smile at Monique as he reached the imposing solid dark wood doors to the suite of corporate rooms. He was clutching the food bill and his notes, rehearsing in his mind his message to the directors, when he felt a touch on his arm.

'Please Mr Ohara,' Marco said solemnly. 'Let me play for the Pitties. I've seen the *Seven Samurai* five times.'

The directors were a good ten minutes late for the meeting. The eminent undertaker and club chairman had to deliver a small gift to the manager of Siddley and District Health Authority ahead of the influenza season and Geoffrey Osborne had needed a nap after his lunch with the board of county sanitary inspectors. Harry Patel was helping his sons modify the labels on a consignment of running shoes and Councillor Townrow was in a suite of the Corn Exchange Hotel, listening attentively to a petition from a friend of a friend for a licence to open an adult goods shop next to the convent of St Prudencia. Sir Reginald Pitt sent apologies, as usual. David Broody came in with a spring in his step, a smirk on his face and a thick folder under his arm. The Russians had just paid a million pounds 'for advisory and consultancy services' via the Aphrodite Bank of Cyprus into his account at the Siddley Co-op Bank as an expression of good faith and a downpayment on the purchase of the Pitt Lane property. He wanted to punch the air: he could now meet the interest payment deadline on the usurious bridging loan he had taken out in extremis from the Banco Cristobal Colon, Cayman Islands, a financial institution owned by interests in Florida and Cali. Sitting smugly at one end of the table, set simply by Monique with ashtrays and bottles of carbonated water, the folder and his mobile phone before him, there was something exciting he had to tell the board, as executive officer.

Walter Hardcastle declared this extraordinary meeting open with a false cough and continued with self-important pomposity. 'David will take the minutes as usual. I understand Ken wishes to give us an early report on his findings at Siddley United.'

Broody raised a hand. 'May I say something first, chairman,' and without waiting for a reply he looked at Ken Ohara who sat on Hardcastle's right at the grand, polished table. 'It's been confirmed to me that Japanese television's going to relay the semi-final of the Golden Mousetrap Trophy match live to Japan.' The directors gasped and shook hands. They took Ohara's immobility and straight face for zen stoicism.

'How about that?' Chairman Hardcastle beamed. 'How many clubs, even the top flight lads in the Premiership, can say they've played live in Japan?'

'I heard some talk about it,' Ohara remarked flatly. Rika Yamaguchi had just confirmed it from an internet news site. 'Which company?'

'NH something,' Broody said, extracting a fax from the folder.

'NHK,' Ohara sighed. 'Nippon Broadcasting Corporation. Our equivalent of your BBC.'

'If we kick off at three, what time is it in Japan?' Harry Patel wondered.

Ohara touched his watch instinctively. 'Nine hours ahead now. But why wasn't I asked?'

'Midnight over there,' Geoffrey Osborne calculated smartly. This'll put Siddley on the global map.'

Indeed it will, Walter Hardcastle mused silently. As soon as David Broody called and told him he was considering a request from NHK to televize the game in Japan he considered what long, stretched advertising billboards along the touchlines would look like. He'd like to see the slogan, 'towards a global funeral,' in that funny Japanese writing.

David Broody paraphrased a clutch of notes and faxes in an irritating nasal drawl. 'NHK will obtain the necessary permits from the respective football associations, telecom people, et cetera and bring their own special production team. The game will not be televized live in this country obviously.'

'In case it has a pejorative effect on the attendances at all the other Saturday games,' councillor Townrow explained to Ohara, without a trace of irony.

'But nobody told me what was happening and—'

Broody went on. 'And even better, NHK has generously offered to pay two hundred thousand pounds, which sadly we must split with Yattock, of course. I've agreed to it and prepared the necessary documents for the Football Association, the local authorities, the police, whatever. It's not much money until you remember we're at the bottom of the food chain. We must be grateful.'

'The mayor will be delighted,' Councillor Ronald Townrow confirmed. 'She will, of course, be at Pitt Lane on the day in her regalia.'

For the first time, Broody thought, and if things moved forward as he planned, the last. The Russians had started paying and were getting very impatient to take legal possession of their land. All of it, not just the slums. And for Broody, the development plans were drawn up, the bulldozers a phone call away. He really must show his own sincerity and goodwill and begin the process that would put an end to the Pitties' occupation of Pitt Lane, even though he hadn't so far found the document that would prove it could be sold under the conditions of Sir Abraham's covenant. It would turn up. It had to, whatever the cost.

While the club's chief executive and the directors back-slapped and laughed and cheered their good fortune, Ohara closed his eyes and saw the faces of at least 50 million Japanese, sleepy but excited, staying up late to see a local hero who had left the motherland with great national fanfare and hope. The shared World Cup in Japan and Korea had left the country with an insatiable desire for worldwide recognition and acceptance as a football power. Their stars were playing in Europe, some with top clubs. What will they think of their national coach in waiting when they get their first sight of the old, weathered stands, the weeds on the empty, cracked terraces and the scruffy patches of turf at Pitt Lane, when they hear the silence of the crowd? When the Tokyo Giants play a three game series in the roofed Tokyo Dome baseball stadium, 50,000 fans turn out each night, even though the games are televized nationally. How can the Japanese spectator watching the Golden Mousetrap Trophy semi-final game begin to comprehend and compare the status of the 92 professional football teams in England, not to mention the Conference semi-pros, with the hundreds of minor league teams like the Pitties who play for fun and pennies as they battle to move up the divisions and leagues? Ohara sighed, overwhelmed by a desire to crawl under a *futon* and sleep through the living nightmare.

Through the boardroom wall, in the confines of the directors' pantry and private drink store, Monique Wainwright listened to the conversation and banter through her earphones. An Albanian electrician called Eric rewiring the offices two years earlier also fitted surveillance equipment 'upon request' and responding to Monique's close, very close, interest demonstrated how easy it was by threading a wire from the pantry into the cavity of the wall, along the path of the main cable up to and crossing the ceiling where it exited through a fitting and connected to a tiny receiver hidden in the circle of dangling crystal teardrops surrounding an ornate, gilded chandelier hanging over the centre of the boardroom table.

Councillor Townrow's voice crackled through the earphones. 'I think, gentleman, we deserve a long weekend away, on a golf-course somewhere warm, courtesy of our Nipponese friends.'

'La Manga, at least,' Geoffrey Osborne trumpeted.

Harry Patel. 'Indeed, indeed.'

'A splendid idea,' Chairman Hardcastle agreed. 'I haven't been to Spain since that convention on the ethics of post-mortem removal of implanted dental precious metals.'

'What do you think, Ken?' David Broody asked the heavy-hearted Japanese.

Ohara's languid eyes fell on the property developer. 'Excuse me?'

'About spending our little windfall from your television pals. When the Pitties get thumped by Yattock and go out of the Golden Mousetrap competition we'll all go off to Spain and plan the future of the club with clear heads.'

Bastard, Monique mouthed, stamping a stiletto heel incautiously. 'They're all bastards, except for—'

The smiling faces of his parents, bursting with pride at the farewell party for the national team before they left for France all those 9 years ago flashed through Ohara's senses. His mother would be watching the Yattock game now only in spirit but his father and younger sister, maybe the neighbours too, would fill the cramped living room in the little detached house in Yokohama's Kohoku ward. How could he let them down? Head clearing a little, he said to David Broody, 'Go out? I am truly sorry, but I don't understand the English in this case.'

'Go out,' Broody enunciated loudly and slowly. 'Get eliminated. Lose the game.' He drew a cigar cylinder from the jacket pocket and pretended to study the Montecristo label. 'I love this club as much as the next man, but let's face reality.'

'But the Pitties do not *go out* yet,' Ohara declared. 'We have not even played Yattock. Perhaps we will win?'

Walter Hardcastle banged the table, the vibration tinkling the crystal pendants on the chandelier so that it rang in Monique's ears like shattering glass. 'Oh, such innocent optimism, lad. It's bloody wonderful to hear. The spirit of the *sam you ray*. The Pitties are on the move, I know it.'

The old butcher Osborne chuckled patronisingly. 'But not in the semifinal. You see, Ken lad, Yattock are arguably the best team in the Conference and they're certainly the best cup team. They regularly knock out Premiership teams in the FA Cup. We've never been into giant killing at

Siddley. We're tiddlers. I'm sorry, but you won't understand that, will you, being foreign? We're little fish in the pond, ready to be eaten by everything else.'

'We will do our best,' Ohara insisted, blushing with controlled fury.

'Of course you will, lad,' chairman Hardcastle said, accepting a small cigar from Geoffrey Osborne.

'So the motion is passed, then?' Harry Patel concluded. 'We use NHK's generous fee to hold a focus group at an overseas venue to be decided, possibly La Manga.' Sweet, intoxicating cigar smoke hovered over the table. The directors nodded and grunted their agreement.

'*Chotto, chotto,* gentlemen!' Unable to contain his anger and confusion in English, Ohara spluttered his dissent in Japanese, startling Monique, who had to adjust the earphones. 'I cannot agree,' he said, quickly calculating they were talking about 20 million yen. 'We must spend the money for the club.' His impending humiliation in front of half the population of Japan had been bought for a pittance. NHK would have paid 50 times that amount to show Japan's national hero live. Why had Broody sold out for so little?

Broody spread his hands, his mouth cracking into a smirk. 'I'm afraid it's a decision for the board, Ken, and at present you are only the team coach and manager.'

With all the weight of his office, the chairman said: 'Wait a moment or two, David. Let's be fair and hear Ken out, find out what *he'd* do with a hundred thousand pounds. Ken.'

Monique heard someone say: 'hear, hear.' It wasn't David Broody.

Ohara wafted at a hanging plume of smoke and cleared his throat. 'Thank you very much, mister chairman, and I am sorry to take you all away from your important businesses today. First of all, I cannot think about the Golden

Mousetrap Trophy until we have played the next two league games.' He glanced at his notes. 'Home to Grittley Mills on Saturday and away to . . . Moss . . . Moxbottom next week.' He poured a glass of water and drained it, bubbles fizzing in his nostrils. 'I have only been in Siddley a short time and I am impressed by the team and the ground here at Pitt Lane. You must also be proud of your amazing one hundred years of history.'

'Ninety nine years, four months and counting,' Geoffrey Osborne corrected.

Ohara smiled weakly. 'But, to be frank, I was a little surprised to be offered the job as coach at Siddley and it is my fault that I did not know more about your city and football club, and about the many, many teams that play at so many different levels in England. I will certainly reflect on my poor knowledge. It was also a surprise to discover that you gentlemen, as directors, have invested your personal money in the club because it is close to your hearts. This makes you the owners of the club as well, but of course profit is not your motive. In Japan professional sports are businesses. It does not happen that private people give their money and time out of pride and deep love of their town and its sports team. At last I think I understand the situation at Siddley United.'

Chairman Hardcastle cleared his throat emotionally. 'You're right there, lad. Tradition, pride, love: things that matter, things that can't be bought.' In the pantry, through the wall, Monique sniffed to herself. 'We do own the club, Ken, in a manner of speaking, but we hold it in trust for the people of Siddley. We can sell our shares in it, but the integrity of the club and this magnificent ground will remain untouchable and indestructible for ever.'

David Broody pulled on his Havana cigar, hiding the smirk that threatened to explode into uncontrollable laughter. That's what you think, he wanted to bellow. At least Sir

Reginald Pitt stayed away today, honest enough to admit he hated football and was only on the board because of the Pitt tradition. The others, pillars of the Siddley establishment, played out a charade of self-importance, grandiosely parading themselves as philanthropists, preservers of the Pitt Lane football legacy. In under three weeks, with the pitiable Pitties' exit from the Golden Mousetrap Trophy, he would take the fucking directors one by one and twist their balls until they screamed for mercy and begged him to buy their share in Siddley United.

Ohara was talking again. 'You have honoured me with the position of manager and I am finding it a great burden of responsibility.' Broody apart, the others nodded their understanding with pursed lips, none of them wishing it known publicly that they thought they had hired an Irishman. 'So I must do my best to live up to your trust.'

'I'm sure you will, Ken,' Walter Hardcastle said thickly. 'So tell us how *you* would use the one hundred thousand pounds.'

Ohara breathed deeply and tabled his notes and food bill. 'I do not know what the financial situation of the club is, but I have made some expenses already because I want to have fast improvements for the team, especially their fitness. I am also trying to change the eating and drinking habits. The team can train freely at Uno Electronics but the qualified masseuse I have hired for two sessions a week requires a fee.' The directors nodded, their lips pursed in professional understanding. 'I would also like to buy special turf for the pitch. At present, we cannot play good football on it. This will require professional groundsmen to help Mr Charlie Wharton repair and maintain the pitch properly. The team's playing kit must be replaced very soon. And I need Mr Terry Dribble to travel a little and pick up intelligence on our opponents and look for new players. A visit to watch Yattock play is a necessity.' He touched his list 'Just a few more things.' David Broody fidgeted, pretending to study the smouldering tip of his dwindling cigar. 'I want more allowance to pay the players for increased training time and perhaps pay a small bonus if they win. I am not sure if you can understand my poor English.'

'Oh, we can understand your English, Ken,' Broody chimed. 'Only too well. Your demands are impossible. The club's already stretched by your presence here, even if most of your expenses are met by the Japanese football association.' He scoffed loud enough to resound in Monique's earphones. 'At least there's no danger of having to pay the win bonus.'

Chairman Hardcastle was scribbling furiously. He'd already listed seven demands from the Japanese coach: the trip to La Manga was evaporating before his eyes.

'We did use to have a bigger squad,' Councillor Townrow remembered.

'That is my understanding also,' Ohara added. 'At present there are eighteen registered players. Regrettably, Hampton and Blink are unavailable through injury and a man called Hopp is in prison. As you, the directors, were all unable to attend the game at Molecroft on Saturday, you would not know that Dean Slutz is now injured and three more are doubtful. Twelve fit players are not enough. I might have to play myself although that wasn't my intention when I became your manager.'

'Have you identified any potential talent, Ken?' Harry Patel asked, trying to sound really interested. Weekends were the busiest at his three discount outlets and his attendance at a Saturday home game rarely stretched to half-time. He had yet to see an away game.

'I have been too busy to look.'

'We only pay appearance money.' It was Geoffrey Osborne, suddenly enthusiastic. 'So it wouldn't cost us that much to have more players on our books, like we used to have. And Ken being in Siddley is bound to bring the old fans back. Does this make sense, David?'

In the pantry, Monique's body hummed. For his second coming the messiah had chosen Siddley, in the guise of a bow-legged Japanese with a cute, flat bottom. If only he were in the pantry with her. 'But what's this?' She clutched the ear pads. The rat Broody was on the counter attack.

'It certainly does not. Our finances are already on a knife-edge.' Looking at Ohara, he said, 'Do you know what our gate receipts were against Cogworth?' Ohara had no idea. 'Because of the Ohara effect, a ten year record high of seven hundred and two pounds was recorded, which just about covers a quarter of the club's running costs. Do you know what keeps this club afloat?' Ohara shook his head again: he had begun to wonder. 'Eighty per cent of the income comes from the car park, from customers of the Panther Hypermarket across the Talbot Street bridge. If we weren't in the centre of Siddley, with the car park, this football club would be dead.' In his mind he saw the twin-towered hotel and office block dominating central Siddley, visible from the ring-road. The Russians would own the land; he would own the skyline.

Walter Hardcastle was alert, his face a mask of seriousness and concern. 'Dead' was an evocative word. He said: 'I'm afraid that we, as directors, are unable to invest more of our personal resources in these difficult economic times.'

'So it would be most inappropriate,' Harry Patel suggested humbly, 'if we were seen using the television windfall for extravagant purposes. Like junkets in the sun, playing golf and rattling castanets.'

They'd make great Japanese, Ohara mused, bending like bamboo as the wind changed.

Walter Hardcastle said: 'So are we agreed? We make this one hundred thousand pounds available to Ken for general purposes in the interests of the club.'

Four right arms rose in unison. David Broody snorted and noted the decision reluctantly for the record and Monique Wainwright snagged her top on a jug hook in the heat-charged atmosphere of the pantry.

'Thank you all very much,' Ohara said sincerely, gathering his papers. Then he remembered. 'Excuse me, another matter.' The directors slumped back into their seats. 'I owe a great debt to Uno Electronics, especially their president, Mr Ishida, for allowing us to use their gym and playing fields. I must return the favour at some time.'

'You can play him at centre forward,' Broody suggested humourlessly.

'Excuse me? No, I want to offer half price tickets to Uno staff and their families for the Golden Mousetrap Trophy semi-final game, and to all other spectators. And you must also permit Uno to erect advertising free of charge.'

Broody slammed his black, gold-inlaid fountain pen onto the table. Walter Hardcastle saw his own advertising plan under threat. Harry Patel was weighing up the figures. 'We only charge two pounds for a seat and a pound for the terraces,' he told Ohara. 'We'll have no income at all if we halve the prices.'

'As far as I can understand, Yattock will be bringing many supporters to the game and I think many Japanese will come. We must respond very positively. A good home crowd gives us an advantage, so for this match I strongly request we announce special prices for all the fans. May I have your agreement, please?' He waited nervously while they debated the point. He hadn't told them that the main reason he wanted to offer virtually free admission was the fear of playing to the population of Japan in a near empty stadium.

'We've nothing to lose, have we?' Councillor Townrow concluded sensibly. 'That hundred thousand's given us a bit of a cushion.' The three directors quickly agreed.

An acrid stench rose from David Broody's dead cigar.

Not wanting to show his hand yet, he capitulated, looking at Ohara with a cold, empty smile. 'Can I take it you have no further issues on your managerial agenda?'

Ohara rose, thanked the board and bowed from the waist, but when he reached the door he turned, a finger on his cheek. 'A small matter, gentlemen. I think the Pitties must have their own website. I will arrange it.'

Ohara closed the boardroom door gently. Monique was not in the outer office immediately, but emerged from a closet of some sort, jumping when she saw him, then smiling, saying: 'Well done, Mr Ohara.' He did not understand her sentiments, or the origin of the furrow ploughed from ear to ear through her crown of golden hair, and when he asked her to arrange urgent interviews with Radio Siddley and the *Siddley Evening Sentinel* so that he could proclaim the great ticket deal for the trophy match she was unimpressed, as if she'd heard about it before. When she'd finished jotting his instructions, she cornered him between a filing cabinet and the pantry door.

'Can I see you in private, Mr Ohara?' Her deep green, saucer eyes burned into his cold, Japanese facade like acid.

'Tomorrow night, perhaps,' he managed thickly. 'Here at Pitt Lane, about five, when you've finished your work for the day.'

Arranged with dedicated haste by Monique, Ken Ohara went on a PR offensive, visiting first the *Siddley Evening Sentinel*'s Stoolton Road offices. To admiring glances from staffers he opened his heart to Paddy Brick, the chief sports correspondent, a craggy faced veteran with red braces supporting his baggy jeans, requesting through the good offices of Siddley's own newspaper total local support in the two upcoming league games and especially the big one – the trophy semi-final against the Conference giants, Yattock. He told Brick the match would be televized live to Japan, an incredible situation given Siddley's lowly existence, and in honour of this the stands and terraces would be thrown open to spectators at half the normal price.

Then it was Radio Siddley, a short walk over the River Siddleworth to Weirside Plaza, where Karen Saddleback recorded their interview for broadcast with the midday half hour of news and sports. The plea was the same; Karen offered full support, promising to promote the cut-price ticket offer in her hourly sports bulletins and inform her colleagues on the regional television network. Karen wondered on air where the goals were going to come from, and Ohara told her he was looking at several options.

A sprightly breeze played along the course of the shallow river, scuffing his neatly trimmed hair. Ohara hurried back across the bridge to meet the club's odd job man, Charlie Wharton, and his two mates from the municipal parks and gardens department behind the Council House on the riverside promenade. A man with bovine buttocks and a nasty neck twitch which gave him an unintentionally furtive expression drew a patch of grass-topped turf from a plastic carrier bag. With Charlie's help in reassembling his colleague's impenetrable English for Ohara's benefit, it appeared they could acquire and lay the mature, fast-growing deep-root grass in the dimensions required with virtually seamless precision. Council vehicles could probably be available for transport, but given the delicate nature of the grass at this crucially intermediate stage of its life, the removal of existing damaged turf and its replacement would most effectively be accomplished after five o'clock in the evening. To nods of agreement from the others, Charlie also thought it best not to talk too much about this bit of business so as not to give opposing teams forewarning of the condition of the pitch at Pitt Lane. Payment in cash would be very appropriate.

Ohara ate a pie with Charlie in the Market Hall. The wiry old council lavatory cleaner basked in reflected glory as the shoppers, young and old, patted the Japanese coach fondly and sheepishly asked him to sign their shopping lists. 'Turn up for the Golden Mousetrap semi-final game and Mr Ohara will sign your thigh,' Charlie said solemnly, only partly in jest.

He'd been too busy to notice, but it was when he was alone, like now in his car on the way to Uno Electronics for an afternoon training session, that the feeling of isolation gripped him. It wasn't loneliness, every day had been full and eventful: it was simple nostalgia for steaming, sticky rice, a bowl of pungent *miso* soup, a simple piece of grilled, ocean fresh sea-bream, a plate of pickled root vegetables and a pot of cold *sake*. He didn't actually eat this traditional stuff very much in Japan, it was the staple of his parents' generation, but the comfort factor of the imagery evoked everything he missed. Separating the NHK fee from the Pitt Lane board also lightened the journey. The directors were wealthy men who loved the tradition of their football club, but they had no vision for it, no yearning for success in case it disrupted their businesses. Monique Wainwright ran the club day to day, purely out of love for it, but David Broody pulled the strings. Ohara had heard that it was the property developer who had negotiated his contract with Siddley United, but why were so many people surprised to find he, Ohara, wasn't Irish and why wasn't Broody as enthusiastic about Ohara's plans for the club as the others? Monique might know, and he'd ask her tonight.

After changing the captaincy, the other big task was a manager's hardest: to drop a veteran player from the regular first team. Kevin Stopham had been a goalie at Siddley United for 18 years. He was part of the tradition, and so far untouchable. But Ohara saw him as heavy of foot, meeting crosses late, and unsure about how to organize his defence under pressure. Tony McDonald was 23, six feet three inches tall, unemployed with a child to support, and had turned out religiously for the team as reserve goalie: he needed the small playing allowance from the Pitties. Ohara liked his attitude and agility in training and with the Pitties leaking almost three goals a game he may as well make the change now.

The other players heard a door slam and watched Kevin Stopham march across the parking lot to his plumber's van.

Another four players arrived, including the injured Dean Slutz who offered to retrieve the balls, and the team moved to the pitch. With Ohara and Drummond supplying crosses from one side and Omerod and Mandrake from the other, Simon Pitt and Omar Grant competed for headers and volleys, testing McDonald from all angles and heights. At the other end of the ground, players practised cross field passing and control drills. When Ohara ceded his place to Mike Groot he saw a familiar figure waiting for him by a heap of tracksuit tops on the touchline.

'You drive on the left in Japan,' Marco di Rapido remarked when Ohara reached him. He was kitted up in a faded Pitties replica shirt, shorts and football boots. 'I didn't know that until I saw *Godzilla* films.'

Ohara had to smile. 'I didn't order a pizza, Marco.'

'I was just passing Uno Electronics and saw you training.'

'And you carry your kit with you always?'

Marco grinned. 'Always.'

Gavin Rowley, the player manager of Uno's company team, had offered to play a pair of 30 minute halves at the end of their working day and Ohara saw him over Marco's shoulder, emerging from the main building in full sky blue kit with the mixed British and Japanese players. He couldn't see Taro Suzuki among the Japanese, all of whom jigged a respectful head bow in his direction. Jogging on the spot, Marco di Rapido prodded a finger towards the Pitties gathering in the centre circle. 'If you leave out Deano Slutz you're still a player short, even if you play yourself. They've got eleven.'

Ohara's stern face gave way to a smile. 'You win,' he conceded. 'But no commitment from me. You are working out with us. It is not a trial.'

The players were exchanging greetings when a slight figure in a tracksuit ran from the main building and across the field, a whistle dangling from his neck. He acknowledged Ohara with a nod and blew for kick-off. Taro Suzuki.

They played fast, soft tackle football, drawing more and more curious Uno workers to the touchline as the afternoon shifts ended. Marco played up front with Simon Pitt, with Lucas Mandrake just behind them on the left. Ohara, Drummond, Grant and Omerod filled the midfield and Scott Fisher played shallow sweeper behind Diamond, Breakin and Blink. Relishing his call up, Tony McDonald prowled the goalmouth, slapping his gloves together, shouting at his defenders as if it were a serious match. He told his players to put the passing practice into effect and test Marco di Rapido, however close the Uno guys marked him. Drawn from a small pool, the Uno lads were too varied in height, size and fitness to have much shape and at times they made the Pitties look positively professional. Shorter, fitter, the three Japanese on the Uno team were the hardest to track. Ohara guessed they must have been high school or university team players, and he had to acknowledge Marco di Rapido's pace and control were outstanding. He strode the pitch with irritating Italian arrogance, running a hand through his hair after a tussle with an opponent or holding up play with shoe-string control while searching for a team-mate in space. He even scored a goal himself in the first short half, on the volley from an Ohara cross, and made two for Simon Pitt. In the second, everyone wanted to score, and it was Les Diamond who came from the back to hit a 30 yarder for the fourth, then Scott Fisher, who should have been on the half-way line, with a header.

To Ohara's horror, defensive discipline completely cracked in the fading light, and the Uno team hit two breakaway goals. Scoring goals had gone to the Pitties' heads, firing them up like hunting dogs bloodied for the first time. Ohara raced around trying to control them. Then Marco di Rapido completely lost it. He berated his defenders, who he recognized but hardly knew, and chased the soccer fun players of Uno as if it were him against eleven in a World Cup final. Before Taro Suzuki blew for the end of the run-out, Marco reacted to a mistimed tackle by a man who by day drove a delivery truck for Uno and pursued him, taking out his legs and then standing accusingly over him. Ohara raced over and dragged the pasta maker's son from his confused victim. 'It's only a practice, Marco,' he shouted, bowing in apology to the stricken player.

'Am I in the team, boss?' Marco demanded, pursuing the Japanese.

'It's too early to say.'

'You saw my goal. A blinder. You've got to let me play. Please. We were allies in the war.' Shoulders raised forearms spread in supplication, his Italian blood was rising to the surface. Before it erupted, he found himself suddenly immobile, powerful hands clamped over his collar bone.

'Mr Ohara will let you know,' Omar Grant informed Marco's ear.

Ohara was hobbling slightly as he left the pitch. He'd ridden the tackles well and made a few of his own, and the delicate right knee seemed to come through it with all but a dull, burning sensation. Thanking Gavin Rowley for the game, he was heading for his car when a voice in Japanese halted him. Taro Suzuki.

'I want to play for you,' the thin lipped Japanese with the arched eyebrows said. The whistle bobbed against his chest as he fell in line with Ohara's disjointed pace. Taro Suzuki had retired a year after the tackle that finished Ohara's full time playing career but he was still very fit, like the Pitties manager, and still loved to play football. He was half a head taller, a natural battling forward whose prominent weakness was selfishness when on the ball.

Watching him running alongside Marco di Rapido, Ohara realized how similar were the instincts of strikers, whatever the nationality.

'*Hisashiburi*, Suzuku *kun*,' Ohara smiled. 'It's been a while. Too long.'

They were walking slowly towards the Uno Electronics car park, where the Siddley players were dispersing. It looked to Ohara that Marco di Rapido, his arms wind-milling about, was trying to convince his possible team mates.

'Four years and a bit since I—'

'I'd heard you went back to Uno Electronics,' Ohara remarked. 'And keep on playing.'

'They call it Sunday league. We have a knockaround on the local park, kick the shit out of each other, swear a lot and then all go down to the pub. We play for fun.'

They reached Ohara's Honda. 'Did your president, Ishida *san*, ask you to play for me?'

'I saw you with him in the canteen the other day. I'm just as Japanese as you are, Ken-ichi *san*. I can figure out what's going on.' He tossed his head at the Siddley players gathered around the team minibus. Pickwich and Les Diamond were nose-to-nose about something and Scott Fisher was trying to separate poor old Kevin Stopham from his younger replacement. 'They're a hard lot down here at this level, in the feeder divisions. The players never made it or were unsuccessful in the professional leagues and failure makes them harder, makes them behave like bad boy bigshots for ninety minutes a week. I'll play for the Pitties because I want to, and all I ask is that one day you'll get drunk with me and tell me what the fuck *you're* doing in Siddley.'

Ohara tried to read behind his old adversary's eyes. Was his offer to play for the Pitties coming out of guilt, pity, a sense of patriotic obligation, his president's command? Ohara needed to know before he could accept. 'Thank you for your sincerity,' he told Suzuki. 'Please think a little more about whether you want to play for me. You must not make the wrong decision.'

Ohara drove straight to Pitt Lane where Monique was anxious to speak to him. Striking permutations filled his head. He had the untried di Rapido and possibly Taro Suzuki if the Japanese still wanted to play for the Pitties after reconsideration. He decided the Golden Mousetrap Trophy semi-final in less than three weeks was to be his own personal standard by which to measure the progress he had made, or lack of it. The Pitties were second to bottom in their division, and while relegation was an issue, he would use the two upcoming league games to juggle what he hoped would be a fitter, tighter, more tactically aware team for the big test against vastly superior opposition from the Conference.

The phone was ringing as he was entering Monique's cluttered office. Picking it up she smiled, beckoning him to take a seat by her desk. 'The Pitties ticket hot-line, Monique speaking. How may I help you?' A pause. 'Yes, the radio is correct. Pitt and Canal Stand seats will be available at one pound and the terraces at fifty pence . . . And you too, love. Come this Saturday as well, if you can. Grittley Mills. It's Ken Ohara's first game at home.'

While she spoke Ohara turned the *Siddley Evening Sentinel* towards him. Below the main story, entitled Falling Satellite

May Hit Siddley,' he saw his face next to the headline, 'Golden Mousetrap Trophy – Ticket Bonanza to Pack Pitt Lane?' He sighed wearily.

When Monique had hung up, he asked: 'What really happened in the first three rounds of the Golden Mousetrap Cup? We must have won them all to qualify for the semi-final.'

Tapping her slender nose with a pencil, Monique slid back in pensive pose, peach-tinted eyelids dropping like shutters over the swell of her huge pale green eyes. 'Sort of won,' she said finally. 'We were given a bye in the first round, away to Boglington. Six of their players were arrested in a swoop for illegal immigrants on a fruit farm the day before the game. Three others, and the manager, disappeared the same night and only two players actually turned up for the game.'

'What about the second round?' Ohara wondered apprehensively. 'How did the Pitties win that one?'

'The best possible draw, really. We avoided all the Conference teams and drew Neep Fliers. It was very sad,' Monique said genuinely. 'Neep are a nice bunch of lads, a works team mainly, toilet and sanitary equipment. But they announced the closure of the factory on the Friday before the match with us and the lads weren't really up to playing much. Simon Pitt seemed to foul their goalie when he scored the only goal but the Neepies couldn't be bothered to protest it.'

'And the quarter-final?' Ohara asked.

'On penalties,' Monique said proudly. 'Here at Pitt Lane against Port Stanley Garden City. We avoided the Conference sides again. We had almost four hundred people in the ground. Not bad for a Wednesday night in Siddley. We'd drawn 0-0 away to them at the weekend and it was 0-0 here after extra time. We won 2-1 on penalties, Legs Diamond getting one and Omar the winner.'

'So we only actually won one game in open play?'

Monique sighed heavily and nodded forlornly.

'And the other three teams in the semis are Conference teams, like Yattock.'

'That's correct,' Monique affirmed. 'Our luck had to run out sometime. But we've just got to beat two of them and we have our first trophy ever. And it's the fabulous Golden Mousetrap.' The rash optimism in her voice trailed off when she saw it wasn't shared by the manager.

Ohara's life was flashing before him: schoolboy international, full national team player at 21, two league championship medals, the Emperor's Cup, the Nabisco Cup, twice, a hero of the World Cup in France, more trophies as manager of the Kinki Princes and then . . . you're qualified to coach Siddley United of the RoustaRodent Solutions League. 'You wanted to talk to me privately, Monique. Let's go to my room.'

'You look so tired, Ken,' she said, drawing a chair up to the scratched metal desk and placing her crimson tinted talons lightly over his two hands, even as she pierced him with moist compassionate eyes. She loved his smooth, taut, light olive skin, his high, dangerous cheekbones and the casual, slightly off-centre parting in his thick, black hair. And what she wouldn't do to those arrogant lips! 'It must be such a change from playing with them kinky blokes in Japan.'

'The Kinki Princes,' Ohara enunciated patiently, his eyes on the troubled rise and fall of her chest, astounded at the stress placed on the tiny buttons. 'And yes, you're right. I am feeling the pressure a little. Siddley was not quite what I imagined and I did not expect to play myself, but with so few players I might have to.' As if he hadn't enough to think about, he said: 'But something is worrying you, Monique *san*.'

For a moment she wondered whether to open her heart

to this virtual stranger, and a foreign one at that, but then she remembered the way he'd confronted the directors and David Broody, forcing them for once to put the club before their selfish interests. Still, the words did not come easily. 'It's about Mr Broody,' she mumbled, her voice catching in her throat.

'Mr Broody?'

Monique concentrated her gaze on a roundel of rust on the desk. 'David Broody wants to buy out the football club, then sell the Pitt Lane ground. And the car park, and all the houses around it.'

So the rumours were true, Ohara thought, just like the old fisherman Alf something said. 'It might be better for the Pitties to play in a smaller stadium,' he said with a smile of sympathy. He was thinking about the vast, wasted terraces, the tall, crumbling stands and the few hundred spectators who bothered to occupy them. 'The Pitt Lane facilities are just too big for the RoustaRodent League.'

Monique thought about it, but then drew herself up, took a deep breath and rolled into what sounded to Ohara liked a carefully rehearsed speech. 'Siddley United are a sleeping giant with an enormous ground. All we need is good management from the directors and a very good coach and the results and the supporters will return.' She leaned a touch too far forward. 'I think we have fulfilled the second condition.'

'Thank you, Monique *san*,' Ohara said. 'I will do my best. But tell me, how do you know about Mr Broody's plans?'

She paused for thought again. 'Let's just say I know. He's Siddley's best-known property speculator. And notorious. People think he set fire to the old lemonade factory on Inkerman Road when he couldn't get permission to knock it down legally. Now he means to sell the Pitt Lane ground to foreigners. Russians, I think.'

'He can't do anything without the directors' agreement

surely?' He remembered the chairman had told him the directors owned all shares in the club.

'I'm sure he can persuade them,' Monique huffed, remembering Broody's threats in the pub. 'And then he'll let the Pitties fold up, die, just like that.'

Ohara felt no strong emotional tie with Siddley United, the opposite was in fact true, but this English woman's passion was quite touching. 'It would be a pity to disappear in the centenary year. In Japan, anything more than fifty years old is a national treasure. But I don't see what I can do.'

Monique's eyes were orbs of fire. 'No, no, Ken. You can save the Pitties. All you have to do is win the Golden Mousetrap this season and the club can carry on.'

Coach Ohara rubbed his throbbing temples between his fingertips. 'I'm sorry, Monique *san*. My English is too poor to understand what you are saying.'

She leaned forward, this time closing her hand over his. 'Please, Ken, you *must* understand. Broody believes that the club's land can be sold if the Pitties haven't won anything after a hundred years. If it's true, all we can win is the Golden Mousetrap.'

'How can he believe such a silly thing?' Ohara wondered, still not really comprehending.

'He thinks Sir Abraham Pitt left a written proviso when he gave the land to the town for a football club.'

'Proviso?'

'A condition, a proviso. It should be written down, on a bit of paper hidden away somewhere, here at Pitt Lane or in Pitt Manor where Sir Reginald Pitt lives. He's on Broody's side in all this, by the way. They're looking for the document right now. Everybody thinks the land belongs to the town forever, but if Broody can prove it doesn't we'll lose it.' Saying that, Monique could contain the flood no longer. Her bosoms welled, her tender, rouged cheeks twitched uncontrollably, her eyes brimmed with tears and the sound of a woman's tortured sobbing filled the manager's little office. Ohara looked around for help but they were alone, then he found a wedge of tissues in a drawer.

Monique snorted expansively into the fragile paper, bringing the convulsions temporarily to a halt and restoring her capacity to speak, if only shakily. 'You're the only one who can save the Pitties,' she shrieked, leaping to her feet and stepping briskly around the desk to his side, engulfing the Japanese's head in the deliciously suffocating embrace of her satin-coated breasts. 'You've got to win the Golden Mousetrap for us. It's our only hope.'

His collar was damp, his senses intoxicated with Monique's jasmine-scented perfume. His mouth lay against the curl of her ear and his voice emerged as a desperate croak. 'Does anyone else know about Mr Broody's terrible plans?'

'Only you and me,' she sobbed. Then, after a moment or two, she pushed away from him, her face forming a frown. 'No. Wait a minute. I think our last manager, Moby McNally knew something. He loved the Pitties as much as I did. He once blurted something out to me about both of us having to look for another job soon. He said something like, "he wants me to help him do it." Then he shut up very sharpish, and I couldn't get him to tell me more. Then he goes and falls in the canal. And dies.'

Ohara was still in his windowless cell a good hour and a half after ushering the distraught woman into the chilly Siddley night with the forlorn promises to win the Golden Mousetrap for her and the town. His eyes were sore from straining in the feeble light of the single bulb, his senses still heady with her perfume. With the ground dark and deserted, he pulled an illicit cigarette from his jacket, lit it and leaned back in the flexible chair, craving the hot soothing water of a hotspring outdoor bath in the rain, followed by a bowl of noodles infused with *miso* broth, a few slivers of fatty bluefin tuna and a pot of hot *sake*. He was feeling old and stupidly nostalgic for a Japan mostly unfamiliar to him. As a player it was fame and money, and *karaoke* and much more with endless groupies, and later as a manager and occasional player it was fitness, tactics and pressure in the high profile, competitive J-League. Why should it matter a bag of soya beans to him whether this little provincial football club in England went under? He'd have ten job offers waiting for him. So what was keeping him here? Why should it bother him if David Broody had put together a sensible plan to redevelop the decaying core of Siddley, a city he hadn't heard of six months ago? But a vision of Monique's imploring face and her liquid eyes, filled his head. The board of directors owned the shares in the Pitties but she possessed its heart. And now the very thing she loved, Siddley United Football Club, was about to be destroyed.

He wrapped the butt of the dead cigarette in Monique's used ball of tissue paper and forced his attention back to his own pressing matters, a league game in less than 48 hours and a cup tie which had now taken on life and death proportions, at least to Monique. For Ohara it was a job; for the dozens of millions of Japanese who would watch the Yattock game live it was national pride and reputation, not the prospect of a titanic struggle between the losers of Siddley and the semi-pros of the Conference. He'd lost track of time and he was hungry. A plate of spaghetti or risotto at PastaBasta and a couple of glasses of wine beckoned. He'd started to tap Rika Yamaguchi's number into his mobile phone when the subterranean silence was shattered by a muffled crashing noise in a room on an upper level. 'Hello,' he called, stacking his papers, an ear cocked to the open door. Then a metallic clash made him start. Letting the echo fade, he locked his team plans and tactical doodles in a drawer and headed up the stairs to the long lounge and the boardroom suite beyond.

The lights everywhere were off and he found himself fumbling along the walls in unfamiliar surroundings until he found a switch. The first noise had come from the chairman's room: one of the photos had fallen off the wall, shattering the glass that protected it. The place where the picture had hung stood out as a clean white patch against the grimier wall. It was level with his face, and he reached out to touch the brass hook. It held firm. So what had caused the photo to fall, he wondered, dropping to a knee and turning it over, mindful of the shards of glass on the floor and still in the frame? It was one of the very oldest photos, a sepia image of three men, one in baggy football gear, in staid poses on any empty football field and it had become separated from the frame and the backing board in the fall. He was running a finger along it when he touched something wet and sticky. He shuddered when he realised it was blood and when he lifted the frame and picture from among the pieces of glass he saw the floorboards were spotted with dark red blobs that led to the door in a staggered trail.

5

The nights close in and the days shorten under murky, sullen skies. It is football weather, and all over the country the great game flourishes on thousands of park pitches, grimy old grounds and modern stadiums. The fitness of the players is peaking, muscles supple ahead of the busy Christmas fixtures and the hard, energy sapping turf in January. Ken Ohara's mind was far from football when he stepped up the narrow staircase to Monique's office.

'Did you get my message?' he panted. 'About the picture?'

Her face clouded. 'Yes I did.' She led him into the boardroom where he saw the glass and the bloodstains had been cleaned up and the picture reassembled. 'It's weird,' she said, her eyes full of uncertainty and amazement.

'Sorry?'

'Strange. Odd. I looked behind this old photo out of curiosity only a couple of days ago. Now somebody else has had a peek and cut himself in the process.'

'Do you think it was him? Mr Broody?'

Monique suddenly clamped a hand over her mouth, cutting off the inward rush of breath. 'Oh my God! He came up behind me just when I was putting it back together. He must have guessed what I was doing and got suspicious.'

'Whoever did this must have cut himself very badly,' Ohara said. 'There was so much blood.'

'I didn't find anything behind the old picture so neither did he. Perhaps he got angry and dropped it deliberately.'

The identity of the clumsy intruder was revealed an hour before the home against Grittley Mills, and it wasn't David Broody. Ohara was checking the last minute fitness of the team when he heard noises coming from the treatment room. Someone was being massaged and pummelled by Clarissa, emitting simian grunts as her expert fingers dug in deep. Worried about a new injury, Ohara peered into the room. The man's face was turned away, but Ohara's eyes fell to the hand dangling off the table – and froze. It was bound with white tape, not crudely, but a neat application of binding over a proper surgical seal, the kind you'd get in the emergency room at a hospital after stitches had been applied to a deep cut in your palm.

Clarissa looked up and smiled, sweat beading her forehead. To the prone body she said: 'That's it for now. Get out there and show 'em.' Billy Pickwich groaned with mock disappointment and pushed himself upright.

Ohara stuttered: 'Will you be fit to play today, with your hand injury?' He suddenly remembered Pickwich had missed yesterday's training session. He hoped he sounded concerned for the player's well-being and not shocked at seeing him as a suspect.

'No problems, boss. Put me hand through an old nail yesterday, doing a bit of do-it-yourself. Had to take the bleeding thing to Siddley General to get patched up. I'll be fine for the match. The hole's in me hand, not me foot.'

'Good. Please take care of yourself.'

Grittley Mills approached the game exactly in the same violent, nihilistic way Matt Dennis and Terry Dribble had predicted, their behaviour encouraged by a contingent of foulmouthed, bawling, skinhead fans imprisoned behind tall fences in a corner of the Canal Stand. Grittley's team consisted of failed hopefuls or veterans from the higher leagues who sought to expunge the shame of collective deficiencies by battering their way around the Rousta-Rodent Solutions League. The Pitties' just about heeded Ohara's demand for restraint but right back Les Diamond and his opposite on the left side of midfield, Gary Omerod, both picked up yellow cards. The Grittley Mills striker, Dermot Bleach, organized his team's thuggery and was sent off for his second very late tackle on Simon Pitt. Ohara winced when his fragile front-man hit the turf again. With Dean Slutz injured, he was running out of strikers. He hadn't decided about Marco di Rapido and Taro Suzuki hadn't come back after Ohara told him to reflect on his motives in wanting to play for the Pitties. He regretted not accepting his fellow countryman immediately but he didn't want the old Gamba star to play out of guilt and remorse. On the positive side, the squad had picked up two more players when Lenny Hampton was declared virus free and played competently for 15 minutes in substitution for a tired and battered Robby Breakin, and the window cleaner and utility midfielder Clint Hopp, who had been released early from his prison sentence in time to train on Friday, surprised Ohara with his skill as a second half substitute.

Monique put the crowd at around 2,000, six times more than average home attendance. Joined-up spectators at last, the *Sentinel's* Paddy Brick would describe them in his review. The terraced end of Pitt Lane was occupied by a pyramid wedge of noisy Japanese and English supporters, many of them from Uno Electronics. Warming up himself, Ohara saw Taro Suzuki among them with his family, impassive, his face a mask of indifference.

Ohara stood outside the dugout in his tracksuit, rocking on his heels, arms crossed as the game ebbed and flowed. The Pitties were not overwhelmed by the old, cynical professionals and as the scrappy, unpleasantly physical match progressed he thought he saw the first signs of his influence on his team's play. The defence kept its shape under provocative pressure and some of the passing, especially from Les Diamond and Clint Hopp, was as clean as the lunges, elbows and blocks of the Grittley Mills players would allow. The Pitties' goal came from neat passing play, without one fortuitous rebound, the ball from Fisher to Grant, back to Fisher, curled over to Pitt who, with the pass of the match, bent it to the feet of Lucas Mandrake. The sleek lay preacher cut past a ponderous right back and hit a sweet, left foot rising drive, which was snared by the net beyond the goalkeeper's outstretched left arm. A Pittie goal unaided by tussle, bobble, bounce or defensive error.

Grittley Mills' equalizer came with eight minutes left on the clock and only nine of their men remaining on the field. A left-sided defender called Mekon Wilson had flattened Simon Pitt on the edge of his own area. It was his second bookable offence and he was off, but Les Diamond's free kick rebounded off the Grittley Mills' wall and was hoofed up to their lone striker with the Pittie defence caught too far forward. He held it up until support reached him, two-timed Billy Pickwich too easily and unselfishly gave it to a colleague for the tap-in.

Ken Ohara's first home game in charge had ended with a draw. A good draw, Karen Saddleback of Radio Siddley told her listeners, from a display worthy of the three points. Most of the Pitties fans, with the Japanese contingent, stayed to applaud the tender signs of positive, tactical, real football. Ohara congratulated each of his players as they entered the tunnel and asked about injuries. Inflamed patches on Simon Pitt's thighs were already turning purple and he was limping. Seeing the last Pittie off the pitch, Ohara pirouetted in salute to the fans: the hardcore regulars, the noisy Japanese, the returnees and the plain curious, and was about to follow his players when Marco di Rapido's agitated figure appeared at the fence above the tunnel entrance. He held up an empty take-away pizza box on the back of which he had written, 'I love sushi,' in a mimicry of Japanese lettering. Ohara smiled and waved and almost walked away, injuries on his mind again. The Pitties faced an away game at Moxbottom in seven days and then the impossible semi-final trophy fixture against Yattock of the Conference. He looked up at the expectant face.

'Bring your boots to Uno Electronics on Tuesday. Please.'
'Yeeessssss!' Marco erupted.
'But not your Italian temper.'

On Monday evening Charlie Wharton directed ten lads from the Parks and Gardens department as they moved their machines, equipment and great rolls of tough, fast-growing, genetically enhanced turf into Pitt Lane. Under dim-mode floodlights and a hazy, half moon, the moonlighters from Siddley City Council moved with the precision of synchronized swimmers, shaving the historic pitch of its scrawny grass cover, flattening and rolling the bald ground expertly and laying the rich, durable turf with painstaking exactitude. The clank of machinery echoed round the stands and terraces, deserted but for the Japanese manager and Monique Wainwright who sat in the directors' enclosure, wrapped against the chill and eating pizza and sharing a bottle of Chianti.

Ecstatic at joining the Pitties, Marco di Rapido invented the Ohara Super Sorpressimo, a thin and crispy pizza sprinkled with shaved parmesan and mixed Italian herbs and after baking spread with slivers of seared tuna in a star formation on a bed of rocket. It arrived at Pitt Lane, effusing the sapid aroma of fresh bread, tarragon and thyme, with the complimentary bottle of wine. They were eating the last pieces when the machinery suddenly went silent.

Charlie called from the touchline. 'Come down and look at this, Mr Ohara.'

Leading Monique down to the pitch, Ohara followed Charlie to the centre circle where a pair of the workers leaned on their spades.

Charlie pointed to an area of earth, darker, slightly sunken and less compacted than the rest. 'Bloody odd this, boss,' he said, raising his flat cap and scratching his scalp. 'We've had problems with moles over the years but this is the opposite.'

'Looks like someone's been digging up the pitch,' one of the council workers opined.

'Bloody vandals,' Charlie decided. 'It weren't like this for the match on Saturday. They must done it yesterday.'

Monique nodded ruefully. 'I think we can guess who it was,' she told Ohara quietly.

'Do you think they found—?' Ohara started, but Monique lifted a finger to her lips.

'Bloody vandals,' Charlie repeated. 'But it don't matter, does it? We're going to turf it over anyway. Just thought I'd tell the boss.'

'Do you think Broody found anything?' Ohara asked when they were back in the stands, their glasses refilled.

'They dug up most of the centre circle. If Sir Abraham's document was buried there he must have found it.'

The mood of the lone couple in the Pitt Stand turned cold and thoughtful. It looked to them like Billy Pickwich, taxi driver and the team left back, had been used by David Broody to help find Sir Abraham's proviso, by whatever means. It wasn't concealed behind the old photo itself so Broody guessed the clue to its whereabouts was actually in it. Sir Abraham Pitt was pictured standing on the centre spot: you could see the chalk marks and the cathedral tower right behind the trio. If Broody had seen through Sir Abraham's mischievous gesture and found the killer covenant under the pitch he now had the legal validation to sell Pitt Lane to the Russians. Until that moment Ohara had actually felt encouraged by events on the pitch but now, with at least two traitors in the camp, he shared Monique's deflation and pessimism.

When she had left, Ohara prepared the week's training programme in his office and was a lone spectator when, almost at midnight, the light roller finished its task, nudging the joints together, and Charlie opened the sprinklers on Pitt Lane's new, thick, green playing surface. An envelope containing £50 notes changed hands as the lads from the council packed up their gear.

Taro Suzuki still hadn't made up his mind by Thursday, but with Hopp and Hampton back in the squad, and Marco di Rapido unrestrained in his desire to play at Moxbottom, Ohara had the luxury of 14 fit outfield players, 15 including himself. Should he drop Billy Pickwich from the team? Omar Grant told him that Billy was complaining the training was too hard for players with jobs and he was trying to recruit Groot, a mechanic, and Omerod, the shelf stacker at the Put'mup DIY warehouse, into a revolt, a situation squashed in the short term by a doubling of the playing allowance, courtesy of the expected television windfall. Ohara agonized silently, watching the players performing drill passing patterns on the Uno pitch. He decided to put the Pickwich issue on hold, to leave him in the team for the moment. He needed players for Moxbottom and even more for the Golden Mousetrap semi-final in eleven days, for which he was demanding pace, feet-to-feet passing and constant off-the-ball movement.

While the Pitties worked through endurance and skill

drills at Uno, an advance team from the Japanese television company's production contractors fell upon Pitt Lane with their clipboards and measuring gear, locating positions for their fixed cameras and commentators, identifying power sources and potential obstacles. They were still there, testing the light under the floods with meters, when Ohara returned to Pitt Lane, an unwelcome reminder that in just over a week their cameras would expose him to overwhelming ridicule in his homeland.

The entire pitch had received the new, durable turf and four days of mild, wet weather, with prolonged periods of lukewarm sunshine had left it looking well knitted, the grass even, dense and erect. Ohara kept the Friday evening training to touchline aerobics and a gentle jog along the canal, where Alf Widdison was ending his day with the rod, his keep-net live with little jumping and squirming brown fish.

'Drop round and have a look at my old dad's football souvenirs some time,' Alf said, as Ohara jogged on the spot to greet him. 'Three long knocks and a short one on the door will identify you as a friend.'

Moxbottom, a quietly prosperous little market town, lay in a shallow valley where houses tiered along the hillsides gave way to slopes peppered with sheep. The river Mox narrowed enough for Saxon ancestors to ford it with a low, two arch bridge – its ancient stonework now pitted with age – which stretched between strips of water meadow. A home football game was hardly enough to stir the townsfolk from the Saturday shopping rituals so when the Pitties kicked off on a heavy pitch, down the gentle slope towards the wall of the churchyard of St Victor's, the 20 rows of the single covered stand and the touchlines were filled mostly with Pitties fans. The locals looked bemused to see so many Japanese flags.

Monique, as ever, came with the team but no directors were aboard Vinny Vanity's bus for the short ride to Moxbottom. The team already knew Marco di Rapido from his father's restaurant chain and his tiresome efforts to join the club but they were not unhappy to have him with them. Simon Pitt was particularly relieved to have a striking partner since Dean Slutz's injury and as they rolled into the car park of the Calf and Liver, the estate agent remembered something and caught his manager's attention when they stepped off the bus.

'A couple of chaps were asking for you in the car park at Pitt Lane this morning.' The players with cars parked at the ground on away Saturdays and took the communal bus. 'They looked sort of, Japanese.'

'Sort of?' Ohara wondered.

'It was hard to tell. They both wore sunglasses and baseball caps, and one of them was a lot bigger than you'd expect.'

'More Japanese reporters,' Ohara guessed. 'A nuisance for everybody.'

'Possibly,' Pitt said, crooking his head doubtfully. 'But the short, thin one did all the talking and he spoke in that kind of broken, staccato way Chinese waiters do.'

'What did they want?' Ohara asked as they approached Moxbottom's unassuming ground.

'You, apparently. They wanted your home address.'

Terry Dribble's report on Moxbottom commented that eight of the first team were farmers or in the agricultural trade. They played football for fun, the premier division of the RoustaRodent Solutions League being the zenith of their fortunes in 42 years of existence. They trained when they finished milking or ploughing fields. The pitch was kept trim in summer by grazing sheep and its slight but gentle slope caused problems to unfit players kicking up it late in the second half. With half an hour in the game to go, Ohara saw that most of his players had stood up to the heavy turf and the topography well, three weeks of gym and track work visibly improving their strength and endurance. The Pitties were on top from the start and when the ball went out of play he was relaxed enough to let his mind drift to the two Asian men who wanted to make a home visit. Lone wolf Japanese paparazzi, he guessed. If they wanted pictures they could attend his regular photo calls, like everybody else. On the pitch the Pitties were failing to break down the stubborn farmers and as half-time approached his frustrations began to surface.

Marco di Rapido was running from left to right, pulling the Moxbottom defenders around and confusing Simon Pitt and his own winger, Mandrake. His screaming and ball begging irritated his own midfielders and the opposition and when he did take possession the Moxxies delighted in felling him. Marco was quick to retaliate, and received a yellow card after two warnings.

At half time, with the score 0-0, the Pitties were confronted with a really angry Japanese for the first time. Perfectly calm on the surface, betrayed only by a slight twitch in his left cheek, Ohara let them know they were playing like constipated sumo wrestlers, all the tactical talk forgotten, weeks of training wasted. Had they forgotten the passing to feet practice at Uno Electronics and their stylish interpretation of it against Grittley Mills? Against this weak opposition they had for the first time the option of going forward of their own volition, not just counter attacking. He picked out the midfielders Drummond and Omerod for direct criticism and ordered team captain Omar Grant to lead by example, getting the ball to Marco and Simon from midfield or to their heads from the wings. He took off Pickwich, who huffed and swore when he removed his lime-green shirt, and put the newly released felon, Clint Hopp, into the left side of defence, with Scott Fisher to his right. Apart from a brave dive to the feet of a Moxbottom striker, Tony McDonald's first half action had been routine, and so the goalkeeper was very surprised to find the coach's finger in his face, warning against complacency. 'This game is winnable,' Ohara said, slapping a plastic bottle of water against a locker in case his message failed to register.

It wasn't Marco di Rapido who scored the Pitties' goal because he was on the ground, his arms wrapped around the neck of a farmer on the half-way line, the tussle unseen by the match officials who were running with the play towards the Moxxies' goal. Clint Hopp had followed through on a one-two pass with Gary Omerod, who, as practised, dropped back when Hopp overtook him, and to his surprise a lucky rebound carried him beyond the last defender, with Simon Pitt just holding back to avoid the offside. Hopp nudged the ball sideways and Pitt hit it cleanly towards the far corner of the Moxbottom goal. He didn't actually see it hit the back of the net because the late tackle by a salmon and blue clad player broke his right leg above the ankle and the pain froze out all his senses. He was barely in the ambulance before there was more action for an impassioned Karen Saddleback to transmit to listeners on Radio Siddley.

Ohara sent on the versatile Lenny Hampton for Pitt and stripped off his tracksuit bottom in case a third substitute was needed. Omar Grant was up with Marco and Hampton and easily won a low Mandrake fifty-fifty cross. He had it under control when Marco powered up and took it off his captain's foot, the new striker's momentum taking him through a mixed pack of players before he pulled the trigger. He went for power rather than direction and the goalkeeper's fingertip parry could only help the ball into his top right hand corner.

Marco charged towards the Pittie supporters, his arms and hands outstretched imploringly, and he singled out Rika Yamaguchi and Monique Wainwright for a sweaty embrace. When the final whistle blew he fell to his knees in front of his happy Japanese manager and touched his forehead to the ground. Caught up with it all, Ohara didn't notice two Asian men slip away from the celebrations early, scowling as they merged into the misty, darkening afternoon.

The bus with the rowdy, thirsty victors diverted the return to Pitt Lane with a stop at Siddley Royal Infirmary to report the result to Simon Pitt who, with his injury confirmed by X-ray, was probably lost to the team for the rest of the season. After the ritual of the Japanese bath prepared by Charlie, most of the squad and Monique invaded the Pitt Lane Arms to a raucous welcome by the early regulars. Ohara put a credit card behind the bar. How long had it been since the Pitties had been cheered in a public place? Around them the mood was more sombre, no doubt something to do with the notice outside saying the pub would close for ever in three weeks, after 92 years serving Appleton's ales to generations of Pittie players and supporters.

Walter Hardcastle reached Ohara's mobile with unrestrained words of congratulations while the team was still on the bus. Councillor Townrow and Harry Patel made contact while Ohara was enjoying his second pint of lager. Geoffrey Osborne stopped by the pub on his way to a function at the Abattoir Association. From the honorary president, Sir Reginald Pitt, and the chief executive, David Broody, there was only silence. Rika Yamaguchi arrived at the Pitt Lane Arms from her flat across the canal, as players had begun to drift away, some ushered out by Terry Dribble in the cause of temperance and moderation, others to work.

Monique, still in her Pitties shirt, watched suspiciously as the slender, beautiful Japanese woman worked the room, closing in on the manager. The chardonnay turned tart in her mouth, forcing her to employ Marco di Rapido to divert the oriental challenge away from Ohara, telling him Rika wanted desperately to meet the hero of the second goal, remembering his lusty, sweaty embrace.

Marco edged through the drinkers to Rika's side. 'I don't know your name,' he breathed moodily. 'But perhaps angels don't have names.'

The pub patrons erupted as one when Ohara's face appeared on an overhead television screen and a reporter for the regional network described the historic game today at Moxbottom. Ohara was returning from the outside lavatory and negotiating a smokey snug bar when over the top of the frosted window he saw Taro Suzuki crossing the square. He met him outside on the worn threshold stones of the pub. 'We're having a drink or two. For the win. Come and join us. Rika *san's* here.' Suzuki flapped a hand like a fan in a wordless gesture of refusal.

'Rika called and told me you'd all come here to celebrate, but Eri's mother's here from Japan and they're waiting for me in the car.'

'Thanks for taking the time to go to Moxbottom.'

Suzuki produced a rare smile. 'Membership of the Pitties supporters' club at Uno is mandatory.'

'Are we getting any better?' Ohara wondered.

'The defence is catching up. Good stuff in the second half. I like the captain's work.'

'They'll have to concentrate for ninety minutes. If they don't, Yattock will tear them apart next Saturday.'

'The new striker looked sharp,' Suzuki remarked.

'Marco? Yeah. Not bad. A bit of a showman.'

'Like you were,' Suzuki chuckled.

Ohara managed a thin smile. 'He was lucky to stay on the pitch today.'

'You'll need him against Yattock, now you've lost Pitt.'

'I don't want to, but I'm ready to play myself if I have to.' Psychosomatic or real, memories of Suzuki's tackle induced a throbbing sensation in Ohara's right knee. 'We're still a bit light up front.'

Suzuki glanced at his watch. 'Must go. Can't upset mother-in-law.' He looked up, avoiding eye contact. 'I've been put on day shift duties for the time being. It frees me for training. And I suppose I can play on Saturday, if you've room in the squad, and if the rules allow foreigners.'

Ohara's head slumped in a bow of sincere appreciation. Words weren't needed. He waved Suzuki off and returned to the lounge bar. 'Thank you for your co-operation and helpful intervention with Taro Suzuki,' he told Rika Yamaguchi while Marco was deeply distracted, scribbling his mobile phone number on a PastaBasta business card. Ohara guessed she was personally close to Suzuki and his family and had talked through with them the implications of a return to football with the man whose playing career he helped end. How would Ohara explain it to the Japanese media?

Then Monique was next to him, an arm threaded through his. 'Some of the team are going over to PastaBasta,' she announced, mostly for Rika's attention, and to exclude her.

The week of the Golden Mousetrap Trophy semi-final started badly for Ohara, with a hangover from the great victory celebration. Worse than the headache, he'd forgotten a lunch date with the Japanese ambassador. The Pitties hadn't trained on Sunday, so Ohara took his foggy head to Rika Yamaguchi's flat in David Broody's Sunriser Heights block overlooking the inner city marina. From the window he could see the lanky, almost bare branches of willow flapping at the black water as they twisted in a capricious breeze, and the silhouette of Siddley cathedral beyond the roof of Pitt Lane's main stand. After a late lunch of salted salmon, seaweed and *tofu* soup and pickles, with sticky Japanese style rice from California, he was ready to announce to the world that Taro Suzuki was returning to serious football by signing for Siddley United Football Club. His vehicle would be Tanaka, the pugnacious reporter from the *Kanto Daily Sports*. It was Rika's idea to neutralize his harshest critic by giving him a real scoop: the Suzuki comeback.

He got through to Tanaka in a room at the journalist's London hotel, and from the rise and fall of the background noise Ohara knew he was watching the Sunday afternoon Premiership football game. He told Tanaka truthfully how Suzuki had agonized over joining the struggling team from the RoustaRodent Solutions League, but it was an awakening of spirit, a feeling that while the incident of the infamous tackle on Ohara was not forgotten, it was forgiven. And no, Ohara told the journalist, he hadn't yet picked his team for the Golden Mousetrap Trophy match and Suzuki wasn't an option until he'd assessed his fitness.

Tanaka agreed not to disclose Ohara as his source, so saving the manager's face for not announcing the Suzuki signing to all the Japanese media as would be the Japanese way. Tanaka's reputation as a formidable journalistic sleuth would soar. He was truly grateful for the scoop, but he had to hurry. It was already past midnight in Japan and while he spoke and listened to Ohara, he was tapping an email into his laptop, ready with the classic, 'hold the front page' line. With a touch of luck the fantastic Suzuki story would make Monday's final edition.

'I'd like to thank you personally,' Tanaka told Ken Ohara.

'It's not at all necessary. I expect you'll be at Pitt Lane on Saturday?'

'Can I meet you briefly tomorrow, before or after your lunch with the ambassador?'

'What lunch? The ambassador?' He looked at Rika, who was crossing the room barefoot, two cups of steaming green tea on a tray, as if she'd have the explanation. Then he remembered, and cuffed his forehead with his free hand. The invitation to a lunch in his honour from the Japanese ambassador, received soon after his arrival in Siddley. It was for tomorrow. 'I don't see why not,' he said warily. 'I'll have to check my travel details.'

'Good. I think I can reciprocate your consideration by giving you some very interesting intelligence.'

David Broody's week could only get better. Monique Wainwright's outright refusal to meet him last Friday and the Pitties' win on Saturday had dealt him a double blow. Worse was to follow on Sunday night when nothing like an airtight container was unearthed from Pitt Lane, even though his men, operating by torchlight, dug down three feet and probed even deeper. His hunch about the clue in the old photo had been wrong. He supposed the Pitties had to win sometime: Moxbottom were a bunch of heavy footed manure shifters, as bovine as their cowshed charges. The semi-pros of Yattock on Saturday would crush the Pitties as if they were eggs. Monique was a different bag of footballs. Was her rebuff something to do with Pitt proviso? Inexplicably she seemed to know about his search for Sir Abraham Pitt's document but for the life of him he couldn't understand how. Had she really been looking for it in the old picture when he surprised her? Using a paid agent, the willing, dumb Pickwich, to check it out proved fruitless, and the oaf almost severed his hand into the bargain.

Things were looking much better by the end of breakfast

when his son Benedict called to say his suspension from Harrow for cheating was for a single term only; and shortly before Camilla left for her *reiki* session their daughter's solicitor telephoned with the news that Davidella was not going to be prosecuted for shoplifting. He was smiling and scheming as he drove along St Loretta's Avenue on his way to his office when he noticed the car behind was flashing its beam lights for no apparent reason. He drove on, but the flashing resumed, this time more urgently. A signal. Curious, he turned the BMW into the Rykneld Pleasure Gardens, circled slowly in the deserted car park and stopped, facing the entrance.

Headlights flaring in the morning murkiness a dark blue Mercedes lumbered over the calming humps and rolled to a stop, bumper to bumper with the front of Broody's car. He shivered. What the hell watched and waited behind those black-tinted windows?

Finally, the rear doors opened together and two broad shouldered men stepped out. One, with cropped dyed blonde hair and sun glasses, stood his ground, turning slowly to take in the trees around the kiddies' paddling pool and the gardens behind the low unkempt hedgerow. The other man pulled a light raincoat from the car and placed it over his shoulders like a cape. He was in his mid thirties, light brown hair perfectly trimmed and parted. Thin feminine lips on his handsome face curled in an enigmatic smile.

'Boris,' Broody said, his shoulders sagging with relief as he recognized the suave Russian merchant banker. 'What are you doing in Siddley? You should have called me.'

'I came to check on my clients' investment,' the Russian said nonchalantly, in a faintly affected American drawl. 'Let's take a little stroll.'

Followed by the silent companion, who kept a hand inside his buttoned jacket, the two men walked across the gravel to the path running beside the paddling pool. Abandoned for the winter, leaves lay plastered over its cracked floor or rotting in pools of rusty rain water.

Born in Moscow, the son of a wealthy Russian father who imported cars and other luxuries for the old Soviet leadership, Boris Rakov was educated at Eton and Harvard and joined the mergers and acquisitions team of the Great Imperial Bank of Russia's branch in London after a year of networking with the new freewheeling entrepreneurs in the now free market country of his birth. He discovered a need among the new government and business elite which he was supremely able to meet, and it entailed finding overseas investment opportunities where the return on capital was less important than the safe and untouchable nature of the money's ultimate repose. Few such places existed inside the emerging Russian state, where the law took a distant second place to the Uzi in the settlement of disputes.

Responding to a particular commission, Rakov's perspicacity and long reach fell upon the quietly prosperous city of Siddley and a property entrepreneur called David Broody, a man who, intelligence gleaned, clearly shared their own ethical standards. Siddley seemed the perfect place to invest $500 million safely, quietly and deeply. The money, including $200 million in new notes, still wrapped in US Federal Reserve Bank seals from the time they were sent to Russia as International Monetary Fund emergency financial aid, was transported to Lebanon, Cyprus and other friendly states and deposited with specially established branches and subsidiaries of trusted financial institutions. Now part of the global money pool, whence trillions of dollars were moved about daily at the touch of keyboard buttons, the Russian funds, travelled under the name of a recognized bank, were transferred electronically to separate accounts in local banks in the Cayman Islands, Belize and Bermuda, then on to receptive financial institutions with better reputations in Hong Kong and Singapore. The gradual legitimatization process, some call it laundering, was completed when the funds appeared as clean, interbank deposits with very respected, globally renowned institutions in London and New York. The ultimate owners of the money, the Russian mafia, entrepreneurs and their bureaucratic collaborators, were several transactions and names removed from their stolen cash and the proceeds of drug dealing and other criminal activities. A million clean pounds of the fortune, a goodwill down payment, had already found its way electronically into the account of the Siddley property entrepreneur who now stood, slightly uneasily, before the Russian broker.

'Things are not moving quite as quickly as my principals desire,' Rakov declared, placing an ambiguously protective arm across Broody's shoulders. The property developer flinched. 'It's very wasteful to have money sitting around in banks, the way interest rates are going. I'm sure you share our concern, don't you David?' What he meant was that hot money had to keep ahead of central banks and other regulatory inspectors and the sooner cash became land or buildings, or in the case of Rakov's last British investment, a complete racecourse in Suffolk and a training stable in Newbury, the better.

'Of course I do,' Broody said, summoning up frowns of sincerity that cut deep ridges across his brow. 'I'll have the Pitt Estate situation completely tidied up in the next few days. The last three tenants are ready to leave and the pub's closing. I'm confident I'll sign the final documents with the freeholders right after they go.' Which was a lie. David Broody already owned the freehold to the entire Pitt housing estate through a nominee offshore company, the purchase financed by a usurious bridging loan from the Cristobal Colon Bank of the Cayman Islands, the first massive interest payment for which was serviced just in time from the Russian's goodwill downpayment. Boris Rakov's clients would actually be buying the land from Broody and he would repay the Caribbean bandidos from the proceeds, leaving Broody with a neat £50 million worth of profit. With venture capital needed to fulfil his grandiose development scheme agreed in principle with a financial consortium based in Andorra he would lease the land from the new Russian owners, using some of his profit to smooth the planning approval process and other tiresome barriers erected by jobsworth bureaucrats and councillors like Ronald Townrow. The architectural plans and designs were already prepared and magnificent scale models of the grand Siddley redevelopment project adorned his house and penthouse flat. Timing was becoming critical: by the end of next week, he needed all of the Russian money to meet the final repayment of the Cayman Islands bridging loan. The bulldozers were secretly booked, ready to rumble across the River Siddleworth. Contracts had been signed, financial commitments made. It only remained to sort out the niggling little problem of the land occupied by Siddley United Football Club and its car park, which he knew was what brought the Russian fixer to Siddley. Here it comes, he was thinking, patting his jacket for a cigar tube.

Rakov rubbed his chin with theatrical weariness. 'You know I'm not really talking about the wretched houses, David,' he said, as if to a naughty child. 'I mean the beluga in the blini, the icing on the fucking golden cake. Either we get the football field and the car park as well or there's no deal. And my clients will want their million pounds back, with accrued interest, pretty sharply.'

Broody's insides stirred. 'I'll own the shares to the football club by Monday night,' he assured the Russian. 'Once Saturday's bloodbath on the pitch is over the way will be perfectly open, the waters ahead clear.' They had circumnavigated the public pool and were on a path between beds of collapsed geraniums and petunias. The bodyguard's footsteps slapped heavily on the moss-slick paving stones, a few paces behind them.

'Very good, spot on. That's what I wanted to hear,' Rakov enthused. He patted the shorter man's shoulder again. 'I think I'll come up for your big game. Whales against plankton, isn't it? Should be fun, your Japanese guy might be on a roll. A draw and a weekend win. It was in *The Times*, you know. And I can take a last look at the grand old stands and the slums before you blow them all up.'

They turned a corner, talking of the glass towers, hotels, leisure centres, shopping malls and executive apartments that would rise over central Siddley. When they reached their cars, Rakov said: 'So I'll call you next Monday night, just to confirm you're on course.' Half into the Mercedes, he remembered something. 'Any chance you can include the cathedral in the deal?'

The train rocked through gentle, bottle green countryside scattered with cows, dark farmhouses and half-bare trees, Ohara working on his speech for the Japanese ambassador and his guests. As always, he smothered his promise to do his best, *gambaritai to omoimasu*, with meaningless, exaggerated politeness, demeaning modesty and baffling honorific glazing. It was what was expected. He soon gave up and returned his mental attention to Siddley United and the big match only five days away. He'd left instructions for Matt Dennis and Terry Dribble to meet Taro Suzuki at Uno Electronics, introduce him to the team, then integrate him on the left side of Marco di Rapido and practise attacking movements, with Drummond the overlapping winger on the right and Mandrake on the left. A defensive approach wasn't an option against Yattock when the reward for a draw at home was the return match away with a Conference club on 21-game unbeaten home streak.

Terry Dribble had taken up his role as scout and snoop with enthusiasm. Ohara opened a slim plastic folder with printouts from Yattock's website and the notes Terry had made on his trip to the Conference town. Dried stains suggested they were scribblings made in a pub, which was just about right. The gossip and the bar room bragging spoke of one man, a striker of prodigious talent called Shane Goodmouth, now the focus of attention from three Premiership clubs. His strike rate of nearly a goal a game in cup and league fixtures made it odds-on he would score against the team from a very inferior division. Scouts from many clubs would attend the Golden Mousetrap Trophy semi-final at Siddley, just to watch Goodmouth. Ohara jotted the names of a pair of his defenders against the Yattock striker's name. Terry's notes described Goodmouth as an 'English centre forward' and for Ohara's enlightenment he added 'lanky', 'poacher', whatever they meant. He also wrote that he was a good header, a target man not easily knocked off the ball. So Goodmouth was not a pace ace, Ohara noted, like Suzuki and di Rapido. Yattock's defence will be weakened on the left side by the absence through injury of a key player at left back, Dribble's scrawl noted hopefully. Ohara mentally moved di Rapido from a central position to the right with Suzuki, who was naturally left sided, alongside him.

The lunch was a pleasant, unnecessary interlude for Ohara, enjoyable more for Ambassador Tokunaga and the senior bureaucrats in London, like the Bank of Japan representative, and bureau heads from the tame national daily newspapers, who all got to bask in Ohara's aura as a national icon. They congratulated him on his first win as manager, though politely no one named Siddley United or remarked on their position near the foot of the Rousta-Rodent Solutions League. The embassy chef served expatriate comfort food, a collage of raw turbot and yellowtail with a little mound of golden yellow sea urchin and a fat, sliced scallop to start, followed by a selection of *tempura* fish and vegetables. *Sake* and Japanese beer were offered but only the journalist from the *Yomiuri* drank. Had they been invited, the awkward, free-wheeling weekly magazines and the sensationalist tabloids would have been less restrained with the after-lunch questions and the alcohol. By 3.30p.m. with the lunch over, speeches delivered, good wishes for Saturday's big game extended, Ohara found himself in Shepherd's Market, a short walk from the Japanese Embassy, having declined invitations from the media men by claiming to have a train to catch. Tanaka was smoking at a table in the little sandwich cum coffee shop opposite a Lebanese restaurant in a narrow, cobbled street. Ohara nodded a brief bow to the Japanese journalist and then noticed another customer in the cafe, a burly man waiting for his order at the counter.

Tanaka stood and showed the top of his head in a deeper bow. 'Thank you for consideration, Mr Manager,' he said genuinely. 'Thanks to you, my newspaper achieved a major scoop.'

'Did you make it for today in Japan?' Ohara wondered.

'*Okagesama,*' he said again. 'Thanks to you. The midday edition. The rest of the media went wild, apparently. Television programmes were interrupted to give the news about Suzuki.'

Ohara managed a thin smile and checked his watch. 'I must catch the train to Siddley soon. You said you had something to tell me.'

'Something? Not exactly something. First, what can I get you?' Tanaka asked, standing smartly.

'Small capuccino, please.'

Tanaka approached the counter and the gurgling expresso machine. He ordered, waited and then returned with the drinks – and the other man. 'Ken Ohara,' he said, his eyes on his fellow Japanese. 'Meet Ken O'Hara.' Tanaka's English was slow, broken and humourless.

Ohara thought he'd misheard. 'Ken-ichi Ohara,' he said hesitantly, a hand outstretched across the table.

'Pleased to meet you, Ken,' the other said jovially, reaching out. 'Kenneth O'Hara. Call me Ken.'

Ohara looked at Tanaka, his face contorted. The foreigner with them was smiling as he raised his cup. He was older than Ohara by a decade and a half, with grey ragged hair curling over his ears. It reached low on his forehead, almost touching the thick, unruly eyebrows overhanging a sallow, lined face. He wore a corduroy jacket over a green turtleneck jersey and pronounced O'Hara exactly like the Japanese's own name, as if mocking him by imitation. Then he produced a card. Ohara stared at it: the man's name was spelt like his own, except for the gap and apostrophe.

'Uncanny, isn't it?' the man said, his dialect strange to Ohara's ears, not helped by a slight slur. The coffee cup tilted ominously in his unsteady fingers. 'Forgetting I'm Irish and you're Japanese, we've got the same surname. And we're both called Ken.'

Ohara was aware that O'Hara had turned to Tanaka and they were finding something amusing, but his mind was racing back to that phone call from the Japan Football Association in early July, not long after the rainy season lifted the lid on another blistering summer. 'An English club wants you for its manager.' He'd known it wasn't easy to place a Japanese as team manager in the competitive European leagues but when the name of Siddley United was announced nobody in the Japanese soccer world could bring themselves to admit they had never heard of the team or even the city. He guessed he was just like the rest of them, still full of pretend respect and innate shame, still scared of standing out, petrified of losing face by admitting ignorance, even if it was shared by all the others.

The popular, unrestrained press, like Tanaka's sports and sex tabloid, were free to mock the establishment as they rooted out the truth, or, in its elusiveness, invented a speculative substitution. Unlike the journalists at the ambassador's lunch, Tanaka wasn't afraid to ask why a former star international player and successful coach should find himself near the very bottom of the vast English football system.

Kenneth O'Hara's mood was deteriorating, creeping towards darkness as the beer he'd had with his lunch soured his spirit. 'We've both been well and truly shafted, Ken me lad,' he spluttered vehemently, spittle oozing from the corners of his mouth.

'Shafted?' Ohara queried. Tanaka reached for his pocket-sized computer dictionary.

'Shafted,' the Irishman growled, his face now damson with vexation. 'Fucked. Knifed in the back.'

Tanaka said something in explanation to Ohara, who nodded grimly. Kenneth O'Hara had played for seven English professional league clubs and one Scottish. He'd been a useful defender in the seventies and early eighties, slipping down the leagues as drink and a bad attitude took its toll. He was a better manager than player at first, starting in the third division of the football league and displaying a knack for leading a club up to a higher division and the flaw of taking it down again a couple of seasons later. As his dreams and skills slipped away, it was up one division and down two until his big league managerial ambitions ended for ever when he led a second division league team down to the Conference in successive years. He never made it back, and turning 50 he finally reached the timeless, unsung world below the Conference, where the clubs survived on enthusiasm, hope and a handful of supporters. After two seasons in the Rumpo Mattress League he saw the chance to move up a couple of levels to the premier division of the RoustaRodent Solutions League at Pitt Lane. Siddley United the oddity, with its hundred years of history, a real football ground with stands and terraces and desperate for success. It was irresistible to a man who had once played before 60,000 people.

'You see, Kenny,' O'Hara declared, tapping out a cigarette and showing his cracked, stained teeth. 'I was in line for Moby McNally's job at Pitt Lane, you know the poor bloke that went scuba diving without a tank. That chairman of yours, the old body planter, Hardcastle. He said I was just the man they were looking for. Then, I swear to God, I didn't hear from him again, because suddenly the worst team in the RoustaRodent Solutions League had hired a famous Japanese. Where I come from, we call this a very rum situation.'

Ohara was twisting the Irishman's card in his fingers as he listened. Now he knew what those little quips he'd overheard in the changing room and the street meant. Things like, 'He doesn't look very Irish.'

'So what's your story, Kenny?' O'Hara asked. 'The RoustaRodent League's big in Japan, is it?'

Ken Ohara from Japan showed his namesake a pair of palms. 'Wait a moment, Mr O'Hara. I am happy and honoured to be manager of the Pitties, whatever their situation.'

'Of course you are, Kenny,' O'Hara said, smoke dribbling from his nostrils. 'Anyone would be. But there's been some serious skulduggery in the English Football Association.' His eyes sparkled for an instant. 'You can bet on it.'

'I don't understand. Perhaps a mistake.'

The Irishman was quivering on his chair, the veins in his

temples bulging. 'No mistake, Kenny. I was shoved out of the way to let you in. And you were let in for reasons I don't know why.'

Ken-ichi Ohara breathed long and deep, the rush of air calming his heart beat while the pieces spinning in his head came together, secreting as they did the stench of hoax and deception and the devious presence of David Broody. He bought more time by sipping at the frothy residue on the lip of the empty coffee cup. It all made sense, just as Monique had said. Broody was doing everything he could to stop the Pitties winning the league championship or a cup competition trophy. When had he started his systematic undermining of Siddley United FC? The directors were nice enough but they were busy men, content to let the scheming chief executive lead them by the nose, like when he reduced the playing staff to an almost unworkable level and starved the Pitties of training and gym facilities. Was former manager Moby McNally's demise just a fortuitous accident from Broody's point or view? Or was there more to it? Monique said Broody had tried to buy McNally's co-operation and the manager had refused. Surely he wasn't murd—? His death left a space Broody needed to see filled with someone who wouldn't be a threat, so who better than a foreigner, an Asian at that, and a rookie, innocent to English football, who've have no idea what was happening off the field and wouldn't have time to produce results to keep the club alive on it. He lowered the cup abruptly and faced the Irishman. 'Please excuse me for a moment, Mr O'Hara, I must speak to Mr Tanaka in Japanese.'

'Sure, you do that, Kenny,' O'Hara said, contemplating the smouldering tip of his cigarette. 'My friend Tanny'll tell you what's been happening.'

'*Honto desu ka?*' Is it true? Ohara asked Tanaka, pressing forward. 'Should he be the real manager of Siddley United?'

'I think so,' the other Japanese said.

Ohara's head was shaking with disbelief. 'How do you know all this? How did you find Mr O'Hara?'

Tanaka lit a new cigarette and sucked in air and smoke noisily. 'If you're being honest, you were as surprised as the whole of Japan when you were appointed the manager of Siddley, so when the deal was agreed I investigated. To be honest, I struggled to find anything about the club at all.'

'We're on the web from tomorrow,' Ohara broke in.

'Great. Well, I was searching around the clubs in the leagues down there with Siddley, a lot of them have good websites, lots of detail on players, coaches, the directors, when the name Ken O'Hara jumped out of the screen. I had to look many times. I thought it was you. It said the club hoped to sign imminently a replacement for manager Ken O'Hara whose contract wasn't renewed at the end of last season. It seemed nothing at the time, but my curiosity was aroused by the coincidence with your name. You were always Ken Ohara in your playing days, never Ken-ichi. So I emailed the English Football Association as a journalist writing about you and they were very kind to help my research. They said the FA often acts as the intermediary, putting clubs without managers in touch with candidates. In a later message to my new contact in the Football Association I said I was confused because I'd read there was another Ken Ohara who used to manage in the Rumpo Mattress League. He thought it was very funny, but said the other man was Kenneth O'Hara, an Irish player turned manager.'

'And you made contact with him,' Ohara remarked.

'By letter, yes. The FA gave me his address. When I arrived in England three weeks ago I got in touch. And here he is, a very unhappy man. He believes your chairman offered him the manager's position at Pitt Lane but it was suddenly withdrawn. Then it was given to you.'

'Didn't your friend at the Football Association explain what happened?'

Tanaka crooked his head, a slow groan of bewilderment leaking from his throat. 'That's the very strange thing,' he said finally. 'I asked to meet him in London, if only to thank him for his co-operation, but his tone had changed and he said he was unavailable to see me. I've telephoned and left messages but my calls have not been returned.'

'What's his name?' Ohara demanded.

6

Returning from morning training, Ohara found Monique standing behind the ponytailed, dome-headed youth from the CyberSiddley Cafe as he clicked around the new Pitties website with the intensity and concentration of a surgeon. Monique clapped when the lime green and tangerine squares on the opening page broke up and turned into stars, spiralling around before reforming into a Pitties strip on a plain pale blue background. While they were watching, a courier from the printers delivered a glossy, multi-paged match programme, the first at Pitt Lane in living memory and a one-off for the Golden Mousetrap Trophy semi-final. It was filled with players' profiles, tables, fixtures and football quizzes, the Japanese manager's views and comments featuring prominently around a stern-looking portrait photograph. He told of his admiration for Siddley and its football club and the tremendous responsibility he felt as he tried to earn the respect of the fans.

Leaving the manager with the website and the match programme, Monique returned to Lavinia and Sal, seriously fanatical Pitties fans taken on temporarily to help with the preparation and distribution of actual numbered tickets, another new experience at Siddley United. When 300 made a crowd at Pitt Lane, it had never been necessary to issue an instrument of admittance, although faded numbers could still be seen on seats in the Pitt and Canal stands, reminders of bygone days. The win at Moxbottom and the Ohara effect triggered the bomb, and what with the half-price ticket deal and the signing of an international star, albeit Japanese and professionally retired, it threatened to become a *tsunami* of demand. 'Think of it, Lavvy,' she gushed to Lavinia. 'We might get thousands at Pitt Lane on Saturday.'

The precious semi-final match tickets for the two covered stands featured an intaglio impression of the famed Golden Mousetrap itself, which, with the pitch improvements, website creation, increased players' incentives, new strip, and programmes, pushed the television fee close to exhaustion. The directors had agreed the expenditure and it was left to David Broody to temper the euphoria, though the welfare of the club was the last thing on his mind.

'It'll be a hard landing when the bubble bursts on Saturday afternoon,' he told Chairman Hardcastle and Councillor Townrow when they met at the Thousand Years of Siddley cocktail party in the Heritage Centre. 'We should have taken the money and buggered off to Spain. Lost causes are not for me.'

Seeing Monique flicking through a stack of tickets, Ohara drew two bank notes from his wallet. Monique eyed them warily. She had never known a £50 note to be used in a legal transaction in Siddley.

'Please give me a hundred tickets for the Pitt Stand,' Ohara requested. 'One pound each, I believe.'

Monique wanted to reach out to him. 'You don't need to do this, Ken.' His knuckles touched hers as she held on to the notes a tad longer than needed. A surge of warmth engulfed her. 'We can charge them to manager's expenses,' she breathed.

'Absolutely not,' he insisted 'These are for my personal gifts.' He shook off her protestations and insisted on giving her the money in exchange for a batch of tickets. Drawing closer, and suffused with her perfume, he said: 'Resist all requests from the directors or others for free tickets. Especially from a certain person. Please.'

Monique nodded, face pinched knowingly. She made coffee for her support team and took hers and Ohara's to the chairman's suite where she found him examining the old photo, the object of Billy Pickwich's vandalism.

'Can I ask you something?' he said, sensing her presence and turning.

'Of course,' Monique beamed, taking the big leather seat behind the chairman's desk.

'It's difficult for me to explain in English,' he said, lowering himself into an armchair.

'Please try,' Monique urged, crossing her legs demonstratively.

'I have a lot to do before Saturday, perhaps it is not important.'

'Is it about David Broody and this secret document thing?'

Ohara's head rocked gently. 'Perhaps.' Then the light came on for him and he looked straight at her. 'Do you have the letters from the English Football Association concerning my appointment to Siddley United?'

Monique frowned, her eyes screwed. 'The chairman keeps the appointment files on the players but I don't think . . .' She was trying to put her thoughts in sequence, it was months ago, after all. David Broody handled recruitment and money matters. Some months before Ohara arrived, Broody told her to present Mr Hardcastle with a certain file concerned with the hiring of the new manager so that the club chairman, who was always busy and distracted, could see it and sign it when he passed through Pitt Lane. Hardcastle hardly looked at the papers, she thought, being professionally occupied with the aftermath of a multi-vehicle bypass accident. Monique reassured him with the message that Mr Broody was happy with the conditions agreed with the English Football Association and so Mr Hardcastle just signed the contract.

'Did they talk about me at all?' Ohara wondered. 'Being Japanese.'

'You?' Monique had been so engrossed in her consuming affair with Broody that it affected her application at work, leaving a few blanks in her memory bank, which she now regretted. 'Possibly. I can't remember. It wasn't really my responsibility.' She badly wanted to help. 'I wonder,' she said, slowly uncrossing her legs and striding from the office. Returning promptly with a set of keys she stooped behind the chairman's ornate desk to open a drawer. Ohara looked around furtively. 'It's all right,' she smiled. 'I have the run of the office. I'm here all the time, not like the directors.' When the sound of slapping paper stopped, she looked over the desk at Ohara. 'Funny. The appointments records aren't here. Not yours or the others.'

'Perhaps Mr Hardcastle keeps them at the funeral shop, or at home,' Ohara suggested.

'Absolutely not. All football matters are confined to the ground. What exactly are you looking for, Ken?' she asked, straightening things on the chairman's desk.

Ohara sighed. 'I'm not sure. I think another man should be the manager here but Mr Broody wanted me because I am a stupid foreigner.'

'Another man?'

'An Irish person. His name sounds like mine. I met him yesterday.' Monique remembered the chairman's surprise when she told him an oriental man was at the gate, claiming to be the new manager. 'I think Broody tricked Mr Hardcastle into hiring me.'

Monique recoiled. 'So you wouldn't cause him any trouble, unlike poor Moby McNally.'

'Right.'

'And he's taken the staff files to cover his tracks?'

'Oh, yes. And to hide the name of the person in the Football Association who helped him.'

Tiny furrows blemished Monique's pert nose as a scheme insinuated itself into her head. 'Leave it to me,' she said finally. 'What's his name? The other bloke. The one who should be manager.'

Ohara turned slowly from the doorway. 'It's Ken. Ken O'Hara.'

When the Japanese had left Monique closed the door and sat deep in the chairmen's soft leather chair. Finally, she leaned forward and pecked out a number stored on her mobile phone, shaking her head and nestling the handset under her luxurious hair.

'David?' she said, when the line connected instantly. 'I can't hold out any longer. I must see you.'

Ohara drove to Uno Electronics with a heap of Japanese and British newspapers on the passenger seat. The thought of facing the Conference team on Saturday with his small squad of part-timers, and with the Japanese people as witness, still overawed him, but less so than a week ago, such had been the psychological effect of the win over Moxbottom. Siddley had started to emerge from an endless night, aroused by Simon Pitt's lunging, leg-breaking goal and Marco di Rapido's poetical striker's strike, all trumpeted and exaggerated with uncompromising bias by Radio Siddley and the *Evening Sentinel*. Players rode the winning streak of one, some of them cockily proud to be recognized for the first time. Ohara had pushed them hard and most had responded to his organized, focused training, and it was showing in their fitness and hungry attitude. He thought they understood his call for tactics that had to be followed, like measured passing to feet and movement off the ball that didn't include physical assault on opponents. But sometimes westerners were very difficult to understand, their mentality as well as their language.

The local British press saw the humour of it all, marvelling at the capriciousness of fate that had brought two famous Japanese, both former international football players, one carrying a career-ending injury, the other playing Sunday league for a factory team, to a post-industrial city in the heart of England to play in a match that would have gone unnoticed without their presence. '*Touchrine Samurai*' was how one tabloid unpleasantly headed its back page, showing a picture of an ancient Japanese suit of armour with Ohara's face imposed inside the Darth Vader-like helmet. 'Where's the Big Game on Saturday?' another headline chortled. 'Old Trafford? Stamford Bridge? No, It's Pitt Lane, Siddley.'

Uno workers were drifting home when he reached the car park. He kitted up and carried a windbreaker into a fresh, breezy evening. It was getting colder by the day, enough to fog the breath by sunset. He knew all wasn't well when he passed the tennis courts and saw the silhouettes of the players on the football field under the hazy lighting. They were kicking balls around aimlessly. The two goalkeepers were scuffing a ball around in a goalmouth while Suzuki and di Rapido exchanged listless passes. Pickwich and Drummond, sat on the turf, propped on their arms. Lucas Mandrake squatted alone, reading his Bible. Seeing Ohara approach, Terry Dribble met him on the touchline, joined by captain Omar Grant.

'I'm sorry I'm late,' Ohara said. 'I had to give an interview to a Japanese magazine and record a programme on Radio Siddley.' He looked past them, at the stillness 'Is there a problem?'

Hands on hips, Omar looked down on his manager mournfully. 'That's just it, boss. The lads are feeling a bit, like, well, pissed off.'

'Pissed off? Not happy, you mean?'

'It's the training. Some of them say they're still knackered from the Moxbottom game.'

'I'm sorry. I thought Simon Pitt was the only serious injury.'

'It's not just the knocks,' Grant explained. 'They're finding the training a bit tough, specially the lads with jobs. They're not full-time professionals.'

Ohara sighed. 'We can only get better if we are fitter, and there are no short cuts to fitness.'

Omar Grant threw a thumb over a shoulder. 'Gazza Omerod was sacked today.'

'Sacked?'

Grant drew a finger across his throat for effect. 'He works nights stacking shelves, or he stacked shelves, at the Put'mup Do It Yourself over in Crilton but he kept falling asleep after football practice.' Grant was already a fit man before Ohara arrived but he said that even he was feeling a bit jaded lately.

Ohara rubbed a non-existent itch on his neck. He'd rested the team on Sunday, hadn't he? After returning from London on Monday, he'd joined them under the floodlights at Uno Electronics for what turned out to be a three hour session. Last night he'd led six players on a five kilometre run followed by an hour of crossing and shooting practice while the others worked out in the gym or submitted to Clarissa's supple fingers on the treatment table. Maybe he'd taken out his anger at David Broody's efforts to destroy the football club on the players, pushing them too hard, forgetting they were part-timers being paid a few pounds to turn out. He had something to prove. Saturday should be a no-hope confrontation but it had become Ohara's obsession, not only to thwart Broody by actually prolonging the possibility of winning a trophy but to save face in front of the Japanese nation watching the match on television. 'I'm sorry about Gary,' he told the two men genuinely. 'I will ease up on the physical side but we must be as fit as possible against Yattock on Saturday and mentally alert.'

On the pitch, the players had stirred, coming together and moving towards the touchline, silver shadows in the floodlights, like slow-motion zombies from the grave. Ohara watched them draw near. One of them was limping badly. He thought it was Les Diamond.

'That's not all, is it?' the manager said fearfully.

Grant sniffed uncomfortably. The team captain exchanged glances with coach Dribble. 'You tell him, Terry,' he said.

Dribble raked his clammy scalp. 'It's not easy to put into words,' he mumbled. 'What with you being very foreign and that.'

'Please try,' Ohara insisted, as a semi-circle of players gathered around them.

Dribble coughed uneasily and spoke through a corner of his mouth. 'One or two of the lads, can't name names obviously, but some of the lads sort of think you ought to be playing in the team with them.'

'Playing?'

'You're the player-manager,' Grant said bluntly. 'And we're short of fit players.'

Another detail from the rudely manipulated contract, Ohara thought, involuntarily searching out Suzuki, who was standing outside the circle, pretending lack of interest. 'I'm not fit enough to play regularly,' he told the players.

'You'd be fitter if you weren't doing fuckin' interviews all the time,' an anonymous voice called.

Ohara thought it was the unreliable Pickwich but he didn't pursue the source. After a deep breath, he said: 'But in an emergency I would turn out.'

'Will you play on Saturday?' Grant asked politely.

'I don't think so. I know Scott Fisher's shin is bruised and Lenny Hampton is still not a hundred per cent recovered from the virus, but Clint Hopp is back and Suzuki is an option up front.'

'Only an option?' a high voice whined.

This is stupid, Ohara told himself in English, stepping between Dribble and Omar Grant. 'Taro hasn't played competitive soccer for four years. I will watch him train in the next two days and decide the strategy for Saturday.' With Dean Slutz and Simon Pitt injured, he only had one out-and-out striker in Marco di Rapido and with Yattock expected to overrun the Pitties he might not be able to afford the luxury of playing two men up front. And he wasn't about to divulge his desperate strategy in front of Billy Pickwich, whose loyalty he suspected. A compromise occurred to him. Whether it would quell the revolt he didn't know. 'We train lightly tomorrow at Pitt Lane but Friday night training is cancelled,' he announced. 'The club will be crowded with visitors from the television company and friends of the directors. It is not a good atmosphere for the players on the day before a big game so we will talk strategy and game plan instead.'

The players nodded and grunted. Mollified, Ohara hoped. Lucas Mandrake, a towel lagging his neck and his Bible clamped in his armpit, raised a tentative hand.

'Yes, Lucas,' Ohara said, thankful for the intervention.

The long-legged winger shrugged nervously. Finally, looking down at his boots, he said: 'The Pitties are a little team who happen to play in a big town but we didn't used to get much of this publicity stuff outside Siddley.' His head jerked upright. 'Then suddenly you come along and we've a famous Japanese as the boss. Now we can't move for the people from the papers, the radio, the telly.'

'Yeah,' Robby Breakin agreed from Mandrake's shoulder. 'It won't matter when we get stuffed by Yattock ten to nothin' on Saturday. Everyone's here for the circus, the massacre. We're just the fall guys in it all.'

Mandrake nodded his agreement. 'When the cameras have gone and you've had enough of Siddley we'll still be here playing for peanuts.'

'Peanuts? Stuffed?' Ohara was falling behind the conversation.

'Well beaten,' Dribble translated. 'Lose the game ten goals to nil.'

'Perhaps we will lose but not by ten goals. And peanuts?'

'Peanuts, small change,' Mandrake explained, only marginally clearer. 'We're glad to have the extra money from you,' he said, bringing his hands together in what he believed was an eastern ritual of thanks. 'But, with respect, you're getting all the big money here.'

'I see,' the Japanese said solemnly, zipping his jacket. At that moment the floodlights shut down with a dull thudding noise.

With a bitter taste in their mouths, and rumbling dissatisfaction in their numbers, neither players nor coaches felt like resuming play in the grey murkiness and they bunched up and headed for the dressing room. The exceptions were Marco di Rapido and Taro Suzuki who walked a few yards apart, exchanging passes with a well scuffed practice ball.

In the dressing room, Ohara changed slowly, waiting until all his players were ready to leave, and then stood on a bench to impose himself over giants like Omar Grant and Les Diamond. The captain read the situation and bellowed the players into silence.

'I think I understand your situation,' Ohara said solemnly, nervously, holding a coat hook for support. 'I will try and explain mine, so please excuse my poor English. When I asked Taro Suzuki to play for the Pitties he wanted me to tell him one day what brought me to Siddley. To tell the truth, I don't know.' More than a few players chuckled.

Ohara looked across at his compatriot who returned a thin smile. 'I was sent to England to manage a football team and gain experience for my country. Frankly speaking, I was not familiar with the Pitties, just as you had not heard of my team, the Kinki Princes, so I looked for you in the league tables on the internet. I started with the Premiership.' This time the whole team erupted with guffaws and cheers. 'I went down the leagues, visiting many websites, Needless to say, I could not find Siddley United until finally I reached the minor divisions. It was a big shock to find you in the RoustaRodent Solutions League. It is not well known in Japan. But I am here anyway and I am very happy to manage the Pitties.'

Terry Dribble led an outburst of applause. When it subsided, Ohara continued: 'Soccer in Japan is a young sport. Baseball and sumo wrestling are our traditional sports but professional football is only ten years old. The players copy foreign players, behaving very badly and showing off. When Taro and I played in the J-League he had short hair coloured blond and I had very long hair dyed brown. Look at us now.' He paused until a ripple of laughter faded, and drew a deep breath. 'Taro was a leading Japanese player but he gave up professional soccer to take responsibility for injuring me very badly with a tackle.' Jaws dropped, faces turned towards Taro Suzuki, whose head had dropped, his eyelids closed. 'That is the Japanese way and it does not matter whether you are young or old. Taro gave up much money and fame, but I suppose it was better than *hara-kiri*' More chuckles. 'So when the Kinki Princes were asked to release me they could not refuse and neither could I. It's the Japanese way. We must support Japan, whatever the circumstances. That is why Uno Electronics allow us to use sports facilities here. It's because of me and Japan.'

He wiped a clammy hand on his tracksuit and returned it to the coat hook. 'I do not understand why Siddley United was chosen.' It wasn't the time to tell them at this very moment Monique was trying to discover the truth behind his appointment in the apartment of David Broody, using her own unique skills. 'But because I am Japanese, I must do my best in all circumstances. That is why I want to win every game, and the semi-final trophy match on Saturday is just another game.' Of course it wasn't. He'd pushed his players to be fitter, healthier and better out of professional duty; but Saturday was all about face.

'I am sorry if I have misunderstood your personal situations. I am paid a salary by the Japanese soccer association because I suppose I am working for Japan as much as the Pitties. I now realise you give up your free time to play football and you earn very little for it. This was not explained to me. I can only now understand your complaints about my salary, the media and the hard training programme. I will reflect on my position and try to bring us closer together with more understanding.'

Heads nodded appreciatively. 'Can't say fairer than that,' Lenny Hampton mumbled to those around him. Only Billy Pickwich seemed to disagree, his scowling face hidden in the shadow of a locker.

Ohara cleared his throat theatrically. 'But we must face Yattock on Saturday and, according to everybody outside Siddley, it means certain defeat.'

'No fuckin' way, boss.' It sounded like Clint Hopp.

Ohara pressed on. 'In the few weeks I've been at Pitt Lane I've seen that you can play as a team. You're fitter than when I arrived and you pass the ball better, and move well off the ball. I think you can win the game on Saturday.'

'Bloody 'ell,' Mike Groot told Marco di Rapido and Omar Grant, as the team gathered their bags. 'I thought he was going to cry.'

Ohara was filling his bag when he found the envelope. 'I

almost forget,' he called, blocking the doorway. 'I have a small present for you.' As his players trooped into the night, he handed each of them four tickets for the Golden Mousetrap Trophy semi-final, asking them to invite their families or friends, courtesy of Siddley United, to attend the big game. In the car park he sought out Gary Omerod and drew him aside. 'Tomorrow I will visit Put'mup shop. Please tell me the name of the senior manager.'

Whirring smoothly upwards to the Sunriser Heights penthouse, Monique loathingly atomised a dash of Calentissimo into the generous cleavage that plunged beneath the cerise satin jacket, her heart torn with hatred for the man she had trusted and who now plotted to destroy the football club she loved. David Broody was waiting as the door slid open, wearing his referee's outfit and clutching two flutes of iced Bollinger. His arms were spread for an embrace but he received nothing more passionate than a passing air kiss as Monique jigged to evade him.

The huge bedroom and functional kitchen apart, the penthouse was a single, large room, divided by two steps into Broody's working space and the living area which was furnished in white, with a soft leather couch and matching armchairs around a glass coffee table, a corner bar and a range of seductive lighting options. The penthouse's working area was also largely in white and centred with a tubular legged desk on which lay a laptop computer, telephone and compact photocopier. Around it stood an easel with a flipchart and on its own desk a small scale mock-up of a high-rise development. Screwed to the wall behind the desk were three plain white shelves supporting books and boxes. Two sides of the apartment comprised ceiling-to-floor glass, one offering access through sliding doors to a balcony with an iron garden table and four chairs and a view beyond the cathedral tower of the tiny orange lights on the Siddley ring-road.

Broody handed over the champagne with a leer, executed an expansive spin and used a remote control to activate a mechanism which drew a lacy mesh slowly across the windows. Camilla wasn't sure why her husband needed his 'space' when their home had 16 rooms of it and insisted only that a friend *feng shui* the penthouse flat before he used it. All that negative energy from the canal needed redirecting. When the woman had gone, Broody flushed the soothing goldfish down the lavatory and put the furniture back where he wanted it.

Camilla believed David watched porn films with his male friends in the flat but guessed wrongly in believing that her husband's sexual needs could satisfactorily be sated by a swift and invasive union between husband and wife, although she would have preferred any congress to be tantric. David Broody had been hugely unfaithful, though impeccably discreet, but his affair with Monique was, until recently, uniquely pleasurable. The freedom he had given her to run the Pitt Lane football club earned him her absolute loyalty and devotion and it wasn't hard to lure a girl so full of gratitude into his private life and secret perversions. To his delight he found she shared his fetish for live fantasy football, and many had been the times when, in the afterglow of provocation, punishment and intolerable ecstasy he'd come close to taking her into his confidence about his great plans for Pitt Lane. But he always held back, even as he drowned in her exotic scents, for while he was thinking dilapidated shed populated by semi-literate petty thieves and pond life, she spoke of Pitt Lane as if of a pantheon where lime green and tangerine gods performed miracles every other Saturday. Could he ever again entrust his body to her ministrations if he told her bulldozers were about to flatten the place?

Monique clutched the flute of fizzy wine, twirling and gaping, pretending a new interest in the luxury furnishing and fittings of the lecher's lair, postponing his first unwelcome grope, rehearsing her plan in her head. She stepped up to his study, her eyes searching for places he might keep his private papers. There were no cabinets, nor drawers in the desk, and only the office equipment on it. She was inconspicuously trying to read the labels on the bookshelf filing boxes when hands enveloped her, fingers penetrating the jacket's fabric.

'I can't wait any more,' Broody's hoarse voiced breathed. 'It's been three weeks. Your kit's on the bed, a real Real Madrid home outfit I got off the internet.' He pulled her skirt to her waist with two hands, tipping her off-balance against the table with the miniature buildings.

'Oh, what's this?' Monique gasped, a stray finger toppling Siddley cathedral. 'It wasn't here last time.' True. It had been installed only two weeks ago to show Boris Rakov in private what an architectural marvel awaited the Russian's land. Her interest in the model city wasn't entirely artificial. She leaned over the table, emitting a low hum of curiosity. Broody froze, allowing Monique to slither from his grip. Why in hell hadn't he covered it? The fact that almost nobody was invited to his ultra-private flat had made him complacent. Cursing to himself, he struggled resolutely for a diversion.

'Just a mock-up of central Siddley. Helps me concentrate, when I'm planning a big project. Gives me a feeling for scale. Can we start now?' Hanging on a cord around his neck, the silvery whistle felt cold and useless.

Ignoring him, Monique leaned forward and touched a mauve fingernail to a little squarish blue block. 'Look. This is where we are now, right? Sunriser Heights. On the canal. It's so accurate,' she enthused. 'So realistic'

'Isn't it?' he said with cold indifference, noticing the untouched champagne in her glass was flat. His state of arousal was going the same way.

Monique's lips pursed into a pink tulip. 'Something's very odd, David,' she queried, a finger darting among the tiny eruptions of glass and plastic. 'Here's the cathedral, there's the marina. Oh, and that must be Church Street. But I can't see the football ground. Your designer must have made a mistake. He's put little towers slap where the pitch and the car park are.'

Broody's mind backpedalled furiously. Then he slapped his forehead brutally. 'Monique, my precious, you're not supposed to see that. Nobody is. It's my dream for the future of Siddley United.'

'Not much of a future without a pitch, I wouldn't have thought.'

'That's the point,' Broody breathed, his head turning furtively, as though they were not alone. 'I don't want people to see my plans and start a landslide of speculation.'

'But where's the football ground in your plans?' she teased. She knew perfectly well the Pitt Lane ground was history, now that he'd dug up Sir Abraham Pitt's spiteful proviso. She smelled Broody behind her, all avocado shower gel and hyperventilating pores. Hands touched her shoulders, warm cigar-foul breath washed her ears. She shivered, which he mistook for expectancy and desire.

'Will you swear yourself to absolute secrecy my hot-tempered, gorgeous little wing back?'

'Of course,' she lied, turning and releasing his hold. She opened the top button of her jacket and fluttered an irresistible pout. 'You'll have to hurry. I can feel a punishable offence coming on.'

His referee's pants stirred once more. 'You see, my angel in pink, I plan to build a state-of-the-art, thirty thousand seater football stadium on the Pitt Lane site, right there in the centre of Siddley, surrounded by low cost housing for young families and sheltered accommodation for the elderly and handicapped. The project is so secret that until I get the last piece of the package together I dare not announce it or even talk about it. I daren't put anything on the model board yet in case my competitors see them and try to undermine me. There are some real unprincipled bastards out there. You do understand, my love, don't you?'

For a micro-second it sounded plausible: David Broody, the benefactor, the caring property developer. All heart and propriety, looking modestly for a future civic award, a national honour, perhaps. But then a voice rose inside her, reminding her of the conversation she'd overheard in the Duck and Prime Minister, when Broody told Sir Reginald Pitt the football ground and all traces of the Pitties would be gone by Christmas. Choose the real David Broody carefully, the voice screamed silently. She smiled a killer smile. 'Thank you, David. You're a saint. I'm sorry I doubted you.' She tiptoed and brushed his cheek with her lips. Then, taking a step back she snapped two more buttons, exposing the swell of gossamer lace.

'Dear God,' he declared, slithering adroitly to the music centre and stabbing a button. The room was filled the screams and curses of a football crowd, with troughs and peaks of noise to accompany the ebbs and flows of a game. 'Hurry, my little midfield destroyer,' he commanded hoarsely. 'The Real Madrid kit.' Seizing a hand, he led her to the bedroom and gestured proudly at the white shirt, shorts and socks that lay in disembodied human form on the duvet. Monique slid out of the jacket, dangling it provocatively before dropping it. Then she wriggled out of the pink skirt and with one foot on the low *futon* bed began to roll her flesh coloured tights over her hips. Suddenly she froze.

'What's the matter?' Broody cried, eyes bulging, mouth as dry as paper.

'I can't do it in the Spanish kit. I'm not in a latin mood.'

'What? I got it direct from the Bernabeu Stadium. It's Luis bloody Figo. He could excite a fire hydrant.'

'I need something really special today, something personal, close to us both.'

'What?' His high, strained voice trailed into a disbelieving wail. He grasped at the referee's cards in his shirt pocket and wafted the yellow one at her. 'I could book you for time wasting, you know.'

Where normally she would throw herself around his legs, pleading for mercy, offering an intimate penance, this time she slumped in theatrical dejection on the bed, hair collapsed, a thread of it intruding over her upper lip. Her eyes were moist with contrived longing. 'Please, David.'

'Okay, okay,' he groaned, falling to his knees before a veneered chest of drawers, tugging open the lower two. 'Take your pick.' The deep drawers contained three neatly folded heaps of colourful football shirts and shorts. 'Something Greek. You like moussaka.' He fumbled in a pile and produced a plain red shirt with a roundel logo over the left breast. 'Olmypiakos, home strip. My God, this'll make you mad.'

Monique hummed and shook her head. 'I see me in blue, David. I need correcting in blue.'

'Blue?'

'Blue. Dark blue.' Broody rummaged again in the stacks of shirts, frustration forcing a ridge of sweat to bubble up on his forehead. He held up a shirt by its collar, a desperate plea etched on his face. 'Paris Saint Germain. Let me give the frogs a kicking.'

'No way,' she chided 'Look at that fat red stripe down the middle.'

Monique watched him pitifully as he flitted between the drawers with rising desperation, tossing unsuitable shirts onto the carpet 'Hurry please, David,' she panted, a hand moulding a butter soft breast.

He found an azure shirt. 'Leicester City?'

'No, no.'

Leicester joined the rumpled heap 'Ipswich?' Broody wondered with quiet desperation, his own shirt clammy against his back.

'So close, David. Please hurry.'

'There aren't any more,' he raged.

'So there's only one thing to do,' Monique said with resignation.

'You're not leaving. Tell me you're not leaving.' He was close to tears, his senses tormented by anticipation, intoxicated with anticipation.

Monique drew his flushed face to her warm breasts and let him rummage with his nose. 'Silly boy. How could I leave you when I'm so close?' she pouted, before pretending to remember. 'I have the blue shirt I want in my car.'

Broody came up for air and breathed heavily. 'Thank God for that. How come?'

'It's the Japanese national team.'

'Japanese? Where did you get it?'

'They sell replicas in the Market Hall.'

Broody's face formed a cynical scowl. 'Perfect,' he muttered, easing himself painfully to his feet. 'Please go and get it and we'll start again.'

Monique wrapped her arms protectively. 'Undressed, like this? Be a darling, David and pop down to the car park.' Not giving him time to protest, she skipped into the lounge, Broody following as though tethered. She produced a Pitties key ring from an oddly large shoulder bag and dangled a key beguilingly. 'It's dark so nobody'll see you, and you'll only be a minute. It's on the back seat, or perhaps the boot.'

Knees still pink from kneeling, he stood in his black referee's outfit, still staring mesmerised at Monique's luscious body as the doors of the private lift closed. Monique waited until he had reached the ground floor, gave him a few seconds to move away and then twisted the key in the wall control panel, rendering the lift immobile, a Broody security feature. She dashed to the bedroom and dressed quickly. She had seven or eight minutes. Whatever happened with the files, she wasn't staying around to receive the odious David Broody. Then to the shelves with the three filing boxes. The first box contained folded technical drawings, blue prints specifications, the second statements, reports, newspaper cuttings. Quickly to the third box. It contained typed and handwritten letters. 'Let's see here,' she murmured, flicking them expertly: a sequence of correspondence with his solicitor, none of them about Pitt Lane. How she could use another ten minutes! She skimmed each communication at speed reading pace: letters of thanks for his charity work, job requests, offers to buy property, invitations, letters with elaborate headings, like the pair from the Football Association she found near the bottom. No time to read them. She scooped the letters onto the photocopier.

David Broody felt cold and silly in the loose shirt and shorts as he edged along the wall where the glare from the lobby lighting was weakest. He'd almost reached the glass-panelled front doors when he saw the worst possible witnesses pressing in the entry code. Larry and Barry, interior designers, business and bedroom partners and leaseholders of apartment 23. He raised an inadequate collar and retracted his head, tortoise-like.

'Love the whistle, Mr Broody,' Larry cooed, causing Broody to stuff the referee's tool angrily into his shirt.

'Perverts,' Broody muttered when out of earshot. He was shivering as the perspiration effused by his frustrated state of arousal dried. The key was unsteady in his hand when he tried to penetrate Monique's crimson car. 'Where's the bloody shirt?' he groaned, his backside spilling into the cold Siddley night as he knelt in the front, a hand rummaging around the seats. 'In the bloody boot,' he decided finally.

The first copies were in her bag and the last was whirring out of the copier's exit groove when Broody's scrambled voice came through the intercom.

'Are you there, Monique? The bloody lift's not working.'

Ignoring him, she rushed the last of the copied pages into her bag and was returning its original to Broody's file when her eyes fell on the next letter in the box. It wasn't the foreign looking writing in the heading that caught her eye but the subject summarised in bold print above the text of the letter. 'Acquisition of the Pitt Estate.' Sliding it under the copier lid without reading it, she looked up, heart racing, willing the lift to stay at ground level.

Broody's cracking voice came again. 'The lift's not working. Check the override key.'

Still paying no attention to the plea, she replaced the filing box and made ready to leave, fussing with things on the tables. Before hoisting the bag onto a shoulder, she made sure she had the spare car key and removed a note she'd written earlier, anchoring it to the coffee table with a champagne glass. Then, without a word into the intercom, she reactivated the lift with a sharp twist of the master key and made a dash to the kitchen and the door that gave onto the fire-escape steps.

Descending smartly, swirling flurries of wind blushing her

cheeks, she pushed through the emergency door onto the floor below and found herself at the end of a corridor with doors to the flats of both sides. After pausing for breath she made for the stairs beside the lift, reaching them just as it looked like stopping. Her first thought was that Broody must have taken the residents' lifts in frustration and it made her retreat smartly. She backed into a shallow doorway, drawing herself in until her profile was hidden. She heard the lift doors open and incomprehensible, though vaguely familiar, male and female voices spilled into the hallway. The woman sounded happy, and Monique recognized the foreign language from hearing Ken talking to journalists. Japanese. She knew from Broody that Uno Electronics expatriates rented flats in Broody's prestigious Sunriser Heights and so, irresistibly and feeling safe, she eased a naked eye into the softly lit corridor. Only to melt back into the doorway, her heart in tatters. Ken Ohara had eyes only for Rika Yamaguchi, whose hair swirled as they passed her obliviously.

Broody burst into his penthouse, holding up the Japanese national team shirt, the key of choice to Monique's passion vault, but he knew inside the frustrations and humiliations of the evening hadn't ended. He looked for her in the bathroom and the compact kitchen and when there was nowhere else to go he fell forlornly on the couch, his eyes finally falling on the piece of paper clamped under the champagne flute. He sighed noisily and read the note aloud. 'Dearest David. Please don't be angry at me. I just can't get it on tonight, what with Saturday's big game on my mind. I couldn't bear to see your disappointment so I left before you returned. Please forgive me. Whether the Pitties win or lose, let's meet next week and you can flash your yellow cards at me. And more. I'll wear any strip you want, even Derby. All my love. M. Your naughty little wingback.'

Broody quartered the letter in two murderous movements and leapt to his feet. He balled the Japanese shirt and silenced the raucous, empty crowd with a bellow and a cushioned punch at the stereo's controls. He downed Monique's untouched tepid champagne and paced the penthouse looking for someone to kill.

Seizing a slender, silver letter opener dagger-like he let the azure shirt unravel itself in his other hand. He stared at the name, Ohara, stencilled across the shoulders and when he had conjured up an image of the interfering, bandy-legged little jap inside it he slashed until the blunt knife penetrated the cloth and in a stroke he ripped it apart. It was while he waited for his heart to slow he noticed the green fluorescence seeping from under the lid of the photocopier. He approached it suspiciously, it must have been weeks since he last used the machine, and lifted the lid. A letter in it! Now a different heat engulfed him, first erupting from a surge of anger at the intrusion and then, as the implications unfolded in his mind, from a flush of fear he felt to the icy roots of his hair. He lifted the letter and turned it with awful foreboding. It couldn't have been worse. Somebody, and Monique Wainwright had been his only visitor to the penthouse since Boris Rakov, had found and copied the letter of intent signed by the Russian banker, a confirmation of his syndicate's intention to acquire the Pitt estate, with the absolute condition that the deal includes the land where the football ground and the car park now stand.

'Oh, Monique,' he wailed at the ceiling. 'You shouldn't have done it. You could have had it all, but now you're a major liability, like Moby NcNally when he turned me down. And you know what happened to him.'

7

Alf Widdison double locked the front door with his usual care and sniffed the damp air outside. 'It's a mornin' for perch,' he told the deserted street and empty houses. Tackle box, rod and folding chair in hand, he knew that one day he'd come home and find the door broken in and bailiffs with a warrant to evict him from his home of a lifetime. He was prepared for the moment. The bottle of whisky was lodged in a crevice under a rotten spar spanning the lock where the Pitties' pre-Ohara manager, Moby McNally, had drowned, and he kept the couple of strips of sleeping tablets in his fishing tackle box. He'd swallow the pills, drink the whisky while he fished for the last time and tumble painlessly into eternity.

He normally threw a nostalgic glance at the rusted, silent turnstiles he passed before he reached the canal but today Pitt Lane was already bustling. A mild morning, 48 hours before the semi-final of the Golden Mousetrap Trophy, found lorries and vans bearing a panoply of communications equipment, operatives manhandling a huge satellite dish onto a platform, trimming its transmitter towards the Hotbird satellite, others unloading cameras and unravelling cables or talking into their mobiles. By midday, six camera units had been fixed strategically around the pitch, ready to send their pictures 7,500 miles across the world to an expectant Japan and even other parts of east Asia.

A transport van from a Uno Electronics warehouse brought billboards and posters stored for display at sporting events sponsored by the Japanese giant in Great Britain. One length of multi-stroke, ornate hieroglyphics for the benefit of the Japanese audience had to be reinstalled when a passing NHK engineer noticed it was upside down. A short but intense discussion took place when the prime space behind the goals were found to be already occupied, and only David Broody's diplomacy persuaded staff from Walter Hardcastle & Sons, Funeral Directors, to remove and re-site the undertaker's billboard depicting the motif of a coffin sprouting roses and bearing the slogan in giant letters, 'What Your Loved One Would Have Wanted'. There was also space to promote Harry Patel's cash 'n' carry sports outlets, Geoffrey Osborne's meat empire and Siddley City Council's inward investment programme under the slogan, 'See Siddley and Try'.

A bus and two black saloon cars pulled up at Pitt Lane in the early afternoon, depositing NHK staff from London and Tokyo, among the latter the match commentator, Shinsuke Sudo. To provide expert analysis and support, NHK called on former international footballer Takeo Shito, who hated the ten-year-old Japanese professional soccer league, and all its players, because he'd missed out on its riches. Since no Japanese sports or general discussion panel is complete without its dumb-acting camera candy, 23-year-old Mimi Bando had been brought over to squeal at moments of excitement on the pitch and generally act as a fall girl by asking obvious questions and nodding appreciatively. Mimi Bando wasn't dumb: she just had to act so. It's the Japanese way. While the technicians went to work around the ground, the commentator and his crew sat with Terry Dribble and a local history teacher from Siddley City University. They stayed there until they were able to pronounce the names of the Pittie and Yattock players with reasonable accuracy and receive a potted history of Siddley. On the nights before the big game, the Japanese team would all sleep at the Five Winds Motel, the football pundit, Shito, with Mimi Bando.

Ken Ohara also reached Pitt Lane early, locking his car and tugging up his collar as he hurried past workers and their equipment. The satellite dish, the appearance of Japanese writing around the ground and the marauding presence already of journalists from his country reminded him the live transmission to his homeland wasn't the product of a nightmare. It made the evening with Rika Yamaguchi seem a lifetime ago. After dinner at PastaBasta he'd only lingered long enough in her apartment for a coffee. He wanted to stay, and Rika had sent out the right signals, but he didn't want to be trapped by the smut sniffing Japanese press. Rika had killer eyes, deep ebony, lively, sparkling with intelligence on her angular, porcelain fine face. She was attentive without being obsequious, flattering but always ready to make a point or contest one of his. It was a close call, but he had too much on his mind, including the two men Simon Pitt said wanted his private address. His biggest worry, though, was Monique, and the plot she'd hatched to search David Broody's private apartment. He guessed the two orientals looking for him were paparazzi from the photo-magazines whose interest in football was zero, in the sex lives of their subjects, total. Paranoid or not, he was sure they were following him last night, when he drove Rika home from the restaurant, and knowing the centre of Siddley better than his pursuers he easily shook them off in the one-way system. Shame for them, really. If they'd made it to Sunriser Heights, they might have got an interesting picture of a pervert, dressed in black shirt and shorts, and creeping about in the car park. And then there was the scent, the whiff of fragrance in the hallway outside Rika's flat. Like most Japanese women, Rika Yamaguchi didn't use perfume; it had reminded him of Monique, and the time she'd embraced him and tearfully told him about David Broody's plot to sell the football ground.

He took to the stairs with briskness and trepidation and found Monique alone in her office, wearing a tight but uncharacteristically sombre, dark grey suit.

'Good morning, Mr Ohara,' she said primly. 'How was your evening?'

'Fine, Monique, thank you. A quiet dinner with Rika Yamaguchi. She is co-ordinating Japanese support for Saturday's game.'

I bet she is, Monique thought. While she was risking her physical well-being with a middle-aged pervert on behalf of the Japanese man she adored and respected and who would help her save the Pitties, the very same man was playing oriental ju-jitsu games with a dark-eyed Japanese bimbo only a floor below Broody's penthouse.

As though reading her bruised heart, Ohara tried to ease it. 'I went home quite early, after a coffee.'

'Oh, really, Mr Ohara?'

'Of course. I had to read Mr Dribble's scouting reports again. And I knew you were planning something so I hoped you'd call.'

'You did, Ken?' Monique said, almost choking with surprise.

'Of course. I wanted you to tell me you were fine.'

Monique melted and beamed at the team manager with a broad smile, her teeth raking the sparkling gloss on her lower lip. She reached for the large brown envelope. 'I hope these are helpful,' she breathed, freshly enthused and hopeful. 'I copied them from Broody's private files.'

Ohara's face filled with concern. 'You were not in danger, were you?'

'Not really,' she said, in a voice that didn't convince Ohara at all.

He returned her smile uncertainly and spread the two

photocopied letters from the English Football Association to David Broody on the desk. Monique watched the door. The club directors were in and out of Pitt Lane, seeking out the international visitors, business cards flashing in their fingers. Even that rare bird Sir Reginald Pitt had announced a visit for the afternoon. David Broody would be there too, she knew, boasting about the club while secretly planning its destruction. Ohara nodded ruefully as he read the contents of the letters. Having met Kenneth O'Hara, his so near namesake, it was all falling into place. Monique stood at his shoulder, eyes following his fingers down the text, then watching his lips as he strove to understand the nuances.

In the first letter, dated late March, someone called Campbell Murton, expressed his condolences over the tragic drowning of Moby McNally and hoped that the immediate availability of the capable and experienced manager, Kenneth O'Hara, subject to agreement on terms and conditions, would be to the long-term benefit of Siddley United Football Club. What transpired between Broody and the Football Association in the meantime was not recorded, but the tenor of the second letter, written just over three months after the first, was entirely different, as was the name of the proposed Pitties manager. Ohara read the short, terse message slowly aloud. '"Mr Ken-ichi Ohara, currently manager of the Kinki Princes of the Japanese J-League, could be released under very favourable conditions to Siddley United FC and would be available to the club as early as September. As you will appreciate from the draft contract addressed to your chairman the Japanese FA is willing to pay the greater share of Mr Ohara's emoluments and all of his living expenses whilst in Siddley".' Ohara pushed the letter away and sighed, sharing a caustic smile with Monique, both knowing that between March and July the chief executive of Siddley United FC and this senior FA official, head of international public relations, had conspired to reject a perfectly suitable managerial candidate, Kenneth O'Hara, and bless the Pitties with a Japanese who, aspiring to lead his national team one day after experience of a high-profile English club, neither knew where Siddley was nor understood the barren, hopeless circumstances of a club at the lower end of the RoustaRodent League.

Monique leaned forward. 'Just one little apostrophe separating your names. How do you pronounce yours? In Japanese, I mean.'

'Ohara,' Ohara said flatly, no intonation at all. 'How about the Irish name?'

'The same. I can't see any difference. And you're both called Ken. Well, almost.' She released a cynical scoff. 'It was easy for David Broody to switch your papers with Kenneth O'Hara's and deceive Mr Hardcastle and the board. They were always so busy, the chairman with his coffins, the others with their shops and law offices and council business. They'd sign anything Broody put in front of them. They let him decide everything.' She threw up her hands. 'What does it all mean?'

Ohara sighed again, his head slumping. 'It means, Monique *san*, that Mr Broody thought I was less of a threat to his plans than Mr Kenneth O'Hara. The Pitties will keep losing because I don't have enough players or time to improve things before he sells the land and closes the club.'

'Things will get better, Ken,' Monique pleaded. 'We won last Saturday for the first time in ages.'

'I hope you are right. But first the Pitties will lose on Saturday in front of the entire Japanese nation.' He smacked his forehead with the palms of his hands. 'I think I lose will to live.'

Monique reached to clutch the slumped head, once more drawing it to her. 'It won't happen, Ken, believe me. The Pitties will win for you on Saturday and Broody can't sell the club or the land if we keep on going to the final. It's all up to you and I know you can do it.' But then, as Ohara's head tugged and pulled, she remembered the third letter she'd copied from Broody's private files. Ohara could not see her face drop, or her eyes moisten. 'I took another letter,' she uttered gamely. 'It's not about you but it's got funny writing at the top. Broody got it a few days ago.'

Ohara finally surfaced and took the photocopy from her. He recognized the imposing cyrillic script across the top, translated below it as The Great Imperial Bank of Russia. He caught her eye, then read aloud, as if delivering a death sentence. '"My Dear David. A brief note to confirm the substance of our conversation in Siddley yesterday. I understand that once the forthcoming Golden Mousetrap semi-final match is finished, and your club's interest in it terminated, you will be in a position to immediately sign the necessary protocols to transfer ownership of the Pitt Lane Estate, in its entirety and levelled."' And here Ohara paused to show Monique the raised, bold letters: IN ITS ENTIRETY, '"to the syndicate for which my bank acts as authorized representative."'

'What does "levelled" mean?' Ohara asked.

'Levelled? It means flattened, everything destroyed, taken away.'

They were silent for a moment, Ohara staring at the photographs on the chairman's wall, looking for inspiration, imploring the moustached figures on the Pitt Lane pitch a hundred years ago to reach out from the past and save him and the club. When Lavinia appeared at the door she had to knock to stir them.

'I think it's time for Mr Ohara's press conference. There's twenty Japanese reporters in the hospitality lounge and a lot more on the way tomorrow, I hear.'

*

Fat bellied clouds hung petulantly over the city when David Broody pulled into the Pitt Lane car-park, between Harry Patel's Lexus and a Japanese bull-barred Continental Cruiser decorated with convoluted cursive characters, part of the Japanese media circus here for the game. He'd allowed himself a scowl of pleasure when he'd passed a transport van outside the second last occupied terraced house on the Pitt Lane estate and it was still on his face when he ran the edge of a 50 pence coin along the side of the four wheel drive. Monique Wainwright had been on his mind from the moment he found the letter from Boris Rakov where she'd forgotten it in the photocopier. Questions pinged around his head. What did Monique intend to do with it, and what else did she copy? Did it mean she knows about Sir Abraham's proviso? It would explain her furtive behaviour when he caught her examining the old boardroom photograph. But the only person he'd told was Reggie Pitt. Was he playing a double-cross game as well? He wouldn't let either of them ruin his greatest property deal, especially that cheating bitch. Surely they remembered what happened to Moby McNally? They were all dangerous, untrustworthy and perfectly dispensable, and Broody decided before he left home that he would make a pre-emptive strike. He would emasculate the board of directors of Siddley United before the big match. They could all go down with their bloody football club: the directors, Monique and anyone else who stood in his way.

Broody's first stop on his way to Pitt Lane was the third level of the Hawksworth shopping centre's weathered multi-storey car park. A figure whose face was obscured by the brim of a baseball cap and the collar of a black zip-up jacket stepped from behind a pitted concrete column when he saw the black BMW creeping towards him. Broody stopped and opened a window. 'You know what you have to do,' he said economically, proffering a chunky brown envelope.

The figure nodded with a grunt and melted into the shadows. Mobile in hand, Broody drove across town to the Cornmarket Piazza, whose surface retained the cobbles from bygone Siddley, and made a couple of calls before parking opposite the equestrian statue of Lord Eek whose colonial governor's banana skin hat and moustache were caked with chalky pigeon shit. A man pedalled from a side street and leaned his bicycle against the solid horse. He looked around the square, glimpsed the figure in the black BMW and descended the steps into the men's public convenience behind the statue. Broody followed.

'Nobody 'ere,' the short, full-bellied man in a distressed leather jacket uttered, tilting his square, unshaven face at the row of cubicles. A thin strip of scar tissue split his fat lips. He was standing by a chipped urinal bowl wherein shredded cigarette and lumps of gum floated on the brimming blocked-up piss.

Broody's face was screwed against the stench in the underground lavatory as he fumbled in his jacket pocket. Producing a key and handing it over with a brown envelope he said: 'It'll be in Wolverine Lane, as close to the post office as I can put it. Take out the radio cassette system carefully and don't damage the car. You know where to leave it?'

The man nodded, took the key and the envelope into an inside pocket and left without another word.

The press conference was a PR affair for broadcast on the national broadcasting channel in Japan in the run up to Saturday's match. With the NHK sports journalist, Shinsuke Sudo, and his two commentary box companions nodding compliantly alongside him at the head table, Ohara said everything and nothing in response to the questions they had planted with selected Japanese journalists gathered in the Pitt Lane hospitality lounge. Most of them were happy to collaborate with their country's senior broadcasting system in return for just being allowed to be present at this historic moment in Japan's sporting history. Tanaka of the tabloid *Kanto Daily Sports* and the muckraking weeklies were not invited. After a tour of Pitt Lane, where Ohara was filmed contemplating papers and checking out the kit in the changing room he was finally left alone to prepare for the Golden Mousetrap Trophy semi-final, now less than two days away.

The players trickled in for the light training session coach Ohara had promised. The boss had listened to the team's complaints at Uno Electronics yesterday and for the players the humility and passion he'd shown after the training ground confrontation were not emotions they experienced often and so publicly in Siddley. And when he wasn't talking tactics and calling for commitment he was leading by example in training, pain wracking his knee and showing when he left the field dragging his foot.

The floodlights were turned on and 13 players, 14 with Ohara, took to the Pitt Lane pitch, early evening dew on its new, well bedded-in grass surface sparkling in the dazzle. Two of the small squad were missing. Scott Fisher, the sweeper defender, was still resting from a bruised thigh. Lenny Hampton's absence was more serious. His partner, Renata, called in just before practice to say he had influenza, or the symptoms of something like it. Since his return from a viral infection he'd filled a gap at the back and in midfield which encouraged Ohara to think about more aggressive tactics going forward. If Hampton was out of the semi-final, Ohara would have to start with Billy Pickwich, and his uncertain loyalties, on the left side of defence. He followed the players in a warm-up trot around the touchline and counted off the options on his fingers. Dean Slutz hadn't even resumed training after the ankle injury at Molecroft but Taro Suzuki was now available to play up front alongside di Rapido, with Mandrake just behind on the left, ahead of the attacking midfield option, Clint Hopp. If the situation remained unchanged in the next 24 hours he'd have 16 players, himself included, available. Fifteen realistically, he thought, because one of them was Kevin Stopham, the substitute goalkeeper.

True to his word the workout was light: 40 or so minutes of unopposed breakout practice, the ball spread along the ground by the four man back line of Diamond, Breakin, Fisher and Pickwich, with Fisher to be the designated limpet marker for the big Yattock striker, Shane Goodmouth, through a midfield of Drummond, Grant, Omerod and Hopp to di Rapido and Mandrake up front The three spare players in the practice, Ohara one of them, would try to thwart the advancing strikers with non-contact obstruction. Then he tried a three man forward line, bringing Taro Suzuki in, just, behind di Rapido and Mandrake. He had to go for a win at Pitt Lane on Saturday, however improbable or impossible, because a replay win away at Yattock was even more the stuff of fantasy.

The players changed roles and positions, the forwards finding speed as their confidence grew, allowing them to chance a few audacious moves. The forward runs were unopposed physically, until, that is, Billy Pickwich suffered a rush of blood to the head. Knowing he wouldn't be tackled hard, Taro Suzuki received the ball from Omerod, twisted this way and that with it and glided past Pickwich, who, instead of tracking back and snapping at the striker's heels as the rules of engagement for this exercise required, threw his body between Suzuki and the ball, leaving the business end of an elbow in the right place to impale Suzuki below the sternum.

'Christ, I'm sorry,' Billy pleaded, spreading his hands biblically, as the others rushed to the writhing body of Taro Suzuki. 'I got carried away.'

'You'll get fucking carried away on Saturday if you do that,' Omar Grant snapped. 'And it'll be on stretcher after I clobber you.'

Terry Dribble had rushed over and cradled the small Japanese head.

'*Daijobu ka?*' Ohara asked, crouching beside his fallen countryman.

From the pinched face came the agonized, strangulated moans of a man with severe breathing difficulties. Ushered by Terry Dribble, Lucas Mandrake and Marco di Rapido raised their injured colleague gently to his feet and with his arms over their shoulders shuffled him towards the dressing room. Hands on hips, a dejected manager watched the party and their burden leave. Sighing, he turned to team captain, Omar Grant.

'Please lead the team in a couple of slow laps of the field and the warm-down exercises. I'll talk to everybody in the changing rooms in fifteen minutes.'

Approaching the tunnel in the main stand, he was thinking: 'Maybe now only thirteen outfield players on Saturday,' when a voice called to him from the dark seats.

'Hello, Ken.' It was Simon Pitt. Crutches propped against the fence, he wore a loose tracksuit with a trouser leg bunched at the knee to reveal the cast on his right leg. His thin, boyish face wore a sheepish, pained expression. 'Thank you for sending me the tickets.'

Ohara naturally intended that Simon Pitt should also receive four free tickets, which Monique had had delivered to Pitt Manor. Ohara scaled the low fence and joined Pitt, waiting patiently while the estate agent heaved himself upright, fumbling with his new crutches and struggling to synchronize his body movements.

'Thank you for coming in to support the team so soon after your injury. You should really be at home.'

Pitt was studiously watching the positioning of his feet and crutches on the steps. 'I'd rather be here, with you and the lads.'

'Thank you. I'm sorry you're not playing on Saturday. They say it's going to be the biggest game in Siddley for fifty years. You deserve to be part of it.'

'Can't be helped.' Pitt shrugged philosophically. 'Is Taro going to be fit. It looked like Billy really caught him with his elbow.'

'I'm not sure. I'm going to see how badly he's injured. To be frank, I'm running out of players. Hampton is sick again, Mike Groot's shin still hurts. And we've lost you.'

'I'm sorry,' Pitt said, breathing in sharp, tired bursts.

Ohara liked Simon Pitt, not just for his gentleness as a human being when all around him were hard young men, even the religious Lucas Mandrake not immune from an occasional need to hurt, but for his quiet tenacity and team approach on the pitch. I'm glad you're here,' he told the struggling man when they emerged at the top of the bare concrete steps. Ohara was about to leave him to his own pace when other matters crowded his head and he remembered who Pitt was and what he did for a living.

'May I ask you something not connected to football? As a professional in the real estate business?'

'Ask away,' the young Pitt said, smiling.

'The old houses around Pitt Lane,' the Japanese wondered. 'They will all be destroyed soon?'

'Yes, and not before time, really. They're the last of the terraced houses my great grandfather built for his workers, almost a hundred years ago. It's still called the Pitt Estate but the property's changed hands several times over the years and so far nobody's got round to redeveloping it.'

'But now it's happened,' Ohara concluded. 'Mr Broody will make buildings.'

'You're very well informed,' Pitt remarked. 'If the rumours in my business are true, he's going for an enormous development project.'

'I don't understand,' Ohara said. 'Developer means he is the owner of Pitt Estate?'

Pitt scratched the skin around the top edge of the cast. 'Not necessarily, and I don't know whether David Broody is or not. The ultimate owner of the freehold is probably hidden in an offshore company somewhere.'

Ohara thought he understood. He didn't know about the high interest bridging loan Broody had raised from the Cristobal Colon Bank of the Cayman Islands to buy the Pitt Estate outright, but he knew from the Russian's letter that Monique had copied that Broody had the power to sell the land. 'But Mr Broody is clearing all the houses away.'

Pitt nodded. 'He's been very active arranging for the residents to be re-located, most of them by the council into tower blocks or old people's homes. There are a few objectors but they can't hold out long.'

'Like the old man who fishes in the canal.'

'Excuse me?'

'Nothing. You were saying?'

'David has strong ties with the council, not the least because our very own club director, Ronald Townrow, happens to be an influential city councillor. The old houses have been condemned as unsanitary so the residents can be evicted as a matter of course and re-housed. Whatever happens, it's going to be a big redevelopment project and my own firm wants to get involved with the future letting of the shops and offices.'

Voices filtered up from the dressing rooms; a light in the commentary box above them illuminated shadowy figures and workers around the stadium were completing their special tasks against the clock. Ohara lowered his head with conspiratorial intent. 'Is this football ground, Pitt Lane, included in the development plans?'

'Absolutely not,' Simon Pitt fired back. 'My great grandfather put this bit of his property, which includes what's now the car park, in trust to the town for a football club, in perpetuity.'

'In per . . .?'

'For ever,' Pitt said helpfully.

'Is there a document where this is all written?' the Japanese wondered.

Pitt's forehead furrowed. 'Never really thought about it. There ought to be something but I can't say I've come across anything at home, in Pitt Manor.'

'So it's possible your great grandfather could have made a secret pro . . .' Ohara searched his memory for Monique's word. 'Like a document to say that the club's ground could be sold in some circumstances.'

'A proviso you mean? I suppose it's possible. But why should he do that?'

'I don't know, but why would you buy Pitt Estate without all the best land? The pitch and the car park.'

Simon shrugged. 'You'd have to ask David Broody, but if he tried to include the club's land in his deal the directors would stand absolutely firm. You'd have to exclude my father, he'd love to sell out, but the other four own the majority shareholding. Excluding my father, they're all big Pitties fans. That's why they've put their personal money into the club. They would never agree to sell out if it meant the end of Pitt Lane as the home of the Pitties.'

'Thank you very much,' Ohara said, a hand offered as Pitt eased himself upright.

It was slow progress, this time down stairs, heading to the basement. Pitt's face screwed with concentration as he measured the descent, and all the while Ohara was trying to recall what Monique remembered Broody saying to Sir Reginald Pitt about the directors. Whatever it was, their controlling interest in the club didn't seem to worry the chief executive much.

When Ohara reached the changing room he found Taro Suzuki doing stretching and breathing exercises, supervised by Matt Dennis. 'How do you feel?' he asked in Japanese.

'Still alive, no thanks to the bastard over there. Why was he trying to hurt me deliberately?'

Charlie had prepared the '*ofuro*' water at a moderately hot 42 degrees and the players had washed and soaked in Japanese fashion and were drying off and dressing up. Simon Pitt sat on a bench, his plastered leg outstretched, team mates around him with pens. Ohara bathed quickly and joined them, wondering whether to tell them how many millions of Japanese would watch them on Saturday. Or rather, they'd be watching for him and Suzuki, two men fighting with the spirit of the samurai for Japan in a far and violent land. The football was incidental: Japan was on show, Siddley the world stage of the moment. No, he wouldn't say anything: or he'd have to confess he'd rather be tied to a bullet train track than face the inevitable ridicule when the Japanese nation saw their national hero was managing a part-time team in a town as unknown to them as the capital of Tajikistan.

The team were in better spirits than yesterday, the revolt forgotten, Ohara hoped. If Billy Pickwich's loyalty was wavering, the others were solidly with him, he believed. It hadn't been easy from the start, but he'd got dirty with them on the pitch, sat in the ancient minibus with them, found proper training facilities and cared about their diet, allowances, injuries, lifestyles. In fact, he treated them like a professional manager would a professional team. Young men like Tony McDonald and Robby Breakin boosted their dole money with the now doubled playing allowance; Lucas Mandrake played for the Pitties out of love and with the missionary zeal of his religious calling. Players like Diamond, Breakin and Drummond seemed to realize how well they could play if their strength was used positively, if their aggression focussed on winning the ball fairly. Omar Grant relished the captaincy and showed it in training and in games, able to back up his commands and admonitions with six foot three inches of muscle and a face that was hard to please. Ohara's admiration for the players had also taken him early that morning to the Put'mup Do It Yourself megastore, his local fame and an apology ensuring the manager reinstated Gary Omerod to his job.

Terry Dribble called for silence and passed each player a sheet with the Yattock squad portrayed in their usual playing positions with their height and a pithy comment on their individual skills and dangers. Ohara wondered if Yattock had assessed the danger from the Pitties.

'Goodmouth's the real threat,' Dribble was saying. 'Alert and sharp as a hawk all the time, even when he's not got the ball. He's got height and strength, but his real skill's his control. He drives defenders crackers. He'll hold up the ball in the penalty area, ready to turn and shoot himself or lay it off. The only way to get it off him is to hack him down. He gets a lot of penalties, apparently.'

'So no reckless challenges on the man,' Ohara interrupted.

'So how do we go about tackling him?' big Breakin wondered, speaking for the absent marker, Scott Fisher.

Dribble glanced at coach Ohara for guidance. Ohara sucked in air noisily. The team had come to recognize this peculiarly Japanese slurping to mean the speaker has no bloody idea what to say or do.

'Very difficult. Please hustle him, dance around him. If referee is on blind side, you should . . .'

'Use your discretion,' Terry Dribble guessed for them all.

'Something like that,' Ohara smiled. 'At this moment, we will go with Darren, Omar, Gary and Clint in midfield and Marco up front with Lucas on his left.' He gestured to Taro Suzuki, who was massaging his chest. 'If Taro is recovered enough he will be on the bench with me, Kevin and Mike. Of the four of us only Kevin Stopham is fully fit, and he is a goalkeeper.'

Once upon a time the players would have laughed at the quip. Now they murmured in sympathy.

'Two players have long term leg injuries and Lenny Hampton now has influenza. It gives me only fifteen players for Saturday.' He drew himself up. 'I want complete discipline in holding defensive line, but also personal discipline.' Fixing his eyes on Marco di Rapido before sweeping the musty, steamy room, he said: 'I want no cheap yellow cards for dissent, kicking ball away or bad language at referee. I will not forgive cheap yellow cards. I hope you understand my words.'

'We do, boss, we do,' Grant confirmed. 'Don't we Marco, lads?'

'Yes,' they shouted as one.

'Please continue, Terry.'

Dribble glanced at his notes then pointed at Darren Drummond. 'Their left side of defence is a bit weak so the boss wants us to test it down our right wing.' Everyone looked at Drummond, who looked surprised. Gary Omerod prodded the right sided midfielder. 'Sure, Tel. Got it.'

'I will see what the injury situation is tomorrow and I will talk again before game,' Ohara added in conclusion.

'"I will not forgive cheap yellow cards,"' Billy Pickwich sneered at the nearest Pittie, Lucas Mandrake, in a very bad imitation of Ohara's accent, pulling the skin from the outer edges of his eyes until they became slits. The players were leaving, their breath cloudy as they trooped out of the side gate. 'And what are we doin' with all this fancy tactics stuff?' Pickwich asked loudly. 'They'll be all over us and we'll go to pieces, like we always do under pressure.' Nobody found him funny, and Omar Grant, who was walking behind Pickwich and Mandrake, reached forward and clamped a heavy hand on the taxi driver's shoulder.

'No we fuckin' won't, and if you don't hold the line at the back I'll personally break your fucking neck, even if we're five down at the time. Got that, have yer?'

The wide, coveted car park adjoining the football ground was deserted but for the broadcast technicians' lorries and a scattering of shoppers' cars. Ohara was leaning against his Honda, cigarette between fingers, waiting for the dashboard lighter to pop, when a voice startled him.

'I thought them fags were banned at Pitt Lane.' It was Alf Widdison, returning from a ten hour stint by the canal, rod, chair, net and tackle box lodged in familiar positions about his body. 'Go on, lad, have one,' he said, chuckling. 'I won't tell anybody.'

Ohara returned the old man's smile and offered him a cigarette. When they were lit, he said: 'I always see you by the canal or walking home from it.'

Alf shrugged and released a deep sigh. 'It's warmer out here than in me old house. They've cut off the gas, haven't they?'

'Cut . . .?'

'The gas. I can't cook and can't light the fire. I've got two weeks before they come to evict me by force. The Conthwartons went today, and old Mrs Spector's going on Monday. That'll just leave me on the whole of the bloody Pitt Estate property.'

'Force?' Taking Alf's folded chair and his old canvas army satchel, he set off with him on the short walk home.

'Yes, lad. All appeals have failed, and since I won't move out peacefully they're sending in the bailiffs.'

'They . . . the what?'

'The bailiffs. Men with the legal power to take the house from me.'

'How can they do that?' Ohara wondered.

Alf scoffed, as if talking to an idiot. 'Your pal Broody's behind it, I'm sure of that. He can do what he likes. Got the council in his pocket, ain't he?'

Ohara hummed through a pensive pause then remembered something Alf had said when they first met by the canal. 'I think you were right about the football ground,' he said. 'Mr Broody plans to develop it as well.'

'I expect he'll try,' old Alf said, dropping the tackle box at his front door and fumbling for his keys. 'It'd look bloody ridiculous if you had to put your posh houses and shops around a battered old football ground and car park.' Wheezing at the very thought of it, he managed with uncertain fingers to open the three locks. 'You're welcome to come inside for a cup of tea, lad,' he said. 'I've still got the electric kettle. And there's me father's collection of Pittie memorabilia. You'd like to see that, wouldn't you? Did I tell you me dad, Endymion, played for the Pitties?'

'You did, Mr Widdison,' Ohara said, holding his watch into the pale light from a street lamp. 'And I would very much like to see your father's football souvenirs, but another time. I have to think about Saturday.'

Alf pushed the door over the scuffed edge of a carpet. 'Of course you do. I'll be following the match on me transistor while I'm fishing.'

Ohara was about to turn away when he remembered. Reaching into his jacket he drew out the last of his gift match tickets. 'Mr Widdison. I understand how important the fishing is to you, but would you please be my guest at the semi-final on Saturday?'

The old man stared at the coloured ticket, as if enraptured, or petrified by memories. Finally, he looked into Ohara's slender, oval eyes. 'I wouldn't miss it for the world, lad.'

Ohara walked back to the Pitt Lane car park, Alf Widdison's smile having filled him with so much warmth, temporarily blocking out David Broody and an image of Saturday's carnival from hell. His feeling of well-being lasted precisely 26 minutes.

It was almost ten o'clock when Ohara brought the Honda under the denuded canopy of the lime tree nearest his detached house. Gathering his briefcase, folders and laptop from the rear seat he was not looking out for the two figures emerging from the cover of a tall hedgerow and was startled when two oriental faces filled the driver's window. There was something odd about the hand spread on the glass, but it disappeared before he could see what it was. The larger, squarer of the two faces was flat and pocked with little craters, the nose a bridgeless blimp, the lips thick and rounded, split by a broad, unpleasant smile revealing two rows of uneven, yellowed teeth. His flat head was capped with short, curled, permed hair, the eyes puffed slits. The other face was smaller and rounder, oriental but darker, not Japanese, with wire-rimmed sun glasses and a thin, desperate shadow of a moustache. The two damn paparazzo, Ohara remembered. They'd been tracking him for a couple of days. When he lowered the window the small face gave way to the large.

'Manager Ohara, isn't it?' it said in Japanese. 'We finally catch up with you.' Ohara felt an odd spasm of fear. The Japanese voice was coarse, a thick croak, like a heavy smoker or a *sumo* wrestler with a damaged larynx. Two webs of blunt, rubbery fingers appeared and clamped themselves over the sill of the window. Ohara's breath caught in his chest: the tip of the little finger on the left hand was a stump of cauterized gristle. 'We need to bother you for a few minutes.'

'I'm sorry but it's impossible. I must work. Japanese visitors are welcome at Pitt Lane but—'

The face feigned a yawn 'We've come from afar to pay our respects to Japan's national hero.' The hand slid off the window and snapped open the Honda's door. The man was *yakuza*, a born-to-be-bad gangster, one of about 80,000 affiliated through blood bonds and feudal customs to organized, officially recognized crime syndicates. Violent, nationalistic and high profile, they dealt in drug trafficking, illegal gambling, prostitution, extortion and protection rackets. They also controlled the country's dynamic sex and entertainment industry and, through their white collar wing, blackmailed legitimate top Japanese companies and worked closely with politicians to skim oceans of public funds by helping rig the bidding for lucrative public construction projects. Professional sportsmen with a penchant for *mahjongg*, high-stake golf and a line of cocaine were prime *yakuza* targets in a country where cash was still king, and Ohara had avoided them so far. His luck just ran out. Leading the two men into his English home he wondered what evil karma was at work to bring the *yakuza* across the world to Siddley.

Wearing an open-necked white shirt whose huge collar overlapped the lapels of his rumpled black suit jacket, the *yakuza* slipped off his shoes instinctively. A small rectangular designer purse-like bag, the type beloved of Japanese men, dangled incongruously from a wrist. The short, thin man, carrying a slim, aluminium briefcase, wore his snakeskin loafers into Ohara's living room, where he embedded his sunglasses in the greased wave of his Elvis haircut and looked around with exaggerated admiration at the high ceiling, shag carpet, Windsor chair and homely hearth before sinking into the soft couch with his heavy companion. Ohara's unease overcame the customary requirement to offer tea or stronger refreshment to guests. The Japanese hard man's indelicate fingers unzipped his purse and rummaged inside for cigarettes and a slender wallet. He planted a cigarette in his lips and shook a business card from its case.

'I'm Makino, and this is Mr Ng See Loo, my business colleague from Malaysia. We've come to help you, Mr Japanese Manager.'

'*Gokurosama*,' Ohara said cautiously, taking the card in his fingers as though it were a dead cockroach. 'Thank you for your efforts on my behalf.' Bunsuke Makino, the card read, General Manager, International Division, the Great Japan Prosperity Group. 'I trust you will enjoy the game on Saturday though I may not see you personally.'

'I'm sure we will. *Tokoro de*—'

Ng's short, slender body squirmed on the couch. 'For fuck's sake, Bun, speak English. This is no fucking tea ceremony and he no *geisha*. Just get to business before I fall asleep.' He lifted the silver case onto his knees and thumbed the lock tumblers.

Makino sucked long and gratefully on his cigarette, English words spinning in confusion in his head. 'All of Japan will be watching you on Saturday. The nation is proud.' He waited for an acknowledgement, a response of gratitude or humility in what passes for communication in Japan, even among crooks. The Malaysian Chinese pretended to examine a dog-shaped piece of porcelain on a side table. When Ohara just stared silently from his chair and Makino stared back, his face a vacant landscape, Ng intervened.

'My Japanese friend too polite to give you real opinion about game.' Ohara raised a wrist and held his eyes on the watch. 'What my friend want say is this. It possible you no win game Saturday.'

Ohara was sitting cross-legged in the Windsor chair near the open door. Even for him the truncated, mangled English was barely understandable. 'Excuse me, Mr ... Nur? I—'

'Ng. It possible Siddley United no win Golden Mousetrap semi-final.'

Ohara sighed with fatigue and frustration. 'I would say it is *extremely* possible we will not win tomorrow. If we win it will be a miracle, like Japan winning the next World Cup. So I agree with you. I could almost bet my life on the Pitties not winning against Yattock.'

The two men's face lit up; they raised their hands and smacked out a loud high five. 'Now we all agree,' Ng beamed, returning to face Ohara. 'Game on television all over Asia but specially people in Malaysia will watch it. They like English football very much: Manchester United, Chelsea, Siddley. So they have much fun and bet money on British football.'

'And they bet on the Siddley United–Yattock game?' Ohara said incredulously.

'They bet much money,' Makino guffawed. 'They bet you lose game.' Ohara finally managed a smile, just a weak, almost sarcastic effort. 'Not a very difficult decision for a bet but good luck to you all. I hope you make a big profit.' He looked at his watch again, 'Now, please excuse me, I—'

Makino's fat mouth was open as he framed his next words but the Malaysian Chinese was quicker, 'We know you lose on Saturday, Mr Ohara, but there's more to situation.' His English was staccato clipped, technically deficient, but perfectly and terrifyingly understandable. 'Many my friends in Japan and Malaysia like bet money on your game.'

'I understand,' Ohara said, 'Although it's probably illegal.'

'Fuck law,' Ng See Loo snapped. 'People gamble and when gamble they want win.'

Ohara felt the heat rising to his scalp; his mouth was dry. 'That's natural. As I said, I think you will make a lot of money when we lose on Saturday.'

Ng leaned forward, his arms embracing the case. 'We know you will lose, Mr Ohara, Yattock too good. Pitties shit. But you no understand.' His dangerous feral eyes held Ohara's. 'Hundred million ringit question is, by how much you lose?'

'I don't understand,' Ohara declared honestly.

'My syndicate bet million US dollars you lose by four goals. Four clear goals. We get odds ten to one from stupid Poon syndicate in Kuala Lumpur.' With that Ohara's two visitors broke down into howls of raucous laughter, squeals of unrestrained joy erupting from their heaving, bouncing chests.

Makino's massive body shook uncontrollably. He had to breathe deeply to control the convulsions and speak. 'Old man Poon's going to be one pissed off chink when he has to pay out ten million bucks thanks to the worst footballers in England.' His voice petered out in sobs of delight Ng See Loo wiped a tear with his sleeve, his shoulders still jigging. 'You so bad Yattock score six goals, maybe eight.'

Ohara hadn't moved: the turbulence was all in his head. 'I wish you luck again,' he managed.

'Luck no good only. We need insurance,' Ng barked, suddenly deadly serious. 'Can't take stupid chance with luck. He flicked the briefcase's clasps. The lid sprang open.

Ohara watched as the case was turned slowly in his direction, then froze upright when new, $100 bills appeared in level heaps and rows. Ohara could hear his heart pounding in his chest: his grasp on reality was beginning to slip. Mouth open, he stood up and took two steps forward until he was standing over the briefcase and its grey green contents. Something told him they were not real, that he was being conned by a pair of '*chimpira*' with the old cut-up newspaper trick. He reached down, as if driven by an invisible force, determined to expose them before he called the police. A bound bunch of bank notes slipped easily in his grip. They were all real bills. He grabbed another stack and flicked it. Real notes too. As a disbelieving, rictus grin formed on his face, a flash lit up the room. His head spun. Bunsuke Makino was holding a small digital camera to his face.

'*Sugoi!*' he proclaimed. 'Wonderful! Such a sincere smile holding the money. I didn't even have to say "cheese".'

'What are you doing?' Trapped in a nightmare with no exit, Ohara dropped the money, looking at one man and then the other for an explanation.

There was no more back-slapping mirth from Ng. His eyes narrowed to invisible slivers, his face muscles twitched. 'Mr Japanese manager. You just dirty your fingers on fifty thousand US dollars.'

'I only wanted to—'

'About six million yen,' Bunsuke Makino said helpfully in Japanese.

Ng lifted a small key from a shirt pocket. 'Fifty thousand dollars and this key.' Dropping it among the notes, he snapped the briefcase shut and jumbled the three tumblers. Placing the case on the floor, he turned to Ken Ohara again, who watched with open-mouthed astonishment. 'The combination to this case is zero four zero. Easy remember, right? That key fits coin locker in Siddley railway station. Inside, you find identical case with another fifty thousand dollars.' He gestured at the briefcase on the floor. 'This for you. How to say? A down payment for kind cooperation. When game ends tomorrow, I call, give you combination of case in locker.'

'You know exactly what you must do to earn one hundred thousand dollars, don't you?' Makino asked in Japanese.

'This is crazy,' Ohara said finally, clutching the sides of his head in desperation. 'This is not happening to me. I am not taking bribes.'

Ng brought his face close to Ohara's. Revolted by the reek of stale breath, the Pitties' manager stepped back, into the broad, immovable body of Bunsuke Makino. Ng closed in again. 'You have this money to make sure crap players do right thing Saturday,' Ng scowled. 'For start, you buy goalkeeper for thousand bucks.'

Ohara pulled himself free and sank onto the couch. 'I can't do these things,' he stuttered in Japanese.

'What he say?' Ng demanded from Makino.

'He wants to know what happens if Yattock don't win by four clear goals.'

Ng scoffed. 'Tell him.'

The *yakuza* scowled. 'When we get our money back and your arms and legs have healed, the Japanese and British media will get the picture of you holding the money over the briefcase. They'll like the big smile on your face.'

'So good luck on Saturday,' the Malaysian grinned, taking Makino's cigarette stub and grinding it into the carpet. 'We watch you from seat.'

8

Ken-ichi Ohara twisted, thrashed and hallucinated. His night was a deep, black hole lined with jagged glass. When he came round in the thin light filtering through the flock curtains he was shivering under damp sheets. In one cosmic scene he was playing in the Golden Mousetrap Trophy semi-final, his opponents legless *sumo* wrestlers wielding samurai swords. It had all seemed so real, and as he clung to the stair-rail and stumbled into the living room, he held the thinnest, stupidest of hopes that the Japanese gangster and the Malaysian gambler who had travelled across the world to buy him or destroy him were just devilish characters in his nightmares. He could not remember them leaving, or whether he'd pursued them and thrown the case of money after them, but he hadn't gone back to his match planning because his bag, folders and laptop were untouched on the hall table. He opened the living room door gingerly, a silent prayer on his lips. His eyes fell on the briefcase, onto the carpet where Ng See Loo had dropped the massive stash contemptuously. He sank to his knees and wished to die.

Staring into the bathroom mirror, he was looking at his future. The recipient of everyone's unfettered praise and adoration, the mastermind of Siddley's finest sporting postwar moments, he was now the pivot, the golden key, in a multi-million dollar international gambling scam. If the

Pitties drew, or won, or lost by less than four clear goals, a million real dollars was lost for ever by some very dangerous men and a potential opportunity profit of ten million forfeited. Ohara would then be broken literally, and when the photo of him clutching a fistful of dollars was published in Japan and Britain he'd be destroyed professionally, ruined by inference and innuendo. However much he'd try to explain the instinctive grin on his face as he fingered the money he'd just be digging the grave deeper, burying forever his reputation and prospects. Political and corporate corruption was endemic in his homeland, bribery a national pastime, but he wasn't just another petty participant unlucky enough to be exposed. He was an icon, a national hero, a standard bearer for Japan. He splashed water on his face but he was shaking so much over the basin he dared not risk the razor's caress around his carotid artery.

Hunger eluded him, but he managed a piece of unbuttered toast with coffee. He ignored the English daily where, in the sports section, he'd have found a photo of himself in a story entitled: 'High Noon for Siddley's Samurai'. He gathered his boots and shin pads and was looking for socks in a drawer when he found he had brought an old used blue and white Japanese national team shirt with his name in the roman alphabet and the number six on it. He put it in his sports bag and left for Pitt Lane just after ten, the briefcase with the $50,000 under a pile of logs in the garden shed. Passing an estate of stark council blocks, he wondered if old Alf Widderson was destined for a cell in one of the stacked up high-rises, not a canal or river in sight beyond the tangle of disused railway lines or the scrubby, neglected, rubbish-strewn waste land. Still, he had his own problems, not the least the threat of physical damage and professional ruination. Should he throw himself on the mercy of British justice or should he do nothing and play the game as competitively as possible? Then there was always the *samurai* way to oblivion . . .

Pulling into the Pitt Lane car-park he tapped his head with the heel of a hand as if he could dislodge a solution. He was slumped in the driver's seat, wearing the vacant smile of a man who failed to find a single reason why he shouldn't run a hose in the car from the exhaust pipe, when a persistent tap on the window shook him alert. His heart jumped in his chest.

It was Monique, who had drawn alongside him in her red compact, her smile like a tropical sunrise. 'Two thousand three hundred stand tickets sold already,' she beamed, seizing his arm as they walked to the ground. 'There'll be thousands at Pitt Lane tomorrow.'

Ohara sighed, smiling politely. He thought of 40 million Japanese, about a third of the population, who'd see him on the satellite relay, inspired to watch, even at midnight. He saw absolutely no reason to live any longer.

David Broody was there to meet the board directors, easing their suspicion by greeting them solicitously. To the surprise of the chairman and his three fellow directors, Sir Reginald Pitt, usually a stranger to his ancestor's treasured gift, was already in attendance. No doubt the honorary president saw the temporary attention of the sporting world, or at least the Japanese bit of it, on Siddley was not an opportunity the local toff should miss. Reacting to Broody's urgent summons, the directors had all arrived at Pitt Lane within a few minutes of 10.30a.m., the chairman appropriately first.

Though death obeyed no timetable, Walter Hardcastle's Fridays were usually quiet ahead of the weekend burial and burn rush. It was a time to ponder the transience of life, thumb a trade magazine or two, perhaps drop in to the Carmel Street warehouse and test the interior of a new line of coffins or caskets with his own formidable body. What could be so urgent the day before the Pitties' greatest day? Somewhere, deep down inside his rotund frame, an ache of trepidation stirred. The predators were circling his beloved Pitt Lane, but thanks to the generous, inviolable legacy from Sir Abraham Pitt, God bless him, they would be thwarted.

Harry Patel was most reluctant to surrender a Friday morning, however big the football occasion. The three days from Friday generated mega-income from his super-sports stores around Siddley. Exiled from Uganda 30 years ago, it had taken him only five to build a business empire around his own-brand sportswear and sports goods. The walls of his private offices inside the Patel mansion in Frizams were graced with business and charity awards from the city of Siddley, the local chamber of commerce, the Rotary Club and the Department of Trade and Industry. He had bought a stake in the Pitties for selfish, promotional reasons, but over the years, as their fortunes declined and his soared, he had come to love the club and its ground, its genteel decay, a reminder of an England that was once great, that had colonized the India of his ancestors and then left it like a weary parent.

Councillor Ronald Townrow, his lean body encased in a charcoal grey, three piece suit, his dyed hair creamed and slick, arrived in ebullient mood, having just finalized the historic visit tomorrow of Siddley City's lady mayor to Pitt Lane, where she would record an interview for Japanese television and watch the game from the directors' box. How well it all reflected on Townrow, influential member of Siddley city council and senior partner in the city's largest firm of solicitors, and how long would it be before an overdue royal honour of some sort was forthcoming? With his lawyer's expertise, it was Ronald Townrow who had engineered the takeover that realized the dreams of himself, Walter Hardcastle, Harry Patel and Geoffrey Osborne when they bought their share-holdings in Siddley United FC, thus becoming trustees and guardians, with Sir Reginald, of the century-old Pitt legacy.

Panting hoarsely, shoulders hunched and hips propped precariously on a walking stick, Geoffrey Osborne hobbled behind Ronald Townrow and sat down at the boardroom table with a coffee cup in the tenuous grasp of his arthritic fingers. The effort had left the last few strands of his ratty hair plastered to the damp, liver-spotted dome of his head. Seventy-one now, he'd sat on the terraces at Pitt Lane when an apprentice butcher in his father's shop, sometimes crying, not from the merciless teasing of others but because he couldn't play football or any sport that required speed and agility. But he knew his carcasses. He'd learned about cuts and ageing and recovering offal and, more importantly, the special ways of the meat trade. He eventually took over the business, opened more shops and built cold-storage facilities for the wholesale business that brought the family its real wealth. They did say, though, that he was only really happy when he was sitting in the directors' box at Pitt Lane, watching his heroes in lime green and tangerine on a January Saturday afternoon.

'What a weekend it's going to be,' David Broody said matter-of-factly, drawing a bunch of thin folders from his briefcase, Sir Reggie Pitt safely to his right, Walter Hardcastle in his familiar leather chair. 'We're all very busy people so I'll get to the point,' he said sharply.

'Please,' Harry Patel urged. 'You know what Fridays are like in the retail trade.'

'I do, Harry, I do,' the property man replied, selecting a folder, 'This won't take long.'

'I hope so.' It was the city councillor, Ronald Townrow.

'We need to get out there and mix with the media people. Show them the elite of Siddley are behind the team, all the way to the final.'

'Hear, hear,' Walter Hardcastle intoned. 'Now then. I declare this extraordinary meeting of the board of Siddley United Football Club open. You'll be taking minutes, no doubt, David?'

Broody smiled icily. 'No minutes today and, Ronald, there ain't going to be a Golden Mousetrap Trophy final for the Pitties.' The directors huffed, looked at each other and mumbled their surprise.

The tumblers in Harry Patel's brain spun, searching for Broody's number. 'We probably won't win but Ken Ohara's made sure we'll make a game of it.'

'Let me explain,' Broody said benevolently, flashing a cold smile and clearing his throat for effect. 'Six years ago you gentlemen asked me to run this football club. As a civic duty, if you will, return something to the city.' Sir Reginald Pitt fiddled self-consciously with his signet ring while the others nodded appreciatively. 'You are all self-made men, apart from you, Reggie. You all sit on charities, you vote conservative, you stand up for the national anthem and you sometimes go to church. Or your temple, or whatever, Harry. But sadly, unlike you lot, I am not part of Siddley United out of love for a century of tradition.'

'I'm slowly beginning to understand,' Harry Patel said ruefully.

'Well, I'm not.' It was Geoffrey Osborne.

'Nor me.' The chairman's perplexed face was a mass of quivering purple folds. 'We own the shares in the club out of our deep affection for it but we don't ask for dividends. Pitt Lane is the cherished heart of Siddley.'

Broody huffed. 'And as you know, Walter, this ground and car park are part of the Pitt Estate. And next week, when the Pitt Lane Arms serves its last pint and the last few slum-dwelling old cranks are carried screaming to the geriatric wards where they belong, the housing estate will be entirely empty.'

'And it will be demolished,' Harry Patel declared knowingly.

'Completely. I prefer to call it slum clearance.' Broody gestured to the city councillor. 'Thanks to Ronald's influence with the council's urban planning committee, approval has been readily forthcoming.'

'And who is this brave acquirer of a million tons of Siddley rubble?' Geoffrey Osborne wondered with a resigned smirk. Sir Reginald cleared his throat against the back of his hand.

'An offshore property company, I believe,' Townrow said sheepishly, thin eyebrows raised.

Broody lowered his eyes modestly. 'That's me, of course. I effectively own the Pitt estate, at least for the time being.'

Geoffrey Osborne raised an arm in tribute. 'Good luck to you, lad. This city needs people like you with the guts to look to the future.' Then he sniffed pensively and said: 'But all that machinery and rubble's going to make access to the football ground and the car park very awkward for the fans and shoppers.' Staring ahead, at an old photo on the boardroom wall, Harry Patel's fine, dark features cracked into an imperceptible smile.

'Quite,' Broody agreed, removing several sheets of paper from a folder. 'Which brings me to the very subject. 'I'll pass a three dimensional sketch around later, but let me tell what I've got in mind for our city centre.' Tapping the paper, he began: 'The area now occupied by the slums will be transformed into a triangular shaped development of three-floor executive townhouses and an upmarket shopping mall. My *pièce de résistance* consists of two state-of-the-art, intelligent towers, one containing a luxury hotel, restaurant complex with leisure facilities, the second comprising a business and financial centre for cutting edge enterprises.' He paused and smiled at a spot on the table. 'Of course, I can't guarantee prime space to an undertaker, a butcher or a purveyor of cheap running shoes.' Before any indignation erupted, Broody continued, 'Pitt Lane will henceforth be known as the DB Global Exchange Plaza, in keeping with the aspirations of our city in the twenty-first century.'

A short silence followed, broken finally by Walter Hardcastle's rattling saucer. 'Forgive me my ignorance of local property matters, David, and I'm sure DB doesn't stand for daft bugger.' Hardcastle was struggling for the right words. 'You'll have done your sums, I know, and the Pitt Estate's a chunky piece of land, but it's not that big, if you see what I mean.'

'I don't quite follow . . .'

'Like, where exactly would you fit two bloody great towers?'

'Thirty-two floors in each, actually,' Broody said with pride, holding up the drawing in his fingertips. 'The DB Global Exchange Plaza will be situated here, exactly where we're sitting, on what is now the football pitch and the car park.'

The moment's silence that fell over the room was broken by Geoffrey Osborne's slight but chronic, chesty wheeze. Then Walter Hardcastle made a calming gesture with his hands and turned to Broody, his face twisted in a dismissive smile. 'It has probably slipped your mind, David, but the land on which this ground and the car park is situated is protected by a special covenant which prevents its use for commercial or any other purposes.' Three other heads nodded in agreement. Sir Reginald Pitt stared at the wall. 'We, the shareholders, are the trustees of that covenant,' Hardcastle proceeded, like a triumphant cock. 'The guardians of Sir Abraham Pitt's beneficence.' Broody leaned back in the chair, removed his glasses and pretended to examine them for dust. Hardcastle turned to Sir Abraham's grandson. 'Is that not so, Reggie? This land belongs to the football club for ever.'

Sir Reginald was trapped between closing doors. Was Broody serious when he'd said he could make the board sell their shares in the club to him, or was he bluffing? If it was a bluff, he'd failed. Steepling his fingers, he spoke cautiously, avoiding Broody's eyes. 'It's certainly how the Pitt family have always seen the situation, but it's not carved in tablets of stone.'

'Precisely, Reggie,' Broody said. 'It's not written down at all, on stone or anything else. In my opinion, Siddley United own the land and you four gentlemen, the shareholders, own Siddley United. You are free to dispose of it whenever you wish.'

'I honestly think we've heard enough, David,' the chairman declared. 'We wish you well with your development venture when you've cleared the old estate but now let's just leave Ken Ohara to get on with taking this football club into the Golden Mousetrap Trophy final.' He grasped the plush arm rests on his chair, as if to stand.

Broody sprang up and strode behind Hardcastle, gently easing the undertaker back into the seat. 'You'd better hear me out, Walter, because Siddley United won't be the same when I've finished.'

'Oh, all right,' Hardcastle conceded. 'But make it quick. I've got to put Mrs Thorpe together before the party tonight. Plate glass can do terrible things to a body.'

Broody returned to his chair and stood with his hands on the back. 'Buying the old houses has almost bankrupted me,' he told the board, pausing dramatically. 'But who would be so foolish as to buy a multi-million pound rubbish tip purely on speculation? Certainly not David Broody. No. A reputable investment syndicate represented by a prime

City merchant bank will buy the property from the current owner, namely me, and I will lease it back and turn the heart of Siddley into a major commercial and financial centre.'

'It's a brilliant scheme,' said a flustered Ronald Townrow, 'but what's it got to do with the football club? As Walter says, the ground can't be part of your global thing.' Hardcastle and Osborne nodded vigorously.

Harry Patel sighed. 'What David is trying to say,' he explained, 'is that the sale of the Pitt Estate will not go ahead unless the land this club stands on and the car park are included in the deal.'

'But that's imposs—' the chairman started to say.

'Walter,' Patel said patiently. 'Be quiet. Let him explain.'

'Thank you, Harry,' Broody said, his smile poisonous. 'You are absolutely right. No football ground and car park, no deal, me dead broke.' And perhaps dead, like Walter Hardcastle's clients, he thought, seeing in his mind's eye the icy visage of Boris Rakov and a very large bodyguard. He let them brood while he pierced the tip of a Havana cigar and singed the business end with his gold lighter. Finally, swiping away a fug of smoke, he said: 'We've always assumed the ground to be inviolable, not for sale, ever, but there's no legal evidence to that effect. I have found nothing which legally substantiates the claim that Reggie's grandfather left this land to Siddley United in perpetuity, neither has Reggie. On the contrary, he is prepared to state under oath that his grandfather made a proviso to the effect that the land could indeed be sold if the Pitties failed to win a trophy within a hundred years of its foundation.'

Sir Reginald hid his 'am I?' expression admirably. The other directors were stunned.

'This is our centenary year and the trophy cabinet is still bare so, gentlemen, your final act as directors of Siddley United will be to sell your shareholdings to me. My accountants have prepared a realistic valuation and my lawyers have drawn up the legal documentation.'

It took a few moments for the finality of Broody's ultimatum to penetrate, but finally Walter Hardcastle, seeing the disbelief and revulsion on the faces of his fellow directors said: 'Have you no shame at all? Ken Ohara is working his heart out. Do you seriously wish his efforts should end in failure?'

'Elvis will turn up in the cathedral before the Pitties win tomorrow aftenoon, but I admit the lad's done much better than I thought he would when I picked him,' Broody conceded.

'What do you mean, when *you* picked? I am the chairman of this football club. I and the directors pick the managers.'

'Walter, Walter. Please. You chaps are so occupied running the city you're too busy to pick your own noses, let alone run this club. I can't recall you rejecting any proposal I made for signing players or buying paperclips. I deliberately put the Japanese's file in front of you instead of the Irishman, who had too much of a pedigree for my liking, and you fell for it. You almost choked, Walter, when you met Ken-ichi Ohara instead of Kenneth O'Hara.'

A veil began to lift, revealing a frightening truth. Geoffrey Osborne said: 'Moby McNally didn't fall for it, did he? He fell in it. Did he refuse to help you destroy the club so you helped him follow the lost football into the canal?'

Broody shrugged and presented a thin smile for their interpretation.

They were stunned, until finally Walter Hardcastle spluttered alive, allowing himself, amid his simmering anger, a faint smirk of satisfaction. 'Even if you're right about the ground and the car park, and you most certainly aren't, you'd need a majority shareholding in the club before you could act on its behalf, and you'll never get my fifty per cent, nor the shares of my fellow directors.' He received the nods of Patel, Osborne and Townrow and returned his gaze to Broody. 'You're howling at the moon if you think we would ever betray the birthright of generations of Siddley citizen to a cheap, nasty, murdering property speculator. I take your preposterous remarks as your statement of resignation, which we all accept.'

Broody drew deeply on the cigar. 'Do you see it this way, Reggie?' he asked the honorary club president. 'As guardian of the Pitt name, title and legacy?'

The baronet squirmed; his forehead was beaded with sweat. 'Not really, David. I think that history has taken its course and it's time to move on.'

'It sounds like David's already got your twenty per cent share tucked into his pocket,' Harry Patel opined. 'We have the other eighty so you don't have to be an accountant to know we win. The Pitties stay at Pitt Lane. On their ancestral land.'

'Can we can go now?' Geoffrey Osborne asked the room. 'They're slaughtering a herd in Moxbottom this afternoon and I don't want to be late for the meat auction.'

'Not yet, Geoffrey,' Broody said, resuming his seat and drawing the other folders to him, each with a name on the cover. 'I didn't want it to be like this but you give me no choice. He looked at Harry Patel and selected a file. 'Let's start with you, Harry, since you've just hit Reggie below the belt. Pass this to Harry, will you?' he commanded Ronald Townrow, sliding an enlarged photograph along the table, Osborne leaned forward, catching the image of a smiling child as the monochrome picture turned on the polished surface.

Patel studied it cursorily and showed an angry face to Broody. 'If you're suggesting I'm a paedophile I'll sue the Armani off your back.'

'Harry, Harry, calm yourself. Nobody's saying that at all.

Heaven forbid. Just look at the picture and tell me what you see.'

Patel saw the head and T-shirted torso of a boy leaning against a desk. Behind him sat other children, their heads lowered over a long table, working at machines. The boy's small, dark face was stretched into a huge, innocent smile, only his eyes betraying the weariness usually found in people much older. Broody released a spiral of smoke towards the elaborate crystal chandelier, cleared his throat and said: 'Do you know him, Harry? The young lad in the picture?'

Patel threw a wayward glance at his Rolex. 'Honestly, David, I just don't have time for games on a Friday morning.'

'Of course you don't. Forgive me. I'll be brief. The boy's name is Lao. You can just about read his name on the badge on his shirt.' Broody glanced at his notes. 'Lao is twelve years old and he's production supervisor in a factory on the outskirts of Phnom Penh, the capital of Cambodia. Behind Lao you can see the workers he supervises. Lao is the oldest by two years.'

'Where is all this going?' Walter Hardcastle wondered aloud. 'We're busy men.' Harry Patel stared ahead.

'I'll tell you,' Broody proclaimed, producing a piece of paper from the folder. 'Little Lao's team constructs the Super Patelina Rocket, which, according to this advertising blurb is a top-of-the-range, air-cushioned, stability-sensitized, state-of-the-art running shoe for the jogger or professional runner. It retails in Britain for seventy-six pounds.' He tilted his face to the chandelier. 'Lao gets one pound seven pence for his efforts. Lao works for Harry Patel.'

The Ugandan Asian looked long at the picture of the grinning child. Walter Hardcastle produced a reproachful expression; Geoffrey Osborne coughed, hump throbbing;

Ronald Townrow huffed self-righteously. 'This could be any kid, anywhere,' Patel said finally, shifting on the seat. 'And Asians look a lot younger than they really are.'

Broody examined the smouldering tip of his cigar. 'Not this lad, Harry.' He held up a second photo. 'This is the factory door. Actually, factory's a bit flattering. It's an old Cambodian airforce hanger, no air-conditioning, of course. The name-plate says Speedfoot Aerotronics, which I understand is listed in the accounts of Consolidated Patel as a wholly-owned subsidiary. Correct me if I'm wrong, Harry, but Lao and his little mates most certainly do work for you, twelve hours a day, six days a week.' Patel's neck was hot and damp. Broody removed his glasses with slow, theatrical intent. 'I'm with you all the way, Harry. I'm an entrepreneur, like you. If I were in manufacturing I'd go straight into a Chinese maternity ward and recruit my workers young, before they got any silly ideas about human rights and minimum wages. But I'm not, Harry, and what you're doing in Cambodia is unethical and, sadly, very illegal. So this is the bottom line. You are in breach of British law, European Union legislation, United Nations directives on child labour and everything we, as caring people, believe compassionately in. What will Paul McCartney do, and the *Guardian*, and all those other fucking carrot-eating do-gooders, when they see one of Britain's finest businessmen employs child slave labour? You could be kicked out of the Siddley Rotary Club, and that would be the least of your problems.'

Harry Patel leaned into the soft leather and contemplated the chandelier, his fingers entwined. 'So my ten per cent's the price of your silence?'

'I wouldn't put it as crudely as that, Harry, but yes. With Reggie's twenty that gives me a clean thirty per cent share in the club, and I'm sure my friends and colleagues around this table will join me in guarding your nasty little secret.'

'Now just a minute.' It was Geoffrey Osborne, his domed

head bobbing. 'I sympathize absolutely with Harry's predicament and I condemn your blackmailing tactics. But we've got our reputations to think about. Where would it leave *us* if all this got out?'

'In the shit, Geoffrey. Deep in the shit. So we are all here to make sure it doesn't.' He funnelled another plume of smoke towards the ceiling, then lowered his eyes onto Siddley's most prominent purveyor of meat products. Another folder spread. Osborne's hump felt like a sack of lead on his back.

'Don't tell me there's more of this nonsense,' Walter Hardcastle wondered. The others seemed mesmerized by a photograph slithering towards Geoffrey Osborne. His pigeon chest rested on the rim of the table, his wrinkled stiff fingers spread painfully. He was staring at the enlarged photo of a medium sized white transport vehicle parked against a raised loading bay.

'What do you see there, Geoffrey?' Broody asked, tapping his cigar into the glass ashtray. 'Something familiar?' Except for Sir Reginald, the others craned to see. 'Since you're all interested, I can tell you Geoff's looking at a photo of a plain, unmarked refrigerated van.' Two more pictures crossed the table. 'That one was taken a few seconds after the first. You can tell from the time sequence at the bottom.' The second showed the top of the lorry now level with the awning over the loading bay. The words on the angled roof read: Pampered Pets of Preston. 'Now look at the third photo.' The same place, the van at the bay, but a figure present, his head hidden by the stiff, truncated limbs on a skinned half carcass of meat balanced across a shoulder. 'Notice he's walking towards the open doors of the van.'

'I think I've seen enough,' Osborne declared, pushing the photos away from him.

Broody slapped the table, causing Walter Hardcastle to

wince. 'You haven't Geoffrey, by God, you haven't. I had that van followed from Preston. It turned off the main road at Molecroft and drove up to the reservoir. It was dark by then and bloody hard for my man to keep up. He left his car and followed them into the woods. He got lucky.' He held up the fourth photo. 'This lucky. That's the back of the white van from Preston on the right, parked parallel to a darker van. Can you see the letters on the rear door, Geoffrey?' He offered the photo but Osborne stayed with his hands overlapping, his eyes vacantly fixed on the table. 'You can't read it completely because the right hand door's open, but am I right in guessing the OSB is Osborne, the IMPE, Imperial and ME, Meat? Osborne Imperial Meat, perhaps? Meat went from the white van to the other transit, which was sky blue. Your fleet's sky blue, isn't it, Geoff? I didn't know the Osborne empire included a pet food processing unit. Otherwise, where was that meat, no doubt deemed unfit for human consumption from Pampered Pets of Preston, going?'

'Don't go on, you bastard,' Osborne hissed, his tortured body shaking.

'Have you been putting rotten meat in them lovely game and herb sausages?' Walter Hardcastle clucked, in a voice brimming with mild outrage.

'Not just once,' Broody said, flipping the folder for effect. 'I've been tracking those shipments of maggot fodder for six months. And good investigators don't come cheap.' He leaned across the table and glared at Geoffrey Osborne. 'What's your motto, Geoffrey? Prime cuts for prime people, isn't it? I won't even bother to spell out the fourteen European Union health regulations you have deliberately chosen to ignore and break, conviction for which could not only close you down but put you in prison.'

'But it won't, will it?' Head lowered, Harry Patel was talking to no one in particular. 'Because David's just got hold of another ten per cent of the shares in Siddley United Football Club.'

Sir Reginald Pitt dabbed his broad forehead with the back of his hand. He looked from Walter Hardcastle to Ronald Townrow. 'Perhaps you gentlemen can find yourselves ready to surrender your holdings to David as well. Now that we all understand the situation.'

'The man's a viper,' Ronald Townrow blurted, 'and you're not much better, Reggie, selling your birthright so that David can make a monument to himself, and a fortune. It looks like he's got forty per cent but he's not having my ten at any price.'

It was the wrong thing to say at the wrong moment. The third folder would probably have stayed unopened if the lawyer had surrendered then and there.

'Councillor Ronald Townrow,' Broody intoned, as if presenting the royal award Townrow so desperately coveted. 'If one had to identify a Mr Siddley from all those illustrious and industrious people who have served our community in the last fifty years it would have to be you. From primary to grammar school you were always top achiever, and after national service in the army and a first class honours degree at university the legal profession beckoned. But you didn't become any old solicitor. Partner in a major city practice at thirty-three, senior partner at forty, Law Society man-of-the year, Siddley Rotary Club chairman. The list goes on. Prominent city councillor for thirty years and director of Siddley United, And not forgetting your rock, the blessed Mabel, the mother of your twins, Gretchen and Portia. What more can I say about your exemplary life?'

'Then don't try,' Ronald Townrow declared, pushing back his chair and brushing an imaginary speck off his lapel. 'Let's all go back to work.'

A shadow seemed to descend over David Broody's face and a large photo emerged from a new folder. Four pairs of eyes followed it along the table to Townrow, who looked away disdainfully. 'I'm not standing for this nonsense. I'm going to the police. I'll instruct the best barristers in Britain to defend my friends Harry and Geoffrey if you dare try to expose them.'

'They're already exposed, Ronald, now that you, a legal practitioner, and the others here know about their misdemeanours. You are all accomplices in a conspiracy to cover up crimes, should you choose to ignore them.'

'Bastard,' Townrow uttered under his breath.

Catching sight of two women in the latest photo, Patel patted Townrow's wrist. 'Having a girlfriend on the side's not a crime, Ronny. It's not as if you're a gun runner or, let's say, an exploiter of children.' The women in Councillor Townrow's photo were filmed at night from behind, holding each other's outstretched hands and about to enter a door. Both were slim, one a head taller than the other, with expansive hair reaching their shoulders. With dainty handbags dangling from straps, they both wore close-fitting, short, one-piece dresses and high heels. The door in front of them was slightly open, and the shadowy profile of a face could be seen in the gap between the two women.

'You sly old devil,' the humiliated Osborne said, without humour or malice. He would willingly bear two humps if he could swap his crime for Townrow's peccadillo.

'It won't look good for you in the papers, Ronald,' Patel told the lawyer. 'If it gets out, that is. What is it? A strip club? Singles bar? Ronald? Ronny?'

Ronald Townrow sat primly upright and motionless in the chair, hands together in his lap. If one possessed the ability to terminate life by sheer willpower Ronald Townrow yearned to discover it within himself now.

'Which one's yours, Ronny?' Sir Reginald wanted to know. Witnessing the slow torture of Siddley's finest had cheered the impoverished baronet beyond all expectation.

'The filly on the left's got a lovely, pert little bottom, I bet she's the one you've been rutting with on the side. What's Mabel going to say when she finds out?'

David Broody hid his contempt for the indolent squire of Pitt Manor. 'You're almost right,' he told Pitt. 'But Mabel knows all about it.'

'I find that hard to believe,' Pitt declared. 'Knowing Mabel as I do.'

Broody sighed. 'It's perfectly true, isn't it Ronny? Mabel knows about you and she doesn't care.' Townrow's head dropped.

'How on earth could you know something so personal?' Walter Hardcastle wanted to know, his voice fill of derision. 'Mabel would never condone Ronald's infidelity. She's a Methodist, for goodness' sake.'

Broody scoffed. 'You don't quite understand, Walter. We're not talking about infidelity. The person on the left with the nice arse is not Ronny's girlfriend. It's Ronny.'

Penetrating the long window and the sudden sepulchral silence of the boardroom, came the sound of blunted hammering. The final advertising hoarding was being secured to the venerable Pitt Lane woodwork bordering the Canal Stand fence.

'Bloody 'ell,' somebody said.

Finally, Walter Hardcastle reached for the photo. 'It-it doesn't make sense,' he spluttered. They were talking about a man he'd known for 30 years. Or not known. 'How can you possibility tell it's Ronald in the dress?'

Broody extracted a second picture from the folder and passed it to the club chairman. 'This is two hours later. You can see the time at the bottom, with the date. Recognize the dress? It is now leaving the place, a little private club in Chupworth called Panty Pose. The wig's pretty big and the make-up could be a little less brazen, but I think you, and the good people of Siddley, will recognize that little nose and the thin, kissable mouth as that of their eminent citizen, Councillor Ronald Townrow.' He was speaking as if the solicitor did not exist. 'His friend in the photo, by the way, and fellow transvestite, is Bert Armitage, a farmer from Moxbottom.' He waited for the second picture to make a circuit of the table, then said: 'When did it start, I wonder? Living with Mabel and the twin girls and their scattered clothes probably aroused a mischievous gene and gave him the chance to experiment. He obviously liked it. My investigator tells me that lovely cerise dress in the picture was bought by Mabel at Ramleigh's with Ronald in attendance. Mabel is the shape of a large beer keg, you'll recall, so he thought it must be for a daughter, until, that is, only Ronald entered the changing room. So you see, Mabel actually supports her husband's little diversion. And why not? Why jeopardize such an envied position in society just because hubby likes to wear panty hose and under-wired stuffed bras occasionally? Of course, what the people in his church, the Law Society, his clients and the council will make of it is anyone's guess.'

Mouth tightly closed, Ronald Townrow began to breath noisily, air exiting his nose in short snorts, his slight frame rising and falling with the effort. Finally, he could not contain his emotions any longer, and the sobs emerged in short, jerky bursts that caught in his throat.

Walter Hardcastle reached across with an understanding pat on Townrow's arm, careful not to leave his hand there too long. 'There, there, Ronald.' Turning a florid, angry countenance to Broody he said: 'You will immediately hand over all those dreadful pictures and walk out of this prestigious football ground for ever.'

Broody scoffed, a sarcastic guffaw, full of contempt and derision. 'You can have the pictures now if you want,' he said. 'And when I have all the shares you five possess in

Siddley United you can have the negatives. The transfers will take place on Monday.'

Geoffrey Osborne's lopsided face leaned over the table. 'If my lad, Ian, were here with his industrial cleaver I swear he'd have your bloody head off, Broody.'

Harry Patel raised a hand to subdue the hubbub and the wailing. 'If my assumptions and calculations are right, David, you've got three of us over a barrel, giving you thirty per cent of the shares, and you get another twenty per cent by dint of Reggie's personal treachery. That's only fifty per cent. Walter's got the other fifty and you could tear him limb from limb before he'd sell them to you.' Patel knew he was dooming the chairman even as he spoke and his words trailed to a pointless mumble when he saw Broody's hand move slowly and inexorably to the final unopened folder.

Hardcastle saw the movement too. 'This has gone far enough.' His bellow of rage was curtailed by a painful rippling in his diseased chest. 'Gentlemen, please leave the room while I sort out Mister bloody Broody.' No-one moved: perhaps they shared a perverse desire to know what skeletons the undertaker kept in his cupboard as well as in his graves.

Broody stubbed the cigar in the glass ashtray. 'You were a tough one to crack, Walter. You're so committed to your work as Siddley's disposer of the dead you don't have much time for outside interests, let alone nefarious ones. And you don't have the face or the body to be a womanizer. But there had to be something. I know for a fact some of your business practices stretch the boundaries of ethical practice. You seem to be the first to know where traffic accident victims are taken, courtesy, I think, of your regular little gifts to the ambulance service; you keep well in with Siddley's old people's homes, a cash reward every time they refer a grieving relative towards Hardcastle and Sons; and a lot of friendly doctors make sure you are aware of imminent demises on their patches.'

'You're being absurd,' Hardcastle scoffed. 'There's nothing illegal in anything I've done.'

Broody look hurt. 'I know that, Walter, I know that. 'You're not just a brilliant undertaker you're a frontier breaking entrepreneur. Your CPP profiling data is visionary as well as revolutionary.'

'What's CPP profiling?' Sir Reggie interrupted.

Broody checked his notes. 'It stands for Client Pre-Expiration Profile.' Using his carefully nurtured contacts in the social services, the medical profession and the retirement homes, Walter has built up a computer data base of almost everybody in Siddley and the county over fifty years of age. It tracks their social status, property ownership, financial assets, surgical history and chronic diseases, principal heirs and a few other things that enable him to have the hearse parked outside the home or hospital before the body's gone cold. It works. He holds the record for undertaker of the month title in *Coffin and Casket* and he's twice been on the cover of the *Embalming Times*.'

'Thank you,' Hardcastle said, allowing the flicker of a bitter-sweet smile to cross his face, but feeling the heat welling on his scalp. 'But I've given quite a bit back to the community.'

'Indeed you have Walter.' Broody's hand slipped inside the covers of a beige folder. Hardcastle's less than robust heart momentarily hesitated. 'You have been known to donate a coffin so that the council can dignify the cremation of a pauper or an ex-serviceman fallen on hard times. A coffin like this one, perhaps.' Broody shifted an enlargement to the club chairman. It came from a brochure and showed a plain, darkish, classical coffin-shaped box set on a trestle table before an arrangement of flowers. For the benefit of the others he said: 'This is Walter's cheapest corpse carrier, from his Endless Sleep range. It goes for two hundred and forty pounds before addition of his professional charges and is made of chipboard, the simulated teak effect coming from a paper veneer. Note the three pairs of Canterbury ring handles and the gothic cross head ornament. It's fully lined, as you would expect, in a tasteful blue and white taffeta finish.'

'It's a bargain at the price,' Hardcastle claimed. 'And the most suitable receptacle for a modest crematory conclusion. I hope you're not accusing me of overcharging.'

'No, Walter, no. It's the ideal price for a chipboard box. Now tell us about this little beauty.'

Walter Hardcastle glanced at a new picture, looked away disdainfully then returned for a longer look. It was not from promotional material this time, it was operational, an on-site scenario. Mourners cluttered the entrance to Siddley Crematorium, and the photographer had snapped in fine detail the length of an ornate casket as it emerged from the back of a hearse. Hardcastle flipped at the photo dismissively. 'This represents an outrageous intrusion at a time of immense personal grief.'

Broody snatched at the picture and held it facing the others. 'Do you remember this particular cremation, Walter? In June, I think it was. Mrs Peverall-Byng, wife of the biscuit magnate from Siddleworth Dale. A grand and fitting funeral, indeed. In Siddley cathedral, no less. I was there, of course, as were we all. And while we were left with the nibbles and the sherry, the family hauled the old girl off to the crem for the fiery send off. And what a send off! Let us remind ourselves of the splendour of Mrs P-B's coffin. No, not coffin. Casket. And not just any casket, eh Walter?' Broody held the photo up to the undertaker, who averted his eyes. 'This is Walter's most expensive model, from his Heavenly Supreme range. Prices start at one thousand two hundred pounds. Mrs P-B did not face the furnace in a piece of veneered chipboard. It is solid mahogany, with panelled sides, raised lid and moulded sides and end, and it's fully lined, including double gathered frills and fold out ruffles, all in the finest deep oyster satin.' Holding the picture aloft, he put a finger over the centre of the casket. 'This is Walter's big selling point. Along the side panel you can see a biblical scene in the form of a finely crafted, raised motif. It costs a lot extra. There's a choice of evocative scenes, including the Last Supper, the Jesus-in-the-manger tableau and the very popular raising of Lazarus, most appropriate for a true believer. Walter's also does a tasteful crucifixion scene, with all its promise of resurrection, but it's not everybody's choice, though that is what Mr Peverall-Byng chose for his wife's sending off.' He tossed the photo onto the table.

'Of course, most people go for the cheapest coffins, especially for cremations. What's the point of spending money on something that's going into the fire? But not it seems the elite of Siddley.' Broody read from his notes as he removed a thin wedge of photos from the folder. Hardcastle's mouth was dry. 'My, you are a busy man. Walter. Your firms handles more than a third of all the cremations in Siddley. These are just a few of them.' All depicted caskets about to be carried into the crematorium. 'That one,' Broody said, singling a photo out and pushing it to the centre of the table, 'contains the deputy head of Siddley City University, killed, you may remember, in the sauna tragedy at the Taiwan Lotus massage and healing centre. Notice how the grieving widow also chose the most expensive line of caskets, the Heavenly Supreme, in, coincidentally, the same solid mahogany. Notice that she also paid for an expensive biblical scene in raised motif along the side panel, Can you tell which she picked?' Broody asked Sir Reginald Pitt, his sole ally at the grand table.

Pitt positioned his glasses and examined the photo, moving and turning it. 'I can see three crosses clearly but—'

'Correct. She also chose the crucifixion, like the Peverall-Byngs, I can tell you that the other photos show similar lavish caskets and all hold Siddley's wealthiest defunct citizens.'

'Shame on you, Walter,' Sir Reginald said, 'for taking advantage of bereaved relatives in their moment of greatest sorrow, smooth talking them into buying your top-of-the-range product when the balance of their mind was disturbed?

Patel smiled sardonically, his energy spent.

'I'm with you on this, Walter,' the transvestite city councillor said supportively, his composure restored. 'Business is business. I'm surprised the blackguard's stooping this low to find something to blackmail you with.'

'You're missing the point,' Broody riposted, ignoring the insult. 'Look at the pictures again.' Only Sir Reginald obeyed, fanning the photos in front of him and leaning over them. 'The bodies are all in caskets from the same Heavenly Supreme range, made from solid mahogany with raised lids and panelled sides, all with the embossed crucifixion scene, three sets of handles and oyster satin lining.' He leaned theatrically over the table, eyes popping from a grimacing face. 'The point is, gentlemen the dearly deceased are lying in the same fucking casket.'

Walter Hardcastle clutched his chest. Geoffrey Osborne's jaw dropped. Sir Reginald held his chin, covering a smirk.

'I found it hard to believe as well,' Broody said, 'so I sent my man to Hardcastle and Sons to look for a coffin, something really special he said, to send off his rich Uncle Stanley in. Inevitably he was recommended a casket from the Heavenly Supreme range, an example of which would be available for viewing that very afternoon. Coincidentally, it was the day of the cremation of the deputy head, and when my investigator returned he found a beautiful example of a mahogany casket, with the delicate depiction of the crucifixion of Christ along the side. Strangely, it seemed to him, the name-plate had been removed, and when left alone for a few moments of contemplation he found that the splintered wood around the screw holes was fresh. The close-ups came out very nicely, if you'd like to see them.' No one did, and Broody turned on Hardcastle again. 'Recycling coffins might not be the greatest crime known to man but think what it's going to do to you and your reputation in the body bag business. You'll be exposed as the fat, pompous, cheating hypocrite you always were.'

In the silence that followed Broody glanced at his watch. 'So there you have it, gentlemen. I'm prepared to forgive you the time and money it has cost me to expose your criminal acts and behavioural weaknesses and you are perfectly at liberty to walk away from this room and laugh it off, pretend this meeting never happened, but come next Monday, and there's a refusal by any one of you to part with your shares I will consider it to be a group decision by all of you and the contents of all these folders will reach the media and the police within the day.' He smiled indulgently at the slumped, motionless heads. 'So now let's all go away and come back tonight for the big party. You never know, it might be the last Friday night piss-up at Pitt Lane.'

Broody held Reginald Pitt back while the others left the boardroom and spoke to his ally from behind a cupped hand. 'If that proviso of your grandfather is real and it turns up, and the Pitties get through to the final of the Golden Mousetrap Trophy with a win tomorrow, it won't just put my plans on hold, it will fuck them up completely. And ruin me. The Russians won't wait. They'll take their millions somewhere else, and I won't have the money to repay the bridging loan from those bloodsuckers in the Caribbean. The Russians will also want their million quid deposit back, which I've already used up to pay interest. So you see, Reggie, the Pitties can't win tomorrow and your grandfather's little time-bomb had better stay lost.'

Listening in the earphones through the secret connection with the executive pantry, Monique desperately suppressed the urge to scream as the electronically muffled voices of the directors cursed and bemoaned their fate. She'd dashed to the closet as soon as they mysteriously disappeared into the boardroom without so much as a greeting. Now she knew why. The Pittie directors were crooks, cheats, opportunists, perverts, and one was a nasty little traitor – and they were being blackmailed by a murderer. Broody did not deny killing Moby McNally, did he? She'd have to listen to the tape. Heart thumping in her chest, she reached between food boxes and tins and turned off the recorder, removing the cassette tape and touching it to her lips before slipping it into her dress.

Fluorescent ceiling tubes illuminated the third floor of the Stoolton Road building occupied by the *Siddley Evening Sentinel*. The red-shirted figure of chief sports correspondent, Paddy Brick, was in his cubicle, fingers tapping at his laptop keyboard. Siddley's flagship newspaper would publish a historic special lime green edition on Saturday, reviewing the match as soon as it finished. Because of the time constraint, the match being only a day away, Paddy felt it prudent to write as much of the Siddley Yattock confrontation as possible in advance. The outcome being so predictable, the story wrote itself. He scrolled to the beginning and pondered his latest attempts at an elusive headline.

'Pitties Crash Out Bravely.' 'Pitties Swept Aside.' 'Rising Sun Sets.' Weak, he decided, still searching for words to crown a story of fighting spirit, courage and failure. 'They Were All Heroes.' 'Pitties Defiant As Yattock Cruise.' Better. It would be unprofessional if he failed to prepare for the impossible. 'Ohara Pulls Off Miracle.' 'Ken Ohara–Pitties Rising Son.' 'The World Belongs to Siddley.' 'They Were All Heroes.' Tomorrow, in the journalists' enclosure, he would amend, add, delete and embellish as the game ebbed and flowed. He wouldn't have to change much. He read the early paragraphs again, imaging himself a Pitties fan, close to tears, either of grief or joy.

'A day Siddley will never forget. On a mild (cold), dry (drizzly) afternoon, with the new turf at Pitt Lane trim (slippery under foot), helping (hindering) coach Ohara's splendid new passing game, Siddleans gathered in their hundreds (thousands) to roar on their heroes in the famed lime green and tangerine strip. Televized to millions of fanatical football fans in Japan, where the Pitties' manager is a national hero, Siddley United were always the underdogs against tough, semi-professional opposition from the Conference. The result was inevitable (an absolute shock), and with only one league win in their last fifteen games for the Pitties it was (nothing short of a miracle) only too depressingly familiar. Ken Ohara has worked his magic in his two months at Pitt Lane with slender resources and defeat (victory) was not a disgrace (a just reward).'

The likely and the downright bloody impossible, covered economically and evocatively. He scrolled briskly through the rest of the pre-emptive story, all eventualities accommodated. The first review of the game in the country, it would be picked up by the news services, international sports agencies, television stations, the whole world. The epic story of the Pitties' glorious defeat in the city's greatest game was his passport out of Siddley and as such the most crucial story he'd ever written, certainly the first sports report he'd written before the event.

He read more of his summary aloud. 'Tears were shed at Pitt Lane today. On a torrid, apocalyptic afternoon, tears of pain (joy), strained with the sweat of superhuman endeavour, flowed as though the Siddley Vale dam had burst. Only the die-hard Pittie fan would begrudge Yattock their victory, but only the cynical and cold-hearted would disparage their team's glorious day. For much of the game the Pitties defied (were overrun by) the Conference team, but keeping (getting possession of) the ball was always a problem in the difficult (even in the excellent) playing conditions on the pitch. So it was a surprise to no one when the Yattock goals came. Manager Ken Ohara patrolled the touchline (sat quietly in the dugout), screaming instructions (in a zen-like trance), urging his players to go forward, but an equalizer was never (always) on the cards, and at the end of the day the superior team scored a deserved victory. One day the Pitt Lane trophy cabinet will sparkle with silverware and in the meantime Siddley will always be lime green and tangerine, our own touchline samurai at the helm.'

Ken Ohara stood on the half-way line, arms folded tight on his chest, watching Marco di Rapido, Clint Hopp and Lucas Mandrake fire shots at Tony McDonald, who dived, jumped and stretched. Terry Dribble scampered around retrieving balls, much as the previous manager, Moby McNally, had been doing before he fell or was pushed into the canal. McDonald was bringing up a child on the few pounds he earned from Siddley United and whatever the state gave him in benefits. Would he take a thousand dollars to let in enough goals to win the Malaysian bet? After all, balls hitting the back of the Pitties' net were not exactly a rarity. Would anyone be surprised if a team like Yattock put four clear goals past us?

Just then, di Rapido struck a rolling ball which McDonald

could only fingertip into his net as it curled up and away from him. Gloved fists clenched, the goalie swore at the ground. 'I should have stopped it!' Then he shouted at the strikers. 'Hit me more, hard and high into the corners.'

At the other end of the ground, Scott Fisher, his left thigh strapped, tracked Taro Suzuki, who, with a few ribs aching from Billy Pickwich's wayward elbow, dribbled a ball around an immobile defensive formation made up of reserve goalkeeper Kevin Stopham, Diamond, Breakin, Grant and Omerod. Suzuki jigged around the statue-like Grant and darted painfully for the open goal. Scott had anticipated the break and sprinted across Suzuki's path, just managing to dislodge the ball before they reached the mouth of the goal. The Japanese sank to his knees, playfully appealing for a penalty with his arms outstretched. Rude banter and laughter reached Ohara. Then Omar Grant's voice boomed. 'Okay, lads, let's do it again.' Ohara counted off the rest of his depleted team. Groot and Blink on the treatment table; Drummond at a job interview; Billy Pickwich working late, having swapped shifts with another driver so that he could play tomorrow.

Turning and looking up, Ohara saw the light in the chairman's suite and silhouettes apparently looking out over the pitch. The ritual Friday night party had begun, this one swollen with Japanese and local guests. How could he face the ecstatic directors, as they wallowed in the euphoria of international publicity, knowing that he'd been bribed to lose, and lose very badly? Even worse, he was actually weighing the options. The ten to one, million dollar bet was a done deal, and the gamblers had a dated photo of him grinning over a bundle of bribe money. They'd use it against him if he failed them, if they didn't kill him outright. The Pitties are expected to lose tomorrow anyway, he told himself, setting off on a touchline jog, so why not make sure it's by four goals? Why not give every player $2,000 and slip them the word? After two laps of the pitch, when his body had warmed, the evil thoughts loosened their grip. Omar Grant, Marco di Rapido, Tony McDonald, not to mention the pious Lucas Mandrake, would all shove the money down his throat. Taro Suzuki would walk out on him. He thought of the burglar, Clint Hopp and allowed himself an ironic chuckle. A whistle shrilled across the ground. Terry Dribble had called time on the last training session before the Golden Mousetrap semi-final. Ohara watched as his team approached the tunnel and noticed Scott Fisher seemed to be supporting Taro Suzuki with his arm.

In the changing room, stripping men around him, he was feeling oddly composed, almost serene, like a *kamikaze* pilot who has written his farewell letter, drunk the ceremonial last cup of *sake* and overcome the final barrier of fear. Now the only thing to fear was failure. He invited the team for soft drinks in the hospitality suite and told them the starting line-up would depend on final fitness tests in the morning, particularly for Taro Suzuki. Billy Pickwich wasn't there to hear Robbie Breakin call the taxi driver a bastard.

The long hospitality suite held almost as many Japanese as locals and hummed with chatter and laughter. The old blemished mirror behind the bar had been hung with lime green and tangerine scarves. Florie and Winnie eased their solid, apron-clad bodies around, carrying trays of dips, food on sticks and drinks. The aroma of beer and smoke enveloped the hosts and their guests. Ohara took a glass of warm fruit juice and worked the room with little enthusiasm, greeting those he knew and meeting the business, social and political elite of Siddley, thanking them for their best wishes and support. He intended to leave as soon as seemed polite.

Monique caught him between groups. 'I must speak to you, Ken,' she begged. 'It's really urgent.'

Before they could slip away, Ohara found himself swept into another band of ebullient guests. For reasons he wouldn't understand until later, the chairman and the other directors were oddly subdued. 'Good luck, lad,' was all the usually star-struck Walter Hardcastle could manage before turning away, deep in thought with a large tumbler of whisky. Apart from staff from the national broadcasting corporation, NHK, the only other Japanese journalist there, at Ohara's special request, was Tanaka from the *Kanto Daily Sports*. Ohara introduced him to Karen Saddleback, the frisky sports reporter for Radio Siddley, and Paddy Brick, who had arrived well into the party in a hyperactive state. Eisaku Ishida, chairman of Uno Electronics, took a patrician's interest in the welfare of the Japanese visitors, explaining the culture of Siddley and the role of its football club to Shinsuke Sudo, the match commentator, and his lovely colleague, Mimi Bando.

Harry Patel had decided to sell out to Broody, as had the others, when they stayed behind in the boardroom, wondering whether the oily bastard could be trusted to keep quiet once he had their shares. With murderous thoughts welling inside, Patel was indifferent to the three mature ladies who made up his circle with Takeo Shito, the pony-tailed Japanese football pundit. Shito was nudging the tweed jacket of Mrs Geoffrey Osborne, holding up his business card and demonstrating to the women the subtle intonation and stress required in the correct pronunciation of his surname. When Taro Suzuki had left early, Ohara found himself temporarily alone, between Patel's group and David Broody's. The property man was in expansive mood, gin and tonic in hand, talking football with three well-fed businessmen in suits. Broody's confident voice overwhelmed the others and caught Ohara's ear.

'Bugger strategy,' he brayed. 'We'll be lucky to lose by only ten. Half of 'em are injured, including that new Jap chap from Uno. Or maybe that's just the coach getting his excuses in first.'

His audience laughed, then one of them said: 'That Yattock striker puts it about a bit, I hear. What's his name?'

'Goodmouth,' Broody chuckled. 'Goal a game lad. Should get a hatful tomorrow. Young Fisher's going to mark him. You'll recognize him from the strapping on his thigh.' The others found the remark hilarious.

Ohara turned away. How did Broody know what his tactics were going to be against the Yattock striker? He'd only told the team 24 hours earlier. And Taro Suzuki's injury? Then, amid the noise and smells of the party, familiar images returned. Broken glass from an old photo frame, the cut on Billy Pickwich's hand and the fullback's constant dissent and complaining and the elbow that winded Taro Suzuki yesterday. Was Broody paying him to undermine the team? Asian gangsters, property sharks and now one of his own players. It might be best if the Pitties did lose tomorrow by four goals. Then he could resign as manager and crawl home to Japan, having returned the cash bribe and refused to pick up the case in the locker and hoping he'd be left in peace with his body and reputation, if not his conscience, intact.

He was in his own world of demons when, over the shoulders of a jolly Sir Reginald Pitt, he saw Monique's piled blonde hair turn his way and then disappear through the doors leading to the kitchen. He followed, almost upsetting Florie who was pushing backwards through the doors with a tray of nibbles.

Monique drew the Japanese into a corner. Her hands were shaking. 'He's going to do it, Ken. Broody's going to buy Siddley United from the directors, then sell the ground, the car park, everything. He's blackmailing all of them, except Reggie Pitt, who's selling out willingly. I've got the proof on tape. We've got to do something to stop him before they give him their shares on Monday. And I think he killed Moby McNally. He'll do anything to stop the Pitties getting to the final. If we get through the semi tomorrow, he can't sell the land until the final's been played next year, if he's right about Sir Abraham Pitt's proviso. Then it'd be too late for him. The deal that Russian bloke wrote about in the letter I copied will fall through. Broody will be ruined.'

Monique was panting. Pausing for breath her eyes suddenly flared with passion. 'That's it!' she screamed, eureka-like. 'We'll destroy him. We win tomorrow and *we* find Sir Abraham Pitt's secret message. We'll shove it in his face and prove he can't sell Pitt Lane.'

Ohara sighed, wanting to take the beautiful woman who loved the Pitties more than life into his embrace. His Japaneseness restrained him. All we have to do is beat Yattock, he mused ruefully. He took a daring step forward and held her wrists. 'If Broody hasn't found it already how can we find it by Monday?' He looked into her large, pleading eyes, which threatened to overflow. How could he tell her he'd get $100,000, and keep his body intact, if he rigged the game tomorrow? 'We will win,' he said hoarsely, defiantly, his superficial posture of *tatemae* hiding the real feelings and beliefs in his heart, his *honne*.

'Thank you,' she breathed, planting a kiss on his lips. 'I know we will.'

As he waited while she re-made her face in the thin reflection of a stainless steel cabinet door, the scowling, contemptuous face of Bunsuke Makino flashed across Ohara's mind. 'About the game tomorrow. There is something I have not told you.'

She stood before him, her eyes filled with new hope, smile lines filling her face. 'Yes, Ken?'

Ohara sighed. 'It doesn't matter. It's not important. I've got something for you,' he remembered. He led her through the rear kitchen door and down to the manager's office. Taking the blue and white shirt from his sports bag he held it up by the shoulders. 'I wore this against Argentina in the France World Cup tournament. I want you to have it. Perhaps it bring us good luck tomorrow.'

Monique looked at the shirt as if it were a priceless jewel. Tears welled, this time of sheer helpless pleasure and she sprang forward and pinioned him to the wall.

David Broody saw them rejoin the party. He was making empty promises to Matt Dennis and Terry Dribble, who considered the alcohol ban did not apply to non-playing staff, and offering selectively warm or cold smiles to guests on their way out. Monique was smiling. Sniffling too, but mostly smiling. Had they found the document with Sir Abraham's devastating proviso? He knew she'd copied Boris Rakov's letter and he was sure she'd shown it to the Japanese. The nonsense with the football shirt was just a cover while the cow went through his files. God! The humiliation. So what did Monique and Ohara make of the letter, and anything else she'd found and copied? It wouldn't matter, really. When he had all the shares in the club he'd settle things with the little ball-breaking bitch. Come Monday afternoon, when David Broody was the new owner and chairman, her job at Pitt Lane would be history.

Ohara led Monique towards the friendly figures of Rika Yamaguchi and Manabu Tanaka, telling her how it was the journalist who discovered the existence of Kenneth O'Hara, the real candidate for the manager's job at Pitt Lane.

The party crowd had thinned, mostly to people connected to the football club. Charlie wandered about, gathering ashtrays and finishing off any substantial remnants in abandoned glasses. Ohara was reluctantly drawn into conversation with Sir Reginal Pitt by Walter Hardcastle. If

Monique hadn't told him about the club president's role as accomplice to David Broody and the blackmailing of the chairman and directors, Ohara wouldn't have understood Pitt's sudden friendliness and Walter's Hardcastle's uncharacteristic silence. When Broody appeared at his shoulder, the chairman mumbled something and shuffled sideways to join the other victims of the property developer's boardroom terrorism in a tight group by the fireplace. Geoffrey Osborne appeared to be very drunk.

After a bit of banter about the differences between the cities of Siddley and Tokyo, the reliability of his Mitsubishi Shogun and Camilla Broody's deep interest in Nichiren Buddhism, Sir Reginald, boredom forcing his eyes often to his chunky gold watch, said: 'And how do you fancy our chances tomorrow, Mr Ohara? I hear we're a bit out of our depth.'

'And some,' Broody saw fit to add smugly.

'We are certainly the clear underdogs, but it is a cup game, a one-off, so anything is possible. I really want to win tomorrow so we can go on to the final and bring the Golden Mousetrap to Siddley. We must do something special to celebrate one hundred years since your ancestor gave the city this wonderful football ground.'

9

Charlie Wharton arrived early on match days, his role was to oil a single turnstile, mark out the pitch, test the floodlights, get the old boiler going and set up a keg of beer in the hospitality suite. Today, he knew it would be different, not least because the tall, erect, turbaned figure of constable Mavindra Singh stood in lonely vigil before the players' entrance, a small white, hairless dog huddled shivering at his feet.

'What's up Singy?' Charlie said jovially. 'Are you queuing to get in? There's still six hours to kick off.'

'Eh up, Charlie,' the Sikh police officer replied. 'You skiving off your council duties again?'

Charlie's pale features and thinness belied a public lavatory cleaner of great energy and guile. He'd watched his first Pitties game when he was five and found paradise from doing the small but vital jobs at Pitt Lane since he was 14. Today, he'd be assisted by a 16-year-old youth on community service and a functionary from the Football Association who would observe the game for the official record. Charlie would also have to activate the other turnstiles if what they were saying about the expected crowd was true.

'Something like that,' Charlie told the policeman. 'So what's up with you?'

'We've had word a hardcore of hooligans from Grittley Mills is coming over to cause trouble. I'm the advance deterrent element of the task force that will assemble to combat the threat as we approach the start of the game.'

'Good luck to you, lad,' Charlie said, fiddling with a ring of keys. 'I don't remember seeing the police at Pitt Lane since the fifties, and they were here to watch.'

Organized by Monique, a childminder was found for the 14-month-old baby of Miss Teenage Siddley, Staniella Lumpley, a petite, vivacious red-head. Clad in a Pitties' replica shirt that cascaded over her bountiful under-sprung breasts and kindly hid the almost imperceptible twelve week bump of her second, and as yet undetected, pregnancy, Staniella criss-crossed the city on a horse-drawn dray belonging to Appleton's Brewery. Her voice of innocent timbre resounded through the megaphone, sensually imploring the citizenry of Siddley to join her for an afternoon of passion in the cauldron of football at Pitt Lane.

The official Pitties' supporters club was a moveable feast, based loosely at the Bell and Abattoir where a hard-core met on home match days to play cards, compare the fantasy football results and trudge down to Pitt Lane at ten minutes to three. The Golden Mousetrap semi-final fever had spread beyond the inner city to dormant city suburbs and to pubs and homes in the villages around Siddley and word had it that the remaining members from the brass band of the long-defunct colliery in Bunton Vale would convene at the Blind Dutchman and then march to Pitt Lane. The arrival of a foreign coach had lit a fire under the city's long dormant football *aficion*. The short, proud Japanese had already arrested the Pitties' league slide, revolutionised its playing tactics, fired its ambition and roused the people of Siddley to an outpouring of unrestrained celebration and solidarity. Whether or not the Pitties achieved the impossible and made it to the final of the Golden Mousetrap Trophy, today's semi-final game was going to crown the club's centenary year.

Ken-ichi Ohara had slept improbably well, given that someone had sprayed 0-4 three times in blood red streaky paint along the low brick wall at the front of his house.

'Dratted vandals,' Mrs Ramirez had remarked when she met Ohara as she was walking her poodle and he was returning from Pitt Lane last night. They had stood looking at the numbers, Mrs Ramirez's dog peeing on a wheel of his Honda. 'It's these foreigners, you know. They come over here, go straight on the social services and then vandalize our streets. I expect it's a code.'

Kind of, Ohara had thought to himself. Just a little reminder from Bunsuke Makino and Ng See Loo. He'd read the faxes, cards and e-mails and listened to all the messages of goodwill waiting for him in the house before boiling water for a pot of noodles and green tea. Then he wrote the letter that now stood propped against the milk jug as he tried to find the enthusiasm to spread honey on his breakfast toast. Not really his *yuigon*, the last communication of a Japanese about to die, just a simple explanation of events, from his improbable appointment as player coach at Siddley United and his discovery that the club's chief executive had schemed to install him instead of an Irishman with a very similar name. Then the plan to blackmail the club directors out of their shares (please contact Miss Monique Wainwright for the recorded evidence) and sell Siddley United's valuable land to Russians and how, absurdly, the outcome of the whole affair depended on the existence or not of a secret covenant left somewhere by Sir Abraham Pitt.

Of the appearance of Makino and Ng he wrote exactly as events had unfolded, including the crafty, damning photograph. If, for any reason, Ohara wrote, he should not be alive to explain it himself, the money in the garden shed comprised half of the proposed bribe, the other being in a locker at Siddley railway station. Finally, he told the reader, whoever it might be, of Monique Wainwright's total and uncompromising devotion to Siddley United, even as unscrupulous forces around her were trying to destroy it.

He showered quickly and sent a batch of emails to Japan, thanking friends for their support. Then he telephoned his father.

Nine-twenty in the morning in Siddley made it six-twenty at night in Japan. Father was about to catch a few hours' sleep before the midnight game. 'Just do your best,' his proud father pleaded. 'For your mother's sake.'

The cordless phone at his ear, he drew back the curtain in the lounge and found himself looking into the lens of a camera and a surround of Japanese faces. More reporters, English and Japanese crowded the pavement, cameras mounted on tripods, waving notepads and recorders when they glimpsed the Japanese manager. Chest thumping, he tugged the curtain shut and made ready to leave. Before he faced the cameras and the noise, he lit a stick of incense and bowed in silent prayer before his mother's photograph on the make-shift Buddhist altar.

The first player to reach the ground was Omar Grant, and he approached it through the car-park, his head hidden inside a black balaclava hood. Fast food stalls were being set up in the front of the ground and a couple of early drinkers were clutching their pints in front of the Pitt Lane Arms.

'Is the boss here yet?' Omar asked, his deep, unmistakable voice oddly muted.

'Who are you?' Charlie Wharton demanded to know at the door, fearing a Grittley Mills terrorist assault.

'Let me in. It's me, Omar.'

'Take that bloody thing off, then.'

Omar revealed himself and there, on skin above his left

eye, was a strip of surgical tape, bound with a piece of coarse bandage stained dark purple. The eye itself, as Charlie could see when he puckered his face close to Omar's, was swollen, almost closed.

'Tell me slowly what happened,' Ohara said from behind his desk. It was obvious from Grant's drawn features and slurred voice he hadn't slept much.

'I dunno how it started, really. It was just another Friday night at the Taste of Heaven. The usual big post-pub and curry crowd around eleven, eleven-thirty, trying to get in. A few drunks which me and Carl had to sort out, but nothing out of the ordinary until about two.' His voice trailed away.

'What happened then?' Ohara asked gently.

'Everybody's inside, a few even going home. I'm on me own, aren't I? Carl's inside, where the crowd is. Then these white guys arrive, about ten of them. They're all around me, swearing and dissing. They're not drunk and they don't want to get in the club. I'm distracted and then one of them hits me here. Don't know what with.' He cupped a hand over the wounded eye. 'I went down, half out of it, blood in me eyes. They kicked me a few times in the gut and ran off. Just like that. Must have hit me with something hard because it opened the eye up. Five stitches down at Siddley Royal Infirmary. Left at half six this morning. I've been home to change and have a rest and here I am. Sorry about this, boss.'

Terry Dribble and Matt Dennis appeared in the manager's stuffy little office, their faces telling him brought their own problems, even before they saw Grant's bandaged head.

'Jesus!' Dennis cried when Grant's puffy, burnt out face turned to him.

Ohara explained what had happened.

'Bloody sabotage,' Dribble thought.

Ohara did not understand the word. 'Are you fit to play today?' he asked his central defender, the key to the Pitties' defence,

'I think so, boss. I'm a bit knackered and it hurts like hell, but I don't want to let the lads down.'

'What can you do to protect the stitches?' Ohara asked Matt Dennis.

Dennis cupped his chin and hummed for a moment 'I've got stretch bandage. We can wrap that round his head a few times and hold it tight with cling film stuff. We can change them at half-time.'

Ohara managed a thin smile. 'Good. Omar. Please go and rest on the bed in the treatment room.'

Matt Dennis groaned. 'That's a bit unfortunate, Ken. Mike Groot's just been sick on it.'

'Sick? You mean, vomit?'

'Hmm. Seems he got pissed as a rat last night. He's still sleeping it off but he's a touch unwell.'

'I'll kill him,' Omar bellowed. 'I swear to God I'll—'

'Again please, Matt.' Ohara had started to think about the official team sheet he had to give to the match referee.

'Grooty met up with Billy Pickwich late last night and got seriously drunk.'

Ohara slapped his pen on the desk. 'I thought I told everybody to rest. Take no alcohol.'

'Billy's okay,' Dribble assured. 'He says he didn't have a drop of booze.'

'So why did he let Groot drink?' the Japanese asked angrily, uselessly, fearing he knew the answer already.

When Grant had gone, Ohara turned on his coach and physio. 'What do I write on this, for referee?' he said with a shrug, slapping the official team sheet. 'Please be careful of captain with broken head, sweeper with groin sprain, Italian striker with bad temper; fullback with grudge against own team.' He shook his head in desperation. 'What have we got on the substitutes' bench? Number two goalkeeper; a drunk; Blink with his aches and pains; and a Japanese international striker who hasn't played serious football for four years and thanks to a team-mate can hardly breathe. And there's me, with my bad knee.'

An hour later, it was a relief to Ohara to find his players, except for Omar Grant and indisposed Mike Groot, eating a crispy vegetarian pasta bake and mixed salad for lunch. Lucas Mandrake quietly mumbled grace but nobody seemed to be listening. Drummond and Omerod, heads newly shaved, ate noisily. Pickwich sat cowered, stabbing suspiciously at a twist of sun-dried tomato. Taro Suzuki was the last player to arrive. He wore the tracksuit of his old Pompanol Osaka club and moved among the team with an uncharacteristic smile on his face, showing them the stitches where his left ear had been sewn back after he'd dived through flaying, raking boots to head in a goal in a World Cup qualifier against Uzbekistan.

The mood of the team was decidedly upbeat and positive. Marco di Rapido sang in broken Italian as he served Drummond a limited second portion of pasta. Even the injury situation seemed a little improved. Scott Fisher would keep his thigh strapped during the game but it was more out of comfort than real need. Taro Suzuki said it didn't hurt much when he breathed and he raised his shirt to show the heat-infusing Salompas pads his wife had clamped on his hairless chest. Tony McDonald was the subject of a feature in yesterday's *Sentinel* under Paddy Brick's headline, 'The Man to Stop Yattock'.

Ohara watched and listened to the good-humoured bantering, and for a while, two dangerous blackmailers left his mind. Was he allowing himself a rare, mild sensation of well-being, he wondered, curling cheese around his fork? If it was, it lasted no longer than it took to swallow. Two, stern-faced uniformed police constables, ushered in by a smirking David Broody, came meekly into the room.

'There he is,' Broody said with mock reluctance, pointing to the sullen face of Clint Hopp, sitting at a table with Breakin and Mandrake.

Clint Hopp, the petty thief recently released from prison for too many burglaries, wiped his mouth on his wrist. For the first time in his felonious life he was surprised to see the law after him when he genuinely hadn't done anything illegal. Ohara was momentarily confused: the man who had played so well against Moxbottom and was a key attacking defender in today's game was walking out, gently encouraged by the two policemen. Late last night, a witness leaving the Phuket And Go satay restaurant two doors from the post-office in Wolverine Lane saw a person he claimed he recognized from all the football exposure as Clint Hopp, smashing the window of a black BMW. The car belonged to a Mr David Broody, chairman and chief executive of Broody Associates and chief executive of Siddley United Football Club.

'I don't do cars,' Hopp was repeating loudly as the policemen led him to his locker in the changing room. Inside they found a mobile phone, a gold lighter engraved C to DB and two Montecristo cigars, all the property of Mr Broody.

'The lighter's a fifteenth wedding anniversary from my darling wife, Camilla,' Broody told the policemen: 'Thank God you've found it.'

One of the officers read Hopp his all too familiar rights and gently took his arm.

'Can't you see your way to letting him off for the game, gentlemen?' Broody wondered lamely. 'I'll guarantee he turns himself in afterwards. Of course, if you must take him away please do so.'

'Please, please don't take him,' Ohara begged. The shorter of two law enforcement officers declared himself a Pitties fan but said that, regrettably, once set in motion the process of arrest, statement taking, possible indictment, arrangement of legal representation and bail must continue and might take several hours. Clint Hopp might be available for the post-match party. Ohara followed them outside to the police car, which early fans had surrounded with curiosity. He could only watch with despair as the left side of his attacking midfield disappeared in the direction of Siddley Central Police Station.

Among the first of the die-hard fans to reach Pitt Lane was Lime Green. Christened Roger Green, he changed his name legally to Lime Green during the famous cup run ten years ago when the Pitties reached the quarter-finals. Today, for the mother of all matches, Lime wore the classic lime green shirt over his thermally secure skin-tight tangerine body suit, his face striped in Pitties' colours under a fluorescent green wig.

When Karen Saddleback from Radio Siddley arrived at Pitt Lane she was surprised to find the car park bursting, closed to all but players, officials and the media. It was packed with utility vans and cars, stickers advertising the presence of the national tabloids, a couple of broadsheets and, from the odd writing on window stickers, a good representation from the Japanese press. The *Siddley Evening Sentinel* set up a booth in front of the ground, proclaiming that a special Golden Mousetrap Trophy edition of the *Sentinel* would be on sale within minutes of the final whistle.

Camilla Broody had forsaken solids for two days and was slightly delirious from the deprivation, and only the expectation of meeting the mayor and other dignitaries could lure her to Pitt Lane. Chairman Hardcastle's dear wife would never see a Pitties game again. She rocked in helpless contentment in a nursing home, thumbing through back issues of *Coffins and Caskets*. 'She's got more chance of recovery from senility than seeing another game at Pitt Lane,' Broody told Camilla happily as he drove them to Pitt Lane in his other car, chuckling to himself and imagining Ronald Townrow as a Pitties cheerleader.

Harry Patel was walking morosely from his car, wondering how to extract himself from Broody's fulsome embrace, when the property magnate drew into the car park. Sniffing contemptuously at the smell of frying onions and sizzling burgers, Broody guided his wife around the stalls and the bystanders gathered in front of the decrepit stadium.

'Traitor!' a woman called.

'Bastard,' a man's voice followed. Broody's trademark slim cut suits, oiled hair and square, punchable face were as familiar to the people of Siddley as the shops and buildings that bore his name. The rumours were spreading. Fifteen or so people, Alf Widderson among them, appeared out of Church Street, some carrying 'Save Our Homes' placards. It didn't bother Broody, even when a few Pitties fans decided it was their moment to show who was to blame for the club's decline. 'Broody out, Broody out,' they chorused, their faces flushed with anger.

Police Constable Singh was reading the situation, his worst fears turning real. 'We have a potential flash-point at Pitt Lane,' he said with urgency into his walkie-talkie.

'You ain't seen nothing yet,' Broody muttered towards the protesters. 'You'll be seeing open countryside when I've finished here. I'll swing the first wrecking ball myself, right into Hardcastle's bloody office.'

'What are these common people talking about?' Camilla wondered, a pert nose raised on the stretched skin of her face as her husband nudged her through the entrance.

'Me, apparently,' Broody said, holding back suddenly as

the swing of his head caught something on the edges of his vision. Three tall men, the one in the centre standing as though protected by the others, stood out ominously among the anoraks and replica shirts of the thickening crowd. The figure raised a match programme in salute as his eyes met Broody's. The property entrepreneur showed Boris Rakov a flagging smile, even as a knot of apprehension tightened in his bowels.

Chairs filled the boardroom and journalists without them overflowed into Monique's office, craning to see and hear Ken-ichi Ohara's last press conference before the semi-final match. Millions would watch it later when it was transmitted in the run-up to kick-off. Monique stood against the door frame. She could see the tension on Ohara's face and only she knew it wasn't just pre-match nerves. What was the secret he was keeping from her? The camera rolled and the questions flowed. She felt for the man she had come to trust, who she thought had come to love the Pitties as much as she did. His strange hissing and sucking noises, his nodding head, crooking neck, they must be meaningful Japanese expressions and gestures, she thought. Inside, he was dying, and Monique saw it in the subtle changes in his expressions, his body language and the way the confident demeanour she so liked had turned into grovelling parody. So was this the Japanese way, Monique wondered? You had to appear to be stupid, ignorant, humiliatingly humble. A journalist raised a hand and introduced himself as Kaneko, from a popular weekly tabloid.

'Is is true, Ohara *san*, that the English football authorities made an administrative mistake when they appointed you to Siddley United?'

The senior NHK publicity relations woman cringed on the edges of the camera's reach. This was a friendly production she had earlier advised journalists, meaning that provocative questions would be edited out of the final transmission.

So Tanaka's discoveries had leaked, as Ohara knew they would. Tanaka promised to hold back on the Kenneth O'Hara allegations until after the big match but it was inevitable someone else should be suspicious. Ohara caught Tanaka's eye and was rewarded with a nod and the flicker of a smile. 'I came to Siddley in good faith,' Ohara said truthfully, twisting a pen on the desk. 'As far as I am concerned Siddley is where I will work until my contract expires.'

A pinch-faced character introduced himself nervously, 'Etoh. *The Yomiuri Shimbun.*' He represented the newspaper with the highest daily circulation in the world. 'You are the underdog by a long way in this game, Ohara coach. What is your strategy to contain and subdue Yattock?'

'I will do my best to inspire my team to victory. I think it will be difficult. We have several injuries but . . .' He'd just lost a thief and gained a drunk.

'Will Taro Suzuki be a starting member today?' somebody asked.

'Perhaps, in spite of a slight injury from training.'

'Whaaaaa . . .' A collected sign of relief, of approval. They all took it to mean Japan would definitely see its great soccer star, retired so young and honourably. Mimi Bando applauded, her delicate hands thrashing.

I'm running out of options, Ohara was thinking to himself. Replacing an attacking defender like Clint Hopp with an out-and-out striker, Suzuki, might please Japan but it would please the Yattock forwards more, and when Goodmouth surged forward the hung-over Groot wouldn't give him the hardest of times.

The man from *Fuji Sports* spoke for all of Japan. 'What about you, Ohara *kantoku*? Will you play today?'

Ohara allowed himself a rueful smile, less of eastern mystery than a cover for the terror welling in his gut. If there was going to be a massacre on the pitch he'd rather watch it from the dugout. 'I will be on the substitutes bench and hope my team can do without me and my unhappy knee.'

At 1.10p.m. the press conference was closed, the journalists expelled to the bar or the stands. Ohara passed through the gathering of club officials and their guests in the long suite, greeting the lady mayor of Siddley and the Japanese ambassador fleetingly and returning the shoulder pats of support with a fleeting smile. Thanks to Monique and her secret tape, he knew why the directors looked so distressed. Monique, bless her, showed him a defiant fist when she saw him leaving. He made the lavatory cubicle just in time, throwing up the pasta bake in two noisy retches and then sitting on the lid, head in his hands, waiting for the convulsions to subside. What had he done to deserve all this? He'd accidentally found himself replacing a man who'd drowned, managing a club with no fixture and being blackmailed to throw an unwinable game that wouldn't normally generate the least flicker of interest outside of Siddley. And what *was* his masterplan to beat the Japanese and Malaysian blackmailers? It was simple: he didn't have one. It was a statistical certainty that Yattock would put two goals past the Pitties, a strong probability it would be four or more. His stomach settled, leaving a metallic taste of bile in his dry mouth. He reached for the rusting chain and suddenly had a thought. If he stood on the seat, tied the chain round his neck there was just enough of a drop to break his neck. He was pondering the physics of it all in the shitty stillness when he was aware of a sound in the other cubicle. Then a voice, seeping through a knot hole in the wall.

'You okay boss?' It was Mike Groot. 'It *is* the boss, isn't it?

I'm sorry I went on the piss last night. Fucking Pickwich led me astray, didn't he?'

Ohara lowered his face to the hole. 'Yes. It is me. I said no drink before game. I need you on the pitch today.'

'I'll there boss, don't you worry,' Groot assured his manager.

How many times had his mother's image flashed across his mind? Hundreds. And she was here again, with him in this stinking cubicle. 'Always do your best, Ken *chan*,' he could hear, seeing her oval, lovely face. 'Listen to advice, but don't take it if you think it's wrong.'

'Good. And do your best,' he told the wall.

'Sorry boss,' Mike Groot shouted. 'I can't hear you.'

Ohara shouted, in Japanese; a little colour returning to his cheeks. 'I'm not giving in to them, mother.'

Groot's voice at the knot hole. 'Right, boss. By the way, how many pints of bloody *sake* did you get through last night?'

While the Pitties' manager was recovering gamely, a maroon and cream bus pulled up in front of Pitt Lane, disgorging a stream of smartly dressed, smiling young men in blazers and club ties. A couple of skinheads outside the Pitt Lane Arms with pints of lager booed lazily but most of the early Pitties fans absorbing the pre-match atmosphere just stared in admiration at Yattock Town's luxury vehicle, with its curtains and individual tables with lamps.

The Bunton Colliery band left the Blind Dutchman after a pie and a pint, gathered fans at agreed pubs in a moon shaped sweep of north and west Siddley, finally congregating at the Pitt Lane Arms with military precision at 2.05p.m. The square was already seething. Pungent smoke rose in the still air from the grills of the burger and kebab stalls. People absent from live football games for years snapped up the glossy match programmes and a queue of at least 50 was already jamming the Canal Stand turnstile.

Inside the press box above the directors' enclosure, Shinsuke Sudo, NHK commentator, and his helpers, Takeo Shito and Mimi Bando, were practising the strange foreign names. In seats reserved for the press the man from *World News* opened a sweepstake, and when the *Sentinel's* Paddy Brick arrived he was offered two options: to bet on the outright result and/or Yattock's margin of victory. Ten pounds for entry into either competition, multiple winners to split the pot. Thirty-two British journalists had requested passes for the game and all but one participated in the sweepstake. The Japanese delegation numbered 48 and many of them had a pop at guessing the final result, 32 going for a 1-0 win for the Pitties, six for a 1-1 draw. Karen Saddleback was the only British journalist to forecast a Pitties win, with a 3-2 scoreline, but also covered this rash bet by backing Yattock to outscore the Pitties by three goals in the second wager. Paddy Brick turned his back on his fellow Siddley journalist and put a tenner on a 0-5 scoreline and another precious £10 on the five goal margin.

In the directors' suite, talking property prices with David Broody, Sir Reginald Pitt was very expansive, being only days away from financial security with a lot to spare, thanks to the imminent inflow of Russian money. Monique Wainwright drew Walter Hardcastle from the party that included the lady mayor, Ms Anenome Abadule, who sweltered in ceremonial clothes and a heavy gold chain of office. Monique led the chairman from the boardroom to the window of his office that overlooked the pitch.

'Have you ever seen anything like it?' she asked him, with barely controlled passion. Unable to recall the thirties and the glory days of Len Grate, the undertaker hadn't, but looking to his right he saw nothing but bodies and colour on the slope that was the uncovered terraced end of Pitt

Lane. The entire area swayed with lime green shirts, Japanese and union flags, weird tangerine plastic clackers and banners with strange hieroglyphics. It seemed to vibrate to the sound of rhythmic clanging and synchronized chanting.

'Where in God's name did that lot come from?' Walter Hardcastle uttered.

'That nice girl from Uno Electronics, Rika, organized them,' Monique beamed. Not that there was much to do in the electronically wired Japanese community to bring them to Siddley: Japanese company employees and their families, language students, Japanese married to Britons, embassy and restaurant staff from all over the country had flocked to the ground. It was their patriotic duty to witness and support two Japanese heroes abroad, although above the din of the orchestrated cheerleading they did not hear the announcement over the tinny public address system that neither Ohara nor Suzuki were in the starting line-up.

'Look down there, Mr Hardcastle,' Monique said, indicating the Pitt Stand, and then the long terrace opposite. They were pocked with people, others arriving in a steady stream, as quickly as the ancient turnstiles would allow. 'I think Pitt Lane will be full by three o'clock.'

The chairman sniffed. He was drained from worry and despair. On the greatest day of his chairmanship, on the biggest day for the Pitties in its hundred years of existence, only a defeat would save his professional life and his reputation. 'Have you seen Ken?' he said wearily. 'I knew I'd picked a good lad there.'

'He'll be pepping up the team.'

'Of course,' Walter Hardcastle agreed sadly, puffing out his gut, thumbs inside his waistcoat. 'With a bit of that zen mediation, I expect.'

'Probably.' Monique laid a protective hand on his arm. 'It's going to be all right, Mr Hardcastle. Ken and me will sort it out.'

'Sort? Sort what?'

'We know everything, about David Broody and his plan to sell the ground.'

Hardcastle stared ahead, seeing only the thin outline of his empty reflection in the glass. 'Everything?' His voice was a mere whisper.

'Everything. Your naughty behaviour with the coffins, and the others, Mr Patel's child labour, Mr Osborne's pet food in the pies and Mr Townrow and his stilettos. Broody's blackmailing you, isn't he?'

Hardcastle heaved a heavy sigh, perhaps of relief. He didn't even want to know how she knew. 'It's too late. The Pitties are finished.'

'No they're not,' Monique insisted, now seizing his arm with two hands. 'They're just beginning.'

It was very quiet in the Pitties changing room when Ohara appeared. Even Marco di Rapido's natural breeziness was missing. Nerves, Ohara hoped. Omar Grant had rallied, complaining only of a slight headache. The bandage stretched around his head like the top end of a poorly ravelled mummy. There was no sympathy for Mike Groot, whose headache was sourced from the bottle. 'Fucking idiot' was their kindest greeting. They all turned and watched as their coach stripped from his blazer, white shirt and razor sharp trousers and, for the first time since arriving in Siddley, slipped on the number 15, lime green shirt, which gave his light olive skin a certain eerie luminosity. The tangerine shorts, socks and the boots followed, the shin pads fitted with almost ritualistic precision. How many years had it been, he asked himself, since he'd played more than 15 minutes in a competitive game? Five, six? Then Marco di Rapido sprang into life, pacing around the room that smelled of nervous men, pumping himself up, slapping fist to palm, mumbling in awful Italian. Clarissa finished rubbing a healing unguent into the left calf of Robby Breakin as Omar Grant inspected each of the players, reminding them of the coach's tactics and their individual role in them. Taro Suzuki tied the final knot in his left boot, his eyes burning with concentration. Kitted out, with tracksuit top zipped, Ohara had nothing more to tell his team. He shook hands individually, went next door to the animated visitors' changing room to greet the Yattock manager, and then to another room to meet the match officials.

'We go out now, loosen up,' he said, backtracking to the open doorway of the Pitties' changing room. It was 2.32p.m. on a mild, slightly overcast Siddley Saturday afternoon when the Pitties emerged from the tunnel into an explosion of noise.

'Bloody 'ell,' Les Diamond shouted, emerging among the leaders onto the pitch.

'Jesus Christ!' It was Darren Drummond.

'He's not here,' Scott Fisher laughed. 'But he's the only one who isn't.'

The long open terraces facing the Pitt Stand was a mass of people where there would normally be a sprinkling, sometimes only Lime Green and his friends. The colliery band was drowned out by a sudden outburst of noise from the Japanese contingent with their clackers and drums when the two Japanese among the players made a point of waving at them. Even the sun joined in, breaking weakly through the misty clouds over Pitt Lane. Yattock came out in tracksuits in an orderly, jogging file, positioning themselves in front of the Canal Stand where a part had been cordoned off for their fans who made the long trip to Siddley for the big semi-final.

The noise from the stands and terraces penetrated the long window. Walter Hardcastle looked over at Monique who smiled, nodded and made a 'go for it' expression. He looked around for David Broody and was relieved not to see him. He took a deep rasping breath until the buttons on his waistcoat came under stress, feeling a strange light-headedness. He spread his arm and called his guests to the window.

'There are the new Pitties,' he declared, gesturing at the stretching and trotting figures on the pitch. 'And those are the new fans.' His voice was croaking with emotion, personal ruination now expunged from his mind. 'The future is lime green and Japanese.'

From the directors' enclosure, David Broody looked down and around at the thickening crowd. Rakov wasn't hard to pick out, sitting in the Pitt Stand below him, behind the visiting team's dugout between two men, one in a Russian fur hat, the other, his bodyguard, a man with the broad, square shoulders.

When the Pitties broke into a cross-field sprint and the terraces erupted again, Boris Rakov leaned close to the man on his left, his breath warm in his ear. 'That's where Broody thinks his hotel's going to be,' he told him in Russian.

The other grunted sardonically. 'But it'd better happen soon. The money's been in one place too long. We need to get it to Siddley and get our hands on the deeds. My neck's on the block over this, Rakov. A couple of the Georgians are just waiting for me to fuck up, so if anything happens to their money I'm borscht.'

Rakov produced two silver hip flasks. 'Don't worry my friend. By Monday night this part of Siddley will be part of Russia. Let's drink to it.'

The man in the hat chugged twice on the vodka, smacked his lips and pulled Rakov to him by the collar. 'You think this Broody guy knows we're not going to lease him back the land? Has he worked out there ain't going to be a hotel or a fucking Siddley financial centre?'

Rakov chuckled. 'No. His head's too full of stupendous plans and his stupid little models.' He pulled on his own flask, which contained mineral water. Then said: 'The Middle Eastern buyers need just a little push, a million under the table should be enough. We'll be in and out of this dump in three weeks, with a truck load of nicely cleaned money.'

Cameras tracking him from all angles of the ground, Ohara ordered his players off the field. Fifteen minutes to kick-off. In three minutes, Pitt Lane would be live in Japan. Lucas Mandrake looked conspiratorially at the retreating figures of his team mates before skipping briskly to the long terrace and waving to a party from the Siddley Charismatic Church. Ohara shepherded his 14 men into the tunnel and then looked up at the Pitt Stand with casual deliberateness, oblivious to the ranting of thousands of boisterous fans. They were there, their two burnished faces beaming at him from among the pale, sun-starved countenances of the locals, for whom the $100,000 from the crooked betting syndicate would mean a life of comfort in Siddley. Ng See Loo rose to his feet, his fingers drawing childish circles, followed by the Japanese *yakuza* gangster, Bunsuke Makino, who jigged his huge frame on the spot, his arms pumping the air like pistons. A waving hand caught his eye, a few rows behind the gangsters, to the left. It was old Alf Widdison, in a tawny overcoat and his usual flat cap. Ohara returned the wave with his own, Pulling up at the edge of the steps to the dressing rooms, his eyes moved from Alf up to the directors' enclosure. The chairman was emerging with the lady mayor and the Japanese ambassador. Then he saw Monique. Her face was not distinct as she bobbed about, making her way down the steps, but the bunched, golden hair, the mile wide smile was. And she was wearing Ohara's Japanese national team shirt from the World Cup.

She radiated love for the Pitties. How could he ever think of not doing his best?

In Yokohama, on the Pacific coast of Japan, a 30 minute train ride from the heart of metropolitan Tokyo, it was a cold November night, with a light breeze rustling the leaves of the zelcova trees and flaming red maple in the shinto shrine behind the Kikuna home of Ken-ichi Ohara's father. At 11.45p.m., Saburo Ohara and his friends, and tens of millions of Japanese from Hokkaido to Kyushu, were treated on their screens to a pastoral image of Siddley, the long shadows at sunset, the River Siddleworth tumbling over the weir by the riverside gardens. A voice made a brief passage across the city's history; the grass square in Sidchester, once a Roman encampment; the splinters of wood in the heritage museum from a Viking long-ship; and the very name, Siddley, most likely derived from the Anglo-Saxon, 'sodlee', meaning settlement by river crossing. From market to mill town to city of 200,000 people, and at its heart, founded a hundred years ago with the support of the great industrialist and philanthropist, Sir Abraham Pitt, Siddley United Football Club at Pitt Lane.

The cameras did not dwell on the wooden seats, the corrugated sheeting, the ramshackle roofs. They zoomed in on the noisy fans, the little rising sun flags of the Japanese supporters, the banners with Ohara and Suzuki, Ken and Taro, in huge Japanese and English letters, then switched to Shinsuke Sudo, settled between Mimi Bando and Takeo Shito in the press box, explaining the magic of the Golden Mousetrap Trophy, how its knockout formula conspired to bring together the semi-professionals of Yattock of the superior Conference and Siddley United, strugglers with few resources near the bottom of the RoustaRodent Solutions League. As phonetic *katakana* characters appeared over the image of the pitch, he tortuously read the names of the starting line-ups, the disappointment in his voice palpable because the Pitties did not include Taro Suzuki or coach Ohara himself. When screams, drums and the racket of clackers erupted the camera swung to the tunnel, where two columns of men were emerging from the Pitt Stand onto the pitch, one in the fabled lime green shirts and tangerine shorts, the visitors in chocolate and cream white.

Ken Ohara watched from the touchline, arms folded, a step or two from the bearded Yattock manager whose dugout overflowed with substitutes and coaches. What was going through his mind, Ohara wondered? He might have expected 1,500 spectators in Siddley's famous old ground for this easy cup match but the place was packed, maybe 15,000 or more, almost all Pitties fans? A few Premiership clubs would celebrate if 10,000 turned up for a home game.

The home fans were worth an extra player, the Yattock manager was thinking ruefully, and when he saw the inside of the Siddley dugout he knew they might need one. Yattock won the toss and chose to attack the terraced end where the Pitties' Japanese support was concentrated.

The referee, a short, heavy man with very thin legs, played to the cameras when he blew his whistle with a flourish and pointed theatrically towards the Pitties' goal.

The Yattock forwards, led by the lanky striker, Shane Goodmouth, went straight at the peasants of Pitt Lane, and it was only a hair's-breadth offside call by the linesman in the third minute that ruled out a ball that flew past a nervous Tony McDonald.

Scott Fisher was looking unsettled in his early duels with Shane Goodmouth but the back line was holding steady, commanded by Omar Grant. The Pitties even had their own chance to open the scoring when Lucas Mandrake sauntered past two Yattock players, reaching Marco di Rapido with a swerving ball that just evaded the visitors' left back. Marco controlled it but his arms were flaying like a demented windmill and a Yattock player appeared to be struck by them and went down writhing. The Pitties' striker slid the ball into the net but the ref had already called the foul. Marco squared up to him, a hand pointing to the Yattock player who had recovered with miraculous speed.

The Pitties kept the score level at 0-0 for 22 minutes. Terry Dribble's analysis was exactly right: Shane Goodmouth was hard to knock off the ball legally, but Fisher and the backs had coped. They fouled him twice outside the penalty area, and the resultant free kicks were saved by an agile, now confident, Tony McDonald.

Apart from the away supporters, Broody and the Asian gamblers, the fans at Pitt Lane and watching television in Japan enjoyed the first 15 skirmishes with a feeling of prescient optimism and it seemed that luck was running with the Pitties this torrid afternoon. But then Billy Pickwich was turned for the tenth time by a sleek, wing back whose shot was saved and then turned into the net by a poaching Yattock midfielder called Map, with McDonald splayed helplessly on the compacted goalmouth mud and three Pittie defenders around Goodmouth. Voices erupted in the visitors' enclosure; but the rest of Pitt Lane was in silence, except for a spot in the Pitt Stand, where the yelps from two oriental characters seriously tested the famed good nature and tolerance of their neighbours.

'You're not from around Siddley, are you?' the man next to Ng asked. He had a bloated pasty face, thick neck, a grey toothbrush moustache flecked with egg and cloudy, suspicious eyes.

Under the roof, among the press corps, laptop on his knees, the *Sentinel's* Paddy Brick scrolled down the draft of the game's story. He filled in a name and a couple of adjectives. 'The floodgates opened at precisely 22 minutes past three,' he added.

'What's Pickwich up to?' Terry Dribble said, seated next to Ohara on the bench. 'I've never seen him play as bad as this.'

Ohara sighed and looked across the field at Mike Groot, Clint Hopp's hung-over replacement on the left. The game was underway again, and he was limping, his face the washed-out green of an old Pitties shirt. He was holding his head, staring at the pitch.

Radio Siddley, forbidden by its statutes of foundation to broadcast live football matches, kept the phone link to Pitt Lane open while Nigel Wensleydale conducted a call-in debate on old-age pensions, trying to disengage the cracked, scalding voice of a Mrs Chipley and revive the interest of a government junior minister who sat in the studio beside him. 'Can I stop you there for a moment, Mrs Chipley? There's been another goal at Pitt Lane. I'm sure the government minister here will want to know how far your cold weather allowance went, but first let's hear from Karen in the cauldron at Pitt Lane. Karen.'

'Yes Nigel, game over at Pitt Lane, I think. The goal's gone to Yattock again. I must say, coach Ohara's back four, with young Scott Fisher given the impossible job of man-marking Shane Goodmouth, were doing a terrific job, but another defensive error set up the big striker for his fourth or fifth real chance of the game. Billy Pickwich lost his footing, letting a Yattock man through to whip in a low pass that Goodmouth held up on the penalty spot, the ball literally tied to his boot laces. Scotty was just too afraid to foul him and it gave Yattock's giant striker enough room to turn and poke it through a devastated Tony McDonald's legs. It's all happening here at Pitt Lane, Nigel. Omar Grant is still having a go at Billy Pickwich as they trudge back to the halfway line. Oh, and wait. I think Ken Ohara is going to make a substitution. Make that a double substitution. Alan Blink's ready to come on and yes, Taro Suzuki is stripping off his tracksuit. Is this unbelievably huge crowd, and millions of fans in Japan about to see a Japanese player on the pitch at Pitt Lane? Blinky's knees are strapped up but he'll be on for Grooty. I didn't see what happened to him but he's throwing up on the far touchline. Who else is coming off, I wonder? Back to you in the studio for the moment, Nigel.'

'Halfway to ten million bucks,' Bunsuke Makino shouted at Ng See Loo, the pair standing among the silent, sad Pitties fans. He punched the air and jigged on the spot.

'Thank the gods for that,' Ng said, relieved. He was tapping numbers into his mobile phone. 'We should have at least three goal by now. Goalkeeper make too many saves. Japanese coach being very clever or very stupid.'

Above them, on the top row of the directors' enclosure, David Broody's face twisted into a smirk. He glanced at his watch. Only ten minutes to half time. Aroused by his destruction of the board, and soon to free himself of the curse of Sir Abraham Pitt, he decided to forgive Monique her treachery and imagined them in the big team bath together, up to their necks in £50 notes. Looking down, he picked out the gorgeous crown of golden hair. She was sitting behind the home team dugout. But what the hell was she wearing? It was a blue football shirt, with white stripes on the sleeves and the number six on the back. Her shoulders were jigging as she sobbed shamelessly. But now he understood, and he scoffed. The bandy-legged little Jap meant more to her than he did. So bloody what? The Pitties were two down and 55 minutes from extinction.

Paddy Brick tapped the latest goal details into his laptop. 'It's all over for the Pitties,' he had written yesterday.

Alan Blink trotted over to fill the gap left by Groot,

transmitting on the way Ohara's order for Darren Drummond to play deeper. It was getting worse for the Pitties. Pickwich hit the ground again. Yattock were making an idiot out of him: all they had to do, it seemed, was look at him and he toppled. They were getting the ball to Goodmouth, and it was only Scott Fisher's dogged harassing that kept the big man's shot rate down. Ohara had seen enough. He sprang to his feet and told Dribble to signal the second change. He suddenly felt alone in the stadium, struck by the truth he'd been trying to deny: Billy Pickwich was throwing the game. Broody had recruited the taxi driver, a defender, a player in a position to do as much damage as a traitorous goalkeeper, with a tackle in the penalty area or a phoney fall. He was roused by a familiar but long unheard sound. It came from the hundreds of Japanese supporters.

'What's that?' thousands of Siddley fans wondered. In Japan, millions knew what it was and many joined in. Long distance nostalgia.

'It's the Suzuki call,' Rika Yamaguchi shouted into the ear of a Welsh colleague from Uno. The crescendo was accompanied by the thrash of a *taiko* drum.'

'*Su zu, Su zu, Su zu ki.*'

The British with them took up the chant, then it spread to the long terraces, then to the Pitt Stand. Taro Suzuki jogged on the spot, focused, impatient, hungry, as if impervious to the noise. His baggy tangerine shorts flapped close to his knees, concealing his muscular thighs.

Billy Pickwich jogged to the touchline, eyes to the ground, the game up for him. Suzuki sprinted to the right side of midfield, taking a quick palm slap from Marco di Rapido, and prepared to help defend a Yattock free kick near the far touchline.

In the studios of Radio Siddley, the producer made the 'cut and go to Pitt Lane' sign to Nigel Wensleydale. 'I'm sorry Mrs Pratt. I have to interrupt you for a moment and—'

'I haven't finished yet, young man. My father fought at the Somme. My husband was at Dunkirk. Your generation doesn't seem to understand—'

'Sod the Somme for the moment, Mrs Pratt. Karen? Are you there?'

'Yes, Nigel. Fantastic scenes here at Pitt Lane. Pickwich and Groot are off, replaced by Alan Blink and, guess who? The former Japanese international striker, Taro Suzuki. Two down, manager Ohara is throwing caution to the wind. He now has two out-and-out strikers and two attacking wingbacks. Back to you, Nigel.'

The noise from thousands of Siddleans, stomping their feet, drumming and chanting to the Japanese beat could be heard from the bus station. In the commentary box, Mimi Bando squealed with delight when the Suzuki call reached the narrow, open fronted broadcast room. Shinsuke Sudo's stiff commentator's front collapsed and his voice reached operatic highs. 'Taro Suzuki is on the pitch. Taro Suzuki is back.' It was approaching one o'clock in the morning in Japan but none slept. 'With his team two goals down the Pompanol Osaka ace is back in attack for, for . . . For Siddley United. A comment, Shito *san*?'

Takeo Shito had momentarily lost it. He was staring at the television monitor. The Japanese cameraman had swung his lens to the seats behind the coaches' dugouts to capture the extraordinary sight of a beautiful western woman waving a Japanese national team shirt over her head, revealing a voluptuous figure encased in a lime-green thermal vest.

On the pitch, the Pitties were forming a diagonal wall in front of their goalmouth to defend yet another Yattock free kick. Diamond had held on to Shane Goodmouth's shirt so tenaciously the Siddley player was dragged to the very edge of the penalty area by the giant striker and was lucky to escape with only a yellow card. The free kick skimmed off Lucas Mandrake's shoulder in the wall and was headed solidly off the Pitties goal line by Omar Grant. Pain erupted from the seeping wound above the big man's damaged eye.

As the last minutes of the first half ran out interminably, Siddley struggled to hold Yattock's lead to two goals. Then, with the referee throwing glances at his watch, Les Diamond lifted the ball over the half-way line. Thousands of voices screamed in unison when Suzuki rushed onto the aimless clearance, controlling it slightly off-balance with his first touch. Before he could look for options, two figures in chocolate and cream closed him down and sandwiched him off the ball. Ohara was on the touchline again, screaming at his back line for the passing ball.

Then Siddley had the ball back after a Yattock slip. 'Pass it!' Grant screamed at Lucas Mandrake who found himself on the end of a quick-fire triangular pattern involving Gary Omerod and Blink and he set off down the wing, cutting easily inside a Yattock defender, Mandrake hesitated only slightly, surprised to find the ball still under his control, but just enough for a six feet three centre-back to back-pedal and clatter him.

An elder from the Siddley Charismatic Church shook his Bible. 'Fucking wanker!' he bawled across the pitch at the offending Yattock player.

The tackle on Mandrake was deemed fair, although the Pitties winger came out of it dragging his left leg. Behind him, Gary Omerod was incensed, but before he could exact revenge the ball had rebounded to him, and, by sheer instinct he poked out a foot, pinging the ball off Marco di Rapido to Omar Grant. Tackles flew in, but Omar Grant stood firm, exchanging fluid passes with di Rapido across the left corner of the Yattock penalty area. Darren Drummond was calling for the ball on the touchline, drawing a pair of defenders towards him. Spectators in the corner of the Pitt Stand roared instructions. The ball bobbled to Suzuki who leapt over a two footed challenge and pressed forward. Marco di Rapido was screaming, his arms spread imploringly, just on-side, on the opposite side of the penalty area. Yattock's normally strong and sharp right back was easily beaten by Suzuki and threw himself recklessly between the Pittie striker and the ball. Obstruction, the crowd roared, and the ref agreed. Free kick to the Pitties, their first in Yattock's half of the pitch.

Omar Grant moved towards the ball, but Suzuki was standing with a boot clamped possessively over it. It was 20 maybe 25 yards from the goal. Omar hurriedly reminded the Japanese it was an indirect free kick.

Ohara, who was standing with a hand on the dugout roof, while the referee paced out ten yards for the Yattock wall realised he had not actually designated a free-kick taker for situations in front of the opposition goal, perhaps subconsciously assuming they were improbable. The crowd was desperately expectant, the clackers on the end terraces momentarily stilled.

Ball underfoot, Taro Suzuki stood his ground. He scanned the Yattock line-up then said something to the players around him: di Rapido, Drummond, Grant, the injured Mandrake and Robbie Breakin who had come forward with Les Diamond from the back. The huddle broke and all but Suzuki and Grant fanned into the Yattock penalty area, where they were tugged and jostled as they jigged and feinted. Hands on hips, Suzuki waited while Omar ran a distracting pattern which took him round the Yattock wall. He puffed hard once, took three steps and sent a curving, sinking free kick across the goalmouth. It was heading out of play, past the far goalpost.

They replayed it in Japan 18 times from all available

camera angles during the half-time interval, each time subjecting it to forensic analysis by a panel of experts. Suzuki bent the ball round the outside end of the wall so that it came in fast and bending inwards from the side, like the slider pitch in baseball a commentator in Tokyo noted sagely. It curved more and sank lower than Suzuki meant it to, and its trajectory looked to be taking it behind for a goal kick, but Marco di Rapido threw his body at knee height between two Yattock players and the ball glanced off his right temple.

'We cannot be complacent, Mr Braine,' the minister declared to the invisible caller, glancing at her watch. 'And my government is committed to delivering the improvements in the benefit system we promised in our manifesto but our wrists are tied by European Union legislation and—'

Nigel Wensleydale leapt to his feet, tearing the headphones off his head. 'Get Mr bloody brain-dead off the line,' he mouthed through the studio glass. Clamping his headphones back, he settled down again, his face flushed, brow beaded with sweat, 'Sorry, Karen. Are you there?'

'It's in the net again, Nigel,' Karen Saddleback screamed through his ear piece. 'The ball is in the back of the net.'

'Which net, Karen? There are two nets. Calm down and tell me which fucking net. Oh Christ! Are we live?'

'Siddley have pulled one back. A great goal by Marco di Rapido. Siddley one, Yattock, two.'

Yattock kicked off but there was barely time for a couple of passes between the forwards before the half-time whistle blew, and the Pitties left the field to hysterical screams, as if they'd won the game. Ohara applauded his team into the tunnel but he was looking at Lucas Mandrake, who was unable to bear his weight on his left leg and was leaving the field with an arm drooped over Gary Omerod's shoulder.

In the journalists' enclosure, Paddy needed to pee but the unexpected exigencies of the unfolding drama demanded stoical sufferance. 'Consolation goal for Pitties in defiant defeat,' he improvised on his laptop. He felt cheated. He'd lost £10 on the final score bet. Only two journalists remained in contention to split the final score pool if the score stayed at 2-1 to Yattock.

The home team's changing room hummed with the reek of men pushed to the brink. Lucas Mandrake lay on the treatment table, Matt Dennis in pessimistic attendance with pain killing spray. Headers had taken their toll and blood was seeping through Omar Grant's bandage. Terry Dribble hurried to change the dressing. Billy Pickwich had gathered his clothes and left the ground before Drummond and the more excitable players could help him find the exit. Marco di Rapido paced the room, pounding a fist into a palm, muttering to himself in hypnotic oblivion. 'Si, si, si. Did you see it, Mama?' He was holding a damp cloth to the graze on his cheek where it had been raked by a stud during his suicidal scoring dive.

Ohara hid his anxiety as he called for attention. 'Well done to all of you,' he said genuinely. How could he criticize them when they were only one goal behind instead of four? 'You held Goodmouth very well,' he told Scott Fisher, who looked exhausted. He'd stymied him so well the Yattock striker showed his frustration once by lashing out and getting himself booked. Ohara ordered the defence to hold its shape, with Gary Omerod dropping back to make up five when necessary. Omar's leaking head wound worried him, but the big man had played an inspired first half. 'You scored through their right so keep feeding the ball to Lucas and let him do the forward runs.'

Matt Dennis appeared from the treatment room. 'I think we've got a problem there, boss.' He was in the doorway to the treatment room. 'He's dead-legged in his left peg. I don't think we can get him going for the start of the second half.'

Hearing this, the deposed goalkeeper, Kevin Stopham, leaned towards Breakin. 'Pass me Clint's shirt,' he said, his lips hardly moving. 'It's on the hook, behind Les.'

'What do you want it for? Breakin wondered.

'There's only me left on the bench, and I used to play in the outfield before I found my strength was between the sticks.'

'You know the boss's going to commit *hairy keery* if we don't win, don't yer?' Breakin whispered loudly, handing him Hopp's shirt.

'Getaway.'

'Yeah. He's got a knife down his sock.'

A knock on the door preceded the face of an assistant referee, 'Are you ready lads?'

Walter Hardcastle sipped the last, cold dregs in his tea cup, holding back as the guests funnelled through the door to the directors' enclosure in the Pitt Stand. Monique, back in Ohara's shirt, touched her chairman's arm sympathetically as she passed and gave him a winning smile and a few words of reassurance. Her make-up was smudged from the tears, her voice rough from shouting and screaming. The other three directors victimized by David Broody also waited for the room to empty.

'We're double buggered if the Pitties force a draw from this one,' Geoffrey Osborne moaned. 'The lads'll still be in with a trophy chance until the replay down in Yattock in three weeks and Broody wants it settled the day after tomorrow.'

Ronald Townrow said: 'So if somebody has old Abraham's

proviso on paper now they can hold up the sale of the club's land for three weeks.'

With a rueful smile, William Hardcastle said: 'What happens if the Pitties win today?'

Geoffrey Osborne scoffed. 'Then we're triple buggered.'

Walter Hardcastle invited them to return to the directors' box with a flourish of his hand. 'It hardly matters any more. By the day of the final some of us will be in prison, the others at home, ruined and in public disgrace.'

The flood lighting cast star-burst shadows around the figures on the pitch. Charlie Wharton saw the two team captains at the mouth of the tunnel, rubbing their hands against the afternoon chill. He stamped on a last divot, hoisted his fork on a shoulder and left the pitch.

His mobile phone tinkling, Ng See Loo pushed rudely along the row of seats, jogging Gilbert Mornley's plastic cup of tea. With spectators waiting for the second half it was quiet in the cold corridor under the Pitt Stand, with its heady odour of damp clothes, cigarette smoke and urine. He answered the call with trepidation. Fat Ping's retribution would extend to his own agents if $1,100,000 US had to be sacrificed. Back in his seat, after returning Gilbert Mornley's snarl with a death threat in Chinese, Ng slumped in his seat, all around him the applause, the cheering, the thumping drums and the rhythmic clacking and chanting from the Japanese supporters and their followers. Suddenly, Pitt Lane was full of optimism. Ng had to lift Bunsuke Makino's Mickey Mouse ski hat and tug an ear to his mouth. 'Kuala Lumpur. They hear half time score. Not happy. You go down talk to fellow countryman in little plastic house. Tell him we kill him if—'

The Japanese gangster put a thick finger to his lips then jabbed it towards the pitch. 'Too late.'

Hair neatly parted, a new lime green shirt flapping over

baggy tangerine shorts, Ken-ichi Ohara emerged from the tunnel behind team captain Omar Grant, before the loudspeaker could announce that Lucas Mandrake had been substituted. Kevin Stopham sat sadly alone in the dugout, back in his goalkeeper's jersey. The Japanese fans on the terraces thought the distant figure was Taro Suzuki, like the rest of the crowd, but when the Uno striker appeared with Marco di Rapido at the end of the line they fell quiet, not quite taking in the reality that two Japanese national soccer heroes were together on the pitch. Then Rika Yamaguchi, at the epicentre of the Japanese support, erupted. '*O ha ra, O ha ra.*' The others around her joined in, and when Monique heard the familiar name from her seat behind the dugout she turned and brought the Pitt Stand into unison with flailing arms.

For commentator Shinsuke Sudo and the Nippon Broadcasting Corporation it was justification for bringing the first ever live soccer game from England to Japan at such an unsociable hour. From now the cameras had only two real targets.

In the first 15 minutes of the second half, with the opposition fans behind them, the Pitties faced wave after wave of Yattock attacking movements inspired by their wiry midfielder and captain, Sean Deekett. Scott Fisher was playing out of his skin, arms spread as he jigged around Shane Goodmouth, trying desperately not to foul him, and when the big striker gave him the slip Blink or Breakin were there to clear up. Grant, his new bandage slipping after four solid headed clearances, fell back with Drummond to help cope with the other two Yattock forwards. They were let off once when a volley on the turn from Goodmouth hit the post and skimmed luckily into Tony McDonald's surprised arms. When the Pitties finally pushed forward, Deekett marshalled his defence and dealt firmly with Marco di Rapido and Taro Suzuki.

Ohara was forced to play back on the left side of his mid field, where Mandrake had been. Finally, when the game was entering its last twenty minutes of play, he broke away from Deekett and made a drifting forward run, close to the left touchline, arms hanging loosely. The crowd urged him forward. Taro Suzuki sprinted diagonally across the pitch onto the overlap, taking Ohara's pass two metres from the corner flag. He cut inside a defender and released it accurately towards Marco di Rapido. The Pitties' first goal scorer was closed down smartly and he scuffed his shot three yards wide. But it was enough to raise thousands of Pitties' fans to another frenzied outburst, and in the early hours of Sunday in Yokohama, Ohara's father beamed and pointed at the image of his son filling the screen. If the camera had stayed on his face longer it might have caught the faintest of winces as Ohara felt the lightest twinge of pain in his chronically damaged knee. At that moment the bearded Yattock coach emerged from the away team's dug-out, pointing here and there. He had decided to show his tactical hand. It would be a fulminating decision.

Yattock had forced the Pitties to play at a higher, unknown level, with the quality and pace of a fitter, more professional team, and it was telling on the Siddley players. An injury to a Yattock forward gave them a welcome break. Robbie Breakin cleared his nose and sat on the penalty spot and Scott Fisher hugged a goal post for support. Hands on hips, Gary Omerod's chin was on his chest, his nostrils snorting steam like a race horse in the winner's paddock. Ohara saw a pair of Yattock coaches on the touchline holding up numbers. They used the injury to make a double substitution. He trotted over to the touchline where Terry Dribble was waving desperately.

'They're gonna close up shop,' Terry shouted above the unsympathetic whistles and jeers from the home supporters.

'Shut shop?' Ohara asked, bending an ear.

'Yeah. Close the game down. Hold on to the lead. They're bringing on two defenders.'

Ohara jogged over to the right side of his formation, his eyes taking in the field. Goodmouth's striking partner and the adventurous winger, Clement Doone, shook hands on the way off with their beefy, tall replacements. The injured player, the useful midfielder called Map, was on his feet again, shaking off the knock and heading for a deep position among his own defenders. Di Rapido and a Yattock defender were about to contest a dropped ball just inside the Yattock half, close to the centre circle. Omar Grant had already worked out the opposition's new tactics and wasn't surprised to be told to release Scott Fisher from his sweeper role, maintain a flatter back four and direct right sided attacks through Drummond.

Marco scrapped for the dropped ball which rebounded to his captain. Grant nudged it in front of Darren Drummond on the right. Drummond released Ohara who evaded a lunging tackle. The crowd screamed foul, but the referee played the advantage and Ohara broke down the right, towards the Japanese fans ranked on the end terracing. A shuffle took him past one of the Yattock substitutes but he was forced into the corner, where he was effectively closed down. He swivelled, tilted backwards and crossed aimlessly, happy to see the ball deflected off a defender's boot and go behind, into a pack of Japanese fans.

It was Siddley United's second corner of the match. Ohara prepared to take the kick himself, hoping that Darren Drummond remembered the cross finger signal for pretend short corner scenarios. He did, even inviting the pass with his hands spread and a screaming plea, successfully drawing a pair of Yattock players to him. The ball, in its gentle parabola trajectory, eluded the spiking heads of di Rapido, Grant and the surprised, somewhat static Yattock defence, and fell at the feet of Taro Suzuki. The Japanese striker killed it on the laces of his right boot, an inch or two from the penalty spot. Yattock's Goodmouth had dashed back to defend and was jigging around on the goal line, protecting the right hand corner, when the Japanese pulled the trigger without benefit of a run-up. The ball was rising, curving away from the leaping goalkeeper, towards Goodmouth, who jumped, hands clamped to his sides. It seared his cheek on its way to the back of the net. Two-two, and fire at Pitt Lane.

Paddy Brick checked his watch and hit the keys with rising desperation. 'A draw was as inevitable as it was deserved,' he improvised. 'The Pitties would not follow the script. And so the climax of this thrilling, painfully enthralling Golden Mousetrap Trophy semi-final encounter will be played out on the lush, green fields of Somerset (check county, could be Dorset) in three weeks.'

Japanese self-control was breaking down in the commentary box. 'A goal for Japan,' Shinsuke Sudo told his nation, while Takeo Shito and Mimi Bando actually embraced before remembering they were Japanese. Karen Saddleback was screaming into her microphone; the Pitt Stand crowd was on its feet, Simon Pitt waved his crutch with alarming disregard for his broken leg and his neighbours and old Alf Widdison hugged Kevin Stopham's wife. Two figures stayed seated, one taking a call on his mobile phone from Kuala Lumpur, the other cracking his knuckles. In the directors' enclosure there was much back patting and hand shaking, while the board members threatened with ruin just managed to conceal their anxiety while all around celebrated. Play resumed before Monique could don her Japanese number six shirt for the second time in public. The Pitties were already defending. David Broody had taken himself to the head of the steps and was talking on his mobile while watching a spot among the Yattock supporters in the Canal Stand.

The Yattock manager's defensive tactics had backfired with absurd speed and the defenders, with Shane Goodmouth now the only real target man up front, were forced to protect the draw by attacking. And attack they did. Sixteen minutes of intense pressure had the Pitties chasing shadows, tackling recklessly and clearing wildly. The home team's fans could not cheer and worry at the same time and fell silent as the inevitable end of the dream approached. Goodmouth found himself teasing Fisher and Breakin, rolling the ball under his right foot just outside the corner of the Pitties penalty area. Yattock fans behind the goal screamed for a shot. The exhausted and cramp-ridden Gary Omerod, blood rushing to his head, saw Goodmouth's posturing as piss-taking of the worst kind and lumbered past the referee, barrelling between his team mates and skidding into an unguided two-footed tackle. To his credit he aimed at the football, but the deft ballsmith from Yattock rolled it back with a heel and watched Omerod skim by harmlessly on his backside. Almost. The studs of Omerod's left boot may have grazed the gangly striker's shin pad but to Goodmouth it was a life threatening assault. He screamed imploringly towards the heavens and fell to earth in slow-motion agony, two hands reaching for his ankle as he rolled on the turf.

The Pitties fans screamed cheat as one; Yattock fans behind the goal in the Canal Stand demanded a penalty. The referee seemed unsure as to whether Omerod had committed an immediate red card offence, whether it was in or outside the penalty area or whether Goodmouth had performed an award-worthy dive. Les Diamond tried to help him decide, standing astride the striken striker. 'Get up you cheating wanker,' he snarled, before being seized by two Yattock players and wrestled to the ground. Marco di Rapido went nose to chest with a gaunt, crop-headed fullback and Darren Drummond chased a Yattock player who was bellowing and punching the air in celebratory anticipation in front of the away fans. Ohara was trying to calm his bellowing players, while Yattock's captain, Deekett, was standing on the penalty spot, shouting 'ref, ref' and pointing down at the circle. It was too much for Tony McDonald, who came off his goal line and shoved the provocative Yattock player off balance. Deekett's legs buckled, sadly for Siddley, because Tony's slightly intemperate challenge had caught the confused referee's eye and his card holder left his shirt pocket before Deekett hit the ground. Red. The referee checked the time of the offence. It was seven minutes from full time. Scribbling 'violent conduct' against the number fifteen, he dispatched the disconsolate young netminder with a flourish of the card. Tony stripped off his green jersey and left it on the goal-line before trotting off the field, sobbing, head on chest, to the sympathetic applause of the stunned Pitt Lane faithful who were only slightly appeased that the foul against Goodmouth was judged to have taken place outside the penalty area. Even so, Yattock were gifted a dangerous free kick.

Ohara had the veteran goalkeeper, Kevin Stopham, on the bench but he'd used his three allowable substitutes. A couple of tall defenders had already backed away but Ohara knew who he wanted. He turned on Omerod.

'Gary. You are stupid man to give away free kick. Put on green shirt.'

Yattock had three men over the ball, and Ohara knew they'd test the makeshift goalie. He put his five tallest men in a wall protecting the near post and Grant and Drummond on the goal line, Omerod nervously covering the far post. Up field, the furthest Yattock player was half way inside the Pitties half. They were going for it.

Omerod raised his gloved hands defiantly and was bobbing on the goal line when he felt a sharp, painful blow on the back of his shaved scalp. 'What the f—?' He tore off a glove and reached behind his head. A Yattock player was about to begin his run up to the dead ball. When he removed his hand, Omerod saw a speck of red.

'Watch the fucking ball,' Omar Grant bellowed at his shoulder.

Goalie's gloves on, Omerod had assumed a spring and pounce position. He turned instinctively towards the Yattock supporters when another coin or something sharp struck his shoulder. The Yattock free kick taker saw the goalie's distraction and tapped the ball to a colleague who pinged an arching ball over the wall towards the goal.

'Incoming! Incoming!' Blink bawled from the wall.

It was a competent, hard-hit ball that sizzled between two leaping Pitties heads a split second after three Yattock players burst towards the goal in practised synchronized intimidation. Three more coins, machined into lethal tooth-edged skimming missiles, were launched from among the Yattock fans by the same Grittley Mills yobs paid by David Broody to smash Omar Grant's head outside the Taste of Heaven nightclub. The coins spun into the goalmouth, one deflected harmlessly by the side netting, another embedding itself in the turf, the other stinging Darren Drummond's arm. The wing back was too stunned by events to notice. A hand against the goalpost, he'd taken the ball smack in the side of his face as he jumped and turned reflexively, holding the line by sheer willpower. He tasted dirt, and fiery comets swirled and burned in his head. The ball rebounded off the goalpost, and forgetting he was the goalkeeper, Omerod swung a boot at it as a curtain of chocolate and cream shirts choked out the light and threatened to bundle him and everything in its path into the net. The ball looped skywards, lost in the glare of the floodlights, and cleared the penalty area, which was cluttered with 19 bodies. The only Yattock outfield defender, on the half way line, followed its trajectory and set off towards the Pitt Stand touchline.

Ken Ohara, the first Pittie to react, went in pursuit. He'd burst from the penalty area with the snap exertion of a sprinter out of the blocks, Taro Suzuki two paces behind. The Pitt Stand spectators rose, their imploring voices united with the masses on the terraces. Ohara heard nothing, nor sensed the pain welling in his knee. He was watching the ball with absolute intensity. It bounced high, ahead of a Yattock defender who arched his body backwards, straining to reach the rebounding ball. He failed. It skimmed up his chest and over his head, where Ohara chased it towards the touchline, leaping over it, stopping it with a heel, the forward momentum carrying him into the fence where friendly hands, Monique's among them, reached out to cushion him.

Upright again, he turned, so sharply it released an explosion of pain in his fragile knee. Grimacing, he pushed the ball past a tired Yattock player and jumped a sliding tackle from another. An eye caught a palette of lime-green, orange and brown moving upfield, his Siddley players in disciplined formation, target arms raised, forcing Yattock back in ragged disorder.

Not used to this pace at this level, the referee puffed to stay up with the play. Omar Grant had followed Ohara and Suzuki, racing out of the Siddley penalty area with team mates and opponents, his head thumping with pain, the bandage unravelling, trailing behind him as his long heavy legs pumped up-field. Drums, clackers and screams fused in a crescendo of pulsating noise from the terraces behind the Yattock goal.

Ohara had the Yattock captain at his shoulder, tugging his shirt, steering him away from the penalty area, towards the corner flag. A flash of lime green at the far post gave

Ohara a focus, a target. Taro Suzuki. He passed the ball riskily to Grant, took the one-two return and released the cross. Arms spread for balance, Ohara had been bending backwards and he knew at once he'd overhit the ball, even as another spasm of pitiless agony exploded in his knee and Yattock players appealed optimistically for an offside against anyone in lime green and tangerine. He fell to the turf, clutching his leg to his chest.

But Taro Suzuki had been played on-side by a big defender whose desperate return run had taken him to his own goal line at the precise moment when his team mates moved forward to catch the Pitties offside with a disciplined move to the edge of the Yattock penalty area. The flag stayed down, the linesman was spot-on because he saw the stranded Yattock defender.

Suzuki darted towards the near post because he knew Ohara would get the cross in. Like the old days. He also knew his old national team colleague's knee could not hold out much longer. He was right. Ohara was down, and the cross he'd sent off-balance was going to dip behind Suzuki when he'd expected something on the ground to drive at or a higher ball to head. So he turned instinctively, left side on to the Yattock goal, the defenders and his own team stalled, uncertain, expecting the ball to miss everybody and bounce out of play. But when the ball seared across the goalmouth Suzuki launched himself off his left leg, his right foot following through elastically, meeting the ball in a frozen moment in time, both boots level with his head, an arm's length from the ground. The contact was solid but not quite perfect, the ball forced into the soft earth a metre from the goal line. The goalkeeper saw the danger to the uncovered side of his goal fractionally late, and expecting a clean volley or a header he went for the mid-level leap rather than the low dive. Suzuki's short, hard, scissor volley skimmed tantalizingly under the flying goalie's body.

Three-two to the Pitties, minutes left on the clock.

Siddley's party began the moment the referee's final whistle calmed racing hearts, bringing ecstatic fans from the stands and terraces onto the hallowed turf of Pitt Lane. Two figures stayed seated, their faces lost among the waving arms.

'I have lost face,' Bunsuke Makino shouted at Ng See Loo. 'I must kill my countryman and restore my honour.'

Ng grunted. 'Better you think restore one hundred thousand dollars first. Then kill him.'

10

Driven rain lashed across the river; empty bottles bobbled in the foam below the weir. Beer tins and grease-stained newspaper scuttled and wafted around the dark, deserted riverside pleasure gardens, reminders of the jubilant Pitties fans and citizens who had partied late into the night all over Siddley during Sunday. The city had come together.

Smoke plumed from the chimney of the last occupied terraced house on the Pitt Estate before being shredded in the wind. Alf Widdison added a few lumps of coke to the glowing heap on the fire in the downstairs sitting room where Alice had slept in her last crippling, arthritic years. 'Not much fuel left in the cellar, mother,' he told the silver haired old lady in the walnut framed photo on the mantelpiece. 'But we won't be needing any more, the way things are going.' Noises, a shuffling of bedclothes and a pained, sleepy grunt, made him turn. 'That'll be our unexpected visitor from last night,' he whispered. 'Hope he didn't bother you.'

Ken Ohara stirred, mouth dry, bottom lip swollen and sore to the touch of his tongue. His hair was matted and damp and there was something putrid about his body.

'You're awake then, lad,' the old man said. 'Mornin' to you. I wiped most of the muck off your face and washed your clothes. They're drying by the fire. You wouldn't let me call the doctor.' He pulled the curtains apart, revealing in the thin light, through rain beaded windows, a narrow stretch of lawn. Ohara mumbled something. 'I don't speak Japanese, lad. Only English. If it's an apology, don't bother. You're not keeping me away from the canal. I can't fish on a day like this. I'll make us a nice cup of tea. Three sugars, same as me?' He straightened the spare blankets he'd put on the bed and shuffled off in his well worn brown corduroy trousers and a buttoned up cardigan.

A lifetime in old photographs hung on the faded flower-patterned wallpaper while the bed, bolstered with blankets, and a bow-legged table and an old armchair took up most of the room. A wicker basket, several bags and boxes, a folding chair and rack of rods claimed a corner for Alf's fishing gear.

Ohara saw he was wearing faded cotton, striped pyjamas, the trousers drawn in with a ragged cord. His body ached and what he could see of his chest was specked with dirt. A radio played in another room.

'Get this down you,' Alf ordered pleasantly, setting a cup down with unsteady hands. Then you can tell me how you got where you did.'

Ohara raised himself on an elbow. The hot, sweet tea stung his injured mouth. He winced.

'You musta been partyin' all day.' Alf chuckled, retreating to the armchair with his cup.

'All day? What time is it? What day?'

'Don't excite yourself.' Alf squinted at the clock. 'Just after six on Monday morning.'

Ohara leaned back on the pillow. 'What happened to Sunday?'

Alf cackled again. 'You tell me, lad. Mind you, you deserve a good time after a game like that, the way your mate scored that winning goal. They want to give you the freedom of Siddley.'

Ohara wondered what the freedom of Siddley meant, too

bewildered to pursue it with the kind old Englishman and desperate to remember the events that brought him here, stinking of rotten vegetation and covered with bruises. What happened after Taro Suzuki scissor-kicked the Pitties to victory? 'It feels like a lifetime ago,' he told Alf Widdison.

'Let me brew another cup and you can tell me all about it.'

Taro Suzuki was buried under his team mates, barely able to breathe. Seeing a Yattock player snatch the ball from the net and dash back towards the centre line, Ohara limped over and pulled his entangled team apart. For the last moments of the game, with the Pitties' English fans whistling for the final whistle and the Japanese clacking and drumming insanely, Ohara was a lame passenger in his own penalty area, trapped with his players as Yattock swept towards them in search of the equalizer. Then Omerod made a save. Nothing spectacular: but it was a save by the co-opted midfielder. A scuffed, deflected effort under pressure from Goodmouth bobbled into his arms as he knelt between Suzuki and Drummond. The ref checked his watch: they were into the minute of extra time. Omerod looked at the ball as if it were a dead cat and for an instant Ohara thought he was going to drop it. Instead, he clutched it professionally, ran slowly to edge of the penalty and dropkicked it with flamboyant arrogance. Marco di Rapido reacted first to the ball's blunted trajectory. With rare skill, he twisted his foot and clipped the ball beyond the last Yattock defender. Spinning, he plumbed his last reserves of energy and charged towards the Yattock goal. Ohara didn't hear the final whistle, he remembered.

The Yattock team declined the Siddley United invitation to drinks, and went from dressing room to bus without using the washing facilities. The police invited spectators in the Canal Stand to stay behind while they searched among them for the lethal coin throwers who were quickly identified as the mercenaries from Grittley Mills, hired anonymously by David Broody. In Siddley town centre and suburbs, spontaneous celebrators spilled from pubs and homes to the streets around the Cornmarket and the Arboretum and the die-hards continued throughout Sunday, a blustery mildish day with rain forecast for the evening.

The NHK team had tried to maintain appropriate decorum as they finished their transmission to Japan but they were in tears and almost incapable of commenting at the end. Karen Saddleback relayed her report to Radio Siddley listeners, her shoulder bag heavy with notes and coins as the only winner of the press sweepstake. One man sat alone under the commentary box: Paddy Brick was still tapping his laptop furiously. Two whole paragraphs of his pre-written story had to be deleted. 'It was always on the cards,' he wrote, on the back-foot. 'Tora, Tora, Taro,' screamed one header on the lime green special edition when it finally hit the streets. Not a bad headline in extremis, he thought, heaping special praise on Suzuki for his two goals and his dramatic free-kick assist for Marco di Rapido's breakthrough first.

The Pitties fans were slow to leave the ground, but David Broody stayed in his seat, a cigar smouldering in his fingers, his mind not on a cup final in January but on financial ruin, and when he caught Rakov's eyes as the Russian stood up to edge his way out of the ground he knew that penury was the nicest of possible conclusions. If the Pitties had lost, and he had the proviso on its original paper, he could, as imminent owner of the club, invoke the condition that allowed the club's sale if no cup graced the trophy cabinet by the end of its centenary year. But they'd won today, and were in with a chance for a trophy in January, more than two months away. Too late for David Broody, even if they lost the final. He needed the millions of dollars within three days to repay the bridging loan from the Banco Cristobal Colon of the Cayman Islands he'd been force to take out at horrendous cost in order to buy the Pitt Estate land around the football ground. He'd already used the Russians' million dollar down-payment to meet interest on the loan. If the Pitties still had a chance of a trophy, he'd have to force the sale of their football ground and car park on purely legal grounds, as the club's owner. But if somebody turned up on Monday with Sir Abraham Pitt's covenant, Broody was dead. The cigar tasted bitter on his lips. The Pitt legacy was turning from honey to hemlock.

Monique cheered the Pitties on their lap of honour. She wanted to enfold the exotic Japanese manager in her arms and make blissful love in the Canal Stand penalty area where the day's glory had been crowned. In the changing room, tins were shaken, the tabs snapped, lager fizzing and spraying over the delirious players. Taro Suzuki's stern facade had collapsed and he was incoherently muttering in Japanese as he received unfamiliar beery male kisses. Clint Hopp had been released without charge when it turned out the witness had given a false name and address and he was there to enjoy it as if he'd played, along with the real casualties, Simon Pitt, Dean Slutz and Lennie Hampton.

Warm in Alf Widdison's bed, Ohara remembered sitting on a dressing room bench, an ice pack on his knee, accepting the plaudits with very mixed emotions, looking for the chance to slip away from Pitt Lane inconspicuously. Out there, no doubt looking for him, were two very unhappy Asian psychopaths. He had to get the two briefcases containing the hundred thousand dollar bribe money to the police, make a 'voluntary statement' as they called it in Japan, and hope the Japanese *yakuza*'s threat to destroy him physically and professionally was as empty as his brain. Before Ohara could attempt a getaway he was obliged to meet the Japanese press again, and after a raucous mass bath, and clad in a blazer and tie, he limped into the packed boardroom suite and sat at the chairman's desk, Taro Suzuki at his side, before a battery of microphones, and recorders.

Manabu Tanaka from the *Kanto Daily Sports* stood by the door, notebook in hand, and threw Ohara a victory sign and a friendly smile when their eyes met. Ohara would use him and his tabloid to put the truth about the bribery attempt to the Japanese people. Ohara claimed only modest responsibility for the win while praising his coaches and players, singling out Suzuki, rightfully. How did Suzuki feel about scoring two goals, the last one the game winner? He felt proud; and happy for Ohara and his team-mates. Yes, Ohara only played because of injuries and other indispositions, without actually confessing to Groot's drunkenness and Hoop's arrest. A prediction for the Golden Mousetrap final next year? We will all do our best not to disappoint the people of Siddley and Japan. Plans? Nothing, beyond getting a team fit for the away game next Saturday in the RoustaRodent Solutions League.

'If there are no more questions,' the big-haired PR girl running things told the room, her mobile in a furry pouch dangling on a chain around her neck, 'the chairman of Siddley United invites you all to the hospitality lounge.'

Ohara waited until the boardroom was empty, exchanged formalities of farewell with the NHK team and when he was sure Broody and the rest were in the bar he left through Monique's office and limped down the stairs to the now deserted changing rooms. He could hear the rumble of conversation and muffled laughter above him. The ground outside was in darkness save for a few lights in the stands. Wrapping a Pitties scarf around his face and pulling up the collar of his jacket, he followed the fence to the exit at the terraced end of the ground, slipping through a turnstile gate Charlie Wharton had been told not to close until the ground was safely clear of fans. They were still gathered around the lamplit food stalls. Drinkers from the Pitt Lane Arms, with their pint glasses, were trying to read the *Siddley Sentinel's* special edition whose pale lime-green front page led with: 'King Ken of Siddley'.

Hunched up, Ohara sidled furtively along the wall of the old ground. From a recess in the corrugated boarding he could see his car among the other vehicles. No sign of Ng and Makino, probably because the Siddley police were using the car park as their base and a few officers were still there. He needed help. Should he, the winning player-manager in the greatest football game in the city's history, confront a policeman in the club's car park with the confession that he'd been paid $100,000 to throw the game? In the pale reflected light he checked his mobile. He recognized Rika Yamaguchi's number among the many logged calls and thought of calling her, but he needed a local, and there was only one he could trust. He picked a number from the directory and pressed. 'Monique *san?*'

She'd changed from Ohara's shirt and leggings into a body hugging black and white striped dress and restored her hair and face for the party ahead. They were all looking for him, she said and was surprised at the fear and urgency in his voice. Of course she'd leave the party for him. Meeting him behind the ground, by the cracked steps leading to the canal, she'd pulled on an ankle length coat and turned up the collar. He tugged her under an overhang of thorny foliage and told her all about the attempt to bribe him.

'A hundred thousand dollars?' Recoiling in shock, she lost her balance on an uneven stone and reached out for his arm.

Ohara nodded ruefully. 'You remember you said two men were looking for me. Tuesday, I think?'

'Yes. They were very odd.'

'One is Japanese and he's *yakuza*, like a gangster. The other guy is a Malaysian professional gambler. They make big bet that Siddley will lose by at least four clear goals.'

'How much did they bet?' Monique asked warily.

'One million US dollars.'

'Phweeeeew,' Monique whistled. 'That must be all of what? Seven hundred thousand quid.'

'They bet at ten to one against the Pitties, so they lost potential ten million dollars. In real cash they lose a million.'

'At least they got to keep the bribe money.'

Ohara looked sheepish. 'Not exactly. I have it, in two suitcases.'

'Bloody 'ell!' Monique declared flatly. Hearing men's voices nearby, they hugged for privacy against the prickly hedgerow. A ghostly mist hung over the stagnant water of the canal below them. 'You cheated them,' she hissed. 'You took the bribe and then won the game. They won't like it.'

'It's not like that at all,' Ohara insisted.

'So why did you take the money?' she breathed, her nose to his.

They forced it on me. They just left it on a chair when they came to my house?'

'Your house? Oh God, it gets worse. You've got to get the money to the police and make a statement.'

Ohara was exhausted, all ways up. A kick to his left thigh had left a bruise and a dull ache when he moved and his knee flared in pain when the right leg took the weight. 'That's why I called you.'

Monique's breath steamed sweetly against his face, her body warmth exuding perfume. 'Not your Japanese girlfriend?'

'Rika?' His voice cracked: he cleared his throat. 'No, no. It's too complicated to explain in Japanese.' Monique's lipped swelled to a glossy pout. 'I mean I can trust you.' Her body relaxed against his.

'Let's take the money to the police,' she said hesitantly. 'There's a certain detective inspector down there who will be very happy to do me a favour and help the hero of Siddley out. Where exactly is the money?'

He was about to say it was in the Honda but he remembered he'd hidden the case under a pile of logs in the garden shed before he left home this morning. The other's in a locker at Siddley station, he told her.

She thought about it, then brought her watch close to her face. 'Look. It's getting on for nine o'clock. The police are run off their feet on a Saturday night in Siddley. Let's get together with my detective friend tomorrow when it's a bit quieter. Besides, Ken, you look exhausted. It's been a hell of a day.'

She was right. He ached, and his head felt loose and heavy. There was no way he could explain his predicament with clinical accuracy. But at the same time, lying in his big empty house, with the dark garden, thick bushes and recessed corners and doorways, jumpy at every bump and squeak, didn't make for a very relaxing prospect.

Monique seemed to read his mind. 'You'd better come home with me.'

They left the car park without being recognized and he kept her red compact in the headlights of his Honda until they arrived in a street of small semi-detached suburban houses with a patch of garden at the front, just off a roundabout ringed with neighbourhood shops. Monique's rooms were small, the ceilings low, walls everywhere hung with photos of her Pittie heroes. 'I've got you in my bedroom,' she told him, to his puzzlement, and led him to a lounge with couch, coffee table and elaborate music centre. 'Champagne, Ken?' she breathed, slipping out of the long coat. 'At least we can celebrate your victory.'

She returned with a cold bottle of Krug, courtesy of David Broody's cellar.

'It's your victory as well, Monique,' he told her, popping the cork. 'The directors didn't look very happy, did they?'

Monique sighed, slumping on the couch beside him, two empty flutes clashing in her fingers. A deep breath eased her breasts in a gentle swell. 'Broody's going to force them to sell their shares to him tomorrow. If not, he'll go public with their stories. It might be their last day in Pitt Lane.' Holding the glasses for him to fill, she suddenly giggled.

'Hold steady please,' he said, infected by her laughter.

'I'm trying to imagine old Ronald Townrow in this dress,' she giggled, inviting his eyes to the tight fabric whose hem ended so abruptly below the curve of her hips.

The image of that cold Friday when he arrived at Pitt Lane flashed through his mind, and he was smiling. The face and blustery confusion of the rotund, purple-cheeked undertaker when he found he had hired a Japanese and not an Irishman. The perceptive Indian and the handicapped, super loyal Pittie supporter, Osborne. And Townrow, the suave, prim Siddley dignitary, guilty of nothing more than a penchant for high heels and sexy clothes. Like Monique's now, but . . .

She had moved closer, clipping his glass and fixing him with those green globe eyes. The stripes on her dress turned to dizzying whorls as the creamy softness of her body engulfed his arm like molten lava. Heat surged through his body, purging his aches and pains, and arousing delicious sensations. She kissed his cheek lightly.

'Thank you for today, Ken. From all of Siddley.'

'It was the best day of my life,' he said, his voice thick.

He let her refill his glass. 'But I don't think it is enough to save the club. Broody gets to own it tomorrow and then he's free to sell the land.'

'If only we had the Pitt covenant,' Monique sighed, her head seeking comfort on his shoulder, her soft golden hair suffused with the scent of jasmine against his cheek. 'At least it would postpone the sale until we played the final, which you will win.'

It took all the zen stoicism of his forebears to concentrate. He took a long drag on his champagne. It had been minutes since he'd thought of the gamblers.

'We only have tomorrow to find it,' he said glumly. 'But I must take the bribe money to your policeman friend and make a confession.'

'Not a confession, Ken. A statement. You've done nothing wrong.' Her fingers closed on his inside thigh, fingernails kneading compassionately in slow, clawing movements. I'll come with you to see Kay. She's really nice. A Detective Inspector.' She sipped her drink, put the glass on the table, then released a mischievous chuckle.

'It's not funny, Monique *san*. They are dangerous men.'

'Sorry Ken, I was thinking of something else.' She shifted on the couch, her dress rising even higher, her hand returning to his thigh, lips closing on an ear. 'I wonder if anybody at the party noticed we were missing. They must have done. After all, you are the star, Siddley's hero.'

He turned to face her, his body tingling, floating, quivering at her touch. 'I'm here with you, Monique. Paradise is Siddley.' Suddenly, the room exploded with uncontrolled, urgent, hungry passion, Monique ahead on skill and speed. She sucked his tongue to the root while unbuckling him consummately. He luxuriated in the feel of her soft, living breasts, in the dreamy, intoxicating rise and fall of her pulsating, rhythmic body, the heat in her skin as the dress peeled away. Then, her mouth moved again to his ear, nibbling, kissing, blowing. 'Ken?' she breathed, her sweet, panting breath hot on his skin, a hand deep inside his trousers. 'Ken. Have you ever wanted be a referee?'

It was a bittersweet moment for Walter Hardcastle and the other three victims of David Broody's blackmailing tactics as they stood solemnly on the edges of the raucous post-match party, watching players and supporters celebrating a victory the club had waited decades to achieve. Drink may have been a factor, but Ken-ichi Ohara's absence was only noticed when Walter Hardcastle called for silence and asked him to step forward for a speech. Everyone assumed their hero was partying elsewhere in the crowded room and with so many Japanese there he did not stand out, as usual. They looked for him in the changing rooms, in the boardroom, phoned his home and left a message on his mobile. At some point, it was also noticed that Monique Wainwright was missing and it was only at the end of the evening, when the joyous supporters and the guests began to leave, that a fair few saw the absence of the couple as more than coincidence.

A pale light filled Monique's bedroom when Ohara woke, the empty rumpled sheets next to him warm. The air was heavy with sweet and sour body smells, reminders of the frenzy of their lovemaking, in three long, energy sapping bouts which started on the couch and culminated in blissfully entwined sleep, interrupted impossibly early by the unmuffled bells of St Armeda's church announcing the Sunday morning religious rituals. Monique filled the doorway, with misty, tired eyes and a huge smile, in a floppy sweater and leggings. She brought him a cup of coffee and kissed him. She was bobbing with excitement.

'I'm just popping down to the roundabout to buy all the Sunday newspapers. I'll be back in five minutes, not a second more.'

'What time is it?' Ohara asked thickly.

'A quarter past ten.'

He rolled his head into the pillow, breathing in Monique's scent. 'I must go and get the money from my house and the railway station and take it with us when we see your police friend.'

'I'll call her as soon as I get back.' She kissed him again, long, on the mouth, a hand sliding under the sheets. 'Perhaps not quite as soon as I get back.'

He washed, found a razor, gathered his scattered clothes, and checked the calls logged on his mobile. People at the club were trying to find him. A thin smile died quickly when the image of the Malaysian gambler and his dangerous Japanese partner surfaced again. He wanted to believe they'd left Siddley to face the wrath of their bosses in the East but he knew they were still out there. He found bread and fruit in the kitchen, where Radio Siddley was playing on Monique's football-shaped radio-cassette. He hadn't eaten since the pasta before the match, almost 24 hours ago, but a piece of toast with honey and an apple were enough. A hint of hope returned, invigorated as he was by the victory and satiated by Monique – who had a plan. When he'd handed in the money and unburdened himself officially of the bribery attempt and explained everything to the Japanese people through Manabu Tanaka's tabloid he'd really celebrate, maybe even take a quick trip to Paris or Rome. He was sipping his second cup of coffee when he heard his name coming from the radio.

'And that was Marge Greatorix from the flower-dressing display at the Stoolton Road Methodist Church. Hope the weather holds for you, Marge.' The voice belonged to Radio Siddley's Nigel Wensleydale and it suddenly became serious, as if announcing a royal death. 'And so, it has now been over fifteen hours since Siddley's giant killing hero, Ken Ohara, was last seen. Following a Japanese press conference at Pitt Lane, our conqueror in lime-green and tangerine was to have received all the honours at the post-match celebrations but failed to appear to receive his hard-earned accolades. The doctor at Radio Siddley suggests that Ken may be suffering from exhaustion, perhaps he's even a victim of Ernst's Euphoria Deflation Syndrome by Proxy, an inability to come to terms with one's achievements, which may be expressed in short-term amnesia and irrational behaviour. If you're listening, Ken, our thoughts and prayers are with you. The city of Siddley is waiting to crown . . .'

Ohara suddenly remembered Monique and glanced at the kitchen clock. She'd been gone for half an hour, at least. It wasn't very far to the roundabout and those shops, he remembered. Finding a scarf and wrapping it around his face, he peeked out of the front door, then ventured to the latticed gate. A woman was dragging her dog away from a lamp post near his car, which sat behind Monique's. He could see shop signs where the road met the roundabout and they were not more than two minutes' walk away. He rushed inside, from room to room. Had she taken her mobile? He called her on his, and cursed when he found it ringing under her Pitties scarf on the sofa. Think, think. He felt his heart beat racing, anguish reaching his stomach. She'd met a friend, he decided. Of course she had. He was at the window, pulling back the curtains, peering out, hoping desperately. No. She said she was coming straight back from the newsagents. Then Monique's mobile purred. He watched it. Was it rude to pick it up? It was Monique's privacy. She might not want the caller to know she had a visitor. But then, she might be calling him from the shop. He snatched the phone and clicked on. 'Yes?'

'Ken? Thank God you picked up.'

'Monique. Where are you?' A pause. Then a man's voice. In Japanese. Bunsuke Makino!

'*Nani o yatteru?* Where's Monique *san?*'

'*Oi, oi,* Mr Coach. You didn't think we'd leave this fucking sewer of a town without saying *sayonara.*'

'Where is the lady? Put her on the line.'

'She's fine,' the *yakuza* said soothingly, mockingly, in that coarse, scraped voice. 'What was the *gaijin* body like, coach Ohara? If I can get to Tokyo with her she'll make my fortune. But I couldn't keep her, could I? I'd have to give her to my boss, wouldn't I? It might stop him killing me for fucking up this operation and save me having to chop a bit more of my fucking finger off.'

'I'll kill you myself,' Ohara heard himself shouting. In a pause, Makino must have told Ng See Loo about the threat and Ohara could hear the two men guffaw. Then Makino was back, his voice deadly serious.

'Her price is one hundred thousand dollars. Know what I mean, coach? You got a hundred grand of ours.'

'You can have it. Don't hurt Monique.'

'Listen. Tonight. Six. When it's dark. I'll call you on this mobile at five-thirty to fix the place. And we'll be watching you till then so don't do anything stupid. And don't even think of hitting the recall button on this phone.'

'Let me speak to her,' Ohara begged. A pop: line disconnected. Ohara paced around the house, full of hatred, breathing out of control, hyperventilating, imagining the most horrible things happening to the beautiful, blameless Monique. Her diary, personal organizer. Where? He turned out drawers, cleared shelves, upturned cushions, examined every surface, glancing often at his watch. What was the name of that detective? Please, Monique, he begged telepathically. You've got keep your numbers somewhere. At Pitt Lane, he decided, just as a car released a long, angry honk near the house. Or? He gathered his mobile and their car keys. Locking the house, he dashed to her red car. An elderly man with a newspaper wondered where he had seen the Chinese face before.

It was there, in the driver's door pocket. A thick, personal organizer bound in blue leather. Hiding it inside his jacket, he slid into his Honda, holding his breath until his heart slowed. Two days of meditation and self-reflection with the Kinki Princes in a zen Buddhist temple hadn't taught him much but . . . Focus thoughts into nothing, search for an empty calm, let clarity emerge naturally.

He drove nervously, an eye flashing often to the mirror, and looking for a familiar road sign, and a route home. The wind was picking up, sharp gusts slamming the car like an invisible hammer. He wished he could talk to Bunsuke Makino, to apologise, try to reason with him, explain why he had to win the game yesterday. He'd appeal to the Japanese way of compromise and understanding, even with gangsters. Then regret began to cloud his mind, the triumph of hindsight. He should have stayed at Pitt Lane, starring in the celebrations. Monique would be safe. In his mind he saw only her, and he was promising the gods he would confess to anything if they kept her safe. Then he realised he was lost in Siddley.

'Sacheveral Avenue?' he asked a man with a nose-ring at the Peg and Butter roundabout. 'Yeah. Posh part of Siddley, right? I don't know exactly but keep going along that road to the left till you get to Vimy Ridge Gardens on the right. Turn right just after and you're going in the right direction. Eh? Aren't you . . .?'

He was feeling much calmer when he recognized Killhope Lane, and then his avenue, with its high hedges and denuded lime trees. Another glance at the mirror. He drove slowly, doors locked, remembering how Ng and Makino had jumped out of the hedges that first time. He parked as close as possible to his house and with Monique's diary under his coat made a dash to the door, key ready for insertion. What to do? Turn on lights and announce noisily his arrival or climb over the side gate to get to the woodpile in the shed and leave as stealthily as he'd arrived? But he had to hurry. Scudding clouds were thickening and the sun when it emerged slipped quickly away. In two hours, the early twilight would clamp Siddley in its cold damp grip. He was inside, the kitchen light on long enough to find the torch he'd need in the shed. If they'd searched his house he couldn't tell; the letter with his last message to the world still lay on the table. Outside, he startled a cat skulking in a clump of dead dahlias and it pounced angrily across the path, leaving Ohara with a pounding heart. In the shed, cold and patched with cobwebs, he pulled the heap of plump fire logs apart until he uncovered the silver case. To get to the little blunt key to the coin locker he unscrambled the briefcase's infamous code and snapped the clasps, gazing with sheer hatred at the neat stacks of dollars bills. Opening the shed door very warily his heart seized. He heard the sound of feet crunching lightly on gravel. Backing into the shed, he looked for a weapon, picking a thin, solid piece of firewood. He heard his teeth rattling, smelled his sweat, his fear. Thinking of his mother, he peered through the crack, down the gravel path to the boundary wall. A large fox turned and stared at him with acute, glistening eyes, sensing a human presence. Tail dragging, it scurried urgently along the path, its claws scraping the gravel.

 He sat for a moment shaking in the Honda, the case beside him on the passenger seat, and the car's digital clock racing forward with obscene speed. He needed to study Monique's personal organizer, find her policeman friend. If he failed, should he call the police emergency number? Would mass police action spook Makino and Ng, corner them like rats, endangering Monique? Makino certainly wouldn't go out without a fight, without a victim or two. He was pure *yakuza*. What was the emergency number in England, anyway? Was it one one zero, the same as Japan? He was driving towards central Siddley in light Sunday traffic, the radio tuned to the local station. He wanted a spot where he could wait without interruption, study the telephone numbers and be ready to rush to the appointed exchange place. First, he had to make a stop at Siddley Station.

Parking in the forecourt, he pulled up his collar and wrapped the scarf. How many locations with lockers?

'Only one. Down them steps,' a railway man in a shabby uniform told him. 'Hey! Aren't you . . .?'

He waited while a couple retrieved a backpack from a locker above 168, wondering why the crooks should bother leaving him the other $50,000. Even if he'd kept the first case and performed his part of the bribe, they could leave the second briefcase empty. He wasn't going to cry to the police, was he? *Hayaku, hayaku,* he urged as the couple took something from the backpack. When they'd gone, he reached up to fit the key. It was there, about the same weight as the other, and with the two identical silver briefcases in his car he headed towards the Pitt Lane estate and the streets of abandoned terraced houses. Dead central Siddley, where he could sit in the deserted streets and examine the diary, waiting to race to the meeting place.

'There is still no word on the whereabouts of super-samurai saint of Siddley, Ken Ohara,' Karen Saddleback was saying on her 4.30p.m. sports bulletin. 'A caller to Radio Siddley claimed the ruthless destroyer of Yattock was present last night in a gay club in Lower Hawksley, naked but for a leopard skin posing pouch and a python wrapped around him. He has also been spotted in a lap-dancing club in Iron Gate and a listener called in two hours ago to say a man with oriental features asked for directions to the manager's home from the Peg and Butter roundabout.

Officials of Siddley United are also concerned about the club's executive administrator, Monique Wainwright, who also cannot be contacted.'

Ohara stopped under a lamp in an empty street parallel to Alf Widdison's. Turning off the radio, he lit the interior light and opened Monique's thick diary, feeling like an intruder and apologising to her aloud. Monique knew everybody: pages and pages of years and years of networking. A lot of men, he thought. He looked under p for police, d for detective, e for emergency. What had she said? The person's name? A woman. Yes, she'd talked about a woman. They were on the couch, or in the bedroom. He wasn't much interested in her conversation. No, it was later, just before she went for the newspaper. He was quivering with panic when Monique's mobile shook him alert.

'You got the money?'

'*Hai*. But please let Monique *san* go free. She is completely innocent. Take me, kill me, whatever, but please release her.'

'Listen to this, Ng *san*,' Ohara heard Makino say in thick English, his voice cracking into hilarity. Then Makino again, in Japanese. 'Here's your hot little *gaijin* pussy,' he said.

'Kay? Is that you? Kay? Don't worry about me, Kay. They are not cruel. Do you understand, Kay? I love you.'

'Get that, coach?' Makino drawled. He'd snatched the mobile. 'She's still alive, for the moment anyway, and calling out a nice little pet name. Ken-chan, is it?' The *yakuza's* voice was deep and flat, completely without humour, black or otherwise. 'Now. You know, the place you groped your girlfriend last night? That river behind the football ground.'

'The canal?'

'You've got thirty minutes to bring two suitcases.' The connection was cut.

Kay? Kay? Why had she called him, Kay? She must have meant Ken, which is what everybody called him here. But she'd said 'kay' four times. He opened the diary, with its individual pages on rings. Kay, that was it! First name beginning with K. Concentrate. Concentrate. He flippped the pages: Keith Andrews, Kirsty Donovan, Kafelia Giorgiou, 'K' something, Kath O'Brien, Ken-ichi (Ken) Ohara, Kate Rogers.' The car's clock read 5.54p.m. He recognized his goalkeeper, Kevin Stopham. Kristine Torgson, Kay Valentine. Kay. Underneath, in a clear hand, Monique had written, 'detective inspector' in tiny letters against a mobile and a regular number.

Shoulders slightly hunched with the weight of the two briefcases, Ohara looked past the silent football ground toward the rear turnstile gates and the stone steps to the canal towpath. Nobody was about on Sunday night in central Siddley and just a few vehicles occupied the valuable car park. He breathed deep, full of dread, and decided to approach the rendezvous from the opposite side of the canal, perhaps giving him time to see Monique was there and unhurt. He crossed the Talbot Street bridge, above the spot where he'd first met Alf Widdison. There was no towpath on this side of the canal where horses once pulled the barges, just a sliver of slippery bare earth between the water and the wall of an old mill. The smell of fetid, stagnant water hung in the air, the only light a fleeting pale glow from a fickle moon. He felt strangely calm, imagining the simplicity of an exchange of money he didn't want for a woman whose love for the Pitties was incorruptible. Walking stealthily along the wall, he could hear falling water, and he knew from his training runs he'd reached the old lock where it cascaded through a crack in the ancient wood of the gate. Then he saw three dark figures on the opposite side of the canal, one of them fidgeting, as if bound and tied to the others. Ohara emerged from a recess in the wall.

'I'm here,' he called in Japanese.

'Ken!' Monique called, her sweater billowing.

'Are you all right?' Ohara responded.

'Shut up, for *fock's* sake,' Ng shouted. 'It's not the *focking* love boat.'

'Bring the money,' Makino ordered, showing Ohara the grip he had on Monique's wrist.

When closed, the gates at the canal's upper level side acted as a narrow wooden bridge for pedestrians, with a low, rusted handrail along one side. Looking down, the walker would see the dark, forbidding water in the lock; on the other side he could touch the upper level water with his foot.

'I can't carry two cases at once,' Ohara said honestly, and deviously. With a putrid smell in his nostrils he gripped the rail with one hand, a briefcase in the other, and edged cautiously across the canal, not daring to look down into the rubbish cluttered water 20 feet below in the lock pool.

Ng See Loo stepped onto the narrow bridge and snatched the case from the trembling Japanese.

'Now other,' he ordered. Ohara was barely an arm's length from Monique. She was tugging against Makino's grip, her face drawn, pleading. Ohara crossed back over the canal, his legs suddenly weak. He gripped the rusted rail and breathed deeply. He picked up the other case and returned to the vertiginous bridge.

'Let the lady come over here first,' he commanded hopefully.

Ohara stepped up onto the slippery, rotting plank, his knuckles white as he gripped the rail, his eyes closed to the coal black abyss below. Ng and Makino seemed to have a brief argument but finally agreed and it fell to the hulk Makino to transport the hostage across the canal. He heaved himself on the cross spur, Monique attached to his free wrist. Ng sat on the first briefcase, a knife in his hand, a smirk on his face. Monique's eyes were shut, she was terrified of heights, but it did not seem to bother Makino that only a thin rusty iron bar separated him from a sharp drop into 200 year old filth. He was a very big, bulky man and he had to stretch his short arm to reach the safety rail, while at the same time hold on to an unco-operative Monique. The two parties were closing at the middle point of the makeshift bridge, Ohara feeling the rail shake from the weight of the approaching *yakuza*. He turned sideways and offered the case. Clutching the rail, the big gangster had to release Monique to get the money from Ohara, who, instead of letting go rammed the briefcase against Makino, forcing him off balance, his enormous weight leaning on the fragile, rusty bars. Ng See Loo sprang to his feet, a shriek erupting from his contorted face.

'Get by me,' Ohara screamed to Monique, ramming himself against the gangster.

Monique threw a glance at Ng, already on the edge of the bridge with a long knife in his hand, and made to pass her Japanese hero as he prepared to force himself and their tormentor down together into the filthy water – for her. But she held up; she heard other voices in the darkness, a woman's among them. Kay? Yes. Flashlight beams jigged on the towpath. Ng was a few feet from Ohara, but he'd heard the voices as well, and retreated. Ohara's strength against his *sumo*-sized compatriot was ebbing. He was now being pushed himself, backwards. Makino grunted and bellowed with anger. One, two backward steps, almost to the unguarded water, touchable from here with a stretch at the canal's upper level. Monique gripped the rail, closed her eyes, bunched her small free hand and unleashed a wild swing at the big target presented by Makino's face. She made solid contact with cheek and bone, her arm shuddering at the impact. Makino shook his head in disbelief, more surprised than hurt, but his hold on Ohara's body slackened and for a decisive moment he was stunned, and when Ohara unleashed a knee into his groin he screamed, tottering as if drunk, his bulk carrying him over the rail in slow-motion absurdity down into the lock pool of the Siddley Grand Canal. But he had thrashed out instinctively and a flaying arm caught Ohara who was struggling to hold himself upright on the slender strip of bridge. The Japanese coach, his body weak from injuries and the fight, lost the battle and toppled backwards with the second briefcase into the deep, stagnant water at his feet.

11

'Where's Monique?' Ohara blurted, his head marginally clearer.

'It's all right, lad, she's still asleep. Upstairs, in me and mother's old room.' Alf sat on the edge of Ohara's bed with a bowl of thick vegetable soup and a fresh cup of tea on a tray.

'Why?' Ohara wondered. 'Why am I here?'

Then Monique was in the doorway, wearing an old smock nightdress, her hair unkempt, face pale. She rushed to the bed, falling onto it, smudging Ken Ohara's face to hers, her body heaving as she sobbed with joy.

Alf looked away, at his wife's portrait on the mantelpiece. He had to swallow, what with the memories. 'I was taking a last stroll down there last night,' he said quietly, suggesting the canal. 'It wasn't late but it were bloody dark, and then there were police everywhere.'

Monique cupped Ohara's jaw. 'You got through to Kay, didn't you? She said you told her to go to Pitt Lane, the canal at the back, because I was in danger.' She sniffed happily. 'Kay didn't believe it was you, did she? Thought it was a drunk's prank. She said it was so hard to see anything down there in the dark and they all went to rescue that big bloke first because he was screaming and thrashing about in the lock. They didn't realize you were in the water as well.' Monique moaned, drawing his head to her, making him cough. 'I was a bit hysterical, I think. I thought you'd drowned.'

'Miss Wainwright here was screaming and shouting but nobody took any notice except me,' Alf said proudly. 'You'd taken yourself up the canal a bit and were clinging to the bank when we found you.'

'We pulled you out,' Monique said. 'Alf's house is so close, we brought you here. I stayed as well.'

'You were delirious,' Alf told Ohara. 'You didn't wash, didn't want a doctor, anything. You threw up a bit of canal water, but you just kept asking about Miss Wainwright here. I gave you something for your stomach and a glass of whisky.'

'You're very kind, Alf *san*,' Ohara said, sucking in the soup greedily. 'What happened to the Japanese guy?'

'They're holding him at the police station,' Monique said. 'He's not hurt. For starters, they'll charge him with kidnapping, or whatever they call it. Illegal confinement. Kay says we can make our statements when we're ready.'

'And the Chinese?'

'He got away. They're looking for him.'

Ohara finished the hot, thick life-saving soup and lay back, Monique's warmth arousing delicious sensations. Across from his bed, on the wall over the mantelpiece, his eyes rested on the sepia image of three moustached men on a football pitch, the same picture as that hanging in the Pitties boardroom and which had inspired Broody to dig up the centre circle where the three men of old stood. Behind them and the empty terraces, Siddley cathedral rose timelessly.

Monique brought his clothes. They were wrinkled and smelly and almost dry. A gust of wind rattled the window.

'Is that your father?' Ohara asked when Alf came in. He remembered the fisherman telling him his father played for the Pitties in the early days.

Alf lifted his glasses and squinted at the familiar picture, as if to remind himself. 'No, no. Dear old dad, Endymion his name was, didn't play for the Pitties till just before the Great War. And he were never captain. The bloke in the shorts would be the first club captain. I don't know who the one on the left is, probably the manager. And that's Sir Abraham in the middle, with the scroll.'

'With the what, I'm sorry?'

'The scroll. It's just a ceremonial picture. No people on the terraces, you'll notice.' Alf lifted the picture gently off its hook and held it where the glass was free of reflection, leading Ohara's eyes with a finger to the lap of the unsmiling character in the three piece suit.

'He's definitely holding something,' Monique said.

'It is not easy to see,' Ohara added, squinting close up.

'Dad used to say it were the deeds that gave the land to Siddley for its football club.'

'But that's what we're trying to find,' Monique gasped. She glanced at the mantelpiece clock. 'By about eleven o'clock this morning. Three hours from now.'

Ohara took the picture, feeling the thump in his chest. 'That's what David Broody's been looking for. It's got the proof in it that means he can sell the club.'

'I told you he was up to no good,' Alf said. 'When I first met you down by the canal. You ask that bloody chief executive of yours, I said, if you want to know if all them rumours were true.'

'They *were* true,' Ohara sighed. 'And Broody must have noticed the scroll in the old photo. That's why he dug up the centre spot, where the three men are standing.'

Alf wheezed out a chuckle. 'Then he's a dafter bugger than he looks.'

Ohara was still struggling with the Siddley dialect. 'He's . . . bugger?'

'Silly person,' Monique explained.

Alf scratched his head. 'He doesn't know his history, lad. When the Pitt Stand were erected, in the twenties some time, I think, it were decided to make the pitch bigger, to full international standards, just in case. It were also moved a few yards to the left so that the new Canal Stand could fit properly. I was thinking about it yesterday, when we were 2-0 down. I was sitting just about in line with the centre circle and I noticed the cathedral weren't straight in front of me, like it were in the old photo. Then I remembered about them moving the pitch. And sure enough, there's the cathedral tower in a different place, over to the right. Then we scored, and it were half time.'

Ohara laid the photo on the bed. 'Mr Widdison.'

'Alf,' Alf said.

'Alf. Please help me understand. If they made the pitch bigger and also moved it, where exactly is the old centre spot now?'

Alf scratched his silvery grey scalp and thought for a moment. 'I reckon if Broody were looking for the middle of the old centre circle he'd find it about fifteen feet to the right of the present one, looking from the Pitt Stand.'

'We'll get this over with, shall we?' Broody said, in the manner of an impatient torturer. 'I suppose you won't want to miss the open-topped bus parade this afternoon. You'd think the plonkers had won the bloody Golden Mousetrap already. As the new, proud owner of Siddley United, I'll be there myself, of course. It's a shame the victorious manager has skipped town.' He placed a thin sheaf of papers, the first headed with the elaborate Siddley United logo, at five places around the table. 'You'll have read the draft contracts of sale I had couriered to each of you yesterday. I took your silence to mean you concurred with the contents so the originals of the document selling your shareholdings to me, on the top there, is the same. My cheques to you will be in the post after all the legal formalities.' He took the seat at the head of the table. 'So there's nothing more to discuss, is there? I'm sorry I can't give you any more than you paid for your shares in the first place, apart from you, Reggie, who deserves a good profit for your support. The rest of you had your fun yesterday, at my expense. Little Hirohito had his moment of glory and the club made a lot of money.'

Sir Reginald Pitt sat arms folded, vacantly staring at the chandelier, while Walter Hardcastle, and directors Patel, Osborne and Townrow listlessly toyed with the papers.

'It was you who hired Ken Ohara,' Walter Hardcastle said hoarsely. 'You tricked us, in case you've forgotten. It's not our fault if he didn't dance to your nasty tune on the pitch.'

'Excuse me, Walter. You're right, The little prick was my responsibility. Never thought he'd win that bloody game. I'd hoped to find that proviso of Reggie's grandfather and use it against you if you refused to go along with my development plans. Bloody ironic, isn't it? If it turned up now you could use it to stop me selling the land, at least until the Pitties play the final next year. I can't wait that long, as I told you. I've torn this place apart, and Reggie's manor, and I've even dug up the centre circle. I found bugger all. It's turned out to be just another Pitt Lane legend, so I won't have to wait two and a half months for the final, which, in the present financial circumstances, I'm unable to do anyway. So you see, there's nothing to stop the owner, and that's going to be me in a few minutes when you sign, from selling the club's assets.' Broody thought about a cigar, but he remembered he was in a hurry. Boris Rakov and his lawyer sat waiting in the car park with the Russians' contract for the purchase of the entire Pitt Estate, club land and all, waiting for Broody's signature.

Boris Rakov was indeed waiting in the car-park, but he was a very nervous and angry Russian. There had been a serious administrative mistake, entirely out of his control, and a junior in the foreign currency settlements department of the Great Imperial Bank of Russia had made it. Instructed to inform the Ambrose Lane branch of the Siddley Co-op Bank, out of courtesy, to expect a large transfer in favour of their customer, Broody Associates, within a few days, the Ukranian clerk, a man with a cursory knowledge of English, misunderstood the vague but normal command and actually opened an account with the little branch in Siddley. He then compounded his error a thousand fold by transferring the carefully laundered sterling equivalent of $240 million from the Won Fang Bank of Hong Kong to Siddley Co-op Bank as the opening balance on the Great Imperial Bank of Russia's new account. In Siddley, a £1 million deposit, by nature of its size and rarity, can bring intense joy and professional kudos to a local branch manager. It would also trigger a series of regulatory events designed to prove the impeccable origins or otherwise of the money and the determine the *bona fides* of the ultimate beneficiary, checks which would reach the Bank of England's anti-money laundering bureau and several police and supervisory agencies worldwide. When £190 million hit Siddley Co-op's books a reconciliations clerk thought at first the currency was yen but confirmation proved it really was sterling. He pressed the panic button. Rakov sat in the back of the limo, tapping his fingers on his briefcase. He needed the money off that fucking account and into Broody's. He needed the land. His Middle Eastern clients were also waiting impatiently, with hot money of their own to exchange for a large parcel of very short-term Russian land in central England.

Broody leaned back, watching with contempt as the five men read the documentation. Sir Reginal Pitt threw him a nod and a knowing smirk.

But it wasn't only the Russian gangsters Rakov represented that worried Broody. At 6.32a.m. a creaky, 40 year old DC-8 belonging to Aerolineas Carambolas had landed at Gatwick Airport from Miami, where it had been joined by two young latin men in beige lightweight suits who had connected with it from a short-haul Cayman Islands flight. They were executives of the Banco Cristobal Colon and were in England to ensure the smooth repayment of the high-interest, $150 million short-term loan extended to a paper company lodged in the Turks and Caicos Islands, the ultimate beneficiary of which was a British entrepreneur, David Broody. Unsecured by property, bank or a third party guarantee, the loan was granted on the good word of a trusted contact, Mr Boris Rakov, representative of certain east European interests familiar to their *bancos* and from whom the funds for the repayment would ultimately be forthcoming following the purchase of Broody's considerable property portfolio in the city of Siddley. The two men from warmer climes knew there'd be plenty around to pay back the loan principal, a wild interest charge and substantial arrangement fee, because Broody was looking at a megabuck profit on the deal with the Russians, who only wanted a secure place to lodge their laundered cash. But they had to be sure: the latins did not trust the Russians or the hick from Siddley. The tired and inappropriately dressed men called Broody from the airport terminal to announce their arrival in Britain. Picking up a metallic green turbo Saab, left for them in the short-term airport car park, they headed north for Siddley, checking first that the oil-cloth bundle in the spare-wheel well held the two compact semi-automatic pistols as agreed.

Sir Reginald Pitt nodded ruefully before his pen put an end to a hundred years of family history with a flourish. Harry Patel signed next, pushing the document contemptuously across the table when he'd signed away his shareholding and striding to the window to contemplate the empty pitch and terraces of Pitt Lane for the last time. Geoffrey Osborne reached back and scratched an imaginary itch on his lump, his pen poised reluctantly in his other hand.

'I can't believe I'm doing this,' Ronald Townrow said, emitting a long sigh before putting his signature to the papers.

Broody smiled as Osborne's arthritic fingers finally scribbled his autograph. 'I have respected your privacy, gentlemen, and so I'll have the documents notarized and your signatures witnessed, shall we say, discreetly, if that's acceptable to you. And I want to assure you I am not a vindictive person, whatever you might think, and I'm prepared to forget your intemperate words last Friday. Once your signatures are dry on the share sale contract I might even find it my heart to leave you the evidence of your illegal activities or in your case, Ronald, your little personal indiscretions. Negatives included.' Harry Patel turned from the window, eyes longingly on the stack of incriminating files on a chair by the door. 'So if you'd just like to finish off and sign where indicated, Walter.'

The undertaker felt he had experienced hell and heaven, the destination of his terrestrial clients, on earth. The axe of utter personal and professional ruin was touching the nape of his neck. During the dark night before Saturday's victory he'd contemplated changing places with one of his corpses but the thought of being tipped out of the recyclable casket in front of the furnace was unbearable. Not even the current outbreak of legionnaires' disease at Siddley Royal Infirmary could lighten the dark of his personal depression. Then, before the big game, Monique told him she had taped evidence of Broody's blackmail tactics, and watching Ken Ohara inspire his no-hopers to a victory heard around the world had filled him with the spirit of defiance. At that moment he determined not to sell out his 50 cent stake which Broody needed to get a controlling interest in the club. But here, sitting in the boardroom, smelling as it did of a hundred years of tobacco and polish, he could only wonder whether it really was worth giving up everything for a worn-out old football club? After all, Ken Ohara would be gone at the end of the season and he'd still be here in Siddley, where he wanted to be, with his beloved coffins and caskets.

'Well, Walter? Do you have a problem with the wording, or something?'

'No, David, no.' Hardcastle sighed once and lowered his pen.

'What's going on out there?' Harry Patel called from the tall, rain-splashed window. 'It looks like Ken Ohara's turned up. He's on the pitch with Monique and another chap.' Geoffrey Osborne rose awkwardly, followed to the window by Councillor Townrow and Sir Reginald Pitt.

'Sign the papers, please Walter,' Broody said urgently, as he also crossed to the window. 'How the hell did they get in?' he muttered. 'I've got two of my people on the gate.' They saw three figures, Ohara hobbling with a spade as a crutch and Monique tugging him by a sleeve towards the centre circle. A much older man followed slowly, carrying a fork.

'I've dug it up, you stupid bastards,' Broody chortled. 'It's not there. It's not there.'

Walter Hardcastle joined his fellow directors and the treacherous speculator, staring with disbelief and fascination at the bizarre trio getting soaked in the middle of Pitt Lane.

On the pitch, scuffed and grazed after the epic match, Alf Widdison wheezed his way to the centre circle where Ken and Monique were waiting for his guidance. The rain had flattened their hair, soaked their clothes but it had eased to a misty wind-blown drizzle which they would not notice. It was eerie for the Japanese, standing in the middle of an empty stadium where just over a day earlier 20,000 people had screamed his name. When they reached Pitt Lane, after the short walk from Alf's house in Church Street, they saw two large men turning a protesting Charlie Wharton away from the gate. Ohara and Alf were all for confronting them but Monique led them away, behind the cars parked on meters, to the outer wall of the terracing where the Japanese supporters had stood. She'd been calling out on her mobile all the way from Alf's house. The single turnstile was covered by a screen of corrugated sheeting, secured to the wall with a single lock, for which Monique produced a key. Passing through the dark tunnels and passages, they gathered tools from Charlie's store and emerged onto the pitch through the players' tunnel. The ground was empty but not unobserved. Ohara glanced up to a spot to the right of the directors' enclosure, where figures, motionless, appeared as silhouettes in the window of the boardroom suite.

Alf Widdison's tired eyes squinted as they adjusted to the thin light. He took his bearings, ticking off familiar places and views with a finger, the terraces, the flag pole, the cathedral spire. Then, with his back to the Pitt Stand and the watchers in the boardroom, he turned to the right and paced out what he estimated was a distance of 15 feet. Monique and Ohara followed him reverentially. Alf stopped, took bearings off the tip of the cathedral tower, moved two more paces forward and two to the left and then brought down his fork into the soft Siddley United turf with defiant finality. 'It was here. This was the centre spot in my dad's day.'

David Broody watched with fascinated horror, glancing once behind him at the old photo that had given him inspiration for his own, frustrated excavations. The old man was loosening the earth with his fork, Ohara digging and shovelling it furiously behind him, each armload sending a jolt of pain through his body. Monique finally closed her mobile. The new turf came off in tidy lumps, the earth below it dense but with few obstacles like stones or rubble. Ohara's spade slid easily into it. The patch of ground which a hundred years ago had been the centre spot of Pitt Lane quickly became a wide, deep bowl. Broody watched from the window, heat rising to his scalp. Then, suddenly, the old man lifted his fork to the skies in a heroic and triumphant gesture. Monique's scream of victory echoed around Pitt Lane and penetrated the boardroom window.

'Well, I'll be buggered,' Walter Hardcastle uttered.

Alf's fork had struck a small metal cylinder, it looked like lead, buried length down. Ohara chipped away at the earth around it, sweat stinging his eyes, his heart racing painfully. It was heavy, and he had to kneel in the mud to get a grounding on the slippery surface and dislodge it. He tugged it gingerly, finally raising it from its hundred year grave as if it were an unexploded bomb.

David Broody barked into his mobile. 'Get it, get it. On the pitch.' Then he turned to the table, sweeping the documents towards the centre. 'It's too late,' he stammered, gathering the papers into his briefcase. 'Too late for all you. I'll have these shares transferred to the new owners in ten minutes. They're in the car park now.' He seemed to be laughing in a frenzied, disembodied way, as if he'd found his own words hysterically funny. And then he was gone, the door slamming behind him.

Sir Reginald Pitt cleared his throat self-consciously. 'I'd better be going as well, chaps. I'm sorry it turned out like this, but I suppose it's for the better.' His fellow directors and prominent Siddleans were curiously silent. Walking backwards a few steps, Sir Reginald nodded his farewell and when he turned to face the door he noticed the files with the incriminating photographs on a chair. He moved to scoop them up on his way out.

'Touch them and you're dead.' It was the normally mild, cross-dressing Ronald Townrow. Clutching a blunt, stiletto letter opener from the chairman's desk he was about to make Siddley United's board of directors unanimously felons, assault with a deadly weapon being potentially the most serious offence. Veins bulged on his forehead. 'Just get out of Pitt Lane, Reggie, with that nasty creepy friend of yours.'

Pitt's eyes bulged, his hands opening in surrender. 'Of course, Ronnie. Don't get excited. I'm going.'

When the door had closed, Townrow slumped at the table, the weapon clattering from his shaking hand. He began to sob.

The old, disgraced butcher, Osborne, eased his aching body down next to him and patted his knee. 'Well done, Ronnie. Now go and get yourself a new dress. It'll make you feel better.'

'What have we done?' Townrow stammered.

'It depends what Ken's found buried in the pitch,' Harry Patel said. 'It might be just a time capsule with a pair of old tangerine socks and a whistle.'

Walter Hardcastle muttered pensively. 'And we'll have to see how Mr bloody Broody reacts when he looks at my sale contract.'

'Did you sign in lime-green ink or blood?' Osborne clucked.

'No, Geoffrey. I didn't sign it at all. Broody's still fifty per cent short of full possession of this club.'

The room fell silent as the four men absorbed the magnitude of the chairman's statement. Then, muffled shouting from the pitch jolted them alert: they filled the window again.

Ohara was cradling the cylinder on the edge of the crater,

Alf and Monique beside him, rubbing dirt off the top. It seemed to be welded shut.

'Let's get it into the boardroom,' Monique shouted. 'We might be in time.' She was about to plant another kiss on Alf's rough cheek when:

'Hey, you lot!' Four men, two of them the same huge goons Broody had employed to block entry to Pitt Lane, were lumbering across the pitch from the corners of the ground, with David Broody following the biggest, clutching his briefcase, his hair in disarray. 'Get that canister,' he was shrieking.

Escape to the tunnel, on a short diagonal course was impossible. Alf was not physically capable and the weight of the cylinder would slow Ohara. Alf's rheumy eyes picked out Broody, the man behind all of his troubles, the man behind his forced eviction, behind the death of the city's football club. Legs apart he assumed a defiant stance, his fork now a three-pronged bayonet. 'I said they'd have to carry me out of Pitt Lane, but I'll take that bugger Broody with me.' He made a sweep with the fork, causing the five men to check their charge, and catching Ohara on the arm with a prong, causing him to drop the container. Everybody was shouting and swearing, demanding and threatening. 'Sorry lad,' Alf bawled at Ohara. 'It were them Italians I showed me steel to in Egypt, not your lot.'

Monique crouched between her men, fingernails bared to strike, the cylinder at her feet.

After the physical punishment of Saturday and his near death experience in the foul canal yesterday, Ohara was numbed to pain and danger, feeling suspended in an unreal world, as if gifted by the Shinto gods of his homeland with a superhuman will to survive. After all, wasn't he the hero of Siddley? Emitting a bushido war cry, he snatched the spade and swung it in a wild arc, brushing back the man who was making a lunge for Monique and forcing another onto his back.

'Get it, for chrissake,' Broody was hollering. 'Kick their heads in. It's only an old sod, a woman and a bloody Jap.'

Then Alf did make contact: he was very, very angry at the remark. A flat-faced, crop-headed man turned and snarled a 'you try it then' grimace at Broody and in that moment of inattention a prong pierced his open palm. His scream froze everybody to the spot, at the very instant they were captured in an explosive flash. Charlie Wharton had turned on the floodlights. The overcast skies were banished: the home of the Pitties was now a gladiatorial pit of light.

'That's it,' the injured man said, shaking off a spurt of blood. He reached into his jacket with his functional hand and extracted a knife. A flick, and a blade flashed alive. He had his back to the players' tunnel in the Pitt Stand and couldn't see what had caused David Broody's eyes to bulge and his mouth to slacken.

From the tunnel emerged Omar Grant, alerted by Monique. Behind him, and breaking into a sprint was Lucas Mandrake, called, like the others, by Grant who had triggered the team network. Then, in tracksuits or shorts, Les Diamond, Robbie Breakin, Marco di Rapido, Darren Drummond and Taro Suzuki who had been training under Terry Dribble at Uno Electronics. Gary Omerod had abandoned his shelf-stacking and rushed to the ground. He broke to the right with Scott Fisher and the goalie Tony McDonald, and Alan Blink and Kevin Stopham. Clint Hopp had left his business ladder against a window in Long Ardon and when he returned it had ironically been stolen.

By the time Mike Groot reached Pitt Lane the battle was over. Omar Grant had seized the spade from Ohara and jabbed it at the bleeding knifeman, driving him back until he stumbled. He kicked the knife from his hand and sank to his knees over the prone figure, a huge fist curled over the petrified face. 'I've seen you before,' he said through a huge smile. 'You were in that mob what beat me up outside the club the other night.' Omar was not a vengeful or violent person, but the knifeman would have a problem eating solids for a while.

Lucas Mandrake took out another thug with a rugby tackle but needed help from Suzuki and two heavier team mates to subdue the thrashing bulk and secure his hands with a belt and his feet with a tie. Gary Omerod knocked another man into semi-consciousness with a blow to the jaw, requiring Matt Dennis, who witnessed the short scrap with his physio's bag, to retrieve the man's tongue from deep in his throat. The last of Broody's heavies set off hopelessly towards the Canal Stand, pursued by whooping Pitties who overcame him and stripped him naked. Marco di Rapido was shoving David Broody, who was trying to keep a hold on the briefcase containing all the precious signed documents. Broody turned to run, stumbled and lost his grip on the case as he struggled to stay on his feet. The case hit the ground and sprang open, releasing the papers which skipped off on the wind to be muddied and ruined with dreadful irony by the soaked, ancient turf of Pitt Lane. He chased and scrambled, grabbed and dived, but it was hopeless. He fell to his knees, clutching his face with filthy hands and bursting into heaving sobs.

Retrieving his fork and holding it proudly, Alf reached for Ohara's hand. 'Could've done with you in the desert, lad. On our side, of course.' Now, as on so many occasions during his eventful stay in Siddley, Ken Ohara was again at a loss to know what had actually been said, but he thought he understood the kind old man's sentiments in spite of the language. Monique clutched Ohara's free arm possessively. The Pitties were herding their five prisoners in military order towards the tunnel, Omar Grant with the mud-coated cylinder under an arm.

'What's this?' Monique said, leaning on Ohara to remove a piece of paper speared by a shoe. It was the last sheet of one of the share transfer contracts and it was creased, soggy and torn. A ragged gash from Monique's slender heel had obliterated the place where Harry Patel's signature used to be.

Kevin Stopham was a plumber by trade and he had rushed to Pitt Lane in his van when Grant caught him at the end of a job in Alma Heights. With Broody and his heavyweights locked in the visiting team's changing room pending the arrival of the police and medical services, and guarded by the players, the directors of the club, less Sir Reginald Pitt, gathered in the basement storeroom, with the roller and assorted tools and machinery, watching intensely as Stopham adjusted his mask and lit the acetylene torch. Alf Widdison had found an old folding chair and nobody asked him to leave.

'Stand back,' Walter Hardcastle commanded imperiously, his arms spread, as sparks flew around the raised head of the cylinder which was secured in a vice, tilted at 45 degrees. The lead began to melt. 'Don't damage the contents,' the chairman urged, as if to uphold his status and reinforce his importance.

Stopham's contempt was hidden behind the protective mask. When he was ready, he extinguished the flame and took from Charlie a heavy duty hacksaw which he carefully passed through the soft metal, cutting and twisting until he could tip the lid off the cylinder. 'Don't touch it yet,' he blurted as the directors, Ohara and Monique closed in, faces glowing expectantly.

Walter Hardcastle cleared his throat for attention. 'Thank you, Kevin, Charlie. If you would like to leave us. We will announce the findings to everyone in an appropriate manner.' Disappointed, Stopham gathered up his tools.

'Just a moment, Kevin.' It was Ronald Townrow, with a bundle of folders under his arm. 'Can I borrow your torch for a moment?'

Charlie brought a bucket and councillor Townrow tipped Broody's blackmail evidence into it, compressing the paper and pictures with his foot. 'Please, Kevin. Step back everyone.' Stopham played the welding torch into the bucket long enough for the paper to ignite and the photographs to melt. The witnesses covered their noses against the acrid smell and wafted away the blue grey smoke.

When Kevin and Charlie had left, Ronald Townrow raised a hand, looking at Monique and Ken Ohara, words suddenly difficult to find for the solicitor and city councillor. 'I speak for Walter here, and Harry, Geoffrey and of course myself.' He coughed, blaming the smoke. 'We were just talking about it after David Broody left the meeting today.'

'About what, Mr Townrow?' Monique wondered mischievously. One heel broken, her leggings torn, sweat and dirt splattered, face and hair streaked and spotted with mud, she huddled close to Ken Ohara for warmth and solidarity.

'Mr Hardcastle here, Walter, that is. He says you know about Broody's little attempt to blackmail us.'

She was enjoying their squirming, painful embarrassment, their shame, but didn't smile. 'Yes. I recorded the meeting last Thursday when he pointed out your little professional miscalculations. Shall I play it for you?' Harry Patel's look of horror was matched by Geoffrey Osborne's.

'That won't be necessary,' Ronald Townrow said, his face blanched. Another empty cough. 'My fellow directors have agreed to reflect on their conduct and take measures to compensate those who may have suffered from their ill-considered activities.'

'He means, illegal,' Harry Patel explained, his eyes fixed on a piece of charred paper at his feet.

'Yes, of course. Thank you. Harry will immediately make a generous contribution to a Cambodian children's charity and take measures to improve the status of his work force in that country. Geoffrey will resign from all positions he still holds in the family meat company which will henceforth supply Siddley Royal Infirmary with properly documented, meat, completely free.' Monique's smudged face finally cracked into a real smile. 'Walter regrets deeply the hurt he could have caused to his bereaved clients at a very vulnerable moment in their lives and henceforth all his coffins and caskets will bear a unique, verifiable registration number to avoid repetition of those regrettable incidents. He has also generously agreed to conduct five funerals per month for needy families, supplying free of charge the coffins, service and transport.' Townrow sighed noisily, a bead of sweat across his brow. He looked at Monique and Ohara with pleading eyes.

Monique made them wait a long five seconds. 'Thank you,' she said finally. The sighs of relief were audible. As if remembering, she looked at Ronald Townrow, her expression deadly serious. 'The satin camisoles at Ramleigh's are a bit risque but we can go and try them on together, if you like.'

The cold room, with the lingering smell of burnt synthetic photo paper, was suddenly still. Then Ronald Townrow looked at his fellow directors and erupted in a raucous cackle, joined instantly by the others. Walter Hardcastle, joined in, until finally he called for an end to the much needed release, his expression hardening. He gestured to the lead cylinder, the buried witness to a century of football passion on the precious turf of Pitt Lane.

'I think it's time to uncover the truth about Sir Abraham Pitt's legacy.'

*

Gunshots were heard in Siddley, threatening to mar the perfect ending to a glorious weekend for Siddley United Football Club. Just pops, really, and hardly anyone noticed. While the secret of Sir Abraham Pitt revealed itself and David Broody pondered suicide in the visitors' changing room, Boris Rakov sat in the back of a silver grey Mercedes limo with his bodyguard, lawyer and driver. He was waiting for David Broody to appear from the ramshackle stadium as its new owner when he took a call on his mobile phone that loosened his bowels and sent a shivering spasm of fear through his body. It came from the angry and frightened chief executive of his bank, the Great Imperial Bank of Russia, in London. The account opened in error at the Siddley Co-op Bank and credited with £190 million had been frozen on the orders of the British money laundering counter-measures agency while clarification of the ultimate beneficiary of the funds was made.

'Do you know who that money belongs to?' Rakov's chief executive had barked rhetorically, simply to remind the aggressive, ambitious shit that certain gentlemen in St Petersburg would not be particularly compassionate when they heard the bank might not have the liquid resources to replace their frozen funds. The bank, and its senior personnel, were finished, professionally and quite probably physically, if the money in Siddley was not released.

Warmed with the fear and tension of the occupants, the windows in the Merc steamed, and if the normally assiduously vigilant bodyguard had cleared the rear window with his wrist he would have seen a metallic green Saab creeping along a parallel lane of the sparsely occupied car park, its windscreen wipers on half speed.

'Have we really financed this pile of *mierda*?' the Saab driver said, his eyes wide with amazement, sweeping the ancient, soot darkened joined-up houses, the abandoned mill and the weathered walls of the Pitt Lane football ground. 'I just fixed a big deal on a condo on Key Biscayne,' he said in musical Miami Spanish. 'What the fuck am I doing in Siddley?'

'I know what you mean,' the other man grinned. 'But this is serious money. We never lent so much without good security, but the guy was happy to pay through the nose. Anyway, it won't be for long now. The guy we lent to, Broody. He gets to sell out to the *Rusos* today. Then we get our money back and we'll be home with the *chicas* in a couple of days.' He shivered involuntarily in his tropical suit, in spite of the heater. 'Let's stay in the car.'

'I'd like to, Raulito, but we can't,' the driver said, nudging his companion. 'The Merc over there. It's three times longer than anything else in this goddamn place. It must be the Russians. Let's go and say hello.'

'Okay,' Raul agreed. He took the Beretta semi-automatic from a shoulder holster, disengaged the safety and pulled back the slide. It rebounded with a comforting metallic snap.

'You won't need that,' his partner said sharply. 'These guys are friends of ours this time.'

Raul tucked the gun back into the holster. 'Guess it's just a habit.'

Boris Rakov's driver clutched the steering wheel, not daring to speak or move; the lawyer next to him stared ahead, breathing quickly. The bodyguard behind with Rakov loosened his collar as the heat rose through his neck. Rakov himself, clutching his mobile phone, was hyperventilating, his life flashing before him. A rap on the window occasioned a sharp cardiac reaction. His tough escort reached instinctively inside his jacket while rubbing the window with an elbow. Two swarthy faces, both sporting sunglasses and neat jet black hair, peered in, friendly smiles helping calm the tension inside. The driver lowered the window from a panel. 'You're from where?' Rakov asked the faces in disbelief.

'The Banco Cristobal Colon of the Cayman Islands,' Raul said proudly.

Rakov nodded a vague sort of recognition. 'What the fuck are you doing in Siddley?'

The second Hispanic showed whitened, even teeth. 'All part of our commitment to client service.'

Raul showed the slightest of gaps between his own surgically enhanced teeth. 'We ride shotgun for our investors.'

Another spasm of fear racked Rakov's already weak insides. If the Russian money was not released to David Broody by the Siddley Co-op Bank, these garlic eating scumbags wouldn't get their usurious loan back; Rakov's mafioso clients wouldn't get title to the land he was sitting on and, calamitously for Rakov, they would not even get their millions back when the source was traced. The work, the money, the bribes. All that effort to get those dollars out of Russia and into the legal banking system, all those transfers, all that risk. He wanted to cry. It was now all going to end tragically, like all good Russian stories. Oh God. He wished he'd never heard of Siddley. He was thinking of his bodyguard's Tokarev nine-millimetre semi-automatic when they all heard the unmistakeable, international whir of police sirens. The men from the tropics spun, guns already in their hands.

'Not again, Monique,' Detective Inspector Kay Valentine had sniffed with mock annoyance. 'It's not been twenty-four hours. I'm not your personal—'

'Shut up, Kay. This is for real. We're in Pitt Lane and we've been assaulted by five men, one with a knife and things.'

'Gotcha. We're on our way, and we'll be armed.' Her detective friend clicked off before Monique could tell her the violent miscreants had been disarmed and were locked in a room, guarded by very angry but jubilant football players, so when twenty uniformed policemen from Siddley constabulary, and ten special response officers bearing guns and protective jackets and helmets, descended on Pitt Lane in a dozen vans and cars it wasn't surprising that the armed Colombians and Russians who happened to be in the car park thought they were the object of a police ambush.

Raul jabbed his sunglasses into his black, glistening hair and felt a surge of testosterone, and if he had not held his snub-nosed semi-automatic in a heroic spread-leg two-handed grip and released a shot at the file of British police it is possible they would have bypassed the two cars in their rush to liberate Monique inside the football ground. The Beretta popped, and an empty shell case sizzled over the roof of a blue Fiat. The only person to feel the attack directly was the unarmed policeman at the back of the line whose hair was singed when Raul's wildly aimed bullet passed through his helmet. He called to his colleagues who dispersed for cover and when a much louder explosion announced itself as a definite gunshot, the armed officers knew they had a situation. The echoed shot they'd heard came from a stretch Mercedes, more precisely from the chamber of a Chinese made Tokarev semi-automatic, held very briefly to his right temple by Boris Rakov.

Ng See Loo was creeping between cars towards the football ground with the intention of torching it after collecting a briefcase of bribe money and killing Ken-ichi Ohara. Too bad his friendly Japanese interpreter, Bunsuke, had to be sadly sacrificed to the British penal system. The appearance of police, the gunshots, the commotion, surprised him, arousing defensive instincts, and he drew his long knife demonstratively, a little too close to Raul as it turned out. The Colombian bank enforcer turned on his heels with the dexterity of an anorexic flamenco dancer and shot the Malaysian through the heart, seconds before he himself fell to a sharpshooter from the Siddley rapid response force.

Heading for the canal with a bag of bread for the ducks and a bottle of cider for herself, Ida Grid thought she was witnessing the making of an action film. Figures rolled and fought on the ground and others ran among the parked cars. Nobody called 'cut' and she couldn't see any cameras.

Epilogue

And the secret covenant of Sir Abraham Pitt? The club's chairman, his fellow directors, Ken Ohara, Monique Wainright, and even Alf Widdison, had examined the contents of the sealed container unearthed from the erstwhile centre circle of the Pitt Lane football pitch where it was buried almost a century ago by the benefactor, Sir Abraham Pitt, who mischievously left the clue to its whereabouts in a photograph. All of those present reached the same conclusion: the cylinder contained nothing that would jeopardise the present or future existence of Siddley United Football Club and so it was re-sealed and displayed in a special, glass-fronted cabinet in the hospitality suite, a reminder to anyone nurturing disloyal and malevolent intentions towards the Pitties of Siddley.

A few months after Ken-ichi Ohara had returned to Japan, and two weeks into the new fishing season, Alf Widdison sat in an unfamiliar spot by the Siddley Grand Canal with his pipe, a flask of tea, a box of wriggling, multi-coloured maggots and a lot of memories that occasionally forced a chuckle out of nothing. Mother would have liked his new accommodation, just a couple of rooms, a dining kitchen and a bathroom, on the ground floor of a sheltered housing project on the other side of the canal from Pitt Lane. That's why he fished there, just above the Junction Street lock where his Japanese friend had nearly met his death. It was only a ten minute walk home at his pace and today was a lovely day, perhaps a bit too sunny for the fish. He'd only managed to lure a pair of puny roach in two hours so he decided on a bit of sport, attaching a barbed hook, and with ten pieces of number eight lead shot on a ten pound breaking strength line he cast into six feet of water below the opposite bank, a place in permanent shadow from the converted Victorian mill. There were rumours of pike. He rested the rod on the towpath and poured a cup of tea from his flask.

When the sun briefly dodged behind the old brick factory chimney, a light breeze rose, ruffling his collar and tipping the float, easing it towards the bank. 'Bugger it,' he said aloud, lifting the rod. It was time to change the bait anyway. Reeling in, the line suddenly went taut, the rod bending at the tip. 'Bugger again,' Alf muttered, rising awkwardly to his feet. 'What's it caught on?' He turned the reel with gentle precision, watching the rod bend until it almost touched the water. The hook stayed firmly snagged. Then he felt the line slacken, not freed, but looser. He always used a strong line, just in case it was his turn for the big one, and now it was being tested. Whatever he'd snared was still on the barbed hook and was moving very slowly in open water. He reeled in until the rod and a short length of line lay almost straight, like an extension of each other, taking half a step backwards as the unseen hook and its mysterious burden approached the stone canal wall.

Now the rod was resting on the edge of the bank, the obstacle invisible in the murky water but not far below the surface. It didn't seem so heavy now, must have a bit of buoyancy in it, Alf thought. He looked around, embarrassed at his inability to free his hook from a shopping cart trolley or whatever it was. The towpath was deserted in both directions.

Removing his jacket and rolling up the sleeves of his pullover, careful not to relinquish a grip on the rigid line, he shifted his chair and tackle box aside and laid himself down on the hard, dry path, his head hanging over the edge, almost touching the water. With the line slippery and less secure in the bony fingers of his left hand, he reached into the stagnant water. It was only a few inches below the surface now and he lay still for a moment, his old heart thumping, his fingers around something like a handle, and waited to find the strength for one last effort to straighten and haul the prize onto the towpath. He soon realized he couldn't and was starting to feel dizzy. He had not the strength, balance or co-ordination to find his feet without toppling into the canal. He'd have to sacrifice the line and the piece of rubbish attached to it.

'Are you all right, Alf?' It was Charlie Wharton. 'Need a hand?' Charlie trapped the catch against the canal wall with Alf's keep net and together they pulled a mottled, slimy, once silvery waterproof briefcase onto the towpath. 'What on earth have you caught?' Charlie wondered. The case stank of ancient canal mud and rotted vegetation.

Sitting comfortably on his chair, Alf lodged it between his legs and tried the clasps. Locked. Using a piece of tackle cleaning cloth he rubbed the filth off the combination lock tumblers. He lifted his cloth cap and scratched the fine, white hair on his scalp. 'I wonder what the combination is,' he hummed.

The final of the Golden Mousetrap Trophy between Siddley United of the RoustaRodent Solutions League and Fosterley of the Conference took place at Old Trafford, home of Manchester United of the Premiership, in front of 42,000 people and half the population of Japan. The score? Siddley 1, Fosterley 4. Taro Suzuki scored for the Pitties.